John Timbs

English Eccentrics and Eccentricities

Volume 1

John Timbs

English Eccentrics and Eccentricities
Volume 1

ISBN/EAN: 9783337405854

Printed in Europe, USA, Canada, Australia, Japan

Cover: Foto ©Andreas Hilbeck / pixelio.de

More available books at **www.hansebooks.com**

ENGLISH ECCENTRICS

AND

ECCENTRICITIES.

By JOHN TIMBS,

AUTHOR OF "CLUB LIFE OF LONDON," "A CENTURY OF ANECDOTE," ETC.

IN TWO VOLUMES.

VOL. I.

LONDON:

RICHARD BENTLEY, NEW BURLINGTON STREET,

Publisher in Ordinary to Her Majesty.

1866.

PREFACE.

GENTLE READER, a few words before we introduce you to our MODERN ECCENTRICS. They may be odd company: yet, how often do we find eccentricity in the minds of persons of good understanding. Their sayings and doings, it is true, may not rank as high among the delicacies of intellectual epicures as the Strasburg pies among the dishes described in the *Almanach des Gourmands;* but they possess attractions in proportion to the degree in which " man favours wonders." Swift has remarked, that " a little grain of the romance is no ill ingredient to preserve and exalt the dignity of human nature, without which it is apt to degenerate into everything that is sordid, vicious, and low." Into the latter extremes Eccentricity is occasionally apt to run, somewhat like certain fermenting liquors which cannot be checked in their acidifying courses.

Into such headlong excesses our Eccentrics rarely stray ; and one of our objects in sketching their ways, is to show that with oddity of character may co-exist much goodness of heart; and your strange fellow, though, according to the lexicographer, he be outlandish, odd, queer, and eccentric, may possess claims to our notice which the man who is ever studying the fitness of things would not so readily present.

Many books of character have been published which have recorded the acts, sayings, and fortunes of Eccentrics. The instances in the present Work are, for the most part, drawn *from our own time,* so as to present points of novelty which could not so reasonably be expected in portraits of older date. They are motley-minded and grotesque in many instances; and from their rare accidents may be gathered many a lesson of thrift, as well as many a scene of humour to laugh at; while some realize the well-remembered couplet on the near alliance of wits to madness.

A glance at the accompanying Table of Contents, and the Index to each volume, will, it is hoped, convey a fair idea of the number and variety of characters and incidents to be found in this gallery of MODERN ECCENTRICS.

It should be added, that in the preparation of this Work, the Author has availed himself of the most trustworthy materials for the staple of his narratives, which, in certain cases, he has preferred giving *ipsissimis verbis* of his authorities to "re-writing" them, as it is termed; a process which rarely adds to the veracity of story-telling, but, on the other hand, often gives a colour to the incidents which the original narrator never intended to convey. The object has been to render the book truthful as well as entertaining.

J. T.

Oct. 26, 1866.

CONTENTS OF VOL. I.

𝔚ealth and 𝔉ashion.

Delusions, Impostures, and Fanatic Missions.

* This memoir has been accidentally misplaced.

CONTENTS OF VOL. L

vii

Strange Sights and Sporting Scenes.

MODERN ECCENTRICS.

Wealth and Fashion.

THE BECKFORDS AND FONTHILL.

THE histories of the Beckfords, father and son, present several points of eccentricity, although in very different spheres. William Beckford, the father, was famed for his great wealth, which chiefly consisted of large estates in Jamaica; and the estate of Fonthill, near Hindon, Wilts. He was Alderman of Billingsgate Ward, London, and a violent political partisan with whom the great Lord Chatham maintained a correspondence to keep alive his influence in the City. When Beckford opposed Sir Francis Delaval to contest the borough of Shaftesbury, the latter said—

"Art thou the man whom men famed Beckford call?"

To which Beckford replied—

"Art thou the much more famous Delaval?"

Alderman Beckford died on the 21st of June, 1770, in his second mayoralty, within a month after his famous exhibition at Court, when, after presenting a City Address to George III., and having received his Majesty's answer, he was said to have made the reply which may be read on his monument in Guildhall, but which he never uttered. The day before Beckford died, Chatham forced himself into the house in Soho Square (now the House of Charity), and got away all the letters he had written to the demagogue alderman. His house at Fonthill, with pictures and furniture to a great value, was burnt down in 1755. The Alderman was then in London, and on being informed of the catastrophe, he took out his pocket-book and began to write, and on being asked what he was doing, he coolly replied, " Only calculating the expense of rebuilding it. Oh ! I have an odd fifty thousand pounds in a drawer, I will build it up again ; it won't be above a thousand pounds each to my different children." The house was rebuilt.

The Alderman had several natural sons, to each of whom he left a legacy of 5,000*l*. ; but the bulk of his property went to his son by his wife, who was then a boy ten years old, and is said to have thus come into a million of ready money, and a revenue exceeding 100,000*l*. Three years later, Lord Chatham, who was his godfather, thus describes him to his own son William Pitt—" Little Beckford is just as much com- pounded of the elements of air and fire as he was. A due proportion of terrestrial solidity will I trust come and make him perfect." The promise which his live- liness and precocity had given, was fulfilled by a *jeu- d'esprit*, written by him in his seventeenth year. This was a small work published in 1780, entitled *Bio- graphical Memoirs of Extraordinary Painters*, and originated as follows. The old mansion at Fonthill contained a fine collection of paintings, which the house- keeper was directed to show to applicants ; but she often told descriptions of the painters and the pictures, which were very ludicrous. Young Beckford, therefore, to methodize and assist the housekeeper's memory, wrote their lives, which she received from her youthful master as matters-of-fact. Thus, after descanting on Gerard Douw, she would add the particulars of that artist's patience and industry in expending four or five hours in painting a broomstick. There were other extravagancies which she believed; a few copies of the book were printed to confirm her belief; hence the book is very rare. Beckford, in after-life, spoke of it as his *Blunderbussiana*. It was, in fact, a satire upon certain living artists, and the common slang of connoisseurship.

Young Mr. Beckford had been educated at home: he was quick and lively, and had literary tastes; he had a great passion for genealogy and heraldry, and studied Oriental literature. He had visited Paris, and mixed in the society of that capital, in 1778, when he met Voltaire, who gave him his blessing. He had fine taste for music, and had been taught to play the pianoforte by Mozart.

Mr. Beckford travelled and resided abroad until his twenty-second year, when he wrote in French *Vathek*,* a work of startling beauty. More than fifty years afterwards he told Mr. Cyrus Redding that he wrote *Vathek* at one sitting. "It took me," he said, "three days and two nights of hard labour. I never

---

* *Vathek* was dramatized by the Hon. Mrs. Norton some thirty years since, and was offered to Mr. Bunn for Drury Lane Theatre, but declined; "the exquisite beauties of Mrs. Norton's metrical compositions being overloaded by a pressure of dialogue and a redundancy of scenic effects, the fidelity and rapid succession of which it would have puzzled any scene-painter or mechanist to follow."—*Bunn's Stage*, vol ii., p. 139.

took off my clothes the whole time. This severe application made me very ill. . . . Old Fonthill had a very ample loud echoing hall—one of the largest in the kingdom. Numerous doors led from it into different parts of the house through dim, winding passages. It was from that I introduced the Hall—the idea of the Hall of Eblis being generated by my own. My imagination magnified and coloured it with the Eastern character. All the females in *Vathek* were portraits of those in the domestic establishment of old Fonthill, their fancied good or ill qualities being exaggerated to suit my purpose." An English translation of the work afterwards appeared, the author of which Beckford said he never knew; he thought it tolerably well done.

At twenty-four, Mr. Beckford married the Lady Margaret Gordon, daughter of Charles, fourth Earl of Aboyne, but the lady died in three years. In 1784 he was returned to Parliament for Wells; in 1790 he sat for Hindon; but in 1794 he accepted the Chiltern Hundreds, and again went abroad. He now fixed himself in Portugal, where he purchased an estate near Cintra, and built the sumptuous mansion, the decoration and desolation of which some years afterwards Lord Byron described in the first canto of his *Childe Harold*, in the stanza beginning—

> "There thou too, Vathek! England's wealthiest son,
> Once form'd thy Paradise, as not aware
> When wanton Wealth her mightiest deeds hath done,
> Meek Peace voluptuous lures was ever wont to shun.
> Here didst thou dwell, here schemes of pleasure plan,
> Beneath yon mountain's ever beauteous brow :
> But now, as if a thing unblest by man,
> Thy fairy dwelling is as lone as thou !

Here giant woods a passage scarce allow
To halls deserted, portals gaping wide :
Fresh lessons to the thinking bosom, how
Vain are pleasaunces on earth supplied ;
Swept into wrecks anon by Time's ungentle tide ! "

Many years after, Mr. Beckford published his Travels,
one volume of which was *An Excursion to the Monasteries
of Alcobaça and Batalha*. Of the kitchen of the magnificent Alcobaça, he gives the following glowing picture :—
" Through the centre of the immense and groined
hall, not less than sixty feet in diameter, ran a brisk
rivulet of the clearest water, flowing through pierced
wooden reservoirs, containing every sort and size of the
finest river-fish. On one side, loads of game and
venison were heaped up ; on the other, vegetables and
fruit in endless variety. Beyond a long line of stoves
extended a row of ovens, and close to them hillocks of
wheaten flour whiter than snow, rocks of sugar, jars of
the purest oil, and pastry in vast abundance, which a
numerous tribe of lay-brothers and their attendants
were rolling out and puffing up into a hundred different
shapes, singing all the while as blithely as larks in a
corn-field ! " The banquet is described as including
" exquisite sausages, potted lampreys, strange messes
from the Brazils, and others still more strange from
China (*viz*. birds'-nests and sharks'-fins), dressed after
the latest mode of Macao, by a Chinese 'lay-brother.
Confectionery and fruits were out of the question here ;
they awaited the party in an adjoining still more sumptuous and spacious saloon, to which they retired from
the effluvia of viands and sauces." On another occasion,
by aid of Mr. Beckford's cook, the party sat down to
" one of the most delicious banquets ever vouchsafed a

mortal on this side of Mahomet's paradise. The *macé-doine* was perfection, the ortolans and quails lumps of celestial fatness, the *sautés* and *bechamels* beyond praise; and a certain truffle-cream was so exquisite, that the Lord Abbot piously gave thanks for it."

Mr. Beckford returned to England in 1795, and occupied himself with the embellishment of his house at Fonthill. Meanwhile, he had studied Ecclesiastical Architecture, which induced him to commence building the third house at Fonthill, considering the second too near a piece of water. In 1801, the superb furniture was sold by auction; when the furniture of the Turkish room, which had cost 4,000*l.*, realized only 740 guineas. Next year there was a sale in London of the proprietor's pictures. In 1807 the mansion was mostly taken down, when the materials were sold for 10,000*l.*; one wing was left standing, which was subsequently sold to Mr. Morrison, M.P., who added to it, and adapted it for a country seat.

These proceedings were, however, only preliminary to the commencement of a much more magnificent collection of books, pictures, curiosities, rareties, bijouterie, and other products of art and ingenuity, to be placed in the new "Fonthill Abbey," built in a showy monastic style. Mr. Beckford shrouded his architectural proceedings in the profoundest mystery: he was haughty and reserved; and because some of his neighbours followed game into his grounds, he had a wall twelve feet high and seven miles long built round his home estate, in order to shut out the world. This was guarded by projecting railings on the top, in the manner of *chevaux-de-frise.* Large and strong double gates were provided in this wall, at the different roads of entrance, and at these gates were stationed persons who had strict orders not to admit a stranger.

The building of the Abbey was a sort of romance. A vast number of mechanics and labourers were employed to advance the works with rapidity, and a new hamlet was built to accommodate the workmen. All around was activity and energy, whilst the growing edifice, as the scaffolding and walls, were raised above the surrounding trees, excited the curiosity of the passing tourist, as well as the villagers. It appears that Mr. Beckford pursued the objects of his wishes, whatever they were, not coolly and considerately like most other men, but with all the enthusiasm of passion. No sooner did he decide upon any point than he had it carried into immediate execution, whatever might be the cost. After the building was commenced, he was so impatient to get it furnished, that he kept regular relays of men at work night and day, including Sundays, supplying them liberally with ale and spirits while they were at work; and when anything was completed which gave him particular pleasure, adding an extra 5l. or 10l. to be spent in drink. The first tower, the height of which from the ground was 400 feet, was built of wood, in order to see its effect; this was then taken down, and the same form put up in wood covered with cement. This fell down, and the tower was built a third time on the same foundation with brick and stone. The foundation of the tower was originally that of a small summer-house, to which Mr. Beckford was making additions, when the idea of the Abbey occurred to him; and this idea he was so impatient to realize, that he would not wait to remove the summer-house to make a proper foundation for the tower, but carried it up on the walls already

standing, and this with the worst description of materials
and workmanship, while it was mostly built by men in
a state of intoxication.

To raise the public surprise and afford new scope for
speculation, a novel scene was presented in the works in
the winter of 1800, when in November and December
nearly 500 men were employed day and night to expe-
dite the works, by torch and lamp-light, in time for the
reception of Lord Nelson and Sir William and Lady
Hamilton, who were entertained here by Mr. Beckford
with extraordinary magnificence on December 20, 1800.
On one occasion, while the tower was building, an
elevated part of it caught fire and was destroyed; the
sight was sublime, and was enjoyed by Mr. Beckford.
This was soon rebuilt. At one period, every cart and
wagon in the district were pressed into the service; at
another, the works at St. George's Chapel, Windsor, were
abandoned, that 400 men might be employed night and
day on Fonthill Abbey. These men relieved each other
by regular watches, and during the longest and darkest
nights of winter it was a strange sight to see the tower
rising under their hands, the trowel and the torch being
associated for that purpose. This Mr. Beckford was
fond of contemplating. He is represented as surveying
from an eminence the works thus expedited, the busy
bevy of the masons, the dancing lights and their strange
effects upon the wood and architecture below, and feast-
ing his sense with this display of almost superhuman
exertion.

Upon one memorable occasion Mr. Beckford was
willing to run the risk of spoiling a good dinner, in
order to show that nothing possible to man was impossible to him. He had sworn by his beloved St. Anthony,

that he would have his Christmas dinner cooked in the new Abbey kitchen. The time was short, the work was severe, for much remained to be done. Still, Beckford had said it, and it must be done. So every exertion that money could command was brought to bear. The apartment, indeed, was finished by the Christmas morn-ing, but the bricks had not time to settle readily into their places, the beams were not thoroughly secured, the mortar, which was to keep the walls together, had not dried. However, Beckford had invoked the blessed St. Anthony, and he would not depart from it. The fire was lit, the splendid repast was cooked, the servants were carrying the dishes through the long passages into the dining-room, when the kitchen itself fell in with a loud crash; but it was not a misfortune of any consequence; no person was injured, the master had kept his word, and he had money enough to build another kitchen.

Mr. Loudon, in 1835, collected at Fonthill some curious evidence in confirmation of his idea that Mr. Beckford's enjoyments consisted of a succession of violent impulses. Thus, when he wished a new walk to be cut in the woods, or work of any kind to be done, he used to say nothing about it in the way of prepa-ration, but merely give orders, perhaps late in the afternoon, that it should be cleared out and in a perfect state by the following morning at the time he came out to take his ride, and the whole strength of the village was then put upon the work, and employed during the night and next day, when Mr. Beckford came to inspect what was done; if he was pleased with it he used to give a 5l. or 10l. note to the men who had been employed, to drink, besides, of course, paying their wages, which were always liberal. His charities were performed in the same capricious manner. Suddenly he would order a hundred pairs of blankets to be purchased and given away; or all the firs to be cut out of an extensive plantation, and all the poor who choose to take them away were permitted to do so, provided it were done in one night. He was also known to suddenly order all the wagons and carts that could be procured to be sent off for coal to be distributed among the poor.

Mr. Beckford seldom rode out beyond his gates, but when he did he was generally asked for charity by the poor people. Sometimes he used to throw a one-pound note or a guinea to them; or he would turn round and give the supplicants a severe horse-whipping. When the last was the case, soon after he had ridden away, he generally sent back a guinea or two to the persons whom he had whipped. In his mode of life at Fonthill he had many singularities: though he never had any society, yet his table was laid every day in the most splendid style. He was known to give orders for a dinner for twelve persons and to sit down alone to it, attended by twelve servants in full dress; yet he would eat only of one dish, and send the rest away. There were no bells at Fonthill, with the exception of one room, occupied occasionally by Mr. Beckford's daughter, the Duchess of Hamilton. The servants used to wait by turns in the anti-rooms to the apartments which Mr. Beckford occupied; they were very small and low in the ceiling. He led almost the life of a hermit within the walls of the Fonthill estate; here he could luxuriate within his sumptuous home, or ride for miles on his lawns, and through forest and mountain woods,—amid dressed parterres of the pleasure-garden, or the wild scenery of nature. This garden, the vast woods, and a wild lake, abounded with game, and the choristers of the forest, which were not only left undisturbed by the gun, but were fed and encouraged by the lord of the soil and his long retinue of servants. A widower, and without any family at home, Mr. Beckford resided at the Abbey for more than twenty years, ever active, and constantly occupied in reading, music, and the converse of a choice circle of friends, or in directing workmen in the erection of the Abbey, which had been in progress since the year 1798.

About the year 1822 his restless spirit required a change; besides which his fortunes received a shock from which they never recovered. He now purchased two houses in Lansdown Crescent, Bath, with a large tract of land adjoining, and removed hither. The property at Fonthill was then placed at the disposal of Mr. Christie, who prepared a catalogue for the sale of the estate, the Abbey, and its gorgeous contents. The place was made an exhibition of in the summer of 1822: the price of admission was one guinea for each person, and 7,200 tickets were sold: thousands flocked to Fonthill; but at the close of the summer, instead of a sale on the premises, the whole was bought in one lot by Mr. Farquhar, it was understood, for the sum of 350,000*l.* Mr. Beckford's outlay upon the property had been, according to his own account, about 273,000*l.*, scattered over sixteen or eighteen years. The reason he assigned for disposing of the property was the reduction of his income by a decree of the Court of Chancery, which had deprived him of two of his Jamaica estates. "You may imagine their importance," he added, "when I tell you that there were 1,500 slaves upon them."

Mr. Farquhar, the purchaser of the property, was an old miser who had amassed an immense fortune in India. By the advice of Mr. Phillips, the auctioneer, of Bond Street, in the following year another exhibition was made of Fonthill and its treasures, to which articles were added, and the whole sold as genuine property; the tickets of admission were half-a-guinea each, the price of the catalogues 12s., and the sale lasted thirty-seven days.

In December, 1825, the tower at Fonthill, which had been hastily built and not long finished, fell with a tremendous crash, destroying the hall, the octagon, and other parts of the buildings. Mr. Farquhar, with his nephew's family, had taken the precaution of removing to the northern wing: the tower was above 260 feet high.

Mr. Loudon, when at Fonthill in 1835, collected some interesting particulars of this catastrophe. He describes the manner in which the tower fell as somewhat remarkable. It had given indications of insecurity for some time; the warning was taken, and the more valuable parts of the windows and other articles were removed.

Mr. Farquhar, however, who then resided in one angle of the building, and who was in a very infirm state of health, could not be brought to believe there was any danger. He was wheeled out in his chair on the front lawn about half an hour before the tower fell; and though he had seen the cracks and the deviation of the centre from the perpendicular, he treated the idea of its coming down as ridiculous. He was carried back to his room, and the tower fell almost immediately.

From the manner in which it fell, from the lightness of the materials of which it was constructed, neither Mr. Farquhar, nor the servants who were in the kitchen preparing dinner, knew that it fallen, though the immense collection of dust which rose into the atmosphere had assembled almost all the inhabitants of the village, and had given the alarm even as far as Wardour Castle. Only one man (who died in 1833) saw the tower fall: it first sank perpendicularly and slowly, and then burst and spread over the roofs of the adjoining wings on every side. The cloud of dust was enormous, so as completely to darken the air for a considerable distance around for several minutes. Such was the concussion in the interior of the building, that one man was forced along a passage as if he had been in an air-gun to the distance of 30 feet, among dust so thick as to be felt. Another person, on the outside, was, in like manner, carried to some distance ; fortunately, no one was seriously injured. With all this, it is almost incredible that neither Mr. Farquhar, nor the servants in the kitchen, should have heard the tower fall, or known that it had fallen, till they saw through the window the people of the village who had assembled to see the ruins. Mr. Farquhar, it is said, could scarcely be convinced that the tower was down, and when he was so he said he was glad of it, for that now the house was not too large for him to live in. Mr. Beckford, when told at Bath by his servant that the tower had fallen, merely observed, that it had made an obeisance to Mr. Farquhar which it had never done to him.

One of the last things which Mr. Beckford did, after having sold Fonthill, and ordered horses to be put to his carriage to leave the place for ever, was to mount his pony, ride round with his gardener, to give directions for various alterations and improvements which he wished to have executed. On returning to the house, his carriage being ready, he stepped into it, and never afterwards visited Fonthill. Though Mr. Beckford had spent immense sums of money there, it is said, on good authority, 1,600,000*l*., it did not appear that he had at all raised the character of the working classes: the effect was directly the reverse; the men were sunk, past recovery, in habits of drunkenness; and when Mr. Loudon visited Fonthill, there were only two or three of the village labourers alive who had been employed in the Abbey works.

We now follow Mr. Beckford to Bath, where he was storing his twin houses with some of the choicest articles from his old libraries and cabinets; was forming and creating new gardens, with hot-houses and conservatories, on the steep and rocky slope of Lansdown. On its summit he built a lofty tower, which commands a vast extent of prospect. A street intervened between the two houses, but they were soon united by a flying gallery. One of these houses was fitted up for Mr. Beckford's residence, and here he lived luxuriously; the splendour and state of Fonthill being followed here on a smaller scale. In his wine-cellars he had a portion of the nineteen pipes of the fine Malmsey Madeira, which his father, Alderman Beckford, had bought. The merchant who imported them offered them to Queen Charlotte, who could only purchase one, as the price was so great; the Fonthill Crœsus, however, purchased the remainder of the cargo.

The new proprietor of Fonthill was a very different man from Mr. Beckford. Born in Aberdeen, Mr. John

Farquhar, like many of his countrymen, started in early life to seek his fortune in India. The interest of some relatives procured him a cadetship in the service of the East India Company, on the Bombay establishment; there the young Scotsman had the certainty of slowly but steadily rising in position, and should health be left to him, of enjoying a reputable and independent competency. He, however, received a dangerous wound in the leg, which first caused a painful and constant lameness, and soon after led to general derangement of his health, and even danger to life itself. He now obtained leave to remove to Bengal, partly in hopes of a more salubrious climate, but chiefly in search of that medical talent which was likely to be most abundant at the chief seat of Government. Settled in Bengal, he obtained the advice of the best physicians. He also studied chemistry and medicine; and it was before long generally said that the sickly cadet who was so attached to chemical experiments, was well fitted to be sent into the interior of the country, where was a large manufactory of gunpowder established by the Government, but which was unsuccessful. The shrewd Scotsman took charge of the mill, henceforth the powder was faultless; and shortly after Farquhar became the sole contractor for the Government. The Governor-General, Warren Hastings, reposed much confidence in Farquhar; and this, added to his own indefatigable vigour of mind, soon laid the foundation of a fortune, which was rapidly increased by his penurious habits.

It was the time when war and distresses in Europe kept the funds so low, that fifty-five was a common price for the Three per cents. Accordingly, as

Farquhar's money accumulated, he sent large remittances to his bankers, Messrs. Hoare, of Fleet Street, for investment in the above tempting securities. When he had thus amassed half a million, he determined to return to his native country, and he bade adieu to the East where he had found the wealth he coveted. Landing at Gravesend, he took his seat upon the outside of the coach, and in due time found himself in London. Weather-beaten, and covered with dust, he made his way to his bankers, and there, stepping up to one of the clerks, expressed a wish to see Mr. Hoare himself. But his rough appearance and common make of the clothes about his sunburnt limbs, suggested to the clerk that he must be some unlucky petitioner for charity; and he was left to wait in the cash-office until Mr. Hoare happened to pass through. The latter was some time before he could understand who Mr. Farquhar was. His Indian customer, indeed, he knew well by name, but he had none of that hauteur which was then common with the successful Anglo-Indians. At length, however, Mr. Hoare was satisfied as to the identity of his wealthy visitor, who then asked him for 25*l.*, and saluting him, retired.

On first arriving in England, Mr. Farquhar took up his abode with a relative of some rank, who mixed a good deal in London society, and who proposed to introduce to his circle Mr. Farquhar, by giving a grand ball in honour of his successful return from India. This relative had tolerated Mr. Farquhar's fancies as regarded his every-day attire; but his fashionable mind was horrified when the day of the coming ball was only a week off, and there was, nevertheless, no sign of his intending to provide himself with a new suit of clothes for the gay occasion. He ventured accordingly to hint to him the propriety of doing so; when Mr. Farquhar made a short reply, packed up his clothes, and in a few minutes was driven from the door in a hackney-coach, not even taking leave of his too-critical host.

He then settled in Upper Baker Street, where his windows were ever remarkable for requiring a servant's care, and his whole house notable for its dingy and dirty appearance; at which we cannot wonder when we learn that his sole attendant was an old woman, and that from even her intrusive care his own apartment was strictly kept free. Yet in charitable deeds Mr. Farquhar was munificent to a princely extent, and often, when he had left his comfortless home with a crust of bread in his pocket to save the expenditure of a penny at an oyster-shop, it was to give away in the course of the day hundreds of pounds to aid the distressed, and to cure and care for those who suffered from biting poverty, hunger, and want. But in his personal expenditure he was extremely parsimonious; and whilst he resided in Baker Street, he expended on himself and his household but 200*l.* a year out of the 30,000*l.* or 40,000*l.* which his many sources of income must have yielded him.*

Such was the man who succeeded the luxurious Beckford at Fonthill! He, however, sold the property about 1825, and died in the following year. The immense fortune he had struggled to make, and to increase which he had lived a solitary and comfortless life, he made no disposal of by will; the law dis-

* Mr. Farquhar died July 6, 1826, in York Place, Marylebone, aged 76 years; he was buried in St. John's Wood Chapel, where is a handsome monument to his memory, with a medallion head of the deceased by P. Row, sculptor.

tributed it among his next-of-kin, and those he favoured and those he neglected inherited equal portions. Three nephews and four nieces became entitled to 100,000*l.* each. Fonthill Abbey had been taken down, merely enough of its ruins being left to show where it had stood. Mr. Farquhar possessed Fonthill for so short a time, and it was demolished so soon after he had parted with it, and so many years before Mr. Beckford followed him to the grave, that the latter lived to know that its last proprietor was comparatively forgotten, and the strange glories of the fantastic pile will be connected by the public voice with no name but that of its eccentric architect.

On settling at Bath, Mr. Beckford was frequently seen on horseback in the streets with his groom, and appeared as the plain unostentatious country gentleman: he was no longer the wealthy lord of Fonthill; still his appearance always excited the gaze and speculation of idlers and gossips. A dwarf, an Italian named Piero, was occasionally seen on a pony with the groom, and strange conjectures were hazarded on the history of this human phenomenon. The fact is, Mr. Beckford had taken charge of him in Italy, when he was deserted by his parents and was homeless and friendless; and he was brought to England by a humane patron, who supported him through life.

In 1844, Mr. Cyrus Redding, when at Bath, had several interviews and conversations with Mr. Beckford, whose mind was then vigorous: his spirits were good, and he displayed his wonted activity of body nearly to the last. In his seventy-sixth year he said that he had never felt a moment's *ennui* in his life. He was the most accomplished man of his time: his reading was very extensive;

he used to say that he could easily read and understand an octavo volume during his breakfast. Besides
the classical languages of antiquity, he spoke four
modern European tongues, and wrote three of them
with great elegance. He read Russian and Arabic.
We have said that he was taught music by Mozart, to
whom he was so much attached, that when the great
composer settled in Vienna, Mr. Beckford made a visit
to that capital "that he might once more see his old
master."

Mr. Redding tells us that Mr. Beckford's custom, "in
fine weather, was to rise early, ride to the tower or
about the grounds, walk back and breakfast, and then
read until a little before noon, generally making pencil
notes in the margin of every book, transact business
with his steward; afterwards, until two o'clock, continue
to read and write, and then ride out two or three hours."
Mr. Beckford was never idle. When planning or
building, he passed the larger part of the day where
the work was proceeding. He sometimes expressed
contempt by a sarcastic sneer, peculiar to himself. Few
could utter more cutting things than the author of
Vathek, the delivery with a caustic expression of
countenance that made them tell with double effect.
Mr. Redding once ventured to remark, "It must have
cost you much pain to quit Fonthill." "Not so much
as you might think. I can bend to fortune. I have
philosophy enough not to cry like a child about a play-
thing." Mr. Britton, who had seen much of Mr.
Beckford, tells us that the remarks and opinions in
the novels of *Cecil a Coxcomb* and *Cecil a Peer*,
mostly written by Mrs. Gore when on a visit to Mr.
Beckford at Bath, afford the nearest approach he had

seen in print to the language, the ideas, the peculiar
sentiments of the author of *Vathek*.

Mr. Beckford continued to reside in Bath (except his
annual visits to the metropolis, when he lived in Park
Lane and in Gloucester Place*) for about twenty
years, and died there on May 2, 1844, in the eighty-
fourth year of his age. His intention was to make the
ground attached to the Lansdown tower the place of
his sepulchre, and he had prepared and placed on the spot
a granite sarcophagus, inscribed with a passage from
Vathek; but the ecclesiastical authorities refused to
consecrate the ground, the body was embalmed and
placed in the sarcophagus in the cemetery of Lyncomb,
to the south of Bath. It was afterwards removed to
Lansdown, when the ground was consecrated.

The author of *Vathek* was unquestionably a man of
genius and rare accomplishments. "But his abilities
were overpowered and his character tainted by the
possessions of wealth so enormous. At every stage his
money was like a millstone round his neck. He had
taste and knowledge; but the selfishness of wealth
tempted him to let these gifts of the mind run to seed
in the gratification of extravagant freaks. He really
enjoyed travelling and scenery, but he felt it incumbent
on him, as a millionnaire, to take a French cook with
him wherever he went;† and he found that the Spanish

---

* Three other of Mr. Beckford's town houses were:—1. On the
Terrace, Piccadilly, part of the site of the newly-built mansion of
Baron Rothschild; 2. No. 1, Devonshire Place, New Road; and,
it is said, though we do not vouch how correctly, 3. No. 27,
Charles Street, Mayfair, a very small house, looking over the
garden of Chesterfield House.

† In conformity with an old English custom, Mr. Beckford invariably travelled with his bed among his luggage.

grandees and ecclesiastical dignitaries who welcomed him so cordially valued him as the man whose cook could make such wonderful omelettes. From the day when Chatham's proxy stood for him at the font till the day when he was laid in his pink granite sarcophagus, he was the victim of riches. Had he had only 5,000*l.* a year, and been sent to Eton, he might have been one of the foremost men of his time, and have been as useful in his generation as, under his unhappy circumstances, he was useless."* It may be added, that he was worse : for he so threw about his money at Fonthill as to corrupt and demoralise the simple country people.

Against this judgment must, however, be placed Mr. Beckford's own declaration, that he never felt a single moment of *ennui.*

Mr. Beckford left two daughters, the eldest of whom, Susan Euphemia, was married to the Marquis of Clydesdale in 1810, and became Duchess of Hamilton. The tomb at Lansdown, with its polished granite, emblazoned shields, and bronzed and gilt embellishments, was not long cared for; since in 1850, it presented in its neglected state a lamentable object. *Vathek* will be remembered. Byron, a good judge of such a subject, has pronounced that "for correctness of costume, beauty of description, and power of imagination," it far surpasses all other European imitations of the Eastern style of fiction.

* *Saturday Review.*

ALDERMAN BECKFORD'S MONUMENT SPEECH, IN GUILDHALL.

The speech on the pedestal of Beckford's statue, and referred to at p. 2 *ante*, is the one which the Alderman is said to have addressed to his Majesty on the 23rd of May, 1770, with reference to the King's reply to the Remonstrance address which Beckford had presented :—" That he should have been wanting to the public as well as to himself if he had not expressed his dissatisfaction at the late address." Horace Walpole thus notes the affair : " The City carried a new remonstrance, garnished with my lord's own ingredients, but much less hot than the former. The country, however, was put to some confusion by my Lord Mayor, who, contrary to all form and precedent, tacked a volunteer speech to the ' Remonstrance.' It was wondrous loyal and respectful, but, being an innovation, much discomposed the solemnity. It is always usual to furnish a copy of what is said to the King, that he may be prepared with his answer. In this case, he was reduced to tuck up his train, jump from the throne, and take sanctuary in his closet, or answer extempore, which is not part of the Royal trade ; or sit silent, and have nothing to reply. This last was the event, and a position awkward enough in conscience."—*Walpole to Sir Horace Mann,* May 24, 1770.

Now, at the end of the Alderman's speech, in his copy of the City addresses, Mr. Isaac Reed has inserted the following note :—" It is a curious fact, but a true

one, that Beckford did not utter one syllable of this
speech (on the monument). It was penned by John
Horne Tooke, and by his art put on the records of the
City and on Beckford's statue, as he told me, Mr.
Braithwaite, Mr. Sayer, &c., at the Athenæum Club.—
Isaac Reed." There can be little doubt that the worthy
commentator and his friends were imposed upon. In
the *Chatham Correspondence*, volume iii., p. 460, a letter
from Sheriff Townsend to the Earl expressly states
that, with the exception of the words "and necessary"
being left out before the word "revolution," the Lord
Mayor's speech in the *Public Advertiser* of the preceding
day is verbatim. (The one delivered to the King.)—
Wright—Note to Walpole.

Gifford says (*Ben Jonson*, VI. 481) that Beckford
never uttered before the King one syllable of the speech
upon his monument; and Gifford's statement is fully
confirmed both by Isaac Reed (as above) and by Maltby,
the friend of Rogers and Horne Tooke. Beckford
made a "remonstrance speech" to the King; but the
speech on Beckford's monument is the after speech
written for Beckford by Horne Tooke.—*See Mitford,
Gray, and Mason's Correspondence*, pp. 438, 439.—
Cuningham's Note to Walpole, v. 239.

Such is the historic worth of this strange piece of
monumental bombast, upon which Pennant made this
appropriate comment :—

> " The things themselves are neither scarce nor rare,
> The wonder's how the devil they got there."

BEAU BRUMMEL.

This celebrated leader of fashion in the times of the Regency—George Bryan Brummel—was born June 7, 1778. His grandfather was a pastrycook in Bury Street, St. James's, who, by letting off a large portion of his house, became a moneyed man. While Brummel's father was yet a boy, Mr. Jenkinson came to lodge there, and this led to the lad being employed in a Government office, when his lodger and patron had attained to eminence: he was subsequently private secretary to Lord Liverpool, and at his death, left the Beau little less than 30,000*l.* Brummel was sent to Eton, and thence to Oxford, and at sixteen he was gazetted to a cornetcy in the 10th Hussars, at that time commanded by the Prince of Wales, to whom he had been presented on the Terrace at Windsor, when the Beau was a boy at Eton. He became an associate of the Prince, then two-and-thirty, but who, according to Mr. Thomas Raikes, disdained not to take lessons in dress from Brummel at his lodgings. Thither would the future King of nations wend his way, where, absorbed in the mysteries of the toilet, he would remain till so late an hour that he sometimes sent his horses away, and insisted on Brummel giving him a quiet dinner, which generally ended in a deep potation.

Brummel's assurance was one of his earliest characteristics. A great law lord, who lived in Russell Square, one evening gave a ball, at which J., one of the beauties of the time, was present. Numerous were the applications made to dance with her; but being as proud as she was beautiful, she refused them all, till the young Hussar made his appearance; and he having proffered to hand her out, she at once acquiesced, greatly to the wrath of the disappointed candidates. In one of the pauses of the dance, he happened to find himself close to an acquaintance, when he exclaimed, "Ha! you here? Do, my good fellow, tell me who that ugly man is leaning against the chimney-piece." "Why, surely you must know him," replied the other, "'tis the master of the house." "No, indeed," said the Cornet, coolly; "how should I? I never was invited."

Captain Jesse, the biographer of Brummel, has drawn his portrait at about this time. "His face was rather long and complexion fair; his whiskers inclined to sandy, and hair light brown. His features were neither plain nor handsome; but his head was well shaped, the forehead being unusually high; showing, according to phrenological development, more of the mental than the animal passions—the bump of self-esteem was very prominent. His countenance indicated that he possessed considerable intelligence, and his mouth betrayed a strong disposition to indulge in sarcastic humour: this was predominant in every feature, the nose excepted, the natural regularity of which, though it had been broken by a fall from his charger, preserved his features from degenerating into comicality.. His eyebrows were equally expressive with his mouth; and while the latter was giving utterance to something very good-humoured or polite, the former, and the eyes themselves, which were grey and full of oddity, could assume an expression that made the sincerity of his words very doubtful. His voice was very pleasing."

Brummel was one of the first who revived and improved the taste for dress, and his great innovation was effected upon neckcloths; they were then worn without stiffening of any kind, and bagged out in front, rucking up to the chin in a roll: to remedy this obvious awkwardness and inconvenience, he used to have his slightly starched; and a reasoning mind must allow that there is not much to object to in this reform. He did not, however, like the dandies, test their fitness for use by trying if he could raise three parts of their length by one corner without their bending; yet, it appears that if the cravat was not properly tied at the first effort, or inspiring impulse, it was always rejected. His valet was coming down stairs one day with a quantity of tumbled neckcloths under his arm, and, being interrogated on the subject, solemnly replied, "Oh, they are *our* failures." Practice like this, of course, made Brummel perfect; and his tie soon became a model that was imitated but never equalled. The method by which this most important result was attained, was thus told to Captain Jesse:—" The collar, which was always fixed to his shirt, was so large that, before being folded down, it completely hid his head and face; and the white neckcloth was at least a foot in height. The first *coup d'archet* was made with the shirt-collar, which he folded down to its proper size; and Brummel, then standing before the glass, with his chin poked up to the ceiling, by the gentle and gradual declension of the lower jaw, creased the cravat to reasonable dimensions, the form of each succeeding crease being perfected with the shirt which he had just discarded."

" Brummel's morning dress was similar to that of every other gentleman. Hessians and pantaloons, or

top-boots and buckskins, with a blue coat and a light
or buff-coloured waistcoat, of course fitting to admiration on the best figure in England. His dress of an
evening was a blue coat and white waistcoat, black
pantaloons, which buttoned tight to the ankle, striped
stockings, and opera-hat; in fact he was always carefully dressed, but never the slave of fashion.

" Brummel's tailors were Schweitzer and Davidson in
Cork Street; Weston; and a German of the name of
Meyer, who lived in Conduit Street. The trousers
which opened at the bottom of the leg, and were closed
by buttons and loops, were invented either by Meyer or
Brummel. The Beau, at any rate, was the first who
wore them, and they immediately became quite the
fashion and continued so for some years.''

Brummel was addicted to practical jokes, one of
which may be related. The victim was an old French
emigrant, whom he had met on a visit to Woburn or
Chatsworth, and into whose hair-pouch he managed to
introduce some finely-powdered sugar. Next morning
the poor Marquis, quite unconscious of his head being so
well-sweetened, joined the breakfast-table as usual; but
scarcely had he made his bow and plunged his knife
into the Perigord pie before him, than the flies began to
desert the walls and windows to settle upon his head.
The weather was exceedingly hot; the flies of course
numerous, and even the honeycomb and marmalade
upon the table seemed to have lost all attraction for
them. The Marquis relinquished his knife and fork to
drive off the enemy with his handkerchief. But scarcely
had he attempted to renew his acquaintance with the
Perigord pie, than back the whole swarm came, more
teazingly than ever. Not a wing was missing. More

of the company who were not in the secret, could not help wondering at this phenomenon, as the buzzing grew louder and louder every moment. Matters grew still worse when the sugar, melting, poured down the Frenchman's brow and face in thick streams; for his tormentors then changed their ground of action, and having thus found a more vulnerable part, nearly drove him mad with their stings. Unable to bear it any longer, he clasped his head with both hands, and rushed out of the room in a cloud of powder, followed by his persevering tormentors, and the laughter of the company.

Brummel was the autocrat of the world in which he moved. It has been said that Madame de Staël was in awe of him, and considered her having failed to please him as her greatest misfortune; while the Prince of Wales having neglected to call upon her, she placed only as a secondary cause of lamentation. The great French authoress, however, was not without reason in her regrets: to offend or not to please Brummel was to lose caste in the fashionable world, to be exposed to the most cutting sarcasm and the most poignant ridicule.

Captain Jesse thus tells the story of Brummel's *cutting* quarrel with the Prince of Wales. Lord Alvanley, Brummel, Henry Pierrepoint, and Sir Harry Mildmay, gave at the Hanover Square Rooms a fête, which was called the Dandies' Ball. Alvanley was a friend of the Duke of York; Harry Mildmay, young, and had never been introduced to the Prince Regent; Pierrepoint knew him slightly, and Brummel was at daggers drawn with his Royal Highness. No invitation was, however, sent to the Prince, but the ball excited much interest and expectation, and to the surprise of the Amphytrions, a communication was received from his Royal Highness intimating his wish to be present. Nothing, therefore, was left but to send him an invitation, which was done in due form, and in the name of the four spirited givers of the ball; the next question was how were they to receive the guest, and which, after some discussion, was arranged thus:— When the approach of the Prince was announced, each of the four gentlemen took in due form a candle in his hand. Pierrepoint, as knowing the Prince, stood nearest the door with his wax-light; and Mildmay, as being young and void of offence, opposite. Alvanley, with Brummel opposite, stood immediately behind the other two. The Prince at length arrived, and, as was expected, spoke civilly and with recognition to Pierrepoint, and then turned and spoke a few words to Mildmay; advancing, he addressed several sentences to Alvanley; and then turned towards Brummel, looked at him, but as if he did not know who he was, or why he was there, and without bestowing on him the slightest recognition. It was then, at the very instant he passed on, that Brummel, seizing with infinite fun and readiness the notion that they were unknown to each other, said aloud for the purpose of being heard, " Alvanley, who's your fat friend ?" Those who were in front, and saw the Prince's face, say that he was cut to the quick by the aptness of the remark.

Mr. Grantley Berkeley (in his *Life and Recollections*) relates the story less circumstantially:—"There is a well-known anecdote I am able to correct, given to me by a medical friend of mine, who had it from the late Henry Pierrepoint, brother to the late Lord Manners:—' We of the Dandy Club issued invitations to a ball from which Brummel had influence enough to get the Prince excluded. Some one told the Prince this, upon which his Royal Highness wrote to say he intended to have the pleasure of being at our ball. A number of us lined the entrance-passage to receive the Prince, who, as he passed along, turned from side to side to shake hands with each of us; but when he came to Brummel, he passed him without the smallest notice, and turned to shake hands with the man opposite to Brummel. As the Prince turned from that man—I forget who it was—Brummel leaned forward across the passage, and said, in a loud voice, 'Who is your fat friend?' We were all dismayed; but in those days Brummel could do no wrong."

The following story was supplied to Captain Jesse by a correspondent. The Beau, it appears, had a great *penchant* for snuff-boxes:—"Brummel had a collection chosen with singular sagacity and good taste; and one of them had been seen and admired by the Prince, who said, 'Brummel, this box must be mine: go to Gray's and order any box you like in lieu of it.' Brummel begged that it might be one with his Royal Highness' miniature; and the Prince, pleased and flattered at the suggestion, gave his assent to the request. Accordingly, the box was ordered, and Brummel took great pains with the pattern and form, as well as with the miniature and diamonds round it. When some progress had been made, the portrait was shown to the Prince; who was charmed with it, suggested slight improvements and alterations, and took the liveliest interest in the work as it proceeded. All in fact was on the point of being concluded when the scene at Claremont took place; [where this writer describes the quarrel as originating, through the Prince preventing Brummel from joining a party, on the plea of Mrs. Fitzherbert disliking him.] A day or two after this, Brummel thought he might as well go to Gray's and inquire about the box: he did so, and was told that special directions had been sent by the Prince of Wales that the box was not to be delivered: it never was, nor was the one returned for which it was to have been an equivalent. It was this, I believe, more than anything besides, which induced Brummel to bear himself with such unbending hostility towards the Prince of Wales. He felt that he had treated him unworthily, and from this moment he indulged himself by saying the bitterest things. When pressed by poverty, however, and, as I suppose, broken in spirit, he at a later period recalled the Prince's attention to the subject of the snuff-box. Colonel Cooke (who was at Eton called 'Cricketer Cooke,' afterwards known as 'Kangaroo Cooke'), when passing through Calais, saw Brummel, who told him the story, and requested that he would inform the Prince Regent that the promised box had never been given, and that he was now constrained to recall the circumstance to his recollection. The Regent's reply was: 'Well, Master Kang, as for the box it is all nonsense; but I suppose the poor devil wants a hundred guineas, and he shall have them;' and it was in this ungracious manner that the money was sent, received, and acknowledged. I have heard Brummel speak of the affair of the snuff-box, but I never heard him say that he received the hundred guineas."

Brummel, late in life, stood to his Whig colours. His evening dress consisted of a blue coat, with velvet collar and the consular button; a buff waistcoat, black trousers and boots. His white neckcloth was unexception-

able. The only articles of jewellery about him were a
plain ring and a massive chain of Venetian ducat-gold,
which served as a guard to his watch, and was evidently
as much for use as ornament, only two links of it were
to be seen; those passed from the buttons of his waistcoat to the pocket; the chain was peculiar, and was of
the same pattern as those suspended *in terrorem* outside
the principal entrance to Newgate. The ring was dug
out on the Field of the Cloth of Gold by a labourer,
who sold it to Brummel when he was at Calais. An
opera-hat, and gloves which were held in his hand, completed an attire that being remarkably quiet, could
never have attracted attention on any other person.
His *mise* was peculiar only for its extreme neatness, and
wholly at variance with an opinion very prevalent among
those who were not personally acquainted with him, that
he owed his reputation to his tailor, or to an exaggerated
style of dress.

Brummel, however, maintained his supremacy in the
world of fashion for years after the Prince had *cut* him.
"But though even royal disfavour could not seriously
lower him, he managed in the end to do that which no
one else could do, he ruined himself; the gaming table,
in the long run, deprived him of all his fortune. Then
came bills to supply the deficiencies of the hour, and
with that the consummation which they never fail to
bring about when necessity has recourse to them. A
quarrel ensuing with the friends joined in one of these
acceptances, and who accused him of taking the lion's
share, he was obliged to quit England and take
up his abode at Calais. It has been said, ludicrously
enough, that Brummel and Bonaparte fell together.
The Moscow of the former, according to his own

account, was a crooked sixpence, to the possession of which his good fortune was attached, but which he unfortunately lost.

" But, if he had lost his magical sixpence, he had not yet exhausted all his friends, from some of whom he was continually receiving even large sums of money, so much in one instance as a thousand pounds. He was thus enabled to furnish his lodgings according to his usual refined habits, and living much retired, he set seriously to work in acquiring the French language, and succeeded.

"His resources now decreased. Some friends were lost to him by death, others, perhaps, grew weary of relieving him. A visit of George IV. held out to him a momentary gleam of hope. But the king came to Calais, and did not send for him, or in any way notice him. Still he was not wholly bereft of friends, but continued from time to time to receive remittances from England; and at length, by the intervention of the Duke of Wellington with King William, Brummel was appointed English Consul in the capital of Lower Normandy. By this time he was deeply involved in debt, and when he had settled at Caen, the large deductions made from his income to discharge the arrears of debt incurred at Calais left him an insufficiency for a man of his habits. He became as deeply involved at Caen as he had before been at Calais. Next, upon his own showing of its uselessness, the consulate at Caen was abolished, and he was left penniless. He obtained funds from England. But he had more than one attack of paralysis. He was flung into prison at Caen by his French creditors, and confined in a wretched, filthy den, with felons for his companions. He was enabled by

aid from England to leave his prison, after more than
two months' confinement. Sickness, loss of memory,
absolute imbecility, and finally, inability to distinguish
bread from meat, or wine from coffee, now came with
their attendant ills. His friends obtained him admission
into the hospital of the *Bon Sauveur*, and he was
placed in a comfortable room, that had once been
occupied by the celebrated Bourrienne. Here he died
on the evening of the 30th of March, 1840."*

The different stages of mental decay through which
this unfortunate man passed, before he became hope-
lessly imbecile, it is painful to read of. One of his
most singular eccentricities was, on certain nights some
strange fancy would seize him that it was necessary he
should give a party, and he accordingly invited many
of the distinguished persons with whom he had been
intimate in former days, though some of them were
already dead. On these gala evenings he desired his
attendant to arrange his apartment, set out a whist
table, and light the *bougies* (he burnt only tallow at the
time), and at eight o'clock this man, to whom he had
already given his instructions, opened wide the door
of his sitting-room, and announced the "Duchess of
Devonshire." At the sound of her grace's well-remembered name, the Beau, instantly rising from his
chair, would advance towards the door, and greet the
cold air from the staircase as if it had been the beautiful Georgiana herself. If the dust of that fair creature
could have stood reanimate in all her loveliness before
him, she would not have thought his bow less graceful
than it had been thirty-five years before ; for, despite

* Abridged from Sir Bernard Burke's *Family Romance*, vol. i.

poor Brummel's mean habiliments and uncleanly person, the supposed visitor was received with all his former courtly ease of manner, and the earnestness that the pleasure of such an honour might be supposed to excite. "Ah! my dear Duchess," faltered the Beau, "how rejoiced am I to see you; so very amiable of you at this short notice! Pray bury yourself in this armchair: do you know it was a gift to me from the Duchess of York, who was a very kind friend of mine; but, poor thing, you know she is no more." Here the eyes of the old man would fill with the tears of idiocy, and, sinking into the *fauteuil* himself, he would sit for some time looking vacantly at the fire, until Lord Alvanley Worcester, or any other old friend he chose to name, was announced, when he again rose to receive them, and went through a similar pantomime. At ten his attendant announced the carriages, and this farce was at an end.

Brummel's sayings are not brilliant in point. They doubtless owed their success to the inimitable impudence with which they were uttered. We have thrown together a few of his many repartees.

Dining at a gentleman's house in Hampshire, where the champagne was very far from being good, he waited for a pause in the conversation, and then condemned it by raising his glass, and saying loud enough to be heard by every one at the table, "John, give me some more of that cider."

"Brummel, you were not here yesterday," said one of his club friends; "where did you dine?" "Dine! why with a person of the name of R——s. I believe he wishes me to notice him, hence the dinner; but, to give him his due, he desired that I would make up the party myself, so I asked Alvanley, Mills, Pierrepoint, and a few others; and I assure you the affair turned out quite unique; there was every delicacy in or out of season; the sillery was perfect, and not a wish remained ungratified; but, my dear fellow, conceive my astonishment when I tell you that Mr. R——s had the assurance to sit down and dine with us."

An acquaintance having, in a morning call, bored him dreadfully about some tour he made in the north of England, inquired with great pertinacity of his impatient listener which of the lakes he preferred? When Brummel, quite tired of the man's tedious raptures, turned his head imploringly towards his valet, who was arranging something in the room, and said, " Robinson?" " Sir." " Which of the lakes do I admire ? " " Windermere, sir," replied that distinguished individual. " Ah, yes; Windermere," repeated Brummel; "so it is— Windermere."

Having been asked by a sympathising friend how he happened to get such a severe cold, his reply was, " Why, do you know, I left my carriage yesterday evening, on my way to town from the Pavilion, and the infidel of a landlord put me into a room with a damp stranger."

On being asked by one of his acquaintance, during a very unseasonable summer, if he had ever seen such an one, he replied, " Yes; last winter."

Having fancied himself invited to some one's country seat, and being given to understand, after one night's lodging, that he was in error, he told an unconscious friend in town, who asked him what sort of place it was, " that it was an exceedingly good house for stopping one night in."

On the night that he quitted London, the Beau was

seen as usual at the opera, but he left early, and, without returning to his lodgings, stepped into a chaise which had been procured for him by a noble friend, and met his own carriage a short distance from town. Travelling all night as fast as four post-horses and liberal donations could enable him, the morning dawned on him at Dover, and immediately on his arrival there he hired a small vessel, put his carriage on board, and was landed in a few hours on the other side. By this time the West-end had awoke and missed him, particularly his tradesmen.

It was while promenading one day on the pier, and not long before he left Calais, that an old associate of his, who had just arrived by the packet from England, met him unexpectedly in the street, and, cordially shaking hands with him, said, " My dear Brummel, I am so glad to see you, for we had heard in England that you were dead; the report, I assure you, was in very general circulation when I left." " Mere stock-jobbing, my good fellow—mere stock-jobbing," was the Beau's reply.

We have said that Brummel's grandfather was a pastrycook. His aunt is said to have been the widow of a grandson of Brawn, the celebrated cook who kept ' The Rummer,' in Queen Street, and who had himself kept 'The Rummer' public-house at the Old Mews Gate, at Charing Cross. Brummel spoke with a relish worthy a descendant of 'The Rummer,' of the savoury pies of his aunt Brawn, who then resided at Kilburn. Henry Carey, in the *Dissertation on Dumpling*, assumes Braun, or Braund, as he calls him, to have been the direct descendant in the male line of his imaginary Brawnd, knighted by King John for his unrivalled skill in making dumplings, and who subsequently resided, as he tells us, " at the ancient manor of Brands, *alias*

Braunds, near Kilburn, in Middlesex." Curious the
accident that found Brummel's "Aunt Brawn" a resident at Kilburn, a century after the *Dissertation on
Dumpling* was written.

SIR LUMLEY SKEFFINGTON, BART.

This accomplished gentleman was the son of Sir
William Skeffington, a much respected Baronet of
Bilsdon, in Leicestershire, where he enjoyed considerable
estates and great provincial esteem. He was born in
1778, and was educated at Soho School, and at New-
come's, at Hackney. At the latter he distinguished
himself in the dramatic performances for which the
school was long celebrated. Dr. Benjamin Hoadley,
author of *The Suspicious Husband*, and his brother, Dr.
John Hoadley, were both educated here, and shone in
their amateur performances; at the representation of
1764, there were upwards of " one hundred gentlemen's
coaches." Young Skeffington excelled in Hamlet, as
he afterwards shone in " the glass of fashion." His
hereditary prospects afforded him a ready introduction
to the fashionable world, and during upwards of twenty
years he was considered as a leader of *ton*, and one of
the most finished gentlemen in England. He was a
person of considerable taste in literature: he wrote *The
Word of Honour*, a comedy, and the dialogue and songs
of a highly finished melodrama, founded on the legend
of *The Sleeping Beauty*. In 1818 he lost his father,
who having embarrassed his estates, his son, as an act
of filial duty to rescue a parent from distress, consented

to the cutting off the entail, by which he deprived himself of that substantial provision without which the life
of a gentleman is a life of misery.

Sir Lumley was the dandy of the olden time, and a
kinder, better-hearted man never existed. He was of
the most polished manners; nor had his long inter-
course with fashionable society at all affected that simplicity of character for which he was remarkable. He
was a true dandy, and much more than that, he was a
perfect gentleman. In 1827, a contributor to the *New
Monthly Magazine* wrote: "I remember, long, long
since, entering Covent Garden Theatre, when I observed
a person holding the door to let me pass; deeming him
to be one of the box-keepers, I was about to nod my
thanks, when I found, to my surprise, that it was
Skeffington who had thus good-naturedly honoured a
stranger by his attention. We with some difficulty
obtained seats in a box, and I was indebted to accident
for one of the most agreeable evenings I remember to
have passed.

"I remember visiting the Opera when late dinners
were the rage, and the hour of refection was carried far
into the night. I was again placed near the fugleman
of fashion, for to his movements were all eyes directed,
and his sanction determined the accuracy of all conduct.
He bowed from box to box, until recognizing one of his
friends in the lower tier, 'Temple,' he exclaimed,
drawling out his weary words, 'at—what—hour—do—
you—dine—to-day?' It had gone half-past eleven
when he spoke.

"I saw him once enter St. James's Church, having at
the door taken a ponderous red morocco prayer-book
from his servant; but although prominently placed in

the centre aisle, the pew-opener never offered him a
seat; and stranger still, none of his many friends beckoned him to a place.   Others in his rank of life might
have been disconcerted at the position in which he was
placed; but Skeffington was too much of a gentleman
to be in any way disturbed; so he seated himself upon
the bench between two aged female paupers, and most
reverently did he go through the service, sharing with
the ladies his book, the print of which was more favour-
able to their devotions than their own diminutive
liturgies."

Sir Lumley Skeffington continued to the last to take
especial interest in the theatre and its artists, notwithstanding his own reduced fortunes. He was a worshipper
of female beauty, his adoration being poured forth in
ardent verse.   Thus, in the spring 1829, he inscribed to
Miss Foote the following ballad:—

> When the frosts of the Winter in mildness were ending,
>   To April I gave half the welcome of May;
> While the Spring, fresh in youth, came delightfully blending
>   The buds that are sweet, and the songs that are gay.
>
> As the eyes fixed the heart on a vision so fair,
>   Not doubting, but trusting what magic was there,
> Aloud I exclaim'd, with augmented desire,
>   I thought 'twas the Spring, when in truth 'twas Maria!
>
> When the fading of stars in the region of splendour
>   Announc'd that the morning was young in the east,
> On the upland I rov'd, admiration to render,
>   Where freshness, and beauty, and lustre increas'd.
>
> Whilst the beams of the morning new pleasures bestow'd,
>   While fondly I gaz'd, while with rapture I glow'd,
> In sweetness commanding, in elegance bright,
>   Maria arose! a more beautiful light.

Again, on the termination of the engagement of
Miss Foote, at Drury Lane Theatre, in May, 1826,
Sir Lumley addressed her in the following im-
promptu :—

Maria departs ! 'tis a sentence of dread ;
For the Graces turn pale, and the Fates droop their head !
In mercy to breasts that tumultuously burn,
Dwell no more on departure, but speak of return.
Since she goes when the buds are just ready to burst,
In expanding its leaves, let the willow be first.
We here shall no longer find beauties in May ;
It cannot be Spring when Maria's away !
If vernal at all, 'tis an April appears,
For the blossom flies off in the midst of our tears.

Sir Lumley, through the ingratitude and treachery
of

" Friends found in sunshine, to be lost in storm,"

became involved in difficulties and endless litiga-
tion, and his latter years were clouded with sorrow ;
still his buoyant spirits never altogether left him,
although "the observed of all observers" passed his
latter years in compulsory residence in a quarter
of the great town ignored by the Sybarites of St.
James's.

When Madame Vestris established a theatre of her
own, Sir Lumley thus sang, in the columns of *The
Times*:—

Now Vestris, the tenth of the Muses,
　　To Mirth rears a fanciful dome,
We mark, while delight she infuses,
　　The Graces find beauty at home.

In her eye such vivacity glitters,
　　To her voice such perfections belong,
That care, and the life it embitters,
　　Find balm in the sweets of her song.

When monarchs o'er valleys are ranging,
A court is transferr'd to the green ;
And flowers, transplanted, are changing
Not fragrance, but merely the scene.

'Tis circumstance dignifies places ;
A desert is charming with spring !
And pleasure finds twenty new graces
Wherever the Vestris may sing !

Sir Lumley, who had long been unheard of in fashionable circles, died in London in 1850 or 1851.

"ROMEO" COATES.

This celebrated leader of fashion, who rejoiced in the sobriquets of "Romeo" and "Diamond," obtained the former from his love of amateur acting, and the latter from his great wealth obtained from the West Indies, He was likewise noted by his splendid curricle, the body of which was in the form of a cockleshell, bearing the cock-bird as his crest ; and the harness of the horses was mounted with metal figures of the same bird, with which got associated the motto of "Whilst we live, we'll crow."

By his amateur performances he shared with young Betty (Roscius) the admiration of the town. A writer in the *New Monthly Magazine*, 1827, pleasantly describes one of these performances :—" Never shall I forget his representation of Lothario (some sixty years since), at the Haymarket Theatre, for his own pleasure, as he accurately termed it ; and certainly the then rising fame of Liston was greatly endangered by his Barbadoes rival. Never had Garrick or Kemble in their best times so largely excited the public attention and curiosity. The very remotest nooks of the galleries were filled by fashion; while in a stage-box sat the performer's notorious friend, the Baron Ferdinand Geramb.

"Coates's lean Quixotic form being duly clothed in velvets and in silks, and his bonnet highly fraught with diamonds (whence his appellation), his entrance on the stage was greeted by so general a *crowing* (in allusion to the large cocks, which as his crest adorned his harness), that the angry and affronted Lothario drew his sword upon the audience, and actually challenged the rude and boisterous tenants of the galleries, *seriatim* or *en masse*, to combat on the stage. Solemn silence, as the consequence of mock fear, immediately succeeded. The great actor, after the overture had ceased, amused himself for for some time with the Baron ere he condescended to indulge the wishes of an anxiously expectant audience.

"At length he commenced: his appeals to the heart were made by the application of the left hand so disproportionately lower down than 'the seat of life' has been proposed to be placed; his contracted pronunciation of the word 'breach,' and other new readings and actings, kept the house in a right joyous humour, until the climax of all mirth was attained by the dying scene of

'that gallant, gay Lothario:'

but who shall describe the grotesque agonies of the dark seducer, his platted hair escaping from the comb that held it, and the dark crineous cordage that flapped upon his shoulders in the convulsions of his dying moments, and the cries of the people for medical aid to accomplish his

eternal exit ?   Then, when in his last throes his coronet
fell, it was miraculous to see the defunct arise, and after
he had spread a nice handkerchief on the stage, and
there deposited his head-dress, free from impurity, phi-
losophically resume his dead condition ; but it was not
yet over, for the exigent audience, not content ' that
when the men were dead, why there an end,' insisted
on a repetition of the awful scene, which the highly flattered corpse executed three several times, to the gratification of the cruel and torment-loving assembly."

Coates was destined to be tantalized by the celebrated fête given at Carlton House, in 1821, in honour
of the Bourbons.   Having no opportunity of learning in
the West Indies the propriety of being presented at
Court ere he could be upon a more intimate footing
with the Prince Regent, he was less astonished than delighted at the reception of an invitation on that occasion
to Carlton House.   What was the fame acquired by his
cockleshell curricle ; his theatrical reputation ; all the
applause attending the perfection of histrionic art ; the
flatteries of Billy Finch, a sort of kidnapper of juvenile
actors and actresses of the O. P. and P. S., in Russell Court ;
the sanction of a Petersham ; the intimacy of a Barry
More ; even the polite endurance of a Skeffington to this !
To be classed with the proud, the noble, and the great !   It
seemed a natural query whether the Bourbons' name were
not a pretext for his own introduction to Royalty, under
circumstances of unprecedented splendour and magnificence. It must have been so. What cogitations respecting
dress, and air, and port, and bearing ! What torturing of
the confounded lanky locks, to make them but revolve ever
so little ! Then the rich cut velvet,—the diamond buttons,
—ay, every one was composed of brilliants. The night ar-

rived—but for Coates's mortification. Theodore Hook had contrived to imitate one of the Chamberlain's tickets, and to produce a facsimile, commanding the presence of Coates: he then put on a scarlet uniform, and delivered the card himself. On the night of the fête, June 19th, Hook stationed himself by the screen at Carlton House, and saw Romeo arrive and enter the palace; he passed in without question, but the forgery was detected by the Private Secretary, and Coates had to retrace his steps to the street, and his carriage being driven off, to get home to Craven Street in a hackney-coach. When the Prince was informed of what had occurred, he signified his regret at the course the Secretary had taken; he was sent by his Royal Highness to apologize in person, and invite Coates to come and look at the state rooms; and Romeo went.

Mr. Coates, who by his cockleshell curricle had acquired some of his celebrity, lost his life by a vehicular accident: he died February 23rd, 1848, from being run over in one of the London streets. He was in his seventy-sixth year.

ABRAHAM NEWLAND.

Abraham Newland, who was nearly sixty years in the service of the Bank of England, and whose name became a synonym for a bank-note, was one of a family of twenty-five children, and was born in Southwark in 1730. At the age of eighteen he entered the Bank service as junior clerk. He was very fond of music, which led him into much dissipation. Still, he was very

attentive to business, and in 1782 he was appointed
chief cashier, with a suite of rooms for residence in the
Bank, and for five-and-twenty years he never once
slept out of the building. The pleasantest version of
his importance is contained in the famous song in the
Whims of the Day, published in 1800 :—

> There ne'er was a name so handed by fame,
>   Thro' air, thro' ocean, and thro' land,
> As one that is wrote upon every bank note,
>   And you all must know Abraham Newland.
>   Oh, Abraham Newland !
>   Notified Abraham Newland !
> I have heard people say, sham Abraham you may,
>   But you must not sham Abraham Newland.
>
> For fashion or arts, should you seek foreign parts,
>   It matters not wherever you land,
> Jew, Christian, or Greek, the same language they speak :
>   That's the language of Abraham Newland !
>   Oh, Abraham Newland!
>   Wonderful Abraham Newland !
> Tho' with compliments cramm'd, you may die and be d—d,
>   If you hav'n't an Abraham Newland.
>
> The world is inclin'd to think Justice is blind ;
>   Lawyers know very well they can view land ;
> But, Lord, what of that, she'll blink like a bat
>   At the sight of an Abraham Newland.
>   Oh, Abraham Newland !
>   Magical Abraham Newland !
> Tho' Justice, 'tis known, can see through a millstone,
>   She can't see through Abraham Newland.
>
> Your patriots who bawl for the good of us all,
>   Kind souls ! here like mushrooms they strew land ;
> Tho' loud as a drum, each proves orator mum,
>   If attack'd by an Abraham Newland.
>   Oh, Abraham Newland !
>   Invincible Abraham Newland !

No argument's found in the world half so sound
   As the logic of Abraham Newland!

The French say they're coming, but sure they are mumming;
   I know what they want if they do land;
We'll make their ears ring in defence of our king,
   Our country, and Abraham Newland.
         Oh, Abraham Newland!
         Darling Abraham Newland!
No tricolour, elf, nor the devil himself
   Shall e'er rob us of Abraham Newland.

In 1807, he retired from the office of chief cashier, after declining a pension. He had hitherto been accustomed, after the business at the Bank in his department had closed, and he had dined moderately, to order his carriage and drive to Highbury, where he drank tea at a small cottage. Many who lived in that neighbourhood long recollected Newland's daily walk— hail, rain, or sunshine—along Highbury Place. It was said that he regretted his retirement from the Bank; but he used to say that not for 20,000*l.* a year would he return. He then removed to No. 38, Highbury Place. His health and strength declined, it is said, through the distress of mind brought upon him by the forgeries of Robert Aslett, a clerk in the Bank, whom Newland had treated as his own son. It was well known that Abraham had accumulated a large fortune; legacy-hunters came about him, and an acquaintance sent him a ham as a present; but Newland despised the mercenary motive, and next time he saw the donor he said, "I have received a ham from you; I thank you for it," said he, but raising his finger in a significant manner, added, "I tell you it won't do, it won't do."

Newland had no extravagant expectations that the

world would be drowned in sorrow when it should be his turn to leave it; and he wrote this ludicrous epitaph on himself shortly before his death :—

> " Beneath this stone old Abraham lies :
> Nobody laughs, and nobody cries.
> Where he's gone, and how he fares,
> No one knows, and no one cares ! "

His physician, in one of his latest visits, found him reading the newspaper, when the doctor expressing his surprise, Newland replied, smiling, " I am only looking in the paper in order to see what I am reading to the world I am going to." He died November 21st, 1807, without any apparent pain of body or anxiety of mind, and his remains were deposited in the church of St. Saviour, Southwark.

Newland's property amounted to 200,000l., besides a thousand a-year landed estates. It must not be supposed that this was saved from his salary. During the whole of his career, the loans for the war proved very prolific. A certain amount of them was always reserved for the cashier's office (one Parliamentary Report names 100,000l.), and as they generally came out at a premium, the profits were great. The family of the Goldsmids, then the leaders of the Stock Exchange, contracted for many of these loans, and to each of them he left 500l. to purchase a mourning ring. Newland's large funds, it is said, were also occasionally lent to the Goldsmids to assist their various speculations.

THE SPENDTHRIFT SQUIRE OF HALSTON, JOHN MYTTON.

The extravagant fellows of a family, says Sir Bernard Burke, Ulster, have done more to overturn ancient houses than all the other causes put together; and no case could be more in point to establish the fact than the history of John Mytton, descended from the Myttons of Halston, who represented, in the days of the Plantagenets, the borough of Shrewsbury in Parliament, and filled the office of High Sheriff of Shropshire at a very remote period. So far back as 1480, Thomas Mytton, when holding that appointment, was the fortunate captor of Stafford, Duke of Buckingham, whom he conducted to Salisbury for trial and decapitation; and in requital Richard III. bestowed on " his trusty and well-beloved squire, Thomas Mytton," the Duke's forfeited castle and lordship of Cawes. Halston, to which the Myttons transferred their seat from their more ancient residence of Cawes Castle and Habberley, is called in ancient deeds "Holystone," and was in early times a preceptory of Knights Templars. The Abbey, taken down about one hundred and sixty years ago, was erected near where the present mansion stands. In the good old times of Halston, before reckless waste had dismantled its halls and levelled its ancestral woods, the oak was seen here in its full majesty of form; and it is related that one particular tree, coeval with many centuries of the family's greatness, was cut down by the spendthrift squire in the year 1826, and contained ten tons of timber.

In the great civil war, Mytton of Halston was one of the few Shropshire gentlemen who joined the Parliamentary standard. From this gallant and upright Parliamentarian, the fifth in descent was John Mytton, the eccentric, wasteful, dissipated, open-hearted, open-handed Squire of Halston, in whose day and by whose wanton extravagance and folly, a time-honoured family and a noble estate, the inheritance of five hundred years, was recklessly destroyed.

John Mytton was born September 30th, 1796. His father died when he was only eighteen months old, so that his minority lasted almost twenty years; and during its continuance a very large sum of money was accumulated, which, added to a landed property of full 10,000*l.* a-year, and a pedigree of even Salopian antiquity and distinction, rendered the Squire of Halston one of the first commoners in England. But a boyhood unrestrained by proper control, and an education utterly neglected, led to a course of profligacy and eccentricity, amounting almost to madness, that marred all these gifts of fortune. Young Mytton commenced by being expelled from both Westminster and Harrow; and though he was entered on the books of the two universities, he did not matriculate at either; the only indication he ever gave of an intention to do so was his ordering three pipes of port-wine to be sent to him, addressed " Cambridge." When a mere child, he had been allowed a pack of harriers at Halston, and at the age of ten was a confirmed scapegrace. At nineteen he entered the 7th Hussars, and immediately joined his regiment, then with the army of occupation in France.

Fighting was, however, all over, and the young Cornet
turned at once to racing and gaming, in which he was
a serious loser.

In 1818 he married the eldest daughter of Sir
Thomas Tyrrwhitt Jones, Bart., of Stanley Hall. By
this lady, who died in 1820, he had an only child,
Harriet, married in 1841 to Clement, youngest brother
of Lord Hill. After his wife's decease, the wayward
extravagance which marked the career of John Mytton
has probably no parallel. He would not suffer any one
to advise him. When heavy liabilities had been incurred, but previously to the disposal of the first property he sold, his agent assured Mr. Mytton that if he
would content himself for the following six years with
an income of 6,000*l*., the fine old Shrewsbury estate—
the earliest patrimony of his ancestors—might be
saved; when besought to listen to this warning counsel,
"No, no," replied Mytton; "I would not give a straw
for life if it was to be passed on 6,000*l*. a-year." The
result confirmed the agent's apprehensions: the first
acre alienated led to the gradual dismemberment of the
whole estate; and from this moment may be dated the
ruin of the Myttons of Halston. Such was the pro-
digality of this unfortunate man, that it was said, "If
Mytton had had an income of 200,000*l*., he would have
been in debt in five years." Most certain it is that,
within the last fifteen years of his life, he squandered
full half-a-million sterling, and sold timber—"the old
oaks of Halston"—to the amount, it is stated, of
80,000*l*.

The late Mr. Apperley (Nimrod) wrote a kindly
biography of Mytton, illustrated with coloured plates of
his strange adventures. One gives a view of Halston,

with its glorious plantations, and its noble sheet of water, through which, as the shortest cut, its eccentric owner is riding home. Another illustrates Mytton's "wild duck shooting." "He would sometimes," says Nimrod, "strip to his shirt to follow wild-fowl in hard weather, and once actually laid himself down on the snow to await their arrival at dusk. On one occasion he out-heroded Herod, for he followed some ducks *in puris naturalibus*, and escaped with perfect impunity." The third plate commemorates a practical joke of the frolic-loving squire. One evening, the clergyman and doctor, who had dined at Halston, left to return on horseback. Their host, having disguised himself in a countryman's frock and hat, succeeded, by riding across the park, in confronting them, and then, in true highwayman voice, he called out, "Stand and deliver!" and before a reply could be given, fired off his pistol, which had, of course, only a blank cartridge. The affrighted gentlemen, Mytton used to say, never rode half so fast in their lives as when, with him at their heels, they fled that night to Oswestry.

Another of the plates exhibits Mr. Mytton in hunting dress, entering his drawing-room, full of company, mounted on a bear; and another exemplifies the old saying, "Light come, light go." Mytton, travelling in his carriage, on a stormy night, from Doncaster, fell asleep while counting the money he had won; the windows were down, and a great many of the bank-notes were blown away and lost. The reckless gambler used often to tell the story as an amusing reminiscence.

Another plate represents Mytton with his shirt in flames. "Did you ever hear," asks Nimrod, "of a man setting fire to his own shirt to frighten away the hiccup? Such, however, was done, and in this manner:—'Oh, this horrid hiccup!' said Mytton, as he stood undressed on the floor, apparently in the act of getting into bed; 'but I'll frighten it away;' so seizing a candle, he applied it to the tail of his shirt, and it being a cotton one, he was instantly enveloped in flames." His life was only saved by the active exertions of two persons who chanced to be in the room.

Mytton married, secondly, Miss Giffard, of Chillington, a match of such misery to the lady, that it ended in a separation. The crisis of the spendthrift's fate was now impending. All the effects at Halston were advertised for sale; and very shortly after Mr. Mytton fled to the Continent to escape from his creditors. " On the 15th of November, 1831," says Nimrod, "during my residence in the town of Calais, I was surprised by a violent knocking at my door, and so unlike what I had ever heard before in that quiet town, that, being at hand, I was induced to open the door myself, when, to my no little astonishment, there stood John Mytton. 'In the name of Heaven,' said I, 'what has brought you to France?' 'Why,' he replied, *just what brought yourself to France*'—parodying the old song—'three couple of bailiffs were hard at my brush.' But what did I see before me—the active, vigorous, well-shapen John Mytton, whom I had left some years back in Shropshire? Oh, no; compared with him, 'twas the reed shaken by the wind; there stood before me a round-shouldered, decrepit, tottering, *old-young* man, if I may be allowed such a term, and so bloated by drink! But there was a worse sight than this—there was a mind as well as a body in ruins; the one had partaken of the injury done to the other, and it was at once apparent that the whole was a wreck. In fact, he was a melancholy spectacle of fallen man."

It appeared that Mytton had been arrested for a paltry debt and thrown into prison. "I once more," writes Nimrod, "was pained by seeing my friend looking through the bars of a French prison-window. Here he was suffered to remain for fourteen days; on the thirteenth day, I thought it my duty to inform his mother of his situation, and in four days from the date of my letter she was in Calais. After a time, Mytton returned to England, but only to a prison and a grave. The representative of one of the most ancient families of his country, at one time M.P. for Shrewsbury and High Sheriff for Shropshire and Merioneth, the inheritor of Halston and Mowddwy and almost countless acres, the most popular sportsman of England, died within the walls of the King's Bench Prison, at the age of thirty-eight, deserted and neglected by all, save a few faithful friends and a devoted mother, who stood by his death-bed to the last."

The announcement of the sad event produced a profound impression in Shropshire: the people within many miles were deeply affected; the degradation of Mytton's later years, the faults and follies of his wretched life, were all forgotten; the generosity, the tenderness of heart, the manly tastes of poor John Mytton, his sporting popularity, and his very mad follies, were recalled with affectionate sympathy. His funeral will long be remembered—three thousand persons attended it, and a detachment of the North Shropshire Cavalry (of which regiment the deceased was Major) escorted his remains to the vault in the chapel of Halston; several private carriages followed, and about one hundred of the tenantry, tradesmen, and friends on horseback closed the procession. The body was placed in the family vault, surrounded by the coffins of twelve of his relatives.

The story of John Mytton is appalling. A family far more ancient and apparently as vigorous as the grand old oaks that once were the pride of Halston, was destroyed, after centuries of honourable and historic eminence, by the mad follies of one man in the brief space of eighteen years! The magnificent Lordship of Dinas Mowddwy, with its 32,000 acres—originally an appanage of the dynasty of Powis—inherited through twelve generations from a co-heiress of the Royal Lineage of Powys Wenwynwyn, had been bartered, it is alleged, in adjustment of a balance on turf and gambling transactions.*

What a sad conclusion to the history of a very distinguished race, memorable in the days of the Plantagenets, and renowned in the great Civil War, is the following record, taken from *The Times*, 2nd April, 1834 :—" On Monday, an inquest was held in the King's Bench Prison, on the body of John Mytton, Esq., who died there on the preceding Saturday. The deceased inherited considerable estates in the counties of Salop and Merioneth, for both which he served the office of High Sheriff, and some time represented the borough of Shrewsbury in Parliament. His munificence and eccentric gaieties obtained him great notoriety in the sporting and gay circles, both in England and on the Continent. Two medical attendants stated that the immediate

---

* Abridged from Sir Bernard Burke's very interesting *Vicissitudes of Families.* Second Series. 1860.

cause of his death was disease of the brain (*delirium tremens*), brought on by the excessive use of spirituous liquors. The deceased was in his thirty-eighth year. Verdict—' Natural Death.' "

LORD PETERSHAM.

This eccentric nobleman, who was the eldest son of Charles, third Earl of Harrington, was a leader of fashion some thirty years since; he was tall and handsome; according to Captain Gronow, Lord Petersham very much resembled the pictures of Henry IV. of France, and frequently wore a dress not unlike that of the celebrated monarch. He was a great patron of tailors, and a particular kind of great-coat was called after him a " Petersham." When young, he used to cut out his own clothes; he made his own blacking, which, he said, would eventually supersede every other. He was also a connoisseur in snuff, and one of his rooms was fitted up with shelves and beautiful jars for various kinds of snuff, with the names in gold. Here were also implements for moistening and mixing snuffs, and Lord Petersham's mixture is to this day a popular snuff. He possessed also a fine collection of snuff-boxes, and it was said, a box for every day in the year. Captain Gronow saw him using a beautiful Sèvres box, which, on being admired, he said was " a nice summer box, but would not do for winter wear." He was equally choice of his teas, and in the same room with the snuffs, upon shelves, were placed tea-canisters, containing Congou, Pekoe,

Souchong, Gunpowder, Russian, and other fine kinds. Indeed, his father's mansion, Harrington House, was long famous for its tea-drinking: the Earl and Countess and family, and their visitors, were received upon these occasions in the long gallery, and here the family of George III. enjoyed many a cup of tea. It is told that when General Lincoln Stanhope returned from India after several years' absence, his father welcomed him with " Hallo, Linky, my dear boy! delighted to see you. *Have a cup of tea!* "

Lord Petersham's equipages were unique: the carriages and horses were brown; the harness had furniture of antique design; and the servants wore long brown coats, reaching to their heels, and glazed hats with large cockades. Lord Petersham was a liberal patron of the opera and the theatres; and two years after he had succeeded his father in the earldom (of Harrington), he married the beautiful Maria Foote, of Covent Garden Theatre.

THE KING AND QUEEN OF THE SANDWICH ISLANDS.

In the year 1824, their " savage Majesties " of the Sandwich Islands visited England. They were seen by Miss Berry, who, in her entertaining Journal, has thus graphically described their visit:—

" At half-past ten o'clock, I went with the Prince and Princess Lowenstein, their son, and my sister, to Mr. Canning's, the Secretary of State, who received for the first time the King and Queen of the Sandwich Islands. They arrived in the midst of a numerous assembly, all of the best society, and all *en grande toilette* for a large assembly given at Northumberland House. Mr. Canning entered, giving his hand to a large black woman more than six feet high, and broad in proportion, muffled up in a striped gauze dress with short sleeves, leaving uncovered enormous black arms, half covered again with white gloves; an enormous gauze turban upon her head; black hair, not curled, but very short; a small bag in her hand, and I do not know what upon her neck, where there was no gauze. It was with difficulty that the Minister and his company could preserve a proper gravity for the occasion. The Queen was followed by a lady in waiting as tall as herself, and with a gayer and more intelligent countenance. Then came the King, accompanied by three of his subjects, all dressed, like him, in European costume; and a fourth, whose office I did not know, but he wore over his ordinary coat a scarlet and yellow feather cloak, and a helmet covered with the same material on his head. The King was shorter than his four courtiers, but they all looked very strong, and, except the King, all taller than the majority of those who surrounded them. The two ladies were seated before the fire in the gallery for some time. Mrs. Canning was presented first to them, and then the Duke and Duchess of Gloucester and the Prince Leopold. The Queen took the Duchess of Gloucester by the arm and shook it. One should have pitied them for the way in which all eyes were turned upon them, and for all the observations they occasioned; but it seemed to me that their minds are not sufficiently opened, and that they are not civilized enough either to notice or to suffer from it. From the gallery Mr. Canning, still holding the Queen's hand, conducted them through the apartment and under the verandah of the garden, where the band of the Guards' regiment, in their full uniform, was playing military airs. Her savage Majesty appeared much more occupied by the red-plumed hats of the musicians than by the music. She ought to have been pleased to see that the officers' helmet of her Court surpassed them as to colour. From there they were conducted into the dining-room, where there was a fine collation. The two ladies were seated alone at a table placed across the room, and ate some cake and drank wine. They appeared awkward in all their movements, and particularly embarrassed in their walk; there was nothing of the free step of the savage, being probably embarrassed by the folds of the European dress."

The King and Queen and their suite were wantonly charged with gluttony and drunkenness by persons who ought to have known better. "It is true," observes Lord Byron, in his *Voyage to the Sandwich Islands,* "that, unaccustomed to our habits, they little regarded regular hours for meals, and that they liked to eat frequently, though not to excess. Their greatest luxury was oysters, of which they were particularly fond; and one day, some of the chiefs having been out to walk, and seeing a grey mullet, instantly seized it and carried it home, to the great delight of the whole party; who, on recognizing the native fish of their own seas, could scarcely believe that it had not swum hither on purpose for them, or be persuaded to wait till it was cooked before they ate it." The best proof of their modera-tion is, however, that the charge at Osborne's Hotel, in the Adelphi, during their residence there, amounted to no greater an average than seventeen shillings a-head per day for their table: as they ate little or no butcher's meat, but lived chiefly on fish, poultry, and fruit, by no means the cheapest articles in London, their gluttony could not have been great. So far from their always preferring the strongest liquors, their favourite beverage was some cider, with which they had been presented by Mr. Canning.

The popular comic song of *The King of the Cannibal Islands* was written *à propos* to the above royal visit.

SIR EDWARD DERING'S LUCKLESS COURTSHIP.

Sir Edward Dering, the founder of the Surrenden library, and a distinguished member of Parliament in the troublous times of Charles I., was born in the Tower of London in 1598, his father having been deputy-lieutenant of that fortress. He studied at Magdalen College, Cambridge, and was knighted by James I. in 1618. Sir Edward was thrice married. The story of an unsuccessful courtship, after his second widowhood, is as good as a play, and indeed more amusing than many dramas of the period based upon a similar subject. The object of this enterprise was a city dame, the widow of a well-connected mercer, Richard Bennett by name. The widow Bennett, by the custom of London and the will of her husband, was possessed of two-thirds of the deceased's property, besides all her jewels and chains of pearl and gold, her diamond and other rings, her husband's coach and the four grey coach-mares and geldings, with all things thereunto belonging. In addition to these substantial recommendations, she seems to have had some personal charms of her own, and no other encumbrance than one little boy. In those days it was not necessary to advertise for a husband, and Mistress Bennett could not lack suitors. Three of the most conspicuous were named Finch, Crow, and Raven, much to the amusement of London society in those days. The first was Sir Heneage Finch, Recorder of London, who had been Speaker of the House of Commons in 1626, and owned a handsome house at Kensington, since converted into a Royal Palace. The next was Sir Sackville Crow, who was Treasurer of the Navy, of which office he was subsequently deprived, owing to an unfortunate deficit of which he was unable to give a satisfactory account. The third was one Raven, a physician. This fatuous individual, not having found much success in the way of ordinary courtship, could think of no better expedient to gain his ends than to present himself in the widow's bedchamber after she had retired to rest, when, having woke the lady, he proceeded to press his suit. The widow screamed thieves and murder, the servants rushed in, and the doctor was secured and handed over to the parish constable. On the next day he was brought before Mr. Recorder, who found the proceeding to be "flat burglary," and committed his unlucky rival to gaol. When brought up for trial he pleaded guilty to the "burglary," but under advice of the judge withdrew the plea, and was ultimately found guilty of "ill-demeanour," and was condemned to fine and imprisonment.

It was on the morning after Dr. Raven's mad freak that Sir Edward Dering presented himself as a suitor. How he commenced this important enterprise, and how he sped, we learn from a minute journal which he kept of his proceedings, and which he did not afterwards think it necessary to burn. Here are a few entries. Thus begins the journal:—

"Nov. 20. Edmund, King. I adventured, was denied. Sent up a letter, which was returned, after she had read it."

This repulse rendered it necessary to resort to crooked means. Servants are corruptible, and so we find—

"Nov. 21. I inveigled G. Newman with 20s.
"Nov. 24. I did re-engage him, 20s. I did also oil the cash-keeper, 20s.
"Nov. 26. I gave Edmund Aspull [the cash-keeper] another 20s.
"I was there, but denied sight."

Unpromising this, but Sir Edward does not lose courage.

"Nov. 27. I sent a second letter, *which was kept*."

There is hope, then, but we must not relax. Same day.

"I set Sir John Skeffington upon Matthew Cradock."

Matthew Cradock is a cousin of the widow, and her trusty adviser. Same day.

"The cash-keeper supped with me."
"Nov. 23. I went to Mr. Cradock, but found him cold."

Sir John Skeffington could not have exerted himself much.

"Nov. 39. I was at the Old Jewry Church and saw her, both forenoon and afternoon."

"Dec. 1. I sent a third letter, which was likewise hept."

The widow had a troublesome affair on her hands. It appears that one Steward, under the abominable system of wardships which then prevailed, had obtained a grant from the crown of the wardship of Mrs. Bennett's little boy, then four years old. The widow was in treaty with Steward to buy from him the wardship of her own child, which the rogue refused to release for 1,500*l.*, offered him in hard cash Between this affair, and Dr. Raven and other suitors, the widow had enough to think of. Steward had also made matrimonial proposals, which Mrs. Bennett deemed it not prudent to cut short at once, while the bargaining for the wardship was going on. On the 5th December Sir Edward communicates with one Loe, an influential person with the widow. Loe answers, " that Steward was so testy that she durst not give admittance unto any, until he and she were fully concluded for the wardship—that she had a good opinion of me—that he (Loe) heard nobly of me—that he would inform me when Steward was off—that he was engaged for another—that I need not refrain from going to the church where she was, unless I thought it to disparage myself." Acting on this advice, Sir Edward goes to St. Olave's next Sunday, and on coming out of church George Newman whispers in his ear, " Good news! Good news!" After dinner George calls on Sir Edward, who had taken a lodging in the sight of the widow's house, and tells him that she " liked well his carriage, and that if his land were not settled on his eldest son there was good hope." The bearer of such news certainly merits oiling, so, says Sir Edward, "I gave him twenty shillings." That evening Sir Edward supped with his rival, Sir Heneage Finch, who gave him to understand that he himself despaired of his own suit, and was ready to vacate the field, and even promised to assist the worthy knight.

The plot now thickens. Sir Edward, on New Year's Day, in a fit of injured dignity, demanded back those letters that had "been kept;" they were promptly returned; he afterwards repented him of this rash proceeding; Izaak Walton, angler, biographer, and man-milliner, was enlisted in the cause, and laboured strenuously, like an honest man and an angler, therein; and the widow, Sir Edward, and the enthusiastic Izaak, all had wonderful dreams, which came to nothing. On the 9th of January Sir Edward notes, "George Newman says she hath two suits of silver plate, one in the country and the other here, and that she hath beds of 100l. the bed!" Such a prize deserves striving for, and an attack is commenced in a new quarter. George Newman, with Susan, the widow's nursemaid, and her little child, going into Finsbury Fields to walk, are met by Taylor, Sir Edward's landlord. Taylor inveigles the child to come with him; George Newman and Susan follow, not unwillingly. Sir Edward says, "I entertained the child with cake, and gave him an amber box, and to them, wine. Susan professed that she and all the house prayed for me, and told me the child called me 'father.' I gave her 5s., and entreated her to desire her mistress not to be offended at this, which I was so glad of. She said she thought she would not." The widow's cousin Cradock arrives in town. "Izaak Walton," says Sir Edward, "undertook him at his first, coming, and did his part well. Cradock said he would do his best, if I would be ruled by him," &c. Other suitors now intervene, and occasion much anxiety. They, too, have their canvassers and agents, and the widow's residence becomes a perfect focus of intrigue. The Dean of Canterbury, Dr. Isaac Bargrave, Sir Edward's relative, is brought to bear, and he procures Dr. Featley, a celebrated city divine, to call on the widow and use his influence. The affair begins to assume public importance. The grave Sir Henry Wotton, coming from Eton to pay his respects to his Majesty, meets Sir Edward in the Privy Chamber, and, with a knowing look, wishes him "a full sail," &c. Alas! all this labour and bribery was destined to come to nothing. The comedy ended by the widow, who all along had kept her own counsel, marrying the smooth-tongued Sir Heneage Finch, who had sat quietly in the background, probably knowing his position to be assured. Sir Edward was more successful in a subsequent matrimonial enterprise. He found an excellent and amiable wife, and must, we should think, have often laughed over his adventures with the widow.*

GRETNA-GREEN MARRIAGES.

In the summer of 1753, a young lady at Ranelagh Gardens, Chelsea, became acquainted with a handsome young gentleman. They danced together on another day; they met at the same place, and again

* This very amusing *précis* is slightly abridged from the *Athenæum* journal.

danced. He was a handsome young fellow, and the lady was beautiful and wealthy, as well as high-born. She was sister to the two leading statesmen of England—Mr. Pelham, the Prime Minister; and the Duke of Newcastle, who had been Secretary of State. Her lover was a notorious highwayman, Jack Freeland by name, with many other aliases. He, professing to be a gentleman of fortune, proposed marriage, to which she assented. From reasons suggested about family objections on both sides, they agreed to repair to the Fleet prison to be wedded. At the foot of Fleet Street, matrimonial visitors in that day entered the region of touters, who accosted couples with such addresses as "Married, sir?" "Wish to be married, ma'am?" And by rival touters who asserted, "His parson be no good —only a cove what mends shoes; get married with mine; mine is a regular hordained parson." Perhaps a third assertion, that "Them fellows' parsons be no good; get married respectable; show you in no time to a real Oxford and Cambridge professor." Following these persons up narrow passages on Ludgate Hill, the couples were married for such fees as private bargain regulated in dingy up-stairs rooms of taverns; or going into the Fleet Prison, were united there by clerical prisoners who found the place too lucrative and pleasant as a lodging to make them anxious about paying their debts to get out. Those prisoners, like some other of the "Fleet parsons"—indeed it was from the prison that the term "Fleet marriages" arose—had also their touters stationed in the adjoining streets to bring them customers. Miss Pelham and her gallant highwayman were conducted to a Fleet parson. But a gentleman happened to observe them who knew both. To save

the lady he caused the robber-bridegroom to be arrested,
and carried the tidings to the Prime Minister, her
brother. The case led to much discussion. In the heat
of offended dignity, the Pelhams caused Lord Chancellor Hardwicke to introduce a Bill for the better
regulation and solemnizing of marriage. It passed
hastily through both houses of Parliament, and became
law. Except in the case of Jews and Quakers, it
required all parties to be married by a regularly ordained
clergyman of the Church, and only after a due pro-
clamation of bans.

The Marriage Law of Scotland did not exact that
there should be a religious ceremony, nor even the
presence of a clergyman, though the religious habits of
the people prefer both. To be valid, the Scottish law
required only that the marriage contract should be witnessed. When the Fleet was shut against lovers in
1754, those impatient of parental control, and possessed
of means to defray travelling expenses, repaired to
Scotland. Edinburgh for a time supplied their wants:
the last, we believe, who carried on a regular traffic in
runaway weddings here was Joseph Robertson, who,
several years ago, died miserably of hunger in London.
But it was on the line of the borders adjoining England
that those weddings abounded. At Lamberton Toll,
the nearest Scottish ground to Berwick, the business
was for many years done at a very low price. After
the erection of the suspension-bridge, six miles above
Berwick, marriages were performed there. A " Sheen
Brig " wedding became a common occurrence both to
Northumberland and Berwickshire lovers. At Cold-
stream, also, those marriages were common. But it was
at Gretna Green, and Sark Toll Bar, and Springfield,

nine miles from Carlisle, that the "high-fly" runaways from England tied their nuptial knots in greatest number. All the space between Carlisle and the Border was common land, until of late years, inhabited only by smugglers and persons of unsettled life. The Scottish parish of Gretna on the north side of the Sark stream, which there divides the countries, had a population of a like character. After the act of 1754 had shut the Fleet parsons out of shop in London, one of them paid his debts in the prison, and advertised his removal to Gretna. Thither he was followed by adventurous couples who failed to obtain the consent of parents and guardians to their union. At his death a native of the place, known as "Scott o' the Brig" (Sark Bridge), took up the business. He was succeeded by one Gordon, an old soldier; and Gordon by the notorious Joseph Paisley. Paisley was succeeded by several rivals, of whom Elliot and Laing were the principals. Mr. Linton, of Gretna Hall, became chief priest after Laing's death, which occurred through cold taken in a journey to Lancaster, in 1826, where he was required as a witness in the prosecution of the Wakefields for the abduction of Miss Turner.

In 1841, the writer visited Gretna and Springfield to inspect the registers, and found them a mass of loose papers. At that time the larger part of the matrimonial trade was done—for couples arriving on foot—by Mrs. Baillie, and Miss Baillie, her daughter, who kept Sark Bridge Toll; the post-chaise weddings going to Mr. Linton, of Gretna Hall: his register, unlike the older ones, was a well-written official-looking volume. Peter Elliot, formerly priest, was then an old man. He had in his younger days been a postboy, but was reduced to the office of "strapper" in a stable at Carlisle. Excess of whisky on his part, and the more genteel competition of the occupier of Gretna Hall, had driven him out of the marriage-trade. But in his lifetime he had been concerned in many races and chases over the nine miles between Carlisle and Gretna, and would tell of the beautiful daughters of England, whom, with whip and spur and shout, and wild halloo, he had carried at the gallop across the border; the pursuing guardian, or jilted lover, or angry father in sight behind, urging on post-boys who also whipped and spurred and hallooed, but took care never to overtake the fugitives until too late. Then there were tales of how time was too short even for the brief ceremony, and how the officiating priest broke, off exclaiming, " Ben the house, ben and into bed, into bed my leddy !" They were proud to boast of two Lord Chancellors having been married there, one of whom, Erskine, arrived in the travelling costume of an old lady.

About the year 1794 it was estimated that sixty couples were married annually, they paying an average of 15 guineas each, yielding a revenue of 945*l.* a-year or thereabout. The form of certificate was in latter times printed, the officiating priest not being always sufficiently sober to write; nor when sober was he an adept in penmanship, as the following from the pen of Joseph Paisley may show :—

" This is to sartify. all persons that may be concernid that (A. B.) from the parish of (C.) and in county of (D.) and (E. F.) from the parish of (G.) and county of (H.), and both comes before me and declayred them-selves both to be single persons, and nowe mayried by the forme of the Kirk of Scotland and agreeible to the

Church of England, and givne ondre my hand this 18th day of March, 1793."

Joseph Paisley, writer of this, was originally a weaver, at some other time a tobacconist. He was the so-called "Blacksmith," though there is no record that he, his predecessors, or successors were real blacksmiths. He removed from Gretna to the village of Springfield, half-a-mile distant, in 1791, and attended to his lucrative employment till his death in 1814. He was tall in person, and in prime of life well-proportioned; but before he died had grown enormously corpulent, weighing upwards of 25 stone. By his natural enemies—the parish clergymen—he was said to be grossly ignorant and coarse in his manners, drinking a Scotch pint of whisky in various shapes of toddy and raw drams in a day. On one occasion he and a companion, named Ned the Turner, sat down on a Monday morning to an auker of strong cognac, and before the evening of Saturday they kicked the empty cask out at the door! He was also celebrated for his stentorian lungs and almost incredible muscular strength. He could with one hand bend a strong poker over his arm, and was frequently known to straighten an ordinary horse-shoe with his hands. But he could not break asunder the bands of matrimony which he so easily rivetted. Law stamped his handiwork with the title of sanctity. The Gretna and Sark Toll marriages greatly increased in number through the facilities of railway conveyance. The fugitives, when obtaining a start by an express train, could not be overtaken by another, while the ordinary third-class carried away so many customers for cheap marriages from their English parish clergy, that the Legislature was invoked, and enacted that on and after the 1st January, 1857, no marriage should be valid in Scotland unless the parties had both resided in Scotland for the last six weeks next preceding the wedding-day. In the evidence upon this Bill, one of the *marriers*, Murray, of Gretna, admitted that he had married between 700 and 800 couples in a year; and as there were two or three other of these marriers in good practice, the number of couples married at Sark Toll Bar and at Gretna may be safely estimated at upwards of 1,000 in a year.

The alteration in the law was effected through the happy effort of a magistrate of Cumberland, immediately and ably supported by the magistrates of the county, who signed a petition committed to the charge of Lord Brougham. His Lordship forthwith introduced a Bill, after Easter, 1856, which Bill passed through Parliament without opposition.*

THE AGAPEMONE, OR ABODE OF LOVE.

This strange place, Agapemone (Gr. ἀγαπὴ love, and μονή an abode), was the general residence of a peculiar sect of religionists, established in 1845 at Charlinch, near Taunton, in Somersetshire. They were originally a branch of the sect called Lampeters, and their peculiar tenets are, that the day of grace and prayer is passed, and the time of judgment arrived. They carry out their belief by perpetual praises to God, but do not adopt the use of prayer. The members enter into a community of property, and profess to live

* For the details of the measure, see "Irregular Marriages," *Knowledge for the Time*, 1864, pp. 120–123.

in a state of constant joyousness and mutual love. In
1849 a singular trial, connected with this institution,
occupied the Court of Exchequer for three days. It
was an action brought by Miss Louisa Nottidge, a
maiden lady of large property, against her brother and
brother-in-law, for forcibly abducting her from the
Agapemone, and confining her in a lunatic asylum.
It appeared that the plaintiff and her three sisters, all
ladies of considerable property, had become converts to
the opinions of this sect, and taken up their abode in
the Agapemone, where the sisters were married to
three of the clerical rulers of the establishment; but
Miss Louisa Nottidge, who had remained single, was
forcibly taken away by the two defendants, and sent to
a lunatic asylum; for which alleged wrong she obtained
50*l.* damages; thus showing that she was not insane,
and that the law, as the Chief Baron observed, tolerated
every sect, however absurd, that did not inflict a social
wrong, or openly violate the laws of morality.

Since that period the sect has been sending its
missionaries to different parts of the country, in order
to gain converts. On the 26th of September, 1856, two
of these missionaries called a meeting at the Hanover
Square Rooms, in London, when one of them addressed
the assembled visitors in an unintelligible jargon
relative to the mission of a certain "Brother Prince,"
the head of the Agapemone, who had, he said, been
made a "vessel of mercy" for the human race, and who
was to supersede the Gospel by some new religious
dispensation which he had been specially commissioned
to teach. The other missionary then stated that he
would explain who Brother Prince was. He was by
nature, he said, a child of wrath, but by grace a vessel,

of mercy. The testimony of Brother Prince was concerning what Jesus Christ had done by his own person. Some eleven years ago, he said, the Holy Ghost fulfilled in Brother Prince all that he came to be and to do. The speaker proceeded to allude to a second spiritual manifestation which, he said, occurred at the Agapemone about five years ago, in which case the phenomenon was exhibited in the person of a woman—a prophetess— "not privately, but in the presence of all." These sentiments were uttered in the midst of general execration; and a resolution was unanimously passed, "That the statements which had been made that evening were contrary to common sense, degrading to humanity, and blasphemous towards God."—*English Cyclopædia.*

SINGULAR SCOTCH LADIES.

Lord Cockburn, in his *Memorials of his Time*, speaks of "a singular race of Scotch old ladies," who were a delightful set; warm-harted, very resolute, indifferent about the modes and habits of the modern world, and adhering to their own ways, who dressed, spoke, and did exactly as they chose. Among these examples of perfect naturalness was a Miss Menie Trotter, of whom Miss Grahame, in her *Mystifications*, relates:—" She was penurious in small things, but her generosity could rise to circumstances. Her dower was an annuity from the estate of Mortonhall. She had contempt for securities, and would trust no bank with her money, but kept all her bills and bank-notes in a green silk bag that hung on her toilette-glass. On each side of the table stood a large white bowl, one of which contained her silver, the other her copper money, the latter always full to the brim, accessible to Peggy, her handmaid, or any other servant in the house, for the idea of any one stealing money never entered her brain. Indeed, she once sent a present to her niece, Mrs. Cuninghame, of a fifty-pound note wrapped up in a cabbage-leaf, and entrusted it to the care of a woman who was going with a basket of butter to the Edinburgh market. My friend Mrs. Cuninghame related to me this and the following histories of her aunt :—One day, in the course of conversation, she said to her niece, 'Do ye ken, Margaret, that Mrs. Thomas R—— is dead. I was gaun by the door this morning, and thought I wad just look in and speer for her. She was very near her end, but quite sensible, and expressed her gratitude to God for what He had done for her and her fatherless bairns. She said " she was leaving a large young family with very small means, but she had that trust in *Him* that they would not be forsaken, and that He would provide for them." Now, Margaret, ye'll tell Peggy to bring down the green silk bag that hangs on the corner of my looking-glass, and ye'll tak' twa thousand pounds out o' it, and gi'e it Walter Ferrier for behoof of thae orphan bairns ; it will fit out the laddies, and be something to the lassies. I want to make good the words, " that God wad provide for them," for what else was I sent that way this morning, but as a humble instrument in his hands ? '

Miss Trotter had a strong friendship for a certain Mrs. B——, who had an only son, and he was looked on as a simpleton, but his relatives had interest to get him a situation as clerk in a bank, where he contrived to steal money to the extent of five hundred pounds. His peculations were discovered, and in those days he would have been hanged, but Miss Trotter hearing the report started instantly for Edinburgh, went to the bank, and ascertained the truth. She at once laid down five hundred pounds, telling them, 'Ye maun not only stop proceedings, but ye maun keep him in the bank in some capacity, however mean, till I find some other employment for him.' Then she fitted the lad out, and sent him to London, where she had a friend to whom she wrote, offering another five hundred pounds to any one who would procure him a situation abroad, in which he might gain an honest living, and never be trusted with money. After all this was settled, she went herself and communicated the facts to his mother."

MRS. BOND, OF HACKNEY.

About the year 1771 there died one of the four children of Bond, a jeweller, residing in an alley leading from Wellclose Square to Ratcliffe Highway. She left property, to be divided between Mrs. S. Bond, of Hackney, and a sister. The latter died in the year 1801, and left her property, amounting to about 6,000*l.*, to her surviving sister, Sarah, who bought an annuity of 700*l.* By living in a most parsimonious manner she contrived to scrape together about 13,000*l.* Three per cent., 1,000*l.* Four per cent., and 150*l.* per year Long Annuities.

In 1821 Mrs. Bond, who was of most eccentric habits, died at her residence, Cambridge Heath, Hackney,

leaving, it was said, great wealth, which was to be paid
to King George the Fourth, *if no relative could be
found to claim it.* After her death, vestry and parish
clerks, beadles, sextons, country schoolmasters, and
persons holding any official situations about cathedral
churches, &c.—in short, innumerable persons who had
leisure or opportunity for such inquiry, set about
searching for Mrs. Bond's pedigree; but all to no effect.
Some ludicrous incidents, however, occurred in the
neighbourhood of Mrs. Bond's residence, where persons
arrived from various parts of the country to claim a relationship. Among the number a man and his son arrived
from Sunderland, whence they had walked. He stated
that his name was Bond; he was sure the deceased was
his sister, and he would not quit London without the
money. Upon investigation he could produce no other
authority than being of the same name, and was, therefore, compelled to retrace his steps, almost penniless.

About a week afterwards, a decently-dressed elderly
woman, named Bond, made her appearance. She had
just arrived outside the coach from the environs of
Carmarthen. Her story was that about fifty years
previously (1771), her sister left her and proceeded to
London to seek her fortune. They had never corre-
sponded, but from the name and description of the
deceased, she had no doubt she was her sister, and the
money accordingly belonged to her. It had cost her
nearly all the money she could raise to come from
Wales, fully satisfied of being amply repaid for her
trouble, but she met with the same fate as the preceding
applicant.

The next claimant was a sailor, who had just returned
from the West Indies, where he had been *moored*, he

said, thirty-five years. He had left in England two sisters named Bond : one was of very eccentric manners, particularly for her love of money ; the sailor declared that he had frequently seen her make a meal off cat's meat. The above he considered sufficient proof of his relationship. He insisted upon entering a caveat against the claim of his Majesty, but acknowledging that the King appeared to be the legal claimant, he swore he would go and see his royal master, and ask him if he had any objection to share the money with him !

It would be tedious to enumerate the persons who put in their claims from various parts of the world; but the King's proctor stood first in the Prerogative Court, and nothing had transpired to affect his right in behalf of his Majesty.

The hut on Cambridge Heath wherein Mrs. Bond died was closed for some time; at length it was announced to be let; but such was the anxiety to get possession of it that the notice was removed. The number of applications were, doubtless, made under the impression that hoards of money were yet undiscovered in the hut.

The claimant most likely entitled to the property was a Mr. Bond, a butcher, in Shoreditch, who traced out that he was second cousin to the wealthy spinster, his grandfather having been the only brother of the father of Mrs. Bond ; and the only bar to his administering was that he had not been able to ascertain the church where Mrs. Bond's father and mother were married, a most essential point to prove the legitimacy of Mrs. Sarah Bond. There were no fewer than eight caveats against the administrator.

JOHN WARD, THE HACKNEY MISER.

In Church Street, Hackney, one of the most interesting of our suburban parishes for its antiquarian history, stands a mansion, which, though plain in itself, has long been traditionally conspicuous, from the infamous character of its founder. This was John Ward, a man who was so notorious for his readiness to take advantage of the foibles, the wants, and vices of his fellow-men, that it attracted the satirical acrimony of Pope, who, in his epistle to Allen, Lord Bathurst, *On the Use of Riches*, has placed him in a niche in the Temple of Obloquy, in company with a trio, who seem fit to descend with him to posterity, or rather to accompany him in the descent alluded to in the following lines :—

> " Like doctors thus, when much dispute has pass'd,
> We find our tenets just the same at last :
> Both fairly owning riches, in effect,
> No grace of Heaven or token of the elect :
> Given to the fool, the mad, the vain, the evil,
> To Ward, to Waters, Chartres, and the Devil."

Of Ward's private history little is known. He is said to have been early in life employed in a floorcloth manufactory. The exact period when he built the house at Hackney is uncertain. He resided in it in the year 1727, at which time he sat in Parliament for Melcombe Regis. But having *made a mistake with respect to a name in a deed* in which the interest of the Duchess of Buckingham was implicated, he was prosecuted by her and convicted of forgery, was first expelled the House

of Commons, and then stood in the pillory, on the 17th
of March, 1727. As misfortune seldom comes alone,
about this time Ward was suspected of joining in
a conveyance with Sir John Blunt to secrete 50,000*l.*
of that director's estate forfeited to the South Sea
Company by Act of Parliament. The Company
recovered the 50,000*l* against Ward, and by execution
swept away the whole of the furniture and other effects
in the mansion at Hackney. These being insufficient
to cover even the costs, Ward sought to protect his
other property, set up prior conveyances of his real
estate to his brother and son, and concealing all his
personal, which was computed to be 150,000*l.* Against
these paper fortifications, a bill in Chancery, ten times
as voluminous, and twenty times more zig-zag, was
erected; a countermine of immense depth was sprung,
and however ably his works were defended, they were
at length carried. The conveyances were set aside,
Ward was imprisoned, and hazarded the forfeiture of
his life by not giving in his effects till the last day,
which was that of his examination. During his confinement his amusement was to give poison to dogs and
cats, and see them expire by slower or quicker
torments!

In the *Post-boy* newspaper of the period we find
these records of Ward's career :—In June, 1719, he
recovered 300*l.* damages from one Thomas Dyche, a
schoolmaster of Bow, for printing and publishing a
libel upon Ward, reflecting upon the discharge of his
trust about repairing Dagenham Breach. In May, 1726,
he fled to France or Flanders. In June, 1731, he was
indicted, with certain others, for wounding several
officers of the Commissioners of Bankruptcy ; and in

September, 1732, he surrendered to the Commissioners, and was kept under examination at Guildhall from three o'clock that afternoon till three the next morning, when he was committed to the Fleet for further examination.

To sum up the wealth of Ward at the several eras of his life: at his standing in the pillory he was worth above 200,000*l*.; at his commitment to prison he was worth 150,000*l*., but became so far diminished in his reputation as to be thought a worse man by fifty or sixty thousand.

Among a variety of curious papers of Mr. Ward was found the following extraordinary document, in his own handwriting, which may very appropriately be called *The Miser's Prayer* :—

" O Lord, Thou knowest that I have nine estates in the City of London, and likewise that I have lately purchased one estate in fee simple in the county of Essex; I beseech Thee to preserve the two counties of Middlesex and Essex from fire and earthquakes; and as I have a mortgage in Hertfordshire, I beg of Thee likewise to have an eye of compassion on that county; and for the rest of the counties Thou mayst deal with them as Thou art pleased. O Lord, enable the Bank to answer their bills, and make all my debtors good men. Give a prosperous voyage and return to the ' Mermaid ' sloop, because I have insured it; and as Thou hast said the days of the wicked are but short, I trust in Thee that Thou wilt not forget Thy promise, as I have purchased an estate in reversion, which will be mine on the death of that profligate young man, Sir J. L. Keep my friends from sinking, and preserve me from thieves and housebreakers, and make all my servants so honest and faithful that they may attend to my interests, and never cheat me out of my property, night or day."

"POOR MAN OF MUTTON."

This is a term applied to the remains of a shoulder of mutton, which, after it has done its regular duty as a roast at dinner, makes its appearance as a broiled bone at supper or upon the next day.

The late Earl of B., popularly known by the name of *Old Rag*, being indisposed at an hotel in London, the landlord came to enumerate the good things he had in his larder, hoping to prevail on his guest to eat something. The Earl, at length, starting suddenly from his couch, and throwing back a tartan nightgown, which had covered his singularly grim and ghastly face, replied to his host's courtesy:—"Landlord, I think I *could* eat a morsel of *a poor man*." Boniface, surprised alike at the extreme ugliness of Lord B.'s countenance and the nature of the proposal, retreated from the room, and tumbled down-stairs precipitately, having no doubt that this barbaric chief when at home was in the habit of eating a joint of a tenant or vassal when his appetite was dainty.—*Jamieson's Etymological Dictionary.*

LORD KENYON'S PARSIMONY.

Lord Kenyon studied economy even in the hatchment put up over his house in Lincoln's Inn Fields after his death. The motto was certainly found to be " *Mors janua vita*"—this being at first supposed to be the mistake of the painter. But when it was mentioned to Lord Ellenborough, "Mistake!" exclaimed his lordship, "it is no mistake. The considerate testator left particular directions in his will that the estate should not be burdened with the expense of a *diphthong!*" Accordingly, he had the glory of dying very rich. After the loss of his eldest son, he said with great emotion to Mr. Justice Allan Park, who repeated the words soon after to the narrator:—" How delighted George would be to take his poor brother from the earth, and restore him to life, although he receives 250,000*l.* by his decease!"

Lord Kenyon occupied a large, gloomy house in Lincoln's Inn Fields: there is this traditional description of the mansion in his time—"All the year through it is Lent in the kitchen and Passion-week in the parlour." Some one having mentioned that, although the fire was very dull in the kitchen-grate, the *spits* were always bright,— "It is quite irrelevant," said Jekyll, "to talk about the *spits*, for *nothing* 'turns' *upon them.*" * * He was curiously economical about the adornment of his head. It was observed for a number of years before he died, that he had two hats and two wigs—of the hats and the wigs one was dreadfully old and shabby, the other comparatively spruce. He always carried into court with him the very old hat and the comparatively spruce wig, or the very old wig and the comparatively spruce hat. On the days of the very old hat and the comparatively spruce wig, he shoved his hat under the bench and displayed his wig; but on the days of the very old wig and the comparatively spruce hat, he always continued covered. He might often be seen sitting with his hat over his wig, but the Rule of Court by which he was governed on this point is doubtful.

MARY MOSER, THE FLOWER-PAINTER.

Mary Moser was the only daughter of George Michael Moser, R.A., goldchaser and enameller, and the first Keeper of the Royal Academy of Arts in London. His daughter was a very distinguished flower-painter, and was the only lady besides Angelica Kauffman who was ever elected an Academician: she became afterwards Mrs. Lloyd. Miss Moser, says Smith, in his *Life of Nollekens,* was somewhat precise, but was at times a most cheerful companion: he has printed three of her letters, two to Mrs. Lloyd, the wife of the gentleman to whom she herself was afterwards married; and the other to Fuseli, while in Rome, of whom she was said to have been an admirer. In one to the former, alluding to the absurd fashions of the beginning of the reign of George the Third, she says:—"Come to London and admire our plumes; we sweep the skies! a duchess wears six feathers, a lady four, and every milkmaid one at each corner of her cap. Fashion is grown a monster: pray tell your operator that your hair must measure three-quarters of a yard from the extremity of one wing to the other." The second letter is chiefly on Lord Chesterfield's Advice to his Son: she says to her friend, "If you have read Lord Chesterfield's Letters, give me your opinion of them, and what you think of his Lordship: for my part, I admire wit and adore good manners, but at the same time I should detest Lord Chesterfield, were he alive, young, and handsome, and my lover, if I supposed, as I do now, his wit was the result of thought, and that he had been practising the graces in the looking-glass." In her letter to Fuseli, she gives this account of the Exhibition of the Royal Academy in the year 1770:—"Reynolds was like himself in pictures which you have seen; Gainsborough beyond himself in a portrait of a gentleman in a Vandyck habit; and Zoffany superior to everybody in a portrait of Garrick in the character of Abel Drugger, with two figures, Subtle and Face. Sir Joshua agreed to give a hundred guineas for the picture; Lord Carlisle had an hour after offered Reynolds twenty to part with it, which the Knight generously refused, resigned his intended purchase to the Lord, and the emolument to his brother artist. He is a gentleman! Angelica made a very great addition to the show, and Mr. Hamilton's picture of Briseis parting from Achilles was very much admired; the Briseis in taste, à l'antique, elegant and simple. Cotes, Dance, Wilson, &c., as usual."

Mary Moser decorated an entire room with flowers at Frogmore for Queen Charlotte, for which she received 900l.; the room was called Miss Moser's room. After her marriage, she practised only as an amateur; she died at an advanced age in 1819. When West was re-instated in the chair of the Royal Academy, in 1803, there was one voice for Mrs. Lloyd, and when Fuseli was taxed with having given it, he said, according to Knowles, his biographer, "Well, suppose I did; she is eligible to the office; and is not one old woman as good as another?" West and Fuseli were ill-according spirits.

THE ECCENTRIC MISS BANKS.

Oddities of dress were half-a-century ago much oftener to be seen than in the present day; or, rather, their singularities were more grotesque than the peculiarities of the present day. John Thomas Smith, writing in 1818, says—"It is scarcely possible for any person possessing the smallest share of common observation to pass through the streets in London without noticing what is generally denominated *a character*, either in dress, walk, pursuits, or propensities." At the head of his remarks on the eccentricity of some of their dresses he places Miss Sophia Banks, Sarah, the sister of Sir Joseph, who was looked after by the eye of astonishment wherever she went, and in whatever situation she appeared. Her dress was that of the *Old School;* her Barcelona quilted petticoat had a hole on either side for the convenience of rummaging two immense pockets, stuffed with books of all sizes. This petticoat was covered with a deep stomachered gown, sometimes obscuring the pocket-holes, similar to many of the ladies of Bunbury's time, which he has introduced into his prints. In this dress she might frequently be seen walking, followed by a six-foot servant with a cane almost as tall as himself. Miss Banks, for so that lady was called for many years, was frequently heard to relate the following curious anecdote of herself: after making repeated inquiries of the wall-vendors of half-penny ballads for a particular one which she wanted, she was informed by the claret-faced woman who strung up her stock by Middlesex Hospital gates, that if she went to a printer's in Long Lane, Smithfield, probably he might supply her ladyship with what her ladyship wanted. Away trudged Miss Banks through Smithfield: but before she entered Mr. Thompson's shop, she desired her man to wait for her at the corner, by the plum-pudding stall. "Yes, we have it," was the printer's answer to her interrogative. He then gave Miss Banks what is called a book, consisting of many songs. Upon her expressing her surprise when the man returned her eightpence from her shilling, and the great quantity of songs he had given her, when she only wanted one— "What, then!" observed the man, "are you not one of our characters? I beg your pardon."

This lady and Lady Banks, out of compliment to Sir Joseph, who had been deeply engaged in the production of wool, had their riding-habits made of his produce, in which dresses the two ladies at one period on all occasions appeared. Indeed, so delighted was Miss Banks with this *overall* covering, that she actually gave the habit-maker orders for three at a time, and they were called *Hightum*, *Tightum*, and *Scrub*. The first was her best, the second her second-best, and the third her every-day one.

Once when Miss Banks and her sister-in-law visited a friend with whom they were to stay several days, on the evening of their arrival they sat down to dinner in their riding-habits. Their friend had a large party after dinner to meet them, and they entered the drawing-room in their riding-habits. On the following morning they again appeared in their riding-habits; and so on, to the astonishment of every one, till the conclusion of their visit.

Although Miss Banks paid great attention to many persons, there were others to whom she was wanting in civility. A great genius, who had arrived a quarter-of-an-hour before the time specified on the card for dinner, was shown into the drawing-room, where Miss Banks was putting away what are sometimes called *rattletraps*. When the visitor observed, "It is a fine day, ma'am," she replied, "I know nothing at all about it. You must speak to my brother upon that subject when you are at dinner." Notwithstanding the very singular appearance of Miss Banks, she was, when in the prime of life, a fashionable whip, and drove four-in-hand. Miss Banks died in 1818.

THOMAS COOKE, THE MISER, OF PENTON-VILLE.

At No. 16, Winchester Place, now No. 64, Pentonville Road, lived, for a period of fifteen years, Thomas Cooke, a notorious miser, who heaped up wealth by the most ungenerous means and servility of behaviour:

> " Gold banished honour from his mind,
>   And only left the name behind."

He was born about 1725 or 1726, at Clewer, near

Windsor, and was the son of an itinerant fiddler. He was left to the care of a grandmother, who resided at Swannington, near Norwich. He obtained employment in a factory, where the leading trait of his character manifested itself. His companions in labour clubbed a portion of their week's earnings to form a mess. This Cooke declined, and determined to live more cheaply; and when others went to dine, he went to the side of a neighbouring brook, and made breakfast and dinner one meal, which consisted of a halfpenny loaf, an apple, and a draught of water from the brook, taken up on the brim of his cap. His economy so far seems to have been judicious, as it enabled him to pay a boy who was an usher in the village school to instruct him in the rudiments of education.

When he arrived at manhood, he obtained employment as porter to a drysalter and paper-maker at Norwich; he was next made a journeyman, with increased wages. He then, through his master, got an appointment in the Excise, in a district near London; and his master also gave him a letter of introduction to a sugar-baker in the metropolis. After a tedious journey by wagon, he reached London, with only eight shillings in his pocket. There was some delay and expense before he could act as an exciseman, and his immediate necessities compelled him to take the situation of porter to the sugar-baker. He then became a journeyman, and by his parsimonious habits saved money enough to pay the preliminary expenses, and was enabled to assume the office to which he had so long aspired.

He was then appointed to inspect a paper-mill at Tottenham, where he closely watched a new process in paper-making. During Cooke's official visits to this mill the owner died, and his widow resolved to carry on the business with the aid of a foreman. Cooke had noted here many infractions of the law, which, designedly or otherwise, were daily taking place; and having summed up the penalties incurred thereby, which he set off against the value of the concern, he privately informed the widow that he had complained of these malpractices, and told her that if the fines were levied, they would amount to double the value of the property she possessed, and reduce her to want and imprisonment. This he followed up by an overture of marriage, and assured the lady that he only knew of the frauds of her establishment. The widow consented to become his wife when the appointed days of mourning for her first husband had expired. To this Cooke agreed, but lest she might prove fickle, he required of her a promise in writing. On his marriage, Cooke became possessed of her property, which was considerable, together with the lease of the mills at Tottenham.

He next purchased a large sugar-baker's business in Puddle Dock. His parsimony now became extreme: he kept no table, but obtained the greater part of his daily food by well-timed visits to persons of his acquaintance. He had good conversational powers, and these he usually turned to his profit. Sometimes, when walking the streets, he fell down in a pretended fit, opposite to the house of one whose bounty he sought. No humane person could well refuse admission to a man in apparent distress and of respectable appearance, whose well-powdered wig and long ruffles induced a belief that he was some decayed citizen who had seen better days. For the assistance thus kindly given he would express his gratitude in the most energetic

manner. He would ask for a glass of water, but if wine
was offered, he said, "No, he never drank anything but
water ; " but when pressed by his kind host, would take
it, and exclaim, "God bless my soul, sir, this is very
excellent wine ! Pray, sir, who is your wine merchant ?
for indeed, to tell you the truth, it was the difficulty of
getting good wine that caused me to leave it off entirely."   Upon invitation, he would take another glass,
and thanking his host, depart.   A few days after, he
would call at the house of his kind entertainer just at
dinner-time, professedly to thank him for having saved
his life, and on being invited to dine would at first
demur, urging that "My gruel is waiting for me at
home."   On sitting down to dinner he would take
notice of the children ; and after great pretended kindness, would say to the mother, "God bless them, pretty
dears. Pray, madam, will you have the goodness to give
me all their names in writing ? "   Thus artfully did he
contrive to make his kind entertainers think that he
designed to do some good thing for their children ; and
they now sought the continuance of his friendship by
occasional presents of game or a dozen or two of the
wine he had so much approved.

Many persons were in this way made the victims of
Cooke's sophistries.   By these gifts, his housekeeping
expenses were reduced to fifteen-pence a day, and it was
sinful extravagance if they reached two shillings.   Such
comestibles as he could not consume, he disposed of to
the dealers and others.   He drank only water, but as
for the " gormandizing, gluttonous maids, they could not
drink, not they, what he did ; nothing would serve them
but table-beer."   This he kept in his front parlour,
with a lock-tap to it, of which he held the key, and

at meal-times he drew exactly half-a-pint for each woman.

With all his rigid economy, Cooke found, to his great grief, that by his sugar-bakery he had lost 500*l*. in twelve months. To amend this state of affairs, and to discover some of the secrets of the trade, he invited several sugar bakers to dine with him, and plying them well with wine, wheedled out of the persons in business the coveted information. His wife was alarmed at this seeming extravagance, but he silenced her scruples by telling her he would "suck as much of the brains" of some of the fools as would amply repay them.

Having retired from business, he resided for a time at the Angel Inn, Islington, from whence he removed to Winchester Place. The plot of garden-ground in the rear he sowed with cabbage-seed, and with his own hands manured it. To obtain the manure, he would, on moonlight nights, go out with a shovel and basket and take up the horse-dung which lay in the City Road. This scheming obtained for him the name of "Cabbage Cooke."

The only luxury he allowed his wife was a small quantity of table-beer ; and by his general mal-treatment he caused her so much grief that she died of a broken heart. Soon after his wife's death, he paid his addresses to several rich widows, but none would listen to his suit, especially as he desired all their property should be made over to him.

Cooke was fond of horse-racing, and contrived to be present at Epsom races at the expense of some of his acquaintances. He once had a horse ; but finding it too expensive to keep at livery, for this purpose he converted the kitchen of his house into a stable, and he used to curry and fodder the horse with his own hands.

During his fifteen years' residence in Winchester Place, he never once painted the house inside or outside, nor would he allow the landlord to paint it. He was then served with legal notice to quit; this he disregarded. At last he so implored the landlord not to turn him into the street, that he consented to allow him time to provide himself with a house, and this in presence of an associate whom he brought purposely in the room. The landlord then had him served with an ejectment; but, upon the case being brought to trial, Cooke brought forward in evidence the witness to the promise of the landlord, who was accordingly nonsuited. The landlord, however, brought another action, in which he succeeded; and Cooke removed to No. 85, White Lion Street, Pentonville.

Sickness and old age now compelled Cooke to seek medical advice, when he obtained, by some artifice, a patient's dispensary letter; but his cheat was discovered. Cooke's principle was, "No cure, no pay;" and when a physician, to whom he had been very troublesome, told him he could do nothing more for him, he said, "Then give me back my money, sir. Why did you rob me of my money, unless you meant to cure me?" Yet Cooke was a professing Christian, and a regular attendant at the ordinances of religion, and he seldom failed to receive the sacrament. He died August 26th, 1811, at the age of eighty-six, and was buried on the 30th at St. Mary's, Islington. Some of the mob threw cabbage-stalks on his coffin as it was lowered into the grave.

The wealth that Cooke had amassed during his long

life-time, by meanness, artifice, and pretended poverty, amounted to the large sum of 127,205*l.* in the Three per cent. Consols. During his lifetime his charities were but few. But, as if to atone for a life of avarice, he left by will the bulk of his riches to several charitable societies, and a few trifling legacies to individuals.

THOMAS COOKE, THE TURKEY MERCHANT.

This eccentric gentleman was resident at Constantinople as a merchant at the time Charles XII. of Sweden was in Turkey, in 1714, and contributed in a very munificent manner to the relief of the royal prisoner. Mr. Cooke well knew the Divan wished to get rid of the king, their prisoner, who always pleaded poverty and inability to pay his debts; and they having lent him money, were afraid to lend him any more. He, however, devised a scheme to assist him, and applied to the Lord High Treasurer, who heard the proposal with great satisfaction, but was surprised to be told, "Your excellency must find the money." To this he answered, by a very natural question, "How will you ever pay us?" Mr. Cooke replied, they were building a mosque, and would stand in need of lead to cover it, which he would engage to supply. Next morning the proposal was accepted, and the arrangements concluded.

Mr. Cooke then treated with the King of Sweden, and offered him a certain sum of money upon condition of being repaid in copper, the exportation of which from Sweden had been for some time prohibited, at a stipulated price. The offer was accepted, and the money paid to the king by the hands of La Mortraye, the well-known author of several volumes of *Travels;* and Mr. Cooke received an order upon the states of Sweden to be paid in copper, which he sold to a house in that kingdom, at an advance of 12,000*l.* sterling upon the first cost, besides the profit he obtained upon the sale of his lead. The money lent was not sufficient for the king's liberation; he stayed in Turkey till he had nothing left but a knife and fork. Upon hearing of the king's situation, Mr. Cooke one day surprised him with a present of his whole sideboard of plate; and for this conduct towards their sovereign his name was idolized by the Swedes.

Mr. Cooke was for many years in the commission of the peace for the county of Middlesex, and was three years governor of the Bank of England. He was a man of singular character, very shrewd, but highly esteemed, particularly for his unbounded munificence. Having made his will, whereby he had bequeathed 1,000*l.* to the clerks of the Bank, he resolved on being his own executor, and to give them the money in his lifetime. Accordingly, in the month of February, preceding his death, he sent a note of 1,000*l.* to the governor of the Bank, requesting that it might be distributed among the clerks, in the proportion of one guinea for every year that each person had been in their service, and the remaining 3*l.* to the porters.

Mr. Cooke died at Stoke Newington, 12th of August, 1752, aged eighty. By his own directions he was attended to the grave by twelve poor housekeepers belonging to a box-club at Stoke Newington, of which he had long been a generous and useful member. To each man he bequeathed a guinea and a suit of clothes, and as much victuals and drink as he chose; but if either of the legatees got fuddled, he was to forfeit his legacy, and was only to receive half-a-crown for his day's work. Mr. Cooke's corpse was wrapped in a clean blanket, sewed up, and, being put into a common coffin, was conveyed, with the above attendants, in three coaches, to the grave close to a stile, near Sir John Morden's College, on Blackheath, of which he was a trustee. The corpse was then taken out of the coffin, which was left in the college for the first pensioner it would fit, and buried in a winding-sheet upright in the ground, according to the Eastern custom.

Cooke's widow maintained the same benevolent character with himself, and died at Stoke Newington, January 15th, 1763. They had issue two daughters, both of whom died before their father.

"LADY LEWSON," OF CLERKENWELL.

In Cold Bath Square, for the space of ninety years, lived Mrs. Lewson, commonly called "Lady Lewson," from her very eccentric manner of dress. She was born in the year 1700, in the reign of William and Mary, in Essex Street, Strand, of respectable parents named Vaughan; and she was married at an early age to Mr. Lewson, a wealthy gentleman, then living in Cold Bath Square, in the house wherein she subsequently continued to reside. She became a widow at the age of twenty-six, having only one daughter living at the time. She was left by her husband in affluent circumstances; she preferred to continue single, and remained so, although she had many suitors. When her daughter married, Mrs. Lewson was left alone, and being of retired habits, she rarely went out, or permitted the visits of any person. During the last thirty years of her life, she kept only one servant, an old woman, who died after a servitude of twenty years: she was succeeded by her grand-daughter, who marrying, was replaced by an old man, who attended the different houses in the Square to go of errands, clean shoes, &c. "Lady Lewson" took this man into her house, and he acted as her steward, butler, cook, and housemaid; and with the exception of two old lapdogs and a cat, was her only companion.

The house in which she lived was large and elegantly furnished; the beds were kept constantly made, although they had not been slept in for about thirty years. Her apartment was only occasionally swept out, and never washed; and the windows were so encrusted with dirt, that they hardly admitted a ray of light. She used to tell her acquaintances that if the rooms were washed, it might be the occasion of her catching cold; and as to cleaning the windows, many accidents happened through that ridiculous practice—the glass might be broken, the person who cleaned them might be injured, and the expense would fall upon her. There was a large garden in the rear of the house, which she kept in good order; and here, when the weather was fine, she sometimes sat and read, or chatted of times past with such of her acquaintances as she could be persuaded to admit. She seldom visited, except at the house of a grocer in Cold Bath Square, with whom she dealt. She had survived many years every relative, and was thus left to indulge her odd tastes.

She was so partial to the fashions that prevailed in her youthful days, that she never changed the manner of her dress from that worn in the time of George I., being always decorated

"With ruffs, and cuffs, and fardingales."

She always wore powder, with a large *tache*, made of horsehair, upon her head, over which the hair was turned, and she placed the cap, which was tied under her chin, and three or four rows of curls hung down her neck. She generally wore a silk dress, with a long train, a deep flounce all round, and a very long waist; her gown was very tightly laced up to her neck, round which was a ruff or frill; the sleeves came down below the elbows, and to each of them four or five large cuffs were attached; a large bonnet, quite flat, high-heeled shoes, a large black silk cloak trimmed with lace, and a gold-headed cane, completed her every-day costume for eighty years; in which dress she occasionally walked round the Square. She never washed herself, because she thought those persons who did so were always taking cold, or engendering some dreadful disorder; her method was to besmear her face and neck all over with hog's-lard, because that was soft and lubricating; and because she wanted a little colour on her cheeks, she bedaubed them with rose-pink. Her manner of living was very methodical: she would only drink tea out of one cup, and always sat in her favourite chair. She enjoyed good health, and entertained the greatest aversion to medicine. At the age of eighty-three, she cut two new teeth, and she was never troubled with tooth-ache. She lived in five reigns, and had the events of the year 1715 (the Scottish Rebellion) fresh in her recollection.

The sudden death of an old lady who was a neighbour made a deep impression on Mrs. Lewson: believing her own time had come, she became weak, took to her bed, refused medical aid, and on Tuesday, the 28th of May, 1816, died at her house in Cold Bath Square, at the age of 116; she was interred in Bunhill Fields burying-ground. "At her death," says Mr. Warner, in his MS. *Notes on Clerkenwell*, "I went over the house, and was struck with astonishment at the number of bars, bolts, &c., to the whole of the doors and windows; the ceilings of the upper floor were completely lined with strong boards, braced together with iron bars, to prevent any one getting into the house from the roof. The ashes had not been removed for many years; they were neatly piled up, as if formed into beds for some particular purpose, around the yard. Her furniture, &c., were sold by auction, and persons were admitted to view by producing a catalogue, which was sold at sixpence, and would permit any number of persons at one time."*

PROFITS OF DUST-SIFTING, AND DUST-HEAPS.

Many years ago a *dust-sifter*, named Mary Collins, residing in Bell Street, Lisson Grove, was robbed by a nurse, when her evidence before the police magistrate was remarkable for the extraordinary disclosures it inci-

* Pinks's *History of Clerkenwell*, 1865, p. 115.

dentally afforded of the large profits obtained from the apparently humble vocation of dust-sifting. The articles stolen were in a pocket, and were thus described: one coral necklace, large beads; one ditto, with pearl clasp; several handsome brooches; five gold seals; some gold rings; several gold shirt-pins; a quantity of loose beads; broken bits of gold and silver, &c. Mr. Rawlinson, the magistrate, expressed his surprise at her having such a motley assortment of valuables. Complainant: Your worship, we find them amongs the dust.— Mr. Rawlinson: Indeed! what, all these articles?—Complainant: Oh, your worship, that's nothing; we find many more things than them: we find almost every small article that can be mentioned. We are employed by the dust contractor, who allows us 8*d.* per load for sifting, besides which we have all the spoons and other articles which we may find among the dust.—Mr. Rawlinson: That is dustman's law, I suppose: but pray how many silver spoons may you find in the course of the year?—Complainant: It is impossible to say: sometimes more and sometimes less.

Mr. Rawlinson declared that what she had just related was quite novel to him. The urbane manner of the worthy magistrate won upon the old lady and made her quite communicative. She had followed her occupation eight years, and what with the "perquisites" (*id est*, articles found), and the savings from "hard labour," she had realized sufficient money to think about house-building, and had then a house erecting which she expected would cost her at least 300*l.* She had deposited 100*l.* in the hands of her employer, in part payment, and as a proof that all was not vaunting, she produced her box, in which were thirty-nine sovereigns, two five-pound bank-notes, and several guineas and half-sovereigns.

Early in the present century, the spot of ground on which now stands Argyle Street, Liverpool Street, Manchester Street, and the corner of Gray's Inn Road, was covered with a mountain of filth and cinders, the accumulation of many years, and which afforded food for hundreds of pigs. The Russians bought the whole of the ash-heap, and shipped it to Moscow, to be used in rebuilding that city after it had been burned by the French. The Battle-bridge dustmen had a certain celebrity in their day. The ground on which the dust-heap stood was sold in 1826 to the Pandemonium Company for fifteen thousand pounds; they walled in the whole, and built a theatre, which now remains at the corner of Liverpool Street. The Company's scheme was, however, abandoned, and the ground was let on building leases. The heap is mentioned in the burlesque song, *Adam Bell, the Literary Dustman :**

> " You recollect the cinder heap,
> Vot stood in Gray's Inn Lane, sirs ? "

When the street now called the Caledonian Road was in the fields, there was at the Battle-bridge end of the road a large accumulation of horse-bones, which were stored there by some horse-slaughterers. And in 1833, Battle-bridge was described in the *New Monthly Magazine* as " the grand centre of dustmen, scavengers, horse and dog dealers, knackermen, brickmakers, and other low but necessary professionalists." The dust-heap is described as " that sublime, sifted wonder of cockneys,

* Pinks's *History of Clerkenwell*, p. 501.

the cloud-kissing dust-heap which sold for twenty thousand pounds;" but this is doubtful.

Mr. T. C. Noble has communicated to Pinks's *History of Clerkenwell* the following particulars of the Dust and Cinder Heap, &c.—"The estate at Battle-bridge comprised from seventeen to twenty acres. Of this my grandfather took sixteen small dilapidated houses, and *the dust and cinder heap*, which, it was said, had been *existing on the spot since the Great Fire of London.* He gave about 500*l.* for the lot, although the parties wanted 800*l.* Bricks were then very scarce, so he very soon realized a good sum for the old buildings, while Russia, hearing in some way of this enormous dust-heap, purchased it for purposes in rebuilding Moscow. The site of the mountain of dust is now covered by the houses of Derby Street, and I may add, the names of the thoroughfares erected on this estate were derived from the popular ministers of that day. The rental derived from the property by my grandfather exceeded 1,000*l.* a-year."

John Thomas Smith gives the following notes upon oddities of the above class:—"Within my time many men have indulged most ridiculously in their eccentricities. I have known one who had made a pretty large fortune in business get up at four o'clock in the morning and walk the streets to pick up horse-shoes which had been slipped in the course of the night, with no other motive than to see how many he could accumulate in the course of a year. I also remember a rich soap-boiler who never missed an opportunity of pocketing nails, pieces of iron hoops, and bits of leather in his daily walks; and these he would spread upon a large walnut-tree three-flapped dining-table, with a similar view to that of the horse-shoe collector. This wealthy citizen would often put on a red woollen cap and a wagoner's frock, in order to stoke his own furnace; after which he would dress, get into his coach, and, attended by tall servants in bright blue liveries, drive to his villa, where his hungry friends were waiting his arrival."

SIR JOHN DINELY, BART.

This eccentric baronet, of the family of the Dinelys, of Charlton, descended by the female line from the Royal House of Plantagenet, having dissipated the wreck of the family estates, obtained the pension and situation of a poor knight of Windsor. His chief occupation consisted in advertising for a wife, and nearly thirty years were passed in assignations to meet the fair respondents to his advertisements. His figure was truly grotesque: in wet weather he was mounted on a high pair of pattens; he wore the coat of the Windsor uniform, with a velvet embroidered waistcoat, satin breeches, silk stockings, and a full-bottomed wig. In this finery he might be seen strolling one day; and next out marketing, carrying a penny loaf, a morsel of butter, a quartern of sugar, and a farthing candle. Twice or thrice a year he came to London, and visited Vauxhall Gardens and the theatres. His fortune, if he could recover it, he estimated at 300,000*l.* He invited the widow as well as the blooming maiden of sixteen, and addressed them in printed documents, fearing his signature, in which he specified the sum the ladies must possess; he expected less property with youth than age or widowhood; adding that few ladies would be eligible that did not possess at least 10,000l. a year, which, however, was nothing compared to the honour his high birth and noble descent would confer; the incredulous he referred to Nash's *Worcestershire*. He addressed his advertisements to "the angelic fair" from his house in Windsor Castle (one of the poor knights' houses). He cherished to the last the expectation of forming a connubial connection with some lady of property, but, alas! he died a bachelor in 1808.*

THE ROTHSCHILDS.

In the *Memoirs of Sir Thomas Fowell Buxton*, edited by his son, we find this amusing letter, dated 1834: "We yesterday dined at Ham House, to meet the Rothschilds; and very amusing it was. He (Rothschild) told us his life and adventures. He was the third son of the banker at Frankfort. 'There was not,' he said, 'room enough for us all in that city. I dealt in English goods. One great trader came there, who had the market to himself: he was quite the great man, and did us a favour if he sold us goods. Somehow I offended him, and he refused to show me his patterns. This was on a Tuesday; I said to my father, "I will go to England." I could speak nothing but German. On the Thursday I started. The nearer I got to England, the cheaper goods were. As soon as I got to Manchester, I laid out all my money, things were so cheap; and I made good profit. I soon found that there were

* We know an instance of an old Baronet advertising twenty years for a wife; at last he succeeded in marrying an out-and-out Xanthippe.

three profits—the raw material, the dyeing, and the manufacturing. I said to the manufacturer, "I will supply you with material and dye, and you supply me with manufactured goods." So I got three profits instead of one, and I could sell goods cheaper than anybody. In a short time I made my 20,000*l.* into 60,000*l.* My success all turned on one maxim. I said, I can do what another man can, and so I am a match for the man with the patterns, and for all the rest of them! Another advantage I had. I was an off-hand man. I made a bargain at once. When I was settled in London, the East India Company had 800,000 ounces of gold to sell. I went to the sale, and bought it all. I knew the Duke of Wellington must have it. I had bought a great many of his bills at a discount. The Government sent for me, and said they must have it. When they had got it, they did not know how to get it to Portugal. I undertook all that, and I sent it through France; and that was the best business I ever did.'

"Another maxim, on which he seemed to place great reliance, was, never to have anything to do with an unlucky place or an unlucky man. 'I have seen,' said he, 'many clever men, very clever men, who had not shoes to their feet. I never act with them. Their advice sounds very well; but fate is against them; they cannot get on themselves; and if they cannot do good to themselves, how can they do good to me?' By aid of these maxims he has acquired three millions of money. 'I hope,' said ——, 'that your children are not too fond of money and business, to the exclusion of more important things. I am sure you would not wish that.'—Rothschild: 'I am sure I should wish that. *I wish them to give mind, and soul, and heart, and body,*

and everything to business ; that is the way to be happy.
It requires a great deal of boldness and a great deal of
caution to make a great fortune ; and when you have
got it, it requires ten times as much wit to keep it. If
I were to listen to all the projects proposed to me, I
should ruin myself very soon. Stick to one business,
young man,' said he to Edward; 'stick to your brewery,
and you may be the great brewer of London. Be a
brewer, and a banker, and a merchant, and a manufacturer, and you will soon be in the *Gazette.*

" ' One of my neighbours is a very ill-tempered man ;
he tries to vex me, and has built a great place for swine
close to my walk. So, when I go out, I hear first, grunt,
grunt, squeak, squeak ; but this does me no harm. I am
always in good humour. Sometimes to amuse myself I
give a beggar a guinea. He thinks it is a mistake, and
for fear I should find it out, off he runs as hard as he
can. I advise you to give a beggar a guinea sometimes,
it is very amusing.' The daughters are very pleasing.
The second son is a mighty hunter, and his father lets
him buy any horses he likes. He lately applied to the
Emperor of Morocco for a first-rate Arab horse. The
Emperor sent him a magnificent one; but he died as
he landed in England. The poor youth said very
feelingly, 'that was the greatest misfortune he ever had
suffered ;' and I felt strong sympathy with him. I
forgot to say, that soon after Mr. Rothschild came to
England, Bonaparte invaded Germany. 'The Prince of
Hesse Cassel,' said Rothschild, 'gave my father his
money ; there was no time to be lost ; he sent it to me.
I had 600,000*l.* arrive unexpectedly by the post; and I
put it to such good use, that the Prince made me a
present of all his wine and his linen.' "

A LEGACY OF HALF-A-MILLION OF MONEY.

On the 30th of August, 1852, there died at Chelsea John Camden Neild, a wealthy gentleman, who had bequeathed an immense legacy to Queen Victoria. His father was a native of Knutsford, in Cheshire; as a goldsmith in London he made a large fortune. He was a truly benevolent man, especially in his efforts for the improvement of prisons, and originated the Society for the Relief of Persons imprisoned for Small Debts. He married the daughter of John Camden, Esq., of Battersea, in Surrey, a direct descendant of the great antiquary of the same name. He died in 1814, and was buried at Chelsea.

John Camden Neild, the only surviving son of the above, was born in 1780; educated at Trinity College, Cambridge; studied at Lincoln's Inn, and in 1808 was called to the bar.' In 1814 he succeeded to the whole of his father's property, estimated at 250,000*l.*; but he made a very different use of his wealth. Avarice was his ruling passion; he became a confirmed miser, and for the last thirty years of his life gave himself over to heaping up riches. He lived in a large but meanly furnished house in Cheyne Walk, Chelsea; and he slept on a bare board, and latterly on an old stump bedstead, on which he died. His favourite companion was a large black cat, which was in his chamber when he breathed his last.

He had considerable property at North Marston, in Buckinghamshire, and here he often stayed for days together, besides his half-yearly visits to receive rents. As lessee of the rectory, it was incumbent on him to repair the chancel of the church; the leaded roof having become full of fissures, he had them covered with strips of painted calico, saying they would "last his time." During this odd repair, he sat all day on the roof, to keep the workmen employed, and even ate his dinner there, which consisted of hard-boiled eggs, dry bread, and buttermilk.

His dress was an old-fashioned swallow-tailed coat, brown trousers, short gaiters, and shoes which were generally patched and down at the heels. His stockings and linen were generally full of holes; but when he stayed a night at a tenant's, the mistress often mended them while he was in bed. He was short and punchy in figure, scarcely above five feet in height, with a large round and short neck. He always carried an old green cotton umbrella, but never wore a great coat, which he considered too extravagant for his slender means. He travelled outside a coach, where his fellow-travellers took him for a decayed gentleman in extreme poverty. Once, when visiting his Kentish property on a bitterly cold day, the coach stopped at Farningham, where the other passengers subscribed for a glass of brandy-and-water, which they sent to the poor gentleman, in pity for their thinly-clad companion who still sat on the coach-roof, while they were by the inn fireside.

He often took long journeys on foot, when he would avail himself of any proffered "lift," and he was even known to sit on a load of coal, to enable him to proceed a little further without expense; yet he would give the driver a penny or two for the accommodation; for, miser as he was, he never liked to receive anything without paying for it—however small the scale; nor would he partake of any meal or refreshment when asked by the clergymen of the parishes where his estates lay.   Yet with tenants of a lower grade he would share the coarse meals and lodging of the family.   At North Marston he used to reside with the tenant on the rectory farm ; while staying here, about 1828, he attempted to cut his throat, but his life was saved chiefly by the prompt assistance of the tenant's wife.   This attempt was supposed to have been caused by a sudden fall in the funds, in which he had just made a large investment.

Sometimes he would eat his dinner at a tenant's, where he would beg a basin of milk, and buy three eggs for a penny, get them hard-boiled, and eat two for his dinner, with another basin of milk ; the third egg he would save for next morning's breakfast.   He used to examine minutely the nature of his land, and keep an account of the number of trees on his estates; he had been known to walk from twelve to fifteen. miles to count only a few trees.

Mr. Neild's general answer to all applications for charitable contributions was a refusal ; in some instances it was otherwise.   He once, but only once, gave a pound for the Sunday-school at North Marston ; he promised 300*l.* towards building an infirmary for Buckingham-shire, but withheld it from an objection to the site.

Mr. Neild was not, as stated at the time of his death, " a frigid, spiritless specimen of humanity," for he pos-sessed considerable knowledge in legal and general literature and the classics.   Nor did he entirely pass over merit.   Finding the son of one of his tenants to possess strong natural abilities, he paid wholly or in part the expenses of his school and college education.   This

person is now a distinguished scholar and a dignitary of
the Church of England.

Mr. Neild was buried on the 16th of September,
according to his own desire, in the chancel of North
Marston Church. His will then necessarily came to
light, and great was the sensation which it occasioned.
After bequeathing a few trifling legacies to different
persons, he left the whole of his vast property, estimated
at 500,000*l.*, to "Her Most Gracious Majesty Queen
Victoria, begging Her Majesty's most gracious acceptance of the same for her sole use and benefit, and her
heirs, &c." To each of his three executors he bequeathed
100*l.* The will had excited such curiosity, that, though
his life had passed almost unnoticed, a large concourse
of persons assembled at Chelsea to witness the removal
of his body, and the church and churchyard at North
Marston were crowded with wondering—not lamenting
—spectators. Among his tenants, workmen, and the
poor of the parish where he possessed so much property,
not a tear was shed, not a regret uttered, as his body
was committed to its last resting-place. The only
remark heard was, "Poor creature! had he known so
much would have been spent on his funeral, he would
have come down here to die to save the expense!"

Two caveats were entered against his will, but were
subsequently withdrawn, and the Queen was left to take
undisputed possession of his property. Her Majesty
immediately increased Mr. Neild's bequest to his three
executors to 100*l.* each; she provided for his old housekeeper, to whom he had made no bequest, though she
had lived with him six-and-twenty years; and she
secured an annuity to the woman who had frustrated
Mr. Neild's attempt at suicide.

Her Majesty, in 1855, had restored the chancel of North Marston Church, and inserted an east window of beautifully stained glass, beneath which is a reredos with this inscription: "This Reredos and the Stained Glass Window were erected by Her Majesty Queen Victoria (D.G.B.R.F.D.), in the eighteenth year of her reign, in memory of John Camden Neild, Esq., of this parish, who died August 30th, 1852, aged 72."*

This man of wealth must not be confounded with the Mr. Neeld who came into possession of great wealth on the demise of his uncle, Philip Rundell, the wealthy goldsmith of Ludgate Hill. He died in 1827, at the age of eighty-one; and, according to the *Gentleman's Magazine*, "had never married, and never kept an establishment, but lived much with one niece at Brompton, and another, the wife of John Bannister, the eminent comedian." The eldest son of the latter, on coming of age, was invited to breakfast with Mr. Rundell, who placed in the young man's hands at parting a sealed letter, which he was not to open till he reached home. It was then found to contain a bequest of 10,000*l*., payable on the death of the donor, and of his own marriage. This incident was related to Mr. Britton by Mr. Bannister, who also indulged him by repeating two songs which he had written and sung at Mr. Rundell's, on two birthdays of the aged goldsmith. Bannister also inherited 5,000*l*. for his own life, and then to devolve to his daughter; and his son had an additional legacy from Mr. Rundell. Numerous other large sums of money were bequeathed to other relatives, friends, and public foundations; but the most important

---

* Condensed from *The Book of Days*, vol. ii. pp. 285-288.

item in the will is the residuary clause, whereby the
testator "gives to his esteemed friend, Joseph Neeld,
the younger, all the rest of his real and mixed estate,
which," says the magazine, " it is computed will amount
to not less than 890,000*l.* The personal effects were
sworn at upwards of 1,000,000*l.*, the utmost limit to
which the scale of the probate duty extends."

ECCENTRICITIES OF THE EARL OF BRIDGEWATER.

Forty years since there lived in Paris the Rev.
Francis Henry Egerton, Earl of Bridgewater, of whom
we find this probably overcharged but curious account
in a Parisian journal of the year 1826; than his lordship
no one has a higher claim to a distinguished place in
the history of human oddities :—" Those who have once
seen—nay, those who have never seen this meagre
personage drag himself along, supported by two huge
lacqueys, with his sugar-loaf hat, slouched down over
his eyes, cannot fail to recognize him. An immense
fortune enables him to gratify the most extravagant
caprices that ever passed through the head of a rich
Englishman. If he be lent a book, he carries his
politeness so far as to send it back, or rather have it
conveyed home, in a carriage. He gives orders that
two of his most stately steeds be caparisoned under one
of his chariots, and the volume, reclining at ease in
milord's landau, arrives, attended by four footmen in
costly livery, at the door of its astounded owner. His

carriage is frequently to be seen filled with his dogs. He bestows great care on the feet of these dogs, and orders them boots, for which he pays as dearly as for his own. Lord Bridgewater's custom is an excellent one for the boot-maker; for, besides the four feet of each of his dogs, the supply of his own two feet must give constant employment to several operatives. He puts on a new pair of boots every day, carefully preserving those he has once worn, and ranging them in order; he commands that none shall touch them, but takes himself great pleasure in observing how much of the year has each day passed, by the state of his boots.

"Lord Egerton is a man of few acquaintance, and very few of his countrymen have got as far as his dining-hall. His table, however, is constantly set out with a dozen covers, and served by suitable attendants. Who, then, are his privileged guests? No less then a dozen of favourite dogs, who daily partake of *milord's* dinner, seated very gravely in arm-chairs, each with a napkin round his neck, and a servant behind to attend to his wants. These honourable quadrupeds, as if grateful for such delicate attentions, comport themselves during the time of repast with a decency and decorum which would do more than honour to a party of gentlemen; but if, by any chance, one of them should, without due consideration, obey the natural instinct of his appetite, and transgress any of the rules of good manners, his punishment is at hand. The day following the offence the dog dines, and even dines well; but not at *milord's* table; banished to the ante-chamber, and dressed in livery, he eats in sorrow the bread of shame, and picks the bone of mortification, while his place at table remains vacant till his repentance has merited a generous pardon!"

This eccentric nobleman died in February, 1829, and by his will, dated February 25th, 1825, bequeathed 8,000*l.* for the writing, printing, and publishing of the well-known *Bridgewater Treatises.*

THE DENISONS, AND THE CONYNGHAM FAMILY.

The history of the Denison family, the last representative of which died in 1849, leaving a fortune of more than two millions and a half, affords a lesson which the mercantile world cannot study too curiously. Somewhat more than one hundred and twenty years ago, the elder Denison made his way on foot to London from Skipton-in-Craven, his native place, with a few shillings in his pocket, and, being a parish-boy, not knowing even how to read or write. Another account states that he was a woollen-cloth-merchant at Leeds, and came to London in a wagon, being attended on his departure by his friends, who took a solemn leave of him, as the distance was then thought so great that they might never see him again. He was recommended by a townswoman of his own (of the name of Sykes, whom he afterwards married) to the house of Dillon and Co., where she was herself a domestic servant; and for some time the lad was employed to sweep the shop and go on errands. His zeal and industry recommended him, however, to his employers, and having been taught to read, he rose to a clerkship. After the death of his wife he obtained an independence by marrying one Elizabeth Butler, daughter of a rich hatter in Tooley Street, and set up in business for himself in Princes Street, Lothbury, where by incessant attention to business and strict parsimony, he managed to scrape together a considerable fortune. He finally removed to St. Mary Axe, where he lived and died, after having purchased the estates in Surrey and York-shire (of Lord King and the Duke of Leeds), Denbies and Seamere; by joining the Heywoods, eminent bankers of Liverpool, his wealth rapidly increased. The *Annual Register* of 1806, in recording these facts and his end, states that through life Mr. Denison was a dissenter: he remained to the last an illiterate man.

By his second wife he had one son and two daughters. The son, William Joseph, a man of sound principle and excellent character, though less penurious than his father, who, when he entertained a friend at dinner in St. Mary Axe, used to walk to the butcher's and bring home a rump-steak in a cabbage-leaf in his pocket, was remarkable for his disinclination to detach even the smallest sum from his enormous capital. Thus, when the nephew to whom he bequeathed 85,000*l.* per annum, fell into railway difficulties (the speculation having been undertaken with the sanction of his uncle), he permitted him, to avoid legal proceedings, to with-draw to Boulogne-sur-Mer, and reside there a twelve-month with his young family, rather than pay for him the sum of 2,000*l.*

Mr. Denison, the father, died in 1806; his son, succeeding to the banking business (the firm being now Denison, Heywood, and Kennard), continued to

accumulate ; and at his death, in 1849, he left two
millions and a half of money. He had sat in Parliament for Surrey since 1818. He was a man of culti-
vated tastes, and possessed a knowledge of art and
elegant literature. He feared to be thought osten-
tatious, and could with difficulty be prevailed on to
have a lodge erected at the entrance to a new road
which he had just formed on his estate in Surrey.

Mr. Denison's two sisters were Elizabeth, married in
1794, to Henry, first Marquis Conyngham ; and Maria,
married in 1793 to Sir Robert Lawley, Bart., created,
in 1831, Baron Wenlock. Up to the age of twenty-
seven, Miss Denison resided with her father in St.
Mary Axe. Here the rich and beautiful heiress was
won and wedded in 1794 by the Honourable Henry
Burton, then a captain, twenty-eight years old, and the
eldest son of the fortunate Francis Pierpoint Burton, of
Buncraggy, who succeeded through his mother, after
the death of her two brothers, to the barony and estates
of the old Conynghams, won at the battle of the Boyne
by Sir Albert Conyngham, Lieutenant-General of the
Ordnance of Ireland, and aggrandized by many for-
feitures and marriages subsequently. Captain Burton
carried off his wife to Ireland, and only revisited England in his forty-second year, to kiss hands, in 1808, on
his promotion to a major-generalship. On succeeding
to his father's title and estates, his lordship so improved
their condition that he was justly regarded as one of
the benefactors of his country ; and a visit to his estate
at Slane, on the banks of the Boyne, is recorded by Mr.
Parkinson in his *Experiences of Agriculture* in the same
terms as a visit to Holkham would have been chronicled
in the days of Mr. Coke. The barony of Conyngham

was increased to an earldom as a reward for the spirited conduct of his lordship's father, which led to a reciprocity of trade between Ireland and England. Upon the conclusion of the war with France, when George IV. paid a visit to Ireland, he was hospitably received and entertained at Slane Castle. Here, probably, commenced that more intimate acquaintance between his Majesty and the Marquis Conyngham and his family which induced the King, upon his return to England, to invite the whole family to court, and, after they had accepted the invitation, to retain them in his household. In 1816 his lordship was created Viscount Slane (the restoration of an ancient title forfeited in the Rebellion), Earl of Mountcharles, and Marquis Conyngham; and in 1821 he was enrolled in the British Peerage as Baron Minster, of Minster Abbey, in the county of Kent. The Marchioness was left a widow in 1832, and survived until 1861, having attained the venerable age of ninety-two, and lived to see both her sons peers of the realm—the one in succession of his father; the second, Albert Denison, as the heir to her own father's great fortune and estates, with the title of Baron Londesborough.

"DOG JENNINGS."

This eccentric character, Henry Constantine Jennings, was born in 1731, and was the son of a gentleman possessed of a large estate at Shiplake, in Oxfordshire. He was educated at Westminster School, and at the age of seventeen years became an ensign in the 1st

Regiment of Foot Guards. He held the commission
but a short time, and on resigning it went to Italy in
company with Lord Monthermer, son of the Duke of
Montagu.

While at Rome, young Jennings commenced his first
collection of articles of vertu, and ever after obtained
the coarse and vulgar *sobriquet* of "Dog Jennings," in
consequence of a circumstance which he thus relates:—
"I happened one day to be strolling along the streets
of Rome, and perceiving the shop of a statuary in an
obscure street, I entered it, and began to look around
for any curious production of art. I at length perceived
something uncommon, at least; but, being partly concealed behind a heap of rubbish, I could not contemplate it with any degree of accuracy. After all impedi-
ments had been at length removed, the marble statue
I had been poking for was dragged into open day; it
proved to be a huge, but fine dog—and a fine dog it
was, and a lucky dog was I to discover and to purchase
it. On turning it round, I perceived it was without a
tail—this gave me a hint. I also saw that the limbs
were finely proportioned; that the figure was noble;
that the sculpture, in short, was worthy of the best age of
Athens; and that it must be of the age of Alcibiades,
whose favourite dog it certainly was. I struck a bargain instantly on the spot for 400 scudi; and as the
muzzle alone was somewhat damaged, I paid the artist
a trifle more for repairing it. It was carefully packed,
and being sent to England after me, by the time it
reached my house in Oxfordshire, it had just cost me
80*l.* I wish all my other bargains had been like it, for
it was exceedingly admired, as I well knew it must be,
by the connoisseurs, by more than one of whom I was

bid 1,000*l.* for my purchase. In truth, by a person sent, I believe, from Blenheim, 1 was offered 1,400*l.* But I would not part with my dog; I had bought it for myself, and I liked to contemplate his fine proportions and admire him at my leisure, for he was doubly dear to me, as being my own property and my own selection."

At the Literary Club, one evening, Jennings' dog was the topic of discussion: " *F.* (*Lord Cipper O'Geary.*) 'I have been looking at this famous marble dog of Mr. Jennings', valued at 1,000 guineas, said to be Alcibiades' dog.'—*Johnson.* 'His tail, then, must be docked. That was the mark of Alcibiades' dog.'—*E.* (*Burke.*) 'A thousand guineas! the representation of no animal whatever is worth so much. At this rate, a dead dog would, indeed, be better than a living lion.'—*J.* 'Sir, it is not the worth of the thing, but of the skill in forming it, which is so highly estimated. Everything that enlarges the sphere of human powers, that shows man he can do what he thought he could not do, is valuable.'"

But Mr. Jennings, like many other collectors, owing to a reverse of fortune, was compelled, in 1778, to break up his collection, which being sold by auction, the dog of Alcibiades brought 1,000 guineas, and became the property of Mr. Duncombe, M.P. It is now at Duncombe Park, in Yorkshire, the seat of Lord Feversham.

It is painful to read that the latter days of Mr. Jennings were spent in the King's Bench; and within the rules of that prison he died, February 17th, 1819, at his lodgings in Belvedere Place, St. George's Fields, in his eighty-eighth year.

BARON WARD'S REMARKABLE CAREER.

Perhaps no man of modern times passed a more varied and romantic life than the famed Yorkshire groom, statesman, and friend of sovereigns, and who played so prominent a part at the Court of Parma; his career strongly exemplifying the adage that truth is stranger than fiction.

Thomas Ward was born at York, on the 9th of October, 1810, where he was brought up in the stable, but was shrewd and intelligent far beyond boys of his own station.

He left Yorkshire as a boy in the pay of Prince Lichtenstein, of Hungary; and after a four years' successful career on the turf at Vienna as a jockey, he became employed by the then reigning Duke of Lucca.

He was at Lucca promoted from the stable to be valet to his Royal Highness, which service he performed up to 1846. About that period he was appointed Master of the Horse to the Ducal Court, when he made extraordinary changes in that department: the stable expenses were reduced more than one-half. Yet the Duke's stud was the envy and admiration of all Italy. Eventually, Ward became Minister of the Household and Minister of Finance, and acquired a diplomatic dignity in the disturbances which preceded the revolutionary year, 1848, when he was despatched to Florence upon a confidential mission of the highest importance. This had no less an object than the delivery, to the Grand

Duke of his master's abdication of the Lucchese princi-
pality. At first the Grand Duke hesitated at receiving,
in a diplomatic capacity, one of whom he had only
heard in relation to the races of the Casino. But our
envoy had seen and provided for such an emergency.
He produced from his pocket a commission, making
him Viceroy of the Duke's estates, which was to be
acted upon if the Grand Duke raised any obstacle, or
even if he refused to receive Ward as ambassador of
the states of Parma, at the capital of the Medicis; this,
of course, ended all difficulties.

Ward held the above offices until the Duke's rule was
violently terminated by the great Revolution of 1848.
With some difficulty he escaped with his able and
faithful minister, when they retired to an estate near
Dresden, called Weisstrop. At this period Ward
became an active agent of Austria, and as Austria
triumphed, he recovered the hereditary estates of
Parma and Placentia; but the Duke, disgusted by his
experience, resigned in favour of his own son, with
whom the minister retained the same favour and exhibited the same talents that first raised him to distinction, and made him more than a match for the first of
the Italian diplomatists. Upon one occasion he was
despatched to Vienna as an envoy from his little court,
when he astonished Schwartzenberg by the extent of
his capacity. His acquaintance was specially culti-
vated by the Russian Ambassador, Meyendorff, who
appears to have been very fond of Yorkshire hams.
An English gentleman, supping one night at the
Russian Ambassador's, complimented him upon the
excellence of the ham. "There is a member of our
diplomatic body here," replied Meyendorff, "who sup-

plies us all with hams from Yorkshire, of which county
he is a native."

As prime minister, Ward negotiated the abdication
of Charles II., and placed the youthful Charles III. on
the throne, who, it will be remembered, was assassinated
before his own palace in 1854. It should be observed
that as soon as Charles III. came to the throne, the
then Baron Ward was sent to Germany by his patron
as Minister Plenipotentiary, to represent Parma at the
Court of Vienna. This post he held up to the time of
his royal patron's tragical end.

When the Duchess-Regent assumed state authority,
Ward retired from public life, and took to agricultural
pursuits in the Austrian dominions. Without any
educational foundation, he contrived to write and speak
German, French, and Italian, and conducted the affairs
of state with considerable cleverness, if not with remarkable straightforwardness. But the moment he
attempted to express himself in English, his dialect was
found to retain all the characteristics of his want of
education. Lord Palmerston once declared that Ward
" was one of the most remarkable men he had ever met
with."

Throughout life, Ward was ever proud of his country,
never for a moment attempting to conceal his humble
origin ; and portraits of his parents, in their homespun
clothes, may be seen in the splendid saloon of the Prime
Minister of Parma.

Baron Ward was married to a humble person of
Vienna, and at his death he left four children. From
the stable he rose to the highest offices of a little
kingdom, at a period of great European political
interest, and died in retirement, pursuing the rustic

occupation of a farmer, but carrying with him to the grave many curious state secrets.

The following is a partial list only of the honours to which Ward attained :—Baron of the Duchy of Lucca, and of the Grand Duchy of Tuscany; Knight of the First Class of the Order of St. Louis of Lucca; Knight Grand Cross of the Order of St. Joseph of Tuscany; Knight Senator Grand Cross of the Order of St. George Constantinano of Parma; and Noble, with the title of Baron, in Tuscany; Honorary Councillor of State to his Imperial Highness the Grand Duke of Tuscany; Minister and Councillor of State to H.R.H. Charles Duke of Parma, &c.*

A COSTLY HOUSE-WARMING.

Fifty years ago, there lived in Edward Street, Portman Square, one Parmentier, confectioner to the Prince Regent. From his emporium, and that of Romualdo, in Duke Street, the *routs* given in the neighbouring squares were sumptuously supplied. In this quarter lived keepers of china and glass shops, who undertook, at a few hours' notice, to supply all the movables and ornaments for large *routs*, as chairs, tables, china and glass, knives and forks, extra plate, looking-glasses, mirrors, girandoles, chandeliers, wax-lights, candelabra-lamps, Aurelian shades, transparencies, vases, and other decorative items for a complete suite of rooms; together with exotics and green-house plants, and a corps of artists

* *Family Romance.* By J. Bernard Burke. Vol. ii.

to chalk the floors. It was by this almost magical aid that the Earl of Shrewsbury gave his magnificent house-warming to the *haut ton* at his new mansion in Bryan-stone Square, which was then in so unfinished a state that the walls in many of the apartments were not even plastered. To the astonishment and delight of the guests, the whole mansion was thrown open, and every room was furnished and decorated in the most. superb style. The principal drawing-room, with its numerous lamps and large looking-glasses, appeared one blaze of light; in contrast to which, another room, in sombre gloom, re-sembled an Arcadian grove of orange and lemon trees and myrtles, part natural and part artificial. The amusements consisted of a dramatic representation, a concert, a dress-ball, a masquerade, and a sumptuous supper of three hundred covers. These elegant festivi-ties cost the Earl several thousand pounds.

In the same neighbourhood, at the corner of George Street, Mohammed, a native of Asia, opened a house for giving dinners in the Hindustanee style. All the dishes were dressed with currie-powder, rice, cayenne, and the finest spices of Arabia. A room was set apart for smok-ing from hookahs with Oriental herbs. The rooms were furnished with chairs and sofas made of bamboo canes, and the walls were hung with Chinese pictures and other Asiatic embellishments. Either Sidi Mohammed's capital was not sufficient to stand the slow test of public encouragement, or the scheme failed at once; for Sidi became bankrupt, and the undertaking was relinquished.

DEVONSHIRE ECCENTRICS.

Some years since, there lived a gentleman in Tavistock, very charitably disposed, who entertained an especial good will and kind feeling towards old sailors. Any old sailor, by calling at his door, received the donation of a shilling and a glass of grog. It was marvellous to see what a number of veteran blue jackets paid him a visit in the course of a year. At last, the servant who opened the door observed that all these sons of the sea had a particular patch on one and the same part of one and the same arm. She began, at length, to fancy that the old patch must be some badge of honour in the service, yet she thought it a very odd distinction in his Majesty's navy. The circumstance awakened her suspicion. The next old blue jacket that appeared, decorated with the order of the patch, was therefore watched and followed to his retreat. He was observed to retire to the house of a certain old woman, and in a little while he was seen to come forth again in his own natural character, that of a street beggar, clothed in rags. The cheat was apparent; and suffice it to say, that on further examination it appeared that the old woman's house was one of friendly call to all the vagabonds and sharpers who paced the country round; and that amongst other masquerade attire for the callers, she kept by her a sailor's old jacket and trousers for the purpose of playing off the imposition. No doubt she was paid for the loan of the dress.

At Tavistock, also, there resided a strange character

in humble life, named Carter Foote. On returning from
Oakhampton, he remounted his horse, after having
enjoyed himself at the public-house, and attempted to
pass the river below the bridge by fording it over.
The day had been stormy, and from the sudden swell
of the river, he found himself in extreme danger. After
endeavouring to struggle with the current, he leaped
from his horse upon a large piece of the rock, and there
stood, calling aloud for help. Some person going by,
ran and procured a rope, which he endeavoured to
throw towards the rock ; but finding it impossible to do
so without further assistance, he begged two men
belonging to Oakhampton, who drew near the spot,
to give him help, and save the stranger, whose life
was in so much peril. One of them, however, very
leisurely looked at the sufferer, and only saying, " 'Tis
a Tav'stock man, let un go," walked off with his companion, and poor Carter Foote was drowned.

Mrs. Bray relates the following of a Devonshire
physician, happily named Vial, who was a desperate
lover of whist. One evening, in the midst of a deal,
the doctor fell off his chair in a fit. Consternation
seized on the company. Was he alive or dead? What
was to be done? All help was given ; hartshorn was
poured almost down his throat by one kind female
friend, whilst another feelingly singed the end of his
nose with burning feathers; all were in the breathless
agony of suspense for his safety. At length, he showed
signs of life, and retaining the last fond idea which had
possessed him at the moment he fell into the fit, to
the joy of the whole company exclaimed, " What is
trumps ? "

Many years ago, there resided in Devonshire a

certain old gentleman, nicknamed Redpost Fynes, from his having painted all the gates of his fields a bright vermilion. The squire was remarkable for never having been able to learn to spell even the commonest word in his own language; so that on the birth of his daughter, he wrote to a friend that his wife was brought to bed of a fine *gull*. The word *usage* he spelt without one letter belonging to it, and yet contrived to produce something like the word, at least in sound, for he wrote it thus, *yowzitch*. Near his house was a very old and grotesque tree, cut and clipped in the form of a punch-bowl; whilst a table and seats were literally affixed within the green enclosure, to which was an ascent by a little ladder, like the companion-ladder of a ship.

HANNAH SNELL, THE FEMALE SOLDIER.

This extraordinary woman was born in Fryer Street, Worcester, on the 23rd of April, 1723. Her grandfather, embracing the military profession, served under William III. and Queen Anne, and terminated his career at the battle of Malplaquet, where he received a mortal wound. Snell's father was a hosier and dyer.

In 1740, Hannah, having lost both parents, came to London, where she for some time resided with one of her sisters, married to one Gray, a carpenter, in Ship Street, Wapping. Here she became acquainted with a Dutch seaman, named James Summs, to whom she was married early in 1743. Her husband led a profligate life, squandered the little property which his wife possessed, and having involved her deeply in debt, deserted her, leaving her pregnant; in two months she was delivered of a girl, who died at the age of seven months.

For some time she resided with her sister, but soon resolved to set out in quest of the man, whom, notwithstanding his ill-usage, she still continued to love. In order to carry out this strange resolve, as she thought, more safely, she put on a suit of the clothes of her brother in-law, assumed his name, James Gray, and started on the 23rd of November, 1745. Having travelled to Coventry, and being unable to procure any intelligence of her husband, on the 27th of the same month she enlisted into General Guise's regiment, and in the company belonging to Captain Miller. She remained at Coventry about three weeks. The north being then the seat of war, and her regiment being at Carlisle, she left Coventry with seventeen other recruits, and joined the regiment, after a march of three weeks, which she performed with as much ease as any of her comrades. At Carlisle she was instructed in the military exercise, which she was soon able to perform with skill and dexterity. She had not been long in this place, when a man named Davis applied to Hannah to assist him in an intrigue; she appeared to acquiesce in his desire, but privately disclosed the whole matter to the intended victim. By this conduct she gained the young woman's confidence and esteem; they frequently met, which excited the jealousy of Davis, and prompted revenge. He accordingly seized an opportunity of charging his supposed rival before the commanding officer with neglect of duty, and she was sentenced to receive six hundred lashes. Five hundred were inflicted, but the remaining hundred were remitted through the intercession of some of the officers.

Not long after this unhappy occurrence, a fresh recruit, a native of Worcester and a carpenter, who had lodged at the house of her brother-in-law, joined the regiment, when Hannah becoming apprehensive of the discovery of her sex, resolved to desert. Her female friend endeavoured to dissuade her from such a dangerous enterprise; but finding her resolution fixed, she furnished her with money, and Hannah commenced her journey on foot for Portsmouth. About a mile from Carlisle, perceiving some men employed in picking peas, and their clothes lying at some distance, she exchanged her regimental coat for one of the old coats belonging to one of the men, and proceeded on her journey. At Liverpool and Chester, Hannah contrived, by her attentions to a landlady and a young mantua-maker, to obtain some money; but in an intrigue with a widow at Winchester our gallant was less successful, the widow rifling her pockets, and leaving her with but a few shillings to finish her journey on foot. Arrived at Portsmouth, she soon enlisted as a marine in Colonel Fraser's regiment, which in three weeks was drafted for the East Indies, and Hannah, among the rest, was ordered to repair on board the *Swallow* sloop, in Admiral Boscawen's fleet. She soon distinguished herself on board by her dexterity in washing, mending, and cooking for her messmates, and she thus became a great favourite with the crew of the sloop. She was regarded as a boy, and in case of an engagement her station was on the quarter-deck, to fight at small-arms, and she was one of the after-guard; she was also obliged to keep watch every four hours, night and day, and frequently to go aloft.   We read likewise of the *Swallow* being in a violent tempest, and almost reduced to a wreck: Hannah took her turn at the pump, which was kept constantly going, and she declined no office, however dangerous, but established her character for courage, skill, and intrepidity.

The ship then made the best of her way to the Cape of Good Hope, during their voyage from which they were reduced to short allowance, and but a pint of water a day.   The admiral next bore away for Fort St. David, on the coast of Coromandel, where the fleet soon afterwards arrived.   Hannah, with the rest of the marines, being disembarked, after a march of three weeks, joined the English army encamped before Aria-Coupon, which place was to have been stormed; but a shell having burst and blown up their magazine, the besieged were obliged to abandon it.   This adventure gave Hannah fresh spirits, and her intrepid conduct acquired the commendation of all the officers.

The army then proceeded to the attack of Pondi-cherry, and after lying before that place eleven weeks, and suffering very great hardships, they were obliged by the rainy season to abandon the siege.   Hannah was the first in the party of English foot who forded the river, breast-high, under an incessant fire from a French battery.   She was likewise on the picket-guard, continued on that duty seven nights successively, and laboured very hard about fourteen days at throwing up the trenches.   In one of the attacks, however, her career was well-nigh terminated.   She fired thirty-seven rounds during the engagement, and received, according to her account, six shots in her right leg, five in the left, and, what was still more painful, a dangerous

wound in the lower part of her body, which she feared
might lead to the discovery of her disguise to the surgeons. She, however, intrusted her secret to a negress
who attended her, and brought her lint and salve; after
most acute suffering she extracted the ball with her
finger and thumb, and made a perfect cure. Meanwhile
the greater part of the fleet had sailed. She was then
sent on board the *Tartar* pink, and continued to do the
duty of a sailor till the return of the fleet from Madras.
She was soon afterwards turned over to the *Eltham*
man-of-war, and sailed with that ship to Bombay.
Here the vessel, which had sprung a leak on the passage,
was heaved down for repair, which lasted five weeks.
The captain remained on shore, while Hannah, in
common with the rest of the crew, had her turn on the
watch. On one of these occasions, Mr. Allen, the
lieutenant, who commanded in the captain's absence,
desired her to sing a song, but she excused herself,
saying she was unwell; the officer, however, insisted
that she should sing, which she as resolutely refused to
do. She soon had occasion to regret her non-compli-
ance, for being suspected of stealing a shirt belonging
to one of her comrades, though no proof could be
adduced, the lieutenant ordered her to be put in irons.
After remaining there five days, she was ordered to the
gangway, and received twelve lashes, and she was then
sent to the topmast-head for four hours. The missing
shirt was afterwards found in the chest of the man who
complained that he had lost it.

About this time the sailors began to rally Hannah
because she had no beard, and they soon afterwards
jocosely christened her Miss Molly Gray; this alarmed
her, lest some of the crew might suspect that she was a

female; but she took part in their scenes of dissipation with such glee, that she was soon called Hearty Jemmy.

While the vessel remained at Lisbon, on her passage home, she met with an English sailor who had been at Genoa in a Dutch vessel. She took the opportunity of inquiring after her long-lost husband, and was informed that he had been confined at Genoa for murdering a native gentleman of that city, a person of some distinction; and that to expiate his crime, he was put into a sack with a quantity of stones, and thus thrown into the sea. Distressing as this information must have been, Hannah had sufficient command over herself to conceal her emotions.

Leaving Lisbon, Hannah arrived safely at Spithead. At Portsmouth she met her female friend, for whose sake she had been whipped at Carlisle. This girl was still single, and would have married Hannah, had she chosen to discover herself. She, however, proceeded to London, where she was heartily received by her sister. She soon afterwards met with some of her shipmates; and, after receiving her pay, she was about to part with them, when she revealed her sex, and one of them immediately offered to marry her, but she declined.

Hannah's strange career had now acquired her popularity, and as she possessed a good voice, she obtained an engagement at the Royalty Theatre, in Wellclose Square, where she appeared in the character of Bill Bobstay, a sailor; she also represented Firelock, a military character, and in a masterly and correct manner went through the manual and platoon exercises. She, however, quitted the stage in a few months; and as she preferred male attire, she resolved to continue to wear it during the remainder of her life; she usually wore a laced hat and cockade, and a sword and ruffles. There were good portraits of her published in 1750.

Hannah now became an out-pensioner of Chelsea Hospital on account of the wounds she received at the siege of Pondicherry, her pension being 30*l.* She next took a public-house at Wapping ; on one side of the sign-board was painted the figure of a jolly British tar, and on the other the valiant marine ; underneath was inscribed, " The Widow in Masquerade, or the Female Warrior." She continued to keep this house for many years ; and afterwards married one Eyles, a carpenter, at Newbury, in Berkshire. A lady of fortune, who admired Hannah's heroism and eccentricity of conduct, took special notice of her, became godmother to her son, and contributed towards his education. Mrs. Eyles continued to receive her pension to the day of her death. She lived for some time with her son in Church Street, Stoke Newington ; but, about three years before her death, she showed symptoms of insanity, and was admitted as patient at Bethlem Hospital, Moorfields, where she died 8th February, 1792, aged sixty-nine years.

LADY ARCHER.

This lady, formerly Miss West, lived to a good age— a proof that cosmetics are not so fatal as some would have us suppose. Nature had given her a fine aquiline nose, like the princesses of the House of Austria, and she did not fail to give herself a complexion. She resembled a fine old wainscoted painting, with the face and features shining through a thick incrustation of copal varnish.

Her ladyship was for many years the wonder of the fashionable world, envied by all the ladies of the Court of George the Third. She had a well-appointed house in Portland Place. Her equipage was, with her, a sort of scenery. She gloried in milk-white horses to her carriage, the coachmen and footmen wore very showy liveries, and the carriage was lined with silk of a tint to exhibit the complexion to advantage.

Alexander Stephens, amongst whose papers was found this account of Lady Archer, tells us that he recollected to have seen Mrs. Robinson (the *Perdita* of the Prince of Wales's love) go far beyond all this in the exuberance of her genius, in a yellow lining to her landau, with a black footman, to contrast with her beautiful complexion and fascinating figure, and thus render both more lovely. Lady Archer lived at Barn Elms Terrace, and her house had the most elegant ornaments and draperies to strike the senses, and yet powerfully address the imagination. Her kitchen-garden and pleasure-ground, of five acres—the Thames flowing in front, as if a portion of the estate—the apartments decorated in the Chinese style, and opening into hothouses stored with fruits of the richest growth, and greenhouses with plants of great rarity and beauty, and superb couches and draperies, effectively placed, rendered her home a sort of elysium of luxury.

Barn Elms will be remembered as the scene of an older eccentricity—Heydegger's instantaneous light reception of George II., a device worthy of the master of the revels.

Delusions, Impostures, and Fanatic Missions.

MODERN ALCHEMISTS.

IT may take some readers by surprise to learn that there have been true believers in alchemy in our days. Dr. Price is commonly set down in popular journals as *the last of the alchemists.* This is, however, a mistake, as we shall proceed to show; before which, however, it will be interesting to sketch the history of this reputed alchemist.

Towards the close of the last century, Dr. James Price, a medical practitioner in the neighbourhood of Guildford, Surrey, acquired some notoriety by an alleged discovery of methods of transmuting mercury into gold or silver. He had been a student of Oriel College, Oxford, where he obtained the degree of Bachelor of Physic. In 1782 he published an account of his experiments on mercury, silver, and gold, performed at Guildford, in that year, before Lord King and others, to whom he appealed as eye-witnesses of his wonder-working power. It seems that mercury being put into a crucible, and heated in the fire with other ingredients (which had been shown to contain no gold), he added a red powder; the crucible was again heated, and being suffered to cool, amongst its contents, on examination, was found a globule of pure gold. By a similar process with a white powder, he produced a globule of silver. The character of the witnesses of these manifestations gave credit and celebrity for a time to Price, who was honoured by the University with the degree of Doctor of Physic, and he was also elected a Fellow of the Royal Society. Dr. Price had now placed himself in a perilous position; for persons acquainted with the history of alchemy must have conjectured how the gold and silver in his experiments might have been procured with any transmutation of mercury or any other substance. The Royal Society authoritatively required that the pretensions of the new associate should be properly sifted, and his claim as a discoverer be clearly established, or his character as an impostor exposed. A repetition of the doctor's experiments before a committee of the Royal Society was commanded on pain of expulsion; when the unfortunate man, rather than submit to the ordeal, took a draught of laurel-water, and died on July 31, 1783, in his twenty-fifth year.

At the beginning of the present century, some persons of eminence in science thought favourably of alchemy. Professor Robinson, writing to James Watt, February 11th, 1800, says, " The analysis of alkalies and alkaline earth will presently lead, I think, to a doctrine of *a reciprocal convertibility of all things into all* . . . *and I expect to see alchemy revive,* and be as universally studied as ever."

Sir Walter Scott, in his well-known paper on Astrology and Alchemy, in *The Quarterly Review,* tells us that about the year 1801, an adept lived, or rather starved, in the metropolis, in the person of the editor of an evening newspaper, who expected to compound the alkahat, if he could only keep his materials digested in his lamp-furnace for the space of seven years. Scott adds, in pleasant banter, "the lamp burnt brightly during six years, eleven months, and some odd days, and then unluckily it went out. Why it went out, the adept could never guess; but he was certain that if the flame could only have burnt to the end of the septenary cycle, the experiment must have succeeded."

The last true believer in alchemy was not Dr. Price, but Peter Woulfe, the eminent chemist, and Fellow of the Royal Society, and who made experiments to show the nature of mosaic gold. Mr. Brande says: "It is to be regretted that no biographical memoir has been preserved of Woulfe. I have picked up a few anecdotes respecting him from two or three friends who were his acquaintance. He occupied chambers in Barnard's Inn, Holborn (the older buildings), while residing in London, and usually spent the summer in Paris. His rooms, which were extensive, were so filled with furnaces and apparatus that it was difficult to reach his fireside. A friend told me that he once put down his hat, and never could find it again, such was the confusion of boxes, packages, and parcels that lay about the chamber. His breakfast-hour was four in the morning; a few of his select friends were occasionally invited to this repast, to whom a secret signal was given by which they gained entrance, knocking a certain number of times at the inner door of his apartment. He had long vainly searched for the Elixir, and attributed his repeated failures to the want of due preparation by pious and charitable acts. I understand that some of his apparatus is still extant, upon which are supplications for success and for the welfare of the adepts. Whenever he wished to break an acquaintance, or felt himself offended, he resented the supposed injury by sending a present to the offender, and never seeing him afterwards. These presents were sometimes of a curious description, and consisted usually of some expensive chemical product or preparation. He had an heroic remedy for illness; when he felt himself seriously indisposed, he took a place in the Edinburgh mail, and having reached that city, immediately came back in the returning coach to London."

A cold taken in one of these expeditions terminated in inflammation of the lungs, of which Woulfe died in the year 1805. Of his last moments we received the following account from his executor, then Treasurer of Barnard's Inn. By Woulfe's desire, his laundress shut up his chambers, and left him, but returned at midnight, when Woulfe was still alive. Next morning, however, she *found him dead!* His countenance was calm and serene, and apparently he had not moved from the position in his chair in which she had last left him.

Twenty years after the death of Peter Woulfe, Sir Richard Phillips visited "an alchemist" named Kellerman, at the village of Lilley, between Luton and Hitchin. He was believed by some of his neighbours to have discovered the Philosopher's Stone and the Universal Solvent. His room was a realization of the well-known picture of Teniers's Alchemist. The floor was strewed with retorts, crucibles, alembics, jars, and bottles of various shapes, interminged with old books. He gave Sir Richard a history of his studies, mentioned some men in London who, he alleged, had assured him that they had made gold; that having, in consequence, examined the works of the ancient alchemists, and discoved the key which they had studiously concealed from the multitude, he had pursued their system under the influence of new lights; and, after suffering numerous disappointments, owing to the ambiguity with which they described their processes, he had at length happily succeeded; had made gold, and could make as much more as he pleased, even to the extent of paying off the National Debt in the coin of the realm!

Kellerman then enlarged upon the merits of the ancient alchemists, and on the blunders and assumptions of modern chemists. He quoted Roger and Francis Bacon, Paracelsus, Boyle, Boerhaave, Woulfe, and others to justify his pursuits. As to the term Philosopher's Stone, he alleged that it was a mere figure to deceive the vulgar. He appeared to give full credit to the silly story of Dee's finding the Elixir at Glastonbury, by means of which, as he said, Kelly for a length of time supported himself in princely splendour. Kellerman added, that he had discovered the *blacker than black* of Apollonius Tyanus: it was itself "the powder of projection for producing gold."

It further appeared that Kellerman had lived in the premises at Lilley for twenty-three years, during fourteen of which he had pursued his alchemical studies with unremitting ardour, keeping eight assistants for superintending his crucibles, two at a time, relieving each other every six hours; that he had exposed some preparations to intense heat for many months at a time; but that all except one crucible had burst, and that, Kellerman said, contained the true "blacker than black." One of his assistants, however, protested that no gold had ever been found, and that no mercury had ever been fixed; for he was quite sure Kellerman could not have concealed it from his assistants; while, on the contrary, they witnessed his severe disappointment at the result of his most elaborate experiments.

Of late years there have been some strange revivals of alchemical pursuits. In 1850 there was printed in London a volume of considerable extent, entitled, *A Suggestive Inquiry into the Hermetic Mystery*—the work of a lady, by whom it has been suppressed; we have seen it described as "a learned and valuable book."

By this circumstance we are reminded that some five-and-thirty years since it came to our knowledge that a man of wealth and position in the City of London, an *adept* in alchemy, was held *in terrorem* by an unprincipled person, who extorted from him considerable sums of money under threats of exposure, which would have affected his mercantile interests.

Nevertheless, alchemy has, in the present day, its prophetic advocates, who predict what may be considered a return to its strangest belief. A Gottingen professor says, in the *Annales de Chimie*, No. 100, that in the nineteenth century the transmutation of metals will be generally known and practised. Every chemist and every artist will make gold; kitchen utensils will be of silver and even gold, which will contribute more than anything else to prolong life, poisoned at present by the oxide of copper, lead, and iron which we daily swallow with our food. More recently, MM. Dr. Henri Fabre and Franz have placed before the French Academy their discovery of the means of transmuting silver, copper, and quicksilver into gold.

JACK ADAMS, THE ASTROLOGER.

Among the celebrities of Clerkenwell Green was Jack Adams, whose nativity was calculated by Partridge, who affirmed that he was born on the 3rd of December, 1625, and that he was so great a *natural*, or simpleton, as to be obliged to wear long coats, besides other marks of stupidity; and that the parish not only maintained him, but allowed a nurse to attend him to preserve him from harm. Allusion is made to him in a satirical ballad of 1655 :—

" Jack Adams, sure, was pamet (poet) by the vein."

And in the *Wits, or Sport upon Sport,* 1682, we read of his visit to the Red Bull playhouse, where Simpleton, the smith, appearing on the stage with a large piece of bread-and-butter, Jack Adams, knowing him, cried out, " Cuz, Cuz, give me some," to the great pleasure of the audience. Ward thus mentions his celebrity :—

" What mortal that has sense or thought
Would strip Jack Adams of his coat;
Or who would be by friends decoyed
To wear a badge he would avoid."

Jack Adams was a conjurer and professor of the celestial sciences; he was (says Granger's Supplement) " a blind buzzard, who pretended to have the eyes of an eagle. He was chiefly employed in horary questions, relative to love and marriage, and knew, upon proper occasions, how to soothe and flatter the expectations of those who consulted him, as a man might have much

better fortune from him for five guineas than for the
same number of shillings. He affected a singular dress,
and cast horoscopes with great solemnity. When he
failed in his predictions, he declared that the stars did
not absolutely force, but powerfully incline, and threw
the blame upon wayward and perverse fate. He assumed the character of a learned and cunning man;
but was no otherwise cunning than as he knew how to
overreach those credulous mortals who were as willing
to be cheated as he was to cheat them, and who relied
implicitly upon his art." Mr. Warner says: "A short
time after we removed into the house (No. 7, Clerkenwell Green), two young women applied to have their
fortunes told; upon being informed they were under
some mistake, one expressed great surprise, and stated
that was the place she always came to, and she thought
some of Mr. Adams's family always resided there. This
was the first time I ever heard anything of Jack Adams.
Several similar applications were made by other persons, and we afterwards learnt that it had been occupied
by persons of that profession for many years, and they
generally went by the name of Adams."*

In an old print we have Jack Adams in a fantastic
dress, with a tobacco-pipe in his girdle, standing at a
table on which lies a horn-book and *Poor Robin's Almanack*. On one shelf is a row of books, and on
another several boys' playthings, particularly tops,
marbles, and a small drum. Before him is a man
genteelly dressed, presenting five pieces; from his
mouth proceeds a label, inscribed, "Is she a princess?"
This is meant for Carleton, who married the pretended German princess. Behind him is a ragged,

* Pinks's *History of Clerkenwell*, 1865, p. 110.

slatternly woman, who has also a label in her mouth, with these words: "Sir, can you tell my fortune?" In *Poor Robin's Almanack* for 1785 are these lines:

> "Now should I choose t' invoke a Muse—
> Muses are fickle madams;
> Else I could go my poem through
> Ere you could say *Jack Adams.*"

In the City of London Library is an original print of Jack Adams, and a copy by Caulfield.

THE WOMAN-HATING CAVENDISH.

Eccentricity in men of science is not rare. The Hon. Henry Cavendish, who demonstrated, in 1781, the composition of water, was a remarkable instance. He was an excellent mathematician, electrician, astronomer, and geologist; and as alchemist shot far a-head of his contemporaries. But he was a sort of methodical recluse, and an enormous fortune left him by his uncle did little to change his habits. His shyness and aversion to society bordered on disease. To be looked at or addressed by a stranger seemed to give him positive pain, when he would dart away as if hurt. At Sir Joseph Banks's *soirées* he would stand for a long time on the landing, afraid to face the company. At one of these parties the titles and qualifications of Cavendish were formally recited when he was introduced to an Austrian gentleman. The Austrian became complimentary, saying his chief reason for coming to London was to see and converse with Cavendish, one of the greatest ornaments of the age, and one of the most illustrious philosophers that ever existed. Cavendish answered not a word, but stood with his eyes cast down, abashed, and in misery. At last, seeing an opening in the crowd, he flew to the door, nor did he stop till he reached his carriage and drove directly home. Any attempt to draw him into conversation was almost certain to fail, and Dr. Wollaston's recipe for treating with him usually answered best: "The way to talk to Cavendish is, never to look at him, but to talk as if it were into a vacancy, and then it is not unlikely you may set him going."

Among the anecdotes which floated about it is related that Cavendish, the club Crœsus, attended the meetings of the Royal Society Club with only money enough in his pocket to pay for his dinner; that he declined taking tavern soup, picked his teeth with a fork, invariably hung his hat upon the same peg, and always stuck his cane in his right boot. More apocryphal is the anecdote that one evening Cavendish observed a pretty girl looking out from an upper window on the opposite side of the street, watching the philosophers at dinner. She attracted notice, and one by one they got up, and mustered round the window to admire the fair one. Cavendish, who thought they were looking at the moon, bustled up to them in his odd way, and when he saw the real object of attraction, turned away with intense disgust, and grunted out "Pshaw!" the more amorous conduct of his brother philosophers having horrified the woman-hating Cavendish.

If men were a trouble to him, women were an abhorrence. With his housekeeper he generally communicated with notes deposited on the hall-table. He would never see a female servant; and if an unlucky maid showed herself she was instantly dismissed. To prevent inevitable encounters he had a second staircase erected in his villa at Clapham. In all his habits he was punctiliously regular, even to his hanging his hat upon the same peg. From an unvarying walk he was, however, driven by being gazed at. Two ladies led a gentleman on his track, in order that he might obtain a sight of the philosopher. As he was getting over a stile he saw, to his horror, that he was being watched, and he never appeared in that path again. That he was not quite merciless to the sex was proved by his saving a lady from the pursuit of a mad cow.

Cavendish's town house was near the British Museum, at the corner of Gower Street and Montague Place. Few visitors were admitted, and those who crossed the threshold reported that books and apparatus were its chief furniture. He collected a large library of scientific books, hired a house for its reception in Dean Street, Soho, and kept a librarian. When he wanted one of his own books, he went there as to a circulating library, and left a formal receipt for whatever he took away. Nearly the whole of his villa at Clapham was occupied as workshops; the upper rooms were an observatory, the drawing-room was a laboratory. On the lawn was a wooden stage, from which access could be had to a large tree, to the top of which Cavendish, in the course of his astronomical and meteorological observations, and electrical experiments, occasionally ascended. His apparatus was roughly constructed, but was always exact and accurate.

His household was strangely managed. He received

but little company, and the few guests were treated on all occasions to the same fare—a leg of mutton. One day, four scientific friends were to dine with him; when his housekeeper asked him what was to be got for dinner, Cavendish replied, "A leg of mutton."

"Sir," said she, "that will not be enough for five."

"Well, then, get two," was the reply.

Cavendish extended his eccentric reception to his own family. His heir, Lord George Cavendish, visited him once a-year, and was allowed an audience of but half-an-hour. His great income was allowed to accumulate without attention. The bankers where he kept his account, finding they had in hand a balance of 80,000*l*., apprised him of the same. The messenger was announced, and Cavendish, in great agitation, desired him to be sent up; and, as he entered the room, the ruffled philosopher cried, "What do you come here for? what do you want with me?"

"Sir, I thought it proper to wait upon you, as we have a very large balance in hand of yours, and we wish your orders respecting it."

"If it is any trouble to you, I will take it out of your hands. Do not come here to plague me!"

"Not the least trouble to us, sir, not the least; but we thought you might like some of it to be invested."

"Well, well, what do you want to do?"

"Perhaps you would like 40,000*l*. invested."

"Do so, do so! and don't come here to trouble me, or I'll remove it," was the churlish finale of the interview.

Cavendish died in 1810, at the age of seventy-eight. He was then the largest holder of Bank-stock in England. He owned 1,157,000*l*. in different public funds;

he had besides, freehold property of 8,000l. a-year, and a balance of 50,000l. at his bankers. He was long a member of the Royal Society Club, and it was reported at his death that he had left a thumping legacy to Lord Bessborough, in gratitude for his Lordship's piquant conversation at the club meetings; but no such reason can be found in the will lodged at Doctors' Commons. Therein, Cavendish names three of his club-mates— namely, Alexander Dalrymple to receive 5,000l., Dr. Hunter 5,000l., and Sir Charles Blagden (co-adjutor in the water question) 15,000l. After certain other bequests, the will proceeds: "The remainder of the funds (nearly 100,000l.) to be divided: one-sixth to the Earl of Bessborough," while Lord George Henry Cavendish had two-sixths instead of one. "It is, therefore," says Admiral Smyth, in his *History of the Royal Society Club*, "patent that the money thus passed over from uncle to nephew was a mere consequence of relationship, and not at all owing to any flowers or powers of conversation at the Royal Society Club."

Cavendish never changed the fashion or cut of his dress, so that his appearance in 1810, in a costume of sixty years previously, was odd, and drew upon him the notice which he so much disliked. His complexion was fair, his temperament nervous, and his voice squeaking. The only portrait that exists of him was sketched without his knowledge. Dr. George Wilson, who has left a clever memoir of Cavendish, says: "An intellectual head, thinking—a pair of wonderful acute eyes, observing—a pair of very skilful hands, experimenting or recording, are all that I realize in reading his memorials."

MODERN ASTROLOGY—"WITCH PICKLES."

It would be an acquisition to our knowledge if some one competent to the task would collect materials for the history of the men who, within the present century, have made a profession of *judicial astrology*. Attention is occasionally drawn to the practices of itinerant fortune-tellers, many of whom still procure a livelihood. The astrologer, however, or, as he is denominated in some districts of England—more particularly in Yorkshire—a " planet-ruler," and sometimes " a wise man," is of a higher order. He does not itinerate, is generally a man of some education, possessed of a good deal of fragmentary knowledge and a smattering of science. He very often conceals his real profession by practising as a " Water Doctor " or as a " Bone-setter," and some possess a considerable amount of skill in the treatment of ordinary diseases.

The more lucrative part of his business was that which they carried on in a secret way. He was consulted in cases of difficulty by a class of superstitious persons, and an implicit faith was placed in his statements and predictions. The " wise man" was sought in all cases of accident, disaster, or loss. He was consulted as to the probabilities of the return and safety of the distant and the absent; of the chances of the recovery of the sick, and of the destiny of some beloved friend or relative. The consultation with such a man would often have a sinister aim ; to discover by the stars whether an obnoxious husband would survive, or whether the affections of courted or inconstant lover could be secured. Very often long-continued diseases and inveterate maladies were ascribed to an " ill-wish;" and the planet-ruler was sought to discover who was the ill-wisher, and what charm would remove the spell. It is needless to say that the practices of these astrologers were productive, in a large number of cases, of much disturbance among neighbours and relatives, and great mischief to all concerned, except the man who profited by the credulity of his dupes.

Some of these charlatans no doubt were believers in the imposture, but the greater number were arrant cheats. In Leeds and its neighbourhood there were, some five-and-thirty years ago, several " wise men." Among the number was a man known by no other name than that of " Witch Pickles." He was avowedly an Astrological Doctor, and *ruled the planets* for those who sought him for that purpose. He dwelt in a retired house on the road from Leeds to York, about a mile from the Shoulder of Mutton public-house, at the top of March Lane. His celebrity extended for above fifty miles, and persons came from the Yorkshire Wolds to consult him. The man and the house were held in awe by boys and even older persons who had belief in his powers. Little was known of his habits, and he had few visitors but those who sought his professional assistance. He never committed anything to writing. He was particular in inquiring into all the circumstances of any case on which he was consulted before he pronounced. He then, as he termed it, proceeded to *draw a figure*, in order to discover the conjunction of the planets, and then entered upon the explanation of what the stars predicted. Strange things were told of him, such as that he performed incantations at midnight on certain days in the year when particular planets were in the ascendant; and that on such occasions strange sights and sounds would be seen and heard by persons passing the house. These were the embellishments of vulgar rumour. The man was quiet and inoffensive in his demeanour, and was fully sensible of the necessity of a life of seclusion. He is believed to have practised a few tricks to awe his visitors, such as lighting a candle or fire without visible agency, and other tricks far more ingenious than the modern table-rapping.

"Witch Pickles" was only one among the number who derived a large profit from this kind of occupation. He was one of the more respectable of the class, as he never descended to the vile tricks of others of the profession—tricks practised upon weak and credulous women and girls—which will not bear description.*

One of the most celebrated works on Astrology is that of Dr. Sibly, twelfth edition, 1817, in two octavo volumes, containing more than eleven hundred pages. The following will give an idea of the pretensions of the book, which is a remarkable book, if it really went through twelve editions. The owner of a privateer, which had not been heard of, called to know her fate. Dr. Sibly gave judgment on a figure " rectified to the precise time the question was propounded. The ship itself appeared well formed and substantial, but not a swift sailer, as is demonstrated by an earthy sign possessing the cusp of the ascendant, and the situation of the Dragon's Head in five degrees of the same sign." The ship itself was pronounced to have been captured.

* Abridged from *Notes and Queries*, 3rd Series, No. 25.

"From the whole account it is clear that Dr. Sibly's system—how now esteemed by astrologers the writer knows not—has but this alternative: either one and the same figure will tell the fate of all the ships which have not been heard of, including their sailing qualities, or the stars will never send an owner to ask for news except just at the moment when they are in a position to describe this particular ship."[*]

HANNAH GREEN; OR, "LING BOB."

This noted sibyl lived in a cottage on the edge of the moor on the left of the old road from Otley to Bradford, between Carlton and Yeadon, and eight miles from Leeds. She was popularly known as "The Lingbob Witch," a name given her, it is supposed, from her living among the ling-bobs, or heather-tubs. She was resorted to on account of her supposed knowledge of future events; but, like the rest of her class, her principal forte was fortune-telling, from which it is said she for herself realized a handsome fortune.

Many strange tales have been told of her; such as her power of transforming herself, after nightfall, into the shape of any she list; and of her odd pranks in her nightly rambles, her favourite character being that of the *hare*, in which personation she was unluckily shot by an unsuspecting poacher, who was almost terrified out of his senses by the awful screams which followed the sudden death of the Ling-bob witch.

* *Notes and Queries*, 3rd Series, No. 34.

In the year 1785, D——, of Sheffield, being at
Leeds, had the curiosity to pay a visit to the noted
Hannah Green.   He first questioned her respecting the
future fortunes of a near relative of his, who was then
in circumstances of distress, and indeed in prison.   She
told him immediately that his friend's trouble would
continue *full three times three years*, and he would then
experience *a great deliverance*, which, in fact, was on
the point of being literally verified, for he was then in
the Court of King's Bench.

He then asked her if she possessed any foreknowledge
of what was about to come to pass on the great stage of
the world; to which she replied in the affirmative.
She said, war would be *threatened once, but would not
happen*; but the second time it would blaze out in all
its horrors, and extend to all the neighbouring countries;
and that the two countries [these appear to be France
and Poland], at a great distance one from the other,
would in consequence obtain their freedom, although
after hard struggles.   After the year 1790, she
observed, many great persons, even kings and queens,
would lose their lives, and that *not by fair means*.   In
1794, a great warrior of high blood is to fall in the
field of battle; and in 1795, a distant nation [thought
to be negro slaves], who have been dragged from their
own country, will rise as one man, and deliver themselves from their oppressors.

Hannah appears to have been one of a somewhat
numerous class, many of whom were resident in Yorkshire.   Very few of them went beyond the attempt to
foretell the future events in the lives of individuals;
they did not work with such high ambition as drawing
the horoscopes of nations.   Their predictions were always

vague, and so framed as to cover a number of the most probable events in the life of every individual.

Hannah really died on the 12th of May, 1810, after having practised her art about forty years; and Lingbob became a haunted and dreaded place. The house remained some years untenanted and ruinous, but was afterwards repaired and occupied. Her daughter and successor, Hannah Spence, laid claim to the same prescience, but it need hardly be added, without the same success.*

ODDITIES OF LADY HESTER STANHOPE.

This eccentric lady, grand-daughter of the great Lord Chatham, held implicit faith in the influence of the stars on the destiny of men, a notion from which every crowned head in Europe is not, at this day, exempt.

Lady Hester brought her theories into a striking though rather ridiculous system. She had a remarkable talent for divining characters by the conformation of men. This every traveller could testify who had visited her in Syria; for it was after she went to live in solitude that her penetration became so extraordinary. It was founded both on the features of the face and on the shape of the head, body, and limbs. Some indications she went by were taken from a resemblance to animals; and wherever such indications

* See a pamphlet of 1794; *Notes and Queries*, 3rd Series, Nos. 20 and 21.

existed, she inferred that the dispositions peculiar to those animals were to be found in the person. But, independent of all this, her doctrine was that every creature is governed by the star under whose influence it was born.

"Animal magnetism," said Lady Hester, "is nothing but the sympathy of our stars. Those fools who go about magnetizing indifferently one person and another, why do they sometimes succeed and sometimes fail? Because, if they meet with those of the same star with themselves, their results will be satisfactory; but with opposite stars they can do nothing."

"What Lady Hester's *own star* was," says her physician, "may be gathered from what she said one day, when, having dwelt a long time on this her favourite subject, she got up from the sofa, and approaching the window, she called me. 'Look,' said she, 'at the pupil of my eyes; there! my star is the sun—all sun—it is in my eyes: when the sun is a person's star it attracts everything.' I looked, and I replied that I saw a rim of yellow round the pupil. 'A rim!' cried she; 'it isn't a rim—it's a sun; there's a disk, and from it go rays all round: 'tis no more of a rim than you are. Nobody has got eyes like mine.'"

Lady Hester delighted in anecdotes that went to show how much and how justly we may be biassed in our opinions by the shape of any particular part of a person's body independent of the face. She used to tell a story of ——, who fell in love with a lady on a glimpse of those charms which gave such renown to the Onidian Venus. This lady, luckily or unluckily, happened to tumble from her horse, and by that singular accident fixed the gazer's affections irrevocably. An-

other gentleman, whom she knew, saw a lady at Rome
get out of a carriage, her head being covered by an
umbrella, which the servant held over her on account
of the rain; and seeing nothing but her foot and leg,
swore he would marry her—which he did.

Lady Hester delighted in prophecies, some of which,
with their fulfilments and non-fulfilments, are very
amusing.   There is reason to think, from what her
ladyship let fall at different times, that Brothers, the
fortune-teller in England, and Metta, a village doctor
on Mount Lebanon, had considerable influence on her
actions and, perhaps, her destiny.   When Brothers was
taken up and thrown into prison (in Mr. Pitt's time), he
told those who arrested him to do the will of heaven,
but first to let him see Lady Hester Stanhope.   This
was repeated to her ladyship, and curiosity induced her
to comply with the man's request.   Brothers told her
that "she would one day go to Jerusalem and lead
back the chosen people; that on her arrival in the
Holy Land, mighty changes would take place in the
world, and that she would pass seven years in the
desert."   Trivial circumstances will foster a foolish
belief in a mind disposed to encourage it.   Mr.
Frederick North, afterwards Lord Guildford, in the
course of his travels came to Brusa, where Lady Hester
had gone for the benefit of the hot baths.   He, Mr.
Fazakerley and Mr. Gally Knight, would often banter
her on her future greatness among the Jews.   "Well,
madam, you must go to Jerusalem.   Hester, Queen of
the Jews! Hester, Queen of the Jews!" was echoed
from one to another; and probably at last the coinci-
dence of a name, a prophecy, and the country towards
which she found herself going, were thought, even by

herself, to be something extraordinary. Metta took up the book of fate from that time and showed her the part she was to play in the East. This man, Metta, for some years subsequent to 1815, was in her service as a kind of steward. He was advanced in years, and, like the rest of the Syrians, believed in astrology, spirits, and prophecy. No doubt he perceived in Lady Hester Stanhope a tincture of the same belief; and on some occasion in conversation he said he knew of a book on prophecy which he thought had passages in it that related to her. This book, he persuaded her, could only be had by a fortunate conjunction connected with himself; and he said if she would only lend him a good horse to take him to the place where it was, he would procure her a sight of it, but she was never to ask where he fetched it from. All this exactly suited Lady Hester's love of mystery. A horse was granted to him; he went off and returned with a prophetic volume which he said he could only keep a certain number of hours. It was written in Arabic, and he was to read and explain the text. The part which he propounded was, "That a European female would come and live on Mount Lebanon at a certain epoch, would build a house there, and would obtain power and influence greater than a sultan's; that a boy without a father would join her; that the coming of the Mahedi would follow, but be preceded by war, pestilence, famine, and other calamities; that the Mahedi would ride a horse born saddled, and that a woman would come from a far country to partake in the mission." There were many other incidents besides which were told.

"The boy without a father" was thought by Lady Hester to be the Duke of Reichstadt; but when he died, not at all discountenanced, she fixed on some one else. Another portion of the prophecy was not so disappointing, for in 1835 the Baroness de Feriat, an English lady residing in the United States, wrote of her own accord, asking to come and live with her, "When," remarks the discriminating doctor, "the prophecy was fulfilled." For the fulfilment of the remainder of the prophecy, Lady Hester was resolved at least not to be unprepared. She kept with the greatest care two mares, called Laïla and Lulu; the latter for Lady Hester herself, and the former, which was "born saddled," or in other words, of a peculiar hollow-backed breed, was for the Murdah or Mahedi, the coming of whom she had brought herself to expect, by the words of St. John, "There is one shall come after me who is greater than I." These mares she cherished with care equal to that paid by the ancient Egyptians to cats; and she would not allow them to be seen by strangers, except by those whose *stars* would not be baneful to cattle.

HERMITS AND EREMITICAL LIFE.

Men have, in most times, withdrawn themselves from the world and taken up their abode in caverns or ruins, or whatever shelter they could find, and lived on herbs, roots, coarse bread and water. In many cases, such persons have deemed these austerities as acceptable to God, and this has become one of the rudest forms of monastic life. It is not from this class of persons that we propose to introduce a few portraits of hermit life, but rather to those whose peculiarities have taken a more eccentric turn, almost in our own time.

The Hon. Charles Hamilton, in the reign of George II., proprietor of Pain's Hill, near Cobham, Surrey, built a hermitage upon a steep brow in the grounds of that beautiful seat. Of this hermitage Horace Walpole remarks that it is a sort of ornament whose merit soonest fades, it being almost comic to set aside a quarter of one's garden to be melancholy in. There is an upper apartment, supported in part by contorted logs and roots of trees, which form the entrance to the cell, but the unfurnished and neglected state of the whole proves the justness of Walpole's observation. Mr. Hamilton advertised for a person who was willing to become a hermit in that beautiful retreat of his. The conditions were that he was to continue in the hermitage seven years, where he should be provided with a Bible, optical glasses, a mat for his bed, a hassock for his pillow, an hour-glass for his timepiece, water for his beverage, food from the house, but never to exchange a syllable with the servant. He was to wear a camlet robe, never to cut his beard or nails, nor ever to stray beyond the limits of the grounds. If he lived there, under all these restrictions, till the end of the term, he was to receive seven hundred guineas. But on breach of any of them, or if he quitted the place any time previous to that term, the whole was to be forfeited. One person attempted it, but a three weeks' trial cured him.

A Correspondent of *Notes and Queries* describes a gentleman near Preston, Lancashire, as more successful in the above eccentricity. He advertised a reward of 50*l.* a year for life to any man who would undertake to live seven years underground, without seeing anything

human; and to let his toe and finger nails grow, with
his hair and beard, during the whole time. Apartments
were prepared underground, very commodious, with a
cold bath, a chamber organ, as many books as the
occupier pleased, and provisions served from his own
table. Whenever the recluse wanted any convenience
he was to ring a bell, and it was provided for him.
Singular as this residence may appear, an occupier
offered himself, and actually stayed in it, observing
the required conditions, for four years.

In the year 1863 there was living in the village of
Newton Burgoland, near Ashby-de-la-Zouch, Leicestershire, a hermit, whose real name was scarcely known,
though he had resided there nearly fifteen years. Yet he
was no recluse, no ascetic, but lived comfortably, and enjoyed his dinner, his beer, and his pipe ; and, according
to his own definition, he was entitled to be called a
hermit. "True hermits," he said, "throughout every
age, have been the firm abettors of freedom." As regarded his appearance, his fancies, and his habits, he was
a hermit, a *solitaire* in the midst of human beings. He
wore a long beard, and had a very venerable appearance.
He was very fantastic in his dress, and had a multitude
of suits. He had no less than twenty different kinds of
hats, each with its own name and form, with some em-
blem or motto on it—sometimes both. Here are a few
examples :—

No.	Name.	Motto or Emblem.
1.	Odd Fellows	Without money, without friends, without credit.
5.	Bellows	Blow the flames of freedom with God's word of truth.

No.	Name.	Motto or Emblem.
7.	Helmet	Will fight for the birthright of conscience, love, life, property, and national independence.
13.	Patent Teapot . . .	To draw out the flavour of the tea best—Union and Goodwill.
17.	Wash-basin of Reform .	White-washed face and collyed heart.
20.	Bee-hive	The toils of industry are sweet; a wise people live at peace.

The shapes of the hats and the devices on them were intended to symbolize some important fact or sentiment.

He had twelve suits of clothes, each with a peculiar name, differing from the others, and, like his hats, intended to be emblematical. One dress, which he called "Odd Fellows," was of white cotton or linen. It hung loosely over the body, except being bound round the waist with a white girdle buckled in the front. Over his left breast was a heart-shaped badge, bearing the words: "Liberty of Conscience," which he called his "Order of the Star." The hat which he wore with the dress was nearly white, and of common shape, but had on it four fanciful devices, bound with black ribbon, and inscribed, severally, with these words: " Bless, feed—good allowance—well clothed—all working-men."

Another dress, which he called "Foresters," was a kind of frock-coat, made of soft brown leather, slightly embroidered with braid. This coat was closed down the front with white buttons, and bound round the waist with a white girdle, fastened with a white buckle. The hat, slightly resembling a turban, was divided into black and white stripes, running round it.

Another dress, which he named "Military," had

some resemblance to the military costume at the beginning of the present century: the hat was between the old-fashioned cocked-hat and that worn by military commanders ; but, instead of the military plume, it had two upright peaks on the crown, not unlike the tips of a horse's ears. This hat, which he asserted cost five pounds, he never wore but on important occasions.

A mania for *symbolization* pervaded all his thoughts and doings. His garden was a complete collection of emblems. The trees—the walks—the squares—the beds—the flowers—the seats and arbours—were all symbolically arranged. In the passage leading into the garden were "the three seats of Self-Inquiry," each inscribed with one of these questions: "Am I vile ?" "Am I a Hypocrite ?" "Am I a Christian ?" Among the emblems and mottoes which were marked by different coloured pebbles or flowers were these :— "The vessels of the Tabernacle;" "The Christian's Armour—olive-branch, baptismal-font, breastplate of righteousness, shield of faith," &c. "Mount Pisgah;" a circle enclosing the motto, "Eternal Love has wed my Soul;" "A Bee-hive;" "A Church;" "Sacred Urn;" "Universal Grave;" "Bed of Diamonds;" "A Heart, enclosing the Rose of Sharon." All the Implements used in Gardening: "The two Hearts' Bowers;" "The Lovers' Prayer;" "Conjugal Bliss;" "The Hermit's Coat-of-Arms;" "Gossips' Court," with motto, "Don't tell anybody !" "The Kitchen-walk" contains representations of culinary utensils, with mottoes. "Feast Square" contains, "Venison Pasty;" "Round of Beef," &c. "The Odd Fellows' Square," with "The Hen-pecked Husband put on Water-gruel." "The Oratory," with various mottoes ; "The Orchestry," mottoes, "God save our Noble Queen;" "Britons never shall be Slaves," &c. "The Sand-glass of Time;" "The Assembly-room;" "The Wedding-walk; "The Holy Mount;" "Noah's Ark;" "Rainbow;" "Jacob's Ladder," &c. "The Bank of Faith;" "The Saloon;" "The Enchanted Ground;" "The Exit"—all with their respective emblems and mottoes. Besides these fantastical devices, there are, or were, in his garden, representations of the Inquisition and Purgatory; effigies of the Apostles; and mounds covered with flowers, to represent the graves of the Reformers. In the midst of the religious emblems stood a large tub, with a queer desk before it, to represent a pulpit. His garden was visited by persons residing in the neighbourhood, when he would clamber into his tub, and harangue the people against all kinds of real or fancied religious and political oppressions. He declaimed vociferously against the Pope as Antichrist and the enemy of humanity; and when he fled from Rome in the guise of a servant, our old hermit decked his head with laurels, and, thus equipped, went to the Independent Chapel, declaring that "the reign of the man of sin was over." He also raised a mock-gallows in his garden, and suspended on it an effigy of the Pope, whimsically dressed, with many books sticking out of his pockets, which, he said, contained the doctrines of Popery. However, these preachings proved very unprofitable; the hermit grew poor, and gladly accepted any assistance which did not require him to relinquish his eccentric mode of living. In his own words, his heart was in his garden. We abridge this account from a contribution to the *Book of Days*.

It is curious to find many instances of what are

termed "Ornamental Hermits," set up by persons of fortune seeking to find men as eccentric as themselves, to represent, as it were, the eremitical life in hermitages provided for them upon their estates.

Archibald Hamilton, afterwards Duke of Hamilton (as his daughter, Lady Dunmore, told Mr. Rogers, the poet), advertised for "a hermit," as an ornament to his pleasure-grounds; and it was stipulated that the said hermit should have his beard shaved but once a year, and that only partially.

Gilbert White, in his poem, *The Invitation to Selborne*, has these lines:—

> "Or where the Hermit hangs the straw-clad cell,
>   Emerging gently from the leafy dell;
>   By fancy plann'd," &c.

In a note, this hermitage is said to have been a grotesque building, contrived by a young gentleman, who used occasionally to appear in the character of a hermit.

Some fancy of this kind at Lulworth Castle, in Dorsetshire, exaggerated or highly coloured by O'Keefe, was supposed to afford him the title and incident of his extravagant but laughable comedy of *The London Hermit; or, Rambles in Dorsetshire*, first played in 1793.

In *Blackwood's Magazine* for April, 1830, it is stated by Christopher North, in the *Noctes Ambrosianæ*, that the then editor of another magazine had been "for fourteen years hermit to Lord Hill's father, and sat in a cave in that worthy baronet's grounds with an hourglass in his hand, and a beard belonging to an old goat, from sunrise to sunset, with orders to accept no half-crowns from visitors, but to behave like Giordano Bruno. In 1810, a correspondent of *Notes and Queries*, visiting the grounds at Hawkestone, the seat of the Hills, was shown the hermitage there, with a stuffed figure dressed like the hermits of pictures, seen by a dim light; and the visitors were told that it had been inhabited in the daytime by a poor man, to whom the eccentric but truly benevolent Sir Richard Hill gave a maintenance on that easy condition; but that the popular voice against such *slavery* had induced the worthy baronet to withdraw the reality and substitute the figure.

A person advertised to be engaged as *a hermit*, in the *Courier*, January 11th, 1810: "A young man, who wishes to retire from the world and live as a hermit, in some convenient spot in England, is willing to engage with any nobleman or gentleman who may be desirous of having one. Any letter directed to S. Lawrence (post paid), to be left at Mr. Otton's, No. 6, Coleman's Lane, Plymouth, mentioning what gratuity will be given, and all other particulars, will be duly attended."

In 1840, there died in the neighbourhood of Farnham, in Surrey, a recluse or hermit, who had been originally a wealthy brewer, but becoming bankrupt, wandered about the country, and having spent at an inn what little money he had, took up his abode in the cavern popularly known as "Mother Ludlam's Hole," in Moor Park. The "poor man" did not long avail himself of this ready-made excavation, but chose his resting-place just above, in the sandstone rock, upon a spot where a fox had been run to ground and dug out not long since. The hermit occasionally walked out, but was little noticed, although, from the bareness of the trees, his retreat was seen from a distance. He soon excavated for himself twenty-five feet in the sandstone, and about five feet in height, with a shaft to the summit of the hill, for the admission of light and air. Here, in unbroken solitude, with fewer luxuries than Parnell's hermit—

"His food the fruits, his drink the crystal well"—

our Surrey hermit subsisted almost entirely upon *ferns*, which abound in this neighbourhood. On January 11th, 1840, he was seen by two labourers, who described him as not having "two pounds of flesh on all his bones." He was carried to the nearest cottage, placed in a warm bath, next wrapped in blankets, and conveyed to the poor-house of Farnham, where he soon died; his last words being: "Do take me to the cave again."

A few miles from Stevenage, and not more than thirty from the metropolis, there was living, not many years since, in strange seclusion, a man of high intellectual powers, in the prime of manhood, and possessing ample means, yet wasting his days in eremitic misery. A Correspondent of the *Wolverhampton Chronicle* was invited to see this extraordinary character, and here is the result of his visit:—

"I had pictured to my mind a venerable old man, with a beard as white as snow, a massive girdle, and a profusion of books and hour-glass, in a cell of picturesque beauty and neatness. Alas, how soon was I to experience that imagination is one thing and reality another! I shall not venture in future to speculate upon objects so unearthly. At the termination of the road a mansion of no ordinary size met my view, but better and happier times had reigned within; without, all was desolation and ruin; time, that destroyer of all things, had done its work here; every inlet was barricaded by the rude axe and hammer; its portals no mortal had passed for eleven long years; the interior, which was one rich in design and comfort, is now mouldering to decay; no cheering voice is heard within its walls, only the noise of rats and vermin. In tracing my steps to the scene of the hermit's cell, which is situated at the back of the building, and looking through the wooden bars of a window devoid of glass, I perceived a dismal, black, and dirty cellar, with an earth floor; not one vestige of furniture, except a wooden bench and a few bottles, with the remnants of a fire.

With difficulty, by the faint rays of light admitted into this loathsome den, I could trace a human form, clothed only in a horse-rug, leaving his arms, legs, and feet perfectly bare; his hair was prodigiously long, and his beard tangled and matted. On my addressing him he came forward with readiness. I found him a gentleman by education and birth, and most courteous in his manner; he anxiously inquired after several aristocratic families in Staffordshire and adjoining counties. It is evident he had at one period mixed in the first circles, but the secret of his desolate retirement is, and probably ever will remain, a mystery to his neighbours and tenantry, by whom he is supplied with food (chiefly bread and milk). Already eleven weary winters has he passed in this dreary abode, his only bed being two sheepskins, and his sole companions the rats, which may be seen passing to and fro with all the ease of perfect safety. During the whole of his seclusion he has strictly abstained from ablution, consequently his countenance is perfectly black. How much it is to be regretted that a man so gifted as this hermit is known to be should spend his days in dirt and seclusion."

To another class belonged one Roger Crab, a gentleman of fortune, long resident at Bethnal Green, and one of the eccentric characters of the seventeenth century. All that is known of him is gathered from a pamphlet, now very rare, written principally by himself, and entitled, *The English Hermit, or Wonder of the Age:* by this it appears that he had served seven years in the Parliamentary army, and had his skull cloven in their service, for which he was so ill requited that he was sentenced to death by the Lord Protector, and afterwards suffered two years' imprisonment. When he obtained his release, he opened a shop at Chesham, as a dealer in hats. He had not long been settled there before he imbibed a notion that it was a sin against his body and soul to eat any sort of fish, flesh, or living creature, or to drink wine, ale, or beer. Thinking himself at the same time obliged to follow literally the injunction given to the young man in the Gospel, he quitted business, and disposing of his property, gave it among the poor, reserving to himself only a small cottage at Ickenham, in Middlesex, where he resided; he had a rood of land for a garden, on the produce of which he subsisted at the expense of three farthings a week, his food being bran, herbs, roots, dock-leaves, mallows, and grass; his drink water.

How such an extraordinary change of diet agreed with his constitution, the following passage from his pamphlet will show:—" Instead of strong drinks and wines I give the old man a drop of water; and instead of roast mutton and rabbits, and other dainty dishes, I give him broth thickened with bran, and pudding made with bran, and turnip-leaves chopped together, and grass; at which the old man (meaning my body) being moved, would know what he had done that I used him so hardly; then I shew'd him his transgression: so the warre began; the law of the old man in my fleshy members rebelled against the law of my mind, and had a shrewed skirmish; but the mind being well enlightened, held it so that the old man grew sick and weak with the flux, like to fall to the dust; but the wonderful love of God, well-pleased with the battle, raised him up again, and filled him with the voice of love, peace, and content of mind, and is now become more humble; for he will eat dock-leaves, mallows, or grasse."

Little is known of Crab's subsequent history, or whether he continued his diet of herbs; but a passage in his epitaph seems to intimate that he never resumed the use of animal food. It is not one of the least extraordinary parts of his history, that he should so long have subsisted on a diet, which, by his own account, had reduced him almost to a skeleton in 1655—being twenty-five years previous to his death—in 1680: he is buried in Stepney churchyard.

THE RECLUSES OF LLANGOLLEN.

Many years ago, there lived together, in romantic seclusion, in the Vale of Llangollen, in Denbighshire, two ladies, remarkable not only for the singularity of their habits and dispositions, but as the daughters of ancient and most distinguished families in the Irish peerage.

Lady Eleanor Butler was the youngest sister of John,

sixteenth Earl of Ormonde, and aunt of Walter, seventeenth Earl, who died in 1820. Miss Mary Ponsonby was the daughter of Chambre Ponsonby, Esq., and half-sister to Mrs. Lowther, of Bath.

These two ladies retired at an early age, about the year 1729, from the society of the world to the Vale of Llangollen. Lady Butler had already rejected several offers of marriage, and as her affection for Miss Ponsonby was supposed to have formed the bar to any matrimonial alliance, their friends, in the hope of breaking off so disadvantageous a companionship, proceeded so far as to place the former in close confinement. The youthful friends, however, found means to elope together, but being speedily overtaken, were brought back to their respective relations. Many attempts were renewed to entice Lady Butler into wedlock; but on her solemnly and repeatedly declaring that nothing should induce her to alter her purpose of perpetual maidenhood, her friends desisted from further importuning her.

Not many months after this a second elopement was planned. Each lady taking with her a small sum of money, and having confided the place of their retreat to a confidential servant of the Ormonde family, who was sworn to inviolable secrecy, they deputed her to announce their safety at home, and to request that the trifling annuities allowed them might not be discontinued. The message was received with kindness, and their incomes were even considerably increased.

When Miss Seward visited the spot, our heroines had resided in their romantic retirement about seventeen years; yet they were only known to the neighbouring villagers as *the Ladies of the Vale.* The verses which

Miss Seward dedicated to the Recluses, and wherein she celebrated " gay Eleanor's smile," and " Zara's look serene," conclude with this morceau of sentimental affectation : —

> " May one kind ice-bolt from the mortal stores
>   Arrest each vital current as it flows,
> That no sad course of desolated hours
>   Here vainly nurse their unsubsiding woes.
> While all who honour virtue gently mourn
> Llangollen's vanish'd pair, and wreathe their sacred urn."

But they did not vanish for many a long year : they neither married nor died till they were grown too old for the world to care whether they did either or both. On one occasion, indeed, a party of tourists, male and female, unable to procure accommodation at the village inn, requested and obtained admittance at " the cottage," when they proved to be near relatives of Miss Ponsonby. No entreaties, however, could allure their fair cousin from her seclusion.

Lady Eleanor is described as tall, of lively manners, and masculine. She usually wore a riding-habit, and donned her hat with the air of a finished sportsman. Her companion, on the contrary, was fair, pensive, gentle, and effeminate. Their abode was a neat cottage, with about two acres of pleasure-ground. Avoiding every appearance of dissipation or gaiety, they led a life as retired as the situation. Two female servants waited on them, and while Miss Ponsonby superintended the house, my Lady amused herself with the garden. The name of the retreat is Plas Newydd, about a quarter of a mile from Llangollen, hidden among the trees on ascending the Vale behind the church. By some the ladies are said not to have led here a life of absolute seclusion, but to have visited their neighbours and received friends. The cottage was built purposely for them. They died after a life full of good deeds, within eighteen months of each other—Lady Eleanor, June 2nd, 1829, at the patriarchal age of ninety; Miss Ponsonby, December 9th, 1831. Their monument, in Llangollen churchyard, in which they were buried, has three sides, each bearing a touching epitaph; the third to the memory of Mary Carrol, a faithful Irish servant.

SNUFF-TAKING LEGACIES.

On April 2nd, 1776, there died, at her house in Boyle Street, Burlington Gardens, one Mrs. Margaret Thompson, whose will affords a notable specimen of the ruling passion strong in death. The will is as follows:—
" In the name of God, Amen. I, Margaret Thompson, being of sound mind, &c., do desire that when my soul is departed from this wicked world, my body and effects may be disposed of in the manner following: I desire that all my handkerchiefs that I may have unwashed at the time of my decease, after they have been got together by my old and trusty servant, Sarah Stuart, be put by her, and by her alone, at the bottom of my coffin, which I desire may be made large enough for that purpose, together with such a quantity of the best Scotch snuff (in which she knoweth I always had the greatest delight) as will cover my deceased body; and this I desire the more especially as it is usual to put

flowers into the coffins of departed friends, and nothing can be so fragrant and refreshing to me as that precious powder. But I strictly charge that no man be suffered to approach my body till the coffin is closed, and it is necessary to carry me to my burial, which I order in the manner following :—

"Six men to be my bearers, who are known to be the greatest snuff-takers in the parish of St. James, Westminster; instead of mourning, each to wear a snuff-coloured beaver hat, which I desire may be bought for that purpose, and given to them. Six maidens of my old acquaintance, *viz.* &c., to bear my pall, each to bear a proper hood, and to carry a box filled with the best Scotch snuff to take for their refreshment as they go along. Before my corpse, I desire the minister may be invited to walk and to take a certain quantity of the said snuff, not exceeding one pound, to whom also I bequeath five guineas on condition of his so doing. And I also desire my old and faithful servant, Sarah Stuart, to walk before the corpse, to distribute every twenty yards a large handful of Scotch snuff to the ground and upon the crowd who may possibly follow me to the burial-place; on which condition I bequeath her 20*l.* And I also desire that at least two bushels of the said snuff may be distributed at the door of my house in Boyle Street."

She then particularizes her legacies; and over and above every legacy she desires may be given one pound of good Scotch snuff, which she calls the grand cordial of nature.

BURIAL BEQUESTS.

In June, 1864, there died at Drogheda one Miss Hardman, at the advanced age of ninety-two years. She was buried in the family vault in Peter's Protestant Church. The funeral took place on the eighth day of her decease. It is not usual in Ireland to allow so long an interval to elapse between the time of a person's death and burial; in this instance it was owing to the expressed wish of the deceased, and this originated in a very curious piece of family and local history. Everybody has heard of the lady who was buried, being supposed dead, and who bearing with her to the tomb, on her finger, a ring of rare price, this was the means of her being rescued from her charnel prison-house. A butler in the family of the lady, having his cupidity excited, entered the vault at midnight in order to possess himself of the ring, and in removing it from the finger the lady was restored to consciousness and made her way in her grave-clothes to her mansion. She lived many years afterwards before she was finally consigned to the vault. The heroine of the story was a member of the Hardman family—in fact, the late Miss Hardman's mother, and the vault in Peter's Church was the locality where the startling revival scene took place.

The story is commonly told in explanation of a monument in the Church of St. Giles, Cripplegate, London, which is commemorative of Constance Whitney, and represents a female rising from a coffin. "This," says Mr. Godwin, in his popular history of the *Churches of London*, "has been erroneously supposed to commemorate a lady, who, having been buried in a trance, was restored to life through the cupidity of the sexton, which induced him to dig up the body to obtain possession of a ring." The female rising from the coffin is undoubtedly emblematic of the Resurrection, and may have been repeated upon other monuments elsewhere; but there is no such monument at Drogheda, which as above is claimed as the actual locality.

On May 24th, 1837, there died at Primrose Cottage, High Wycombe, Bucks, Mr. John Guy, aged sixty-four. His remains were interred in a brick grave in Hughenden Churchyard: on a marble slab, on the lid of the coffin, is inscribed:

> "Here, without nail or shroud, doth lie,
> Or covered with a pall, John Guy,
> Born, May 17th, 1773.
> Died, „ 24th, 1837."

On his gravestone are the following lines:—

> "In coffin made without a nail,
> Without a shroud his limbs to hide;
> For what can pomp or show avail,
> Or velvet pall to swell the pride?"

Mr. Guy was possessed of considerable property, and was a native of Gloucestershire. His grave and coffin were made under his directions more than a twelvemonth previous to his death; he wrote the inscriptions, he gave the orders for his funeral, and wrapped in separate pieces of paper five shillings for each of the bearers. The coffin was very neatly made, and looked more like a piece of cabinet-work for a drawing-room than a receptacle for the dead.

Dr. Fidge, a physician of the old school, who in early days had accompanied the Duke of Clarence (afterwards William IV.) when a midshipman as medical attendant, possessed a favourite boat; upon his retirement from Portsmouth Dockyard, where he held an appointment, he had this boat converted into a coffin, with the sternpiece fixed at its head. This coffin he kept under his bed for many years. The circumstances of his death were very remarkable. Feeling his end approaching, and desiring to add a codicil to his will, he sent for his solicitor. On entering his chamber he found him suffering from a paroxysm of pain, but which soon ceased; availing himself of the temporary ease to ask him how he felt, he replied, smiling: "I feel as easy as an old shoe," and looking towards the nurse in attendance, said: "Just pull my legs straight, and place me as a dead man, it will save you trouble shortly," words which he had scarcely uttered before he calmly died.

Job Orton, of the Bell Inn, Kidderminster, had his tombstone, with an epitaphic couplet, erected in the parish churchyard; and his coffin was used by him for a wine-bin until required for another purpose.

Dr. John Gardner, "the worm doctor," originally of Long Acre, erected his tomb and wrote the inscription thereon some years before his death. Strangers reading the inscription naturally concluded he was like his predecessor, "Egregious Moore," immortalized by Pope, "food for worms," whereas he was still following his profession, that of a worm-doctor, in Norton Folgate, where he had a shop, in the window of which were displayed numerous bottles containing specimens of tape and other worms, with the names of the persons who had been tormented by them, and the date of their ejection. Finding his practice declining from the false impression conveyed by his epitaph, he dexterously caused the word *intended* to be interpolated, and the inscription for a long time afterwards ran as follows:—

intended
" Dr. John Gardner's last and best bed-room."
^

He was a stout, burly man, with a flaxen wig, and rode daily into London on a large roan-coloured horse.

Not a few misers have carried their penury into the arrangements for their interment. Edward Nokes, of Hornchurch, by his own direction, was buried in this curious fashion :—A short time before his death, which he hastened by the daily indulgence in nearly a quart of spirits, he gave strict charge that his coffin should not have a nail in it, which was actually adhered to, the lid being made fast with hinges of cord, and minus a coffin-plate, for which the initials E. N. cut upon the wood were substituted. His shroud was made of a pound of wool. The coffin was covered with a sheet in place of a pall, and was carried by six men, to each of whom he directed should be given half-a-crown. At his particular desire, too, not one who followed him to the grave was in mourning ; but, on the contrary, each of the mourners appeared to try whose dress should be the most striking. Even the undertaker was dressed in a blue coat and scarlet waistcoat.

Another deplorable case might be cited, that of Thomas Pitt, of Warwickshire. It is reported that some weeks prior to the sickness which terminated his despicable career, he went to several undertakers in quest of a cheap coffin. He had left behind him 3,475*l.* in the public funds.

BURIALS ON BOX HILL AND LEITH HILL.

As the railway traveller passes over Red Hill, on the London and Brighton line, his attention can scarcely fail to be struck with two prominent points in the charming landscape—Box Hill, covered with its patronymic shrub; and Leith Hill, surmounted by a square tower. On each of these elevations is buried an eccentric person: one with his head downwards, and the other in the usual horizontal position; but the fondness for exaggerating things already extraordinary, has led to the common misstatement that one person is buried with his head downwards, and the other standing upon his feet. Of the two interments, however, the following are the true versions.

On the north-western brow of Box Hill, and nearly in a line with the stream of the Mole, as it flows towards Burford Bridge, was interred, some sixty-five years since, Major Peter Labelliere, an officer of marines. During the latter years of his life he had resided at Dorking, and, in accordance with his own desire, he was interred on this spot, long denoted by a wooden stake or stump. This gentleman in early life fell in love with a lady, who, although he was remarkably handsome in person, rejected his addresses. This circumstance inflicted a deep wound on his mind, which, at a later period, religion and politics entirely unsettled. Yet his eccentricities were harmless, and himself the only sufferer. At this time the Duke of Devonshire, who had been formerly fond of the major's society, settled on him a pension of 100*l.* a year. Labelliere then lived at Chiswick, and there wrote several tracts, both polemical and political, but the incoherency of his arguments was demonstrative of mental incapacity. From Chiswick he frequently walked to London, his pockets filled to overflowing with newspapers and pamphlets, and on the road he delighted to harangue the ragged boys who followed him. He next removed to Dorking, and there resided in a mean cottage, called "The Hole in the Wall," on Butter Hill. Among the anecdotes of his eccentricity it is related that, to a gentleman with whom he was intimate he presented a packet, carefully folded and sealed, with a particular injunction not to open it till after his death. This request was strictly complied with, when it was found to contain merely a blank memorandum-book.

Long prior to his decease he selected the point of Box Hill we have named, where, in compliance with his oft-expressed wish, he was buried, without church rites, with his head *downwards;* in order, he said, that as "the world was turned topsy-turvy, it was fit that he should be so buried that he might be *right at last.*"* He died June 6th, 1800, and was interred on the 10th of the same month, when great numbers of persons witnessed his funeral ; and the slight wooden bridge which then crossed the Mole having been removed by some mischievous persons during the interment, many

---

* Honest Jack Fuller, who is buried in a pyramidal mausoleum in Brightling churchyard, in Sussex, gave as his reason for being thus disposed of, his unwillingness to be eaten by his relations after this fashion : " The worms would eat me, the ducks would eat the worms, and my relations would eat the ducks."

had to wade through the river on returning homewards.
The Major earned the not uncommon reward of eccen-
tricity—his portrait being engraved—by H. Kingsbury.
Under Labelliere's name is inscribed in the print—
"A Christian patriot and Citizen of the World."

The interment on Leith Hill is less characterized by
oddity than that of Major Labelliere on Box Hill.   In
a mansion on the south side of Leith Hill lived Mr.
Richard Hull, a gentleman of fortune, who, in 1766, with
the permission of Sir John Evelyn, of Wotton, built a
tower on the summit of Leith Hill, from which the sea
is visible, and it became a landmark for mariners.   It
comprised two rooms, which were handsomely furnished
by the founder, for the accommodation of those who
resorted thither to enjoy the prospect.   Over the
entrance, on the west side, was placed a stone with a
Latin inscription, which may be thus translated:
"Traveller, this very conspicuous tower was erected by
Richard Hull, of Leith Hill Place, Esq., in the reign of
George III., 1766, that you might obtain an extensive
prospect over a beautiful country; not solely for his
own pleasure, but for the accommodation of his neighbours and all men."

Mr. Hull was, by his own direction, interred within
this tower, and an epitaph inscribed on a marble slab
let into the wall, on the ground-floor, stated that he
died January 18th, 1772, in his eighty-third year.   He
was the oldest bencher of the Middle Temple, and sat
many years in the Parliament of Ireland.   He lived, in
his earlier years, in intimacy with Pope, Trenchard,
Bishop Berkeley, and other distinguished men of the
period; "and, to wear off the remainder of his days,
he purchased Leith Hill Place for a retirement, where

he led the life of a true Christian and rural philosopher; and, by his particular desire, his remains were here deposited, in a private manner, under this tower, which he had erected a few years before his death."

After the decease of the founder, the building was neglected, and suffered to fall into decay; but about 1796, Mr. W. Philip Perrin, who had purchased Mr. Hull's estate, had the tower thoroughly repaired, heightened several feet, and surmounted by a coping and battlement, so as to render it a more conspicuous sea-mark; but the lower part was filled in with lime and rubbish, and the entrance walled up. Leith Hill is the highest eminence in Surrey, its extreme point being 993 feet above the sea-level. It commands a view 200 miles in circumference. Dennis, the critic, described this prospect as superior to anything he had ever seen in England or Italy, in its surpassing "rural charms, pomp, and magnificence."

JEREMY BENTHAM'S BEQUEST OF HIS REMAINS.

Bentham's long life was incessantly and laboriously devoted to the good of his species; in pursuance of which he ever felt that incessant labour a happy task, that long life but too short for its benevolent object. The preservation of his remains by his physician and friend, to whose care they were confided, was in exact accord-

ance with his own desire. He had early in life determined to leave his body for dissection. By a document
dated as far back as 1769, he being then only twenty-
two years of age, bequeathed it for that purpose to
his friend, Dr. Fordyce. The document is in the following remarkable words :—

" This my will and general request I make, not out of
affectation of singularity, but to the intent and with
the desire that mankind may reap some small benefit
in and by my decease, having hitherto had small oppor-
tunities to contribute thereto while living."

A memorandum affixed to this document shows that
it had undergone Bentham's revision two months before
his death, and that this part of it had been solemnly
ratified and confirmed. The Anatomy Bill, passed subsequently to his death, for which a foundation had been
laid in *The Use of the Dead to the Living* (first published
in the *Westminster Review*, and afterwards reprinted, and
a copy given to every Member of Parliament), had
removed the main obstructions in the way of obtaining
anatomical knowledge; but the state of the law previous to the adoption of the Anatomy Act was such as
to foster the popular prejudices against dissection, and
the effort to remove these prejudices was well worthy of
a philanthropist. After all the lessons which science
and humanity might learn from the dissection of his
body had been taught, Bentham further directed that
the skeleton should be put together and kept entire ;
that the head and face should be preserved ; that the
whole figure, arranged as naturally as possible, should
be attired in the clothes he ordinarily wore, seated in
his own chair, and maintaining the attitude and aspect
most familiar to him.

Mr. Bentham was perfectly aware that difficulty and even obloquy might attend a compliance with the directions he gave concerning the disposal of his body. He therefore chose three friends, whose firmness he believed to be equal to the task, and asked them if their affection for him would enable them to brave such consequences. They engaged to follow his directions to the letter, and they were faithful to their pledge. The performance of the first part of this duty is thus described by an eyewitness, W. J. Fox, in the *Monthly Repository* for July, 1832:—

"None who were present can ever forget that impressive scene. The room (the lecture-room of the Webb Street School of Anatomy) is small and circular, with no window but a central skylight, and capable of containing about three hundred persons. It was filled, with the exception of a class of medical students and some eminent members of that profession, by friends, disciples, and admirers of the deceased philosopher, comprising many men celebrated for literary talent, scientific research, and political activity. The corpse was on the table in the middle of the room, directly under the light, clothed in a night-dress, with only the head and hands exposed. There was no rigidity in the features, but an expression of placid dignity and benevolence. This was at times rendered almost vital by the reflection of the lightning playing over them; for a storm arose just as the lecturer commenced, and the profound silence in which he was listened to was broken and only broken by loud peals of thunder, which continued to roll at intervals throughout the delivery of his most appropriate and often affecting address. With the feelings which touch the heart in the contemplation of departed greatness, and in the presence of death, there mingled a sense of the power which that lifeless body seemed to be exercising in the conquest of prejudice for the public good, thus co-operating with the triumphs of the spirit by which it had been animated. It was a worthy close of the personal career of the great philanthropist and philosopher. Never did corpse of hero on the battle-field, 'with his martial cloak around him,' or funeral obsequies chanted by stoled and mitred priests in Gothic aisles, excite such emotions as the stern simplicity of that hour in which the principle of utility triumphed over the imagination and the heart."

The skeleton of Bentham, dressed in the clothes which he usually wore, and with a wax face, modelled by Dr. Talrych, enclosed in a mahogany case, with folding-doors, may now be seen in the Anatomical Museum of University College Hospital, Gower Street, London.

———

THE MARQUIS OF ANGLESEY'S LEG.

Among the curiosities of Waterloo are the grave of the late Marquis of Anglesey's leg, and the house in which it was cut off, and where the boot belonging to it is pre-served! The owner of the house to whose share this relic has fallen finds it a most lucrative source of revenue, and will, in spite of the absurdity of the thing, probably bequeath it to his children as a valuable property. He has interred the leg most decorously in the garden of

the inn, within a coffin, under a weeping-willow, and
has honoured it with a monument and the following
epitaph :—

> " Ci est enterrée la Jambe,
> de l'illustre et vaillant Comte d'Uxbridge,
> Lieutenant-Général de S.M. Britannique,
> Commandant en chef la cavalrie Anglaise, Belge, et Hollandaise,
> blessé le 18 Juin, 1815,
> à la mémorable bataille de Waterloo ;
> qui par son héroisme a concouru au triomphe de la cause
> du genre humain ;
> Glorieusement décidée par l'éclatante victoire du dit jour."

Some wag scribbled this infamous couplet beneath
the inscription :—

> "Here lies the Marquis of Anglesey's limb ;
> The devil will have the rest of him."

More apposite is the following epitaph, attributed to
Mr. Canning, on reading the description of the tomb
erected to the memory of the Marquis of Anglesey's
leg :—

> " Here rests,—and let no saucy knave
>   Presume to sneer or laugh,
> To learn that mould'ring in this grave
>   There lies—a British *calf*.

> " For he who writes these lines is sure
>   That those who read the whole,
> Will find that laugh was premature,
>   For here, too, lies a *soul*.

> " And here five little ones repose,
>   Twin born with other five,
> Unheeded by their brother toes,
>   Who all are now alive.

" A leg and foot, to speak more plain,
    Lie here of one commanding ;
Who, though he might his wits retain,
    Lost half his understanding.

" And when the guns, with thunder bright,
    Poured bullets thick as hail,
Could only in this way be taught
    To give the foe *leg bail*.

" And now in England just as gay
    As in the battle brave,
Goes to the rout, the ball, the play,
    With one leg in the grave.

" Fortune in vain has showed her spite,
    For he will soon be found,
Should England's sons engage in fight,
    Resolved to stand his ground.

" But Fortune's pardon I must beg;
    She meant not to disarm :
And when she lopped the hero's leg,
    She did not seek his h—arm.

" And but indulged a harmless whim,
    Since he could *walk* with one :
She saw two legs were lost on him,
    Who never meant to run."

When the Marquis of Anglesey was, for the second time, Lord-Lieutenant of Ireland, he became very unpopular through an unguarded speech ; and Mr. O'Connell, in one of his flowery addresses, quoted the lines:—

" God takes the good, too good on earth to stay ;
And leaves the bad, too bad to take away."

The great orator continued:—

" This couplet's truth in Paget's case we find ;
God took his leg, and left himself behind."

Of a ballad sung in the streets of Dublin, the chorus ran as follows:—

> "He has one leg in Dublin, the other in Cork,
> And you know very well what I mean, O !"

It was stated that he had an artificial leg in cork.

THE COTTLE CHURCH.

' "For more than twenty years," says Mr. de Morgan, in his "Budget of Paradoxes"* in the *Athenæum*, 1865, "printed papers have been sent about in the name of Elizabeth Cottle. It is not so remarkable that such papers should be concocted, as that they should circulate for such a length of time without attracting public attention. Eighty years ago, Mrs. Cottle might have rivalled Lieutenant Brothers or Joanna Southcote. Long hence, when the now current volumes of our journals are well-ransacked works of reference, those who look into them will be glad to see this feature of our time : I therefore make a few extracts, faithfully copied as to type. The Italic is from the New Testament; the Roman is the requisite interpretation :—

"Robert Cottle ' *was numbered* (5196) *with the transgressors*' at the back of the Church in Norwood Cemetery, May 12, 1858—Isa. liii. 12. The Rev. J. G. Collinson, Minister of St. James's Church, Clapham, the then district church, before All Saints was built, read the funeral service *over the Sepulchre wherein never before man was laid.*

"*Hewn on the stone,* 'at the mouth of the sepulchre,' is his name

* We hope to see these interesting accounts of real " curiosities of literature" reprinted in a separate volume.

—Robert Cottle, born at Bristol, June 2, 1774; died at Kirkstall Lodge, Clapham Park, May 6, 1858. *And that day* (May 12, 1858) *was the preparation* (day and year for ' the PREPARED place for you ' —Cottleites—by the widowed mother of the Father's house, at Kirkstall Lodge—John xiv. 2, 3. *And the Sabbath* (Christmas Day, Dec. 25, 1859) *drew on* (for the resurrection of the Christian body on ' the third [Protestant Sun]-day '—1 Cor. xv. 35). *Why seek ye the living* (God of the New Jerusalem—Heb. xii. 22 ; Rev. iii. 12) *among the dead* (men): *he* (the God of Jesus) *is not here* (in the grave), *but is risen* (in the person of the Holy Ghost, from the supper of ' the dead in the second death' of Paganism). *Remember how he spake unto you* (in the Church of the Rev. George Clayton, April 14, 1839). *I will not drink henceforth* (at this last Cottle supper) *of the fruit of this* (Trinity) *vine, until that day* (Christmas Day, 1859), *when I* (Elizabeth Cottle) *drank it new with you* (Cottleites) *in my Father's kingdom*—John xv. *If this* (Trinitarian) *cup may not pass away from me* (Elizabeth Cottle, April 14, 1839), *except I drink it* (' new with you Cottleites, in my Father's kingdom '), *thy will be done*—Matt. xxvi. 29, 42, 64. ' Our Father which art (God) in Heaven, *hallowed be thy name, thy* (Cottle) *kingdom come, thy will be done in earth, as it is* (done) *in* (the new) *Heaven* (and new earth of the new name of Cottle—Rev. xxi. 1 ; iii. 12.)

" . . . . (Queen Elizabeth, from A.D. 1558 to 1566). *And this* WORD *yet once more* (by a second Elizabeth—the WORD of his oath) *signifieth* (at John Scott's baptism of the Holy Ghost) *the removing of those things* (those Gods and those doctrines) *that are made* (according the Creeds and Commandments of men) *that those things* (in the moral law of God) *which cannot be shaken* (as a rule of faith and practice) *may remain, wherefore we receiving* (from Elizabeth) *a kingdom* (of God,) *which cannot be moved* (by Satan) *let us have grace* (in his grace of Canterbury) *whereby we may serve God acceptably* (with the acceptable sacrifice of Elizabeth's body and blood of the communion of the Holy Ghost) *with reverence* (for truth) *and godly fear* (of the unpardonable sin of blasphemy against the Holy Ghost) *for our God* (the Holy Ghost) *is a consuming fire* (to the nation that will not serve him in the Cottle Church). We cannot defend ourselves against the Almighty, and if He is our defence, no nation can invade us.

" In verse 4 the Church of St. Peter is *in prison between four quaternions of Soldiers*—the Holy Alliance of 1815. Rev. vii. 1. Elizabeth, *the Angel of the Lord* Jesus *appears* to the Jewish and Christian body with *the vision* of prophecy to the Rev. Geo. Clayton and his clerical brethren, April 8th, 1839. *Rhoda* was the name of her maid at Putney Terrace who used *to open the door to her Peter*, the Rev. Robert Ashton, the Pastor of 'the little flock' 'of 120 names together, assembled in an upper (school) room' at Putney Chapel, to which little flock she gave the revelation (Acts i. 13, 15) *of Jesus the same* King of the Jews *yesterday* at the prayer meeting, Dec. 31, 1841, *and to-day*, Jan. 1, 1842, *and for ever*. See book of Life, page 24. Matt. xviii. 19 ; xxi. 13-16. In verse 6 the Italian body of St. Peter *is sleeping* ' in the second death ' *between the two* Imperial *soldiers* of France and Austria. The Emperor of France from Jan. 1 to July 11, 1859, causes the Italian *chains of St. Peter to fall off from his* Imperial *hands*.

"*I say unto thee*, Robert Ashton, *thou art Peter*, a stone, *and upon this rock*, of truth, *will I* Elizabeth, the Angel of Jesus, *build my* Cottle *Church, and the gates of hell*, the doors of St. Peter, at Rome, shall not prevail against it—Matt. xvi. 18 ; Rev. iii. 7-12."

" This will be enough for the purpose. When anyone who pleases can circulate new revelations of this kind, uninterrupted and unattended to, new revelations will cease to be a good investment of eccentricity. I take it for granted that the gentlemen whose names are mentioned have nothing to do with the circulars or their doctrines. Any lady who may happen to be entrusted with a revelation may nominate her own pastor, or any other clergyman, one of her apostles; and it is difficult to say to what court the nominees can appeal to get the commission abrogated.

"March 16, 1865. During the last two years the circulars have continued. It is hinted that funds are low: and two gentlemen, who are represented as gone 'to Bethlehem asylum in despair,' say that Mrs. Cottle will ' spend all that she hath, while Her Majesty's ministers

are flourishing on the wages of sin.' The following is
perhaps one of the most remarkable passages in the
whole :—

" *Extol and magnify Him* (Jehovah, the everlasting God, see
the Magnificat and Luke i. 45, 46—68—73—79), *that rideth* (by
rail and steam over land and sea, from his holy habitation at Kirkstall Lodge, Psa. lxxvii. 19, 20), *upon the* (Cottle) *heavens as it were*
(Sept. 9, 1864, see pages 21, 170), *upon an* (exercising, Psa. cxxxi.
1), *horse-*(chair, bought of Mr. John Ward, Leicester-square)."

HORACE WALPOLE'S CHATTELS SAVED BY A TALISMAN.

In the spring of 1771, Walpole's house in Arlington
Street was broken open in the night, and his cabinets
and trunks forced and plundered. The Lord of Strawberry was at his villa when he received by a courier the
intelligence of the burglary. In an admirable letter to
Sir Horace Mann, he thus narrates the sequel :—" I was
a good quarter of an hour before I recollected that it
was very becoming to have philosophy enough not to
care about what one does care for, if you don't care
there's no philosophy in bearing it. I despatched my
upper servant, breakfasted, fed the bantams as usual,
and made no more hurry to town than Cincinnatus
would if he had lost a basket of turnips. I left in my
drawers 270*l.* of bank-bills and three hundred guineas,
not to mention all my gold and silver coins, some inesti-
mable miniatures, a little plate, and a good deal of
furniture, under no guard but that of two maidens.

. . . . When I arrived, my surprise was by no means diminished. I found in three different chambers three cabinets, a large chest, and a glass case of china wide open, the locks not picked, but forced, and the doors of them broken to pieces. You will wonder that this should surprise me when I had been prepared for it. Oh! the miracle was that I did not find, nor to this hour have found, the least thing missing. In the cabinet of modern medals, there were, and so there are still, a series of English coins, with downright John Trot guineas, half-guineas, shillings, sixpences, and every kind of current money. Not a single piece was removed. Just so in the Roman and Greek cabinet; though in the latter were some drawers of papers, which they had tumbled and scattered about the floor. A great exchequer chest, that belonged to my father, was in the same room. Not being able to force the lock, the philosophers (for thieves that steal nothing deserve the title much more than Cincinnatus or I) had wrenched a great flapper of brass with such violence as to break it into seven pieces. The trunk contained a new set of chairs of French tapestry, two screens, rolls of prints, and a suit of silver stuff that I had made for the king's wedding. All was turned topsy-turvy, and nothing stolen. The glass case and cabinet of shells had been handled as roughly by these impotent gallants. Another little table with drawers, in which, by the way, the key was left, had been opened too, and a metal standish that they ought to have taken for silver, and a silver hand-candlestick that stood upon it, were untouched. Some plate in the pantry, and all my linen just come from the wash, had no more charms for them than gold or silver. In short, I could not help laughing, especially as the only two movables neglected were another little table with drawers and the money, and a writing-box with the bank-notes, both in the same chamber where they made the first havoc. In short, they had broken out a panel in the door of the area, and unbarred and unbolted it, and gone out at the street-door, which they left wide open at five o'clock in the morning. A passenger had found it so, and alarmed the maids, one of whom ran naked into the street, and by her cries waked my Lord Romney, who lives opposite. The poor creature was in fits for two days, but at first, finding my coachmaker's apprentice in the street, had sent him to Mr. Conway, who immediately despatched him to me, before he knew how little damage I had received, the whole of which consists in repairing the doors and locks of my cabinets and coffer.

"All London is reasoning on this marvellous adventure, and not an argument presents itself that some other does not contradict. I insist that I have a talisman. You must know that last winter, being asked by Lord Vere to assist in settling Lady Betty Germaine's auction, I found in an old catalogue of her collection this article, '*The Black Stone into which Dr. Dee used to call his spirits.*' Dr. Dee, you must know, was a great conjuror in the days of Queen Elizabeth, and has written a folio of the dialogues he held with his imps. I asked eagerly for this stone; Lord Vere said he knew of no such thing, but if found, it should certainly be at my service. Alas, the stone was gone! This winter I was again employed by Lord Frederic Campbell, for I am an absolute auctioneer, to do him the same service about his father's (the Duke of Argyle's) collection. Among other odd things he produced a round piece of shining black marble in a leathern case, as big as the crown of a hat, and asked me what that possibly could be? I screamed out, ' Oh Lord, I am the only man in England that can tell you! It is Dr. Dee's Black Stone!' It certainly is; Lady Betty had formerly given away or sold, time out of mind, for she was a thousand years old, that part of the Peterborough collection which contained natural philosophy. So, or since, the Black Stone had wandered into an auction, for the lotted paper is still on it. The Duke of Argyle, who bought everything, bought it. Lord Frederic gave it to me; and if it was not this magical stone, which is only of high-polished coal, that preserved my chattels, in truth I cannot guess what did."

At the Strawberry Hill sale, in 1842, this precious relic was sold for 12*l*. 12*s*., and is now in the British Museum. It was described in the catalogue as " a singularly interesting and curious relic of the superstition of our ancestors—the celebrated *Speculum of Kennel Coal*, highly polished, in a leathern case. It is remarkable for having been used to deceive the mob, by the celebrated Dr. Dee, the conjuror, in the reign of Queen Elizabeth," &c. When Dee fell into disrepute, and his chemical apparatus and papers and other stock-in-trade were destroyed by the mob, who made an attack upon his house, this Black Stone was saved. It appears to be nothing more than a polished piece of cannel coal; but this is what Butler means when he says :—

> " Kelly did all his feats upon
> The devil's looking-glass—a stone."

NORWOOD GIPSIES.

Two centuries ago, Norwood, in Surrey, was celebrated as the haunt of many of the gipsy-tribe, who in the summer-time pitched their blanket-tents beneath its shady trees. Thus we find Pepys recording a visit to the place, under the date of August 11th, 1688 :— "This afternoon my wife, and Mercer, and Deb. went with Pelling to the gipsies at Lambeth, and have their fortunes told ; but what they did I did not enquire." [Norwood is in the southern part of Lambeth parish.]

From their reputed knowledge of futurity, the Norwood gipsies were often consulted by the young and credulous. This was particularly the case some sixty or seventy years ago, when it was customary among the working class and servants of London to walk to Norwood on the Sunday afternoon to have their fortunes told, and also to take refreshment at the Gipsy House, said to have been first licensed in the reign of James the First. The house long bore on its sign-post a painting of the deformed figure of Margaret Finch, the Queen of the Gipsies.

The register of Beckenham, under the date of October 24th, 1740, records the burial of Margaret Finch, who lived to the age of 109 years. After travelling over various parts of the kingdom (during the greater part of a century), she settled at Norwood, whither her great age and the fame of her fortune-telling attracted numerous visitors. From a habit of sitting on the ground, with her chin resting on her knees, the sinews became so contracted that she could not rise from that posture.   After her death they were obliged to enclose her body in a deep square box.   Her funeral was attended by two mourning-coaches, a sermon was preached on the occasion, and a great concourse of people attended the ceremony.   There is an engraved portrait of this gipsy queen, from a drawing made in 1739.

In the summer of 1815, the gipsies of Norwood were " apprehended as vagrants, and sent in three coaches to prison," and this magisterial interference, and the increase of houses and population, have long since driven the gipsies from their haunts; but the association is preserved in the Gipsy Hill station of the Crystal Palace Railway.

"CUNNING MARY," OF CLERKENWELL.

Early in the seventeenth century, one Mary Woods, of Norwich, a person who professed skill in palmistry, came to London in the way of her vocation, and lodged at the house of one Crispe, a barber, in Clerkenwell. Having received such a valuable inmate, the barber soon afterwards removed " Cunning Mary " and her husband to the more fashionable neighbourhood of the Strand, and there the barber became a willing agent in procuring subjects or patients for his female lodger. One branch of her business consisted in furnishing ladies who desired to become mothers with charms and medicines which would assist them in attaining their end.   In the next house to Somerset Place dwelt a

Mrs. Isabel Peel, wife of a tradesman, who to her great grief was childless. The barber, at his lodger's suggestion, whispered in her ear, that the very skilful person who was an inmate of his house could provide her with means to help forward her desires. An interview was arranged, and by "fair speech and cozening skill" Mary Woods persuaded Mrs. Peel of her power, but demanded no less a sum than twenty pounds for its exercise. In cash, the amount was beyond the patient's means, but she delivered to her adviser "two lawn and other wrotte (wrought) wares," and received in return a small portion of an infallible powder, which the cunning woman sewed in a little piece of taffeta, and bade the aspirant after maternity wear it round her neck.

The news that a woman of such marvellous skill had come to lodge in Westminster soon spread. Anxious ladies in many of the neighbouring mansions sent for her, and she specially got a footing in Salisbury House. Mrs. Jane Sacheverell, who attended on Lady Cranborne, was one of her victims. The Countess of Essex had several interviews with her in the same friendly mansion, and gave her a diamond ring worth fifty or sixty pounds, sent by her husband, the Earl, out of France, with directions to pawn it, in order to procure a portion of the infallible powder, "which was very costly." The Countess also bestowed upon Mrs. Woods "certain pieces of gold worth between thirty and forty pounds." When the affair was called in question, Mrs. Woods asserted that the Countess gave her these things to procure "a kind of poison that would be in a man's body three or four days without swelling," and that this poison was to be given to the Earl of Essex. But Mrs. Woods was an infamous person, whose uncorroborated assertion was worth nothing, and she had previously mentioned to Mrs. Peel that her employment by the Countess had relation merely to the child-giving powder.

Mrs. Woods possessed other faculties besides those with reference to which she was consulted by Mrs. Peel and Mrs. Sacheverell. She could "help" ladies to husbands, and "cause and procure whom they desired to have, to love them." On this branch of her business she was consulted by Mrs. Cooke, Lady Walden's gentlewoman, who gave her twenty pounds and more, in twenty-shilling pieces of gold; and, finally, also, by Mrs. Clare, who is described as lying in the Court at Whitehall, and as being a waiting gentlewoman in attendance upon the young Lady Windsor. Mrs. Clare, like several other of the ladies named, had no ready money, but the fees paid by her were very handsome. They comprised a standing cup and cover of silver gilt, worth fourteen pounds; a petticoat of velvet, layed with three silver laces, that cost forty pounds; and two diamond rings, the one worth twenty pounds, and the other five pounds.

After the bubble had burst, and Cunning Mary absconded with her plunder, Mrs. Peel says that she "ripped the taffeta to see what powder it was, and found it but a little dust swept out of the flower (floor ?).*

* S. P. Dom. James I., vol. lxxvii., quoted in Pinks's *History of Clerkenwell*, Appendix.

JERUSALEM WHALLEY.

Mr. Whalley was elected for Newcastle, 1785, before he was of age, which was not unusual in Ireland, and sat for it to 1790, and for Enniscorthy from 1797 to June, 1800. He acquired the sobriquet of *Jerusalem Whalley* in consequence of a bet, said to have been 20,000*l.*, that he would walk (except where a sea-passage was unavoidable) to Jerusalem and back within twelve months. He started September 22nd, 1788, and returned June 1st, 1789.

Lord Cloncurry describes Whalley as a perfect specimen of the Irish gentleman of the olden time. Gallant, reckless, and profuse, he made no account of money, limb, or life, when a feat was to be won, or a daring deed to be attempted. He spent a fine fortune in pursuits not more profitable than his expedition to play ball at Jerusalem; and rendered himself a cripple for life by jumping from the drawing-room window of Daly's club-house, in College Green, Dublin, on to the roof of a hackney-coach which was passing.

The lawless behaviour of the yeomanry corps which he commanded obtained for him another and less agreeable appellation, "Bever-chapel Whalley." His residence in Stephen's Green was, in 1855, converted into a nunnery. Sir Jonah Barrington states that 4,000*l.* was paid to Mr. Whalley by Mr. Gould, M.P., for Kilbeggan.

Whalley, "Buck Whalley" as he was sometimes called, is stated to have been the founder of the Hell-fire Club. Having a taste for the fine arts, and means to gratify it, he accumulated a large number of valuable paintings in his mansion at Stephen's Green, Dublin, of which the following account has appeared in the *Dublin University Magazine* :—" In the centre of the south side of St. Stephen's Green stands a noble building, with a large stone lion reposing over the entrance, and finding his legs and tail encroached on by grass and weeds. This mansion belonged to the great Buck Whalley, and witnessed many a noble feast and mad carouse during the viceroyalty of the Duke of Buckingham. At last, when all the pleasures that could be procured on Irish land were tried, and found to result in satiety and disgust, and his tailor and wine-merchant began to disturb him, he sought new excitement in his wager that he would have a game of ball against the walls of Jerusalem; and he succeeded, as already stated. A bard, who contributed to a collection of political squibs, entitled, *Both Sides of the Gutter*, sang the going forth of the expedition : it is entitled, *Whalley's Embarkation*, to the tune of 'Rutland Gigg.' "

FATHER MATHEW AND THE TEMPERANCE MOVEMENT.

No great cause was ever inaugurated with more eccentric or more genuine fervour than the advocacy of the Temperance principles by Father Mathew, the Capuchin Friar. "Here goes in the name of God!" said the Father, on the 10th of April, 1838, when he pledged his name in the cause of Temperance, and, together with the Protestant priest, Charles Duncombe, the Unitarian philanthropist, Richard Dowden, and the stout Quaker, William Martin, publicly inaugurated a movement at Cork, destined in a few years to count its converts by millions, and to spread its influence as far as the English language was spoken.   In this good work, the habitually impulsive temperament of the Irish was acted upon for the purest and most beneficial of purposes ; and one element of its success lay in the unselfishness of the Father, who was himself a serious sufferer by the results of his philanthropic exertions. A distillery in the south of Ireland, belonging to his family, and from which he himself derived a large income, was shut up in consequence of the disuse of whisky among the lower orders, occasioned by his preaching.   But his "Riverance" was most unscrupulously tyrannized over by his servant John, a wizened old bachelor, with a red nose, privately nourished by Bacchus; and he was only checked in his evil doings when the Father, more exasperated than usual, exclaimed, "John, if you go on in this way, I must certainly leave this house."   On one occasion, there was a frightful smack of whisky pervading the pure element which graced the board, which he accounted for by saying he had placed the forbidden liquid, with which he "cleaned his tins," in the jug by mistake.

The Temperance cause prospered, but Father Mathew, through his eccentric love of giving, found it impossible to keep out of debt, which ever kept him in thraldom. The hour of his deepest bitterness was when, while publicly administering the pledge in Dublin, he was arrested for the balance of an account due to a medal manufacturer; the bailiff to whom the duty was entrusted kneeling down among the crowd, asking his blessing, and then quietly showing him the writ.

This is one of the many anecdotes told by Mr. Maguire, in his admirable Life of Father Mathew, who, we learn from the same authority, at a large party attempted to make a convert of Lord Brougham, who resisted, good-humouredly but resolutely, the efforts of his dangerous neighbour. "I drink very little wine," said Lord Brougham; "only half-a-glass at luncheon, and two half glasses at dinner; and though my medical adviser told me I should increase the quantity, I refused to do so." "They are wrong, my lord, for advising you to increase the quantity, and you are wrong in taking the small quantity you do; but I have my hopes of you." And so, after a pleasant resistance on the part of the learned lord, Father Mathew invested his lordship with the silver medal and ribbon, the insignia and collar of the Order of the Bath. "Then I will keep it," said Lord Brougham, "and take it to the House, where I shall be sure to meet the old Lord —— the worse of liquor, and I will put it on him." Lord Brougham was as good as his word; for, on meeting the veteran peer, he said: "Lord ——, I have a present from Father Mathew for you," and passed the ribbon quietly over his neck. "Then I'll tell you what it is, Brougham, by,—— I will keep sober for this day," said his lordship, who kept his word, to the great amusement of his friends.

ECCENTRIC PREACHERS.

Scores, nay, hundreds of volumes have been gathered upon the oddities of character which mankind, in all ages, have presented to the observant writer who loves to " shoot folly as it flies." Voltaire has said, "Every country has its foolish notions. . . . Let us not laugh at any people ;" and it would be difficult to find any age which has not its curiosities of character, to be laughed at and turned to still better account; for, of whatever period we write, something may be done in the way of ridicule towards turning the popular opinion. Diogenes owes much of his celebrity to his contempt of comfort, by living in a tub, and his oddity of manner. Orator Henley preached from his " gilt tub " in Clare Market, and thus earned commemoration in the *Dunciad* :—

" Still break the benches, Henley, with thy strain,
While Sherlock, Hare, and Gibson preach in vain ;
O, worthy thou of Egypt's wise abodes,
A decent priest, where monkeys were the gods !
But Fate with butchers placed thy priestly stall,
Meek modern faith to murder, hack, and haul."

Eccentricity has its badge and characteristics by which it gains distinction and notoriety, and which in some cases serve as a lure to real excellence. The preaching of Rowland Hill is allowed to have been excellent; but his great popularity was won by his eccentric manner, and the many piquant anecdotes and witticisms, and sallies of humour unorthodox, with which, during his long ministry, he interlarded his sermons. However, he thought the end justified the means; and certain it is that it drew very large congregations. The personal allusions to his wife, which Rowland Hill is related to have used in the pulpit, were, however, fictious, and at which Hill expressed great indignation. "It is an abominable untruth," he would exclaim; "derogatory to my character as a Christian and a gentleman. They would make me out a bear."

The success of Edward Irving, the popular minister of the National Scotch Church in London, was of a more mixed character. It is stated, upon good authority, that he first chose the stage as a profession, and acted in Ryder's company, in Kirkaldy, a few miles from Edinburgh, about fifty-five years since. The obliquity of his vision, his dialect, and peculiarly awkward gait and manner, created so much derision, that he left the stage for the pulpit, after about three months' probation.

Irving's sermons were not liked at first; and it was not until he was recognized by Dr. Chalmers that Irving became popular. But he was turned out of his church, and treated as a madman, and he died an outcast heretic. "There was no harm in the man," says a contemporary, "and what errors he entertained, or extravagancies he allowed in connection with supposed miraculous gifts, were certain in due time to burn themselves out. It was not so much the error of his doctrine as the peculiarity of his manner, the torrent of his eloquence, his superlative want of tact, that provoked his enemies, and frightened his friends. The strength of his faith was wonderful. Once, when he was called to the bedside of a dying man late at night he went immediately. Presently he returned, and beckoned one of his friends to accompany him. The reason was, that he really believed in the efficacy of prayer, and held to the promise—"If *two* of you shall agree on earth as touching anything that ye shall ask, it shall be done." It was necessary, therefore, that two should go to the sick man. So, also, he had a child that died in infancy, to whom he was in the habit of addressing "words of godliness, to nourish the faith that was in him." And Irving adds that the patient heed of the child was wonderful. He really believed that the infant, by some incomprehensible process, could guess what he was saying, and profit by it. His love for children was very great; and he, a very popular man in London, might be seen, day by day, marching along the streets of Pentonville of an afternoon, his wife by his side, and his baby in his arms.

His sermons had a large sale, going through many editions. But Irving complains that, in spite of these large sales, he could never get the religious publishers to whom he had entrusted his book to give him anything but a pitiful return. It is amusing to find him in one letter complaining that there is neither grace nor honour in the religious booksellers, and requesting his wife in negotiating the sale of his next venture to "try Blackwood, or some of these worldlings," in the evident expectation that "these worldlings" were a good deal more liberal in their dealings, not to say honest, than those whom he regarded as his peculiar friends.

IRVING A MILLENARIAN.

The Millenarians proudly claim the late Edward Irving as having been one of the most earnest believers in the personal reign of Christ. In his latter days he was a Millenarian in the strictest sense of the word. From the year 1827 to 1830, the Millenarianism question was brought under the notice of thousands of Christians, who, though remarkable for their knowledge of Scripture on other points, had never bestowed a single thought on the question of Christ's personal reign on earth. The cause of this was the prominence given to it by the Rev. E. Irving, then at the summit of his popularity. Solely with the generous view of assisting a Spanish friend, he had, in the previous year, studied the Spanish language, and had made such progress as to be able to translate it into English. Just at this time appeared in Spanish, *The Coming of the Messiah in Glory and Majesty*, with which Irving was much struck, as powerfully expressing his own views on the Millenarian question, that he at once set to work, and translated it into English. Its author professed to have been a Jewish convert to Christianity, and gave the name of Juan Josaphat Ben-Ezra on the title-page. He was, however, a Spanish priest and a Jesuit. It is not known whether Mr. Irving was aware of the fraud which had been thus practised upon the readers of the book; he described it as " the chief work of a master's hand," and " a masterpiece of reasoning," and " a gift which he had revolved well how he might turn to profit."

Irving likewise established *The Morning Watch* for the sole purpose of advocating Millenarian views; but the extravagance of some of the collateral notions which the preacher intermingled with simple Millenarianism rather impeded than promoted the object in view. The doctrine, too, of speaking with tongues, the assertion of the peccability of Christ's humanity, the zealous advocacy of the opinion that the power of working miracles was still vested in the Church, and not the expectation only, but from time to time, the repeated assertion, most emphatically, that *Christ would come immediately to reign personally on the earth*—all these, and other sentiments no less confidently advanced, and earnestly inculcated both from Irving's pulpit and through the press, injured rather than benefited the cause of Millenarianism among the more sober-minded men in the religious world.

Moreover, he retained these momentous errors till his dying hour, and added one more to them. When his physicians and friends, seeing him in the last stage of consumption, prepared him in the spirit of affectionate faithfulness for the solemn event which was at hand, he would not believe that he was dying, or ever would die, but that he would be changed in the twinkling of an eye, and in a transformed body, made unspeakably glorious, be caught up to heaven. The Millenarians therefore do not strengthen their cause by quoting the name of Edward Irving as an authority in favour of their views.

The intense enthusiasm with which Irving entered into the notion of a personal reign of Christ on earth is well described in his Life by Mrs. Oliphant. "The conception," she says, " of a second advent nearly approaching was like the beginning of a new life. The thought of seeing his Lord in the flesh cast a certain ecstasy on the mind of Irving. It quickened tenfold his already vivid apprehension of spiritual things. The burden of his prophetic mystery, so often darkly pondered, so often interpreted in a mistaken sense, seemed to him, in the light of that expectation, to swell into divine choruses of preparation for the splendid event which, with his bodily eyes, undimmed by death, he hoped to behold." It is generally thought that the extravagancies which, towards the close of his career, proceeded both from his lips and his pen, were to be traced to a mind which, through its prophetic studies, had *lost its balance.* Yet, to the last, he made many proselytes to his Millenarian notions.

Irving originated the idea of Christ, with his saints, remaining and reigning in the air after he has caught up his people to meet him there, instead of reigning literally on the earth. Irving also originated the doctrine of *secret rapture,* or the assumption that Christ will come and take up his people who are alive with him into the air when he raises the saints who are in their graves, and summons them to meet him in aerial regions. So deeply did this notion take possession of many of those who adopted Mr. Irving's Millenarian views, in conjunction with this other idea—that *Christ's second coming might be* looked for at any hour—that they were as firmly persuaded they would not see death, as they were of any truth in the Word of God.*

* See *The End of All Things,* by the author of *Our Heavenly Home.* 1866.

A TRIO OF FANATICS.

The names of Sharp, Bryan, and Brothers will not soon be forgotten among the so-called prophets of the present century. The first of this inspired trio was William Sharp, one of the greatest masters in the English school of engraving; Bryan was what is termed an irregular Quaker, who had engrafted sectarian doctrines on an original stock of fervid religious feeling; and Richard Brothers, who styled himself the "Nephew of God," predicted the destruction of all sovereigns, &c.

Sharp was, at one time, so infected with wild notions of political liberty, and so free in his talk, that he was placed under arrest by the Government, and several times examined before the Privy Council, for the purpose of ascertaining whether or not, in his speeches or writings, he had committed himself far enough to be tried with Horne Tooke for high treason; but Sharp, being a handsome-looking, jocular man, and too cheerful for a conspirator, the Privy Council came to a conclusion that the altar and the throne had not much to fear from him. At one of the examinations, when Mr. Pitt and Mr. Dundas were present, after he had been worried with questions, which, Sharp said, had little or nothing to do with the business, he deliberately took out of his pocket a prospectus for subscribing to his portrait of General Kosiusko, after West, which he was then engraving; and handing the paper first to Pitt and Dundas, he requested them to put their names down as subscribers, and then to give his prospectus to the other members of the Council for their names. The singularity of the proposal set them laughing, and he was soon afterwards liberated.

Sharp possessed a fraternal regard for Bryan, had him instructed in copper-plate printing, supplied him with paper, &c., and enabled him to commence business; but they soon quarrelled. A strong tide of animal spirits, not unaccompanied by some intellectual pretensions and shrewdness of insight, characterized the mind of Jacob Bryan; which, when religion was launched on it, swelled to enthusiasm, tossed reason to the skies, or whirled her in mystic eddies. Sharp found him one morning groaning on the floor, between his two printing-presses, at his office in Marylebone Street, complaining how much he was oppressed, by bearing, after the pattern of the Saviour, part of the sins of the people; and he soon after had a vision, commanding him to proceed to Avignon on a Divine mission. He accordingly set out immediately, in full reliance on Divine Providence, leaving his wife to negotiate the sale of his printing business: thus Sharp lost his printer, but Bryan kept his faith. The issue of this mission was so ambiguous, that it might be combined into an accomplishment of its supposed object, according as an ardent or a cool imagination was employed on the subject; but the missionary (Bryan) returned to England, and then became a dyer, and so much altered, that a few years after he could even pun upon the suffering and confession which St. Paul has expressed in his text—"I die daily."

The Animal Magnetism of Mesmer and the mysteries of Emanuel Swedenborg had, by some means or other, in Sharp's time, become mingled in the imaginations of their respective or their mutual followers; and Bryan and several others were supposed to be endowed, though not in the same degree, with a sort of half-physical and half-miraculous power of curing diseases, and imparting the thoughts or sympathies of distant friends. De Loutherbourg, the painter (one of the disciples), was believed by the sect to be a very Esculapius in this divine art; but Bryan was held to be far less powerful, and was so by his own confession. Sharp had also some inferior pretensions of the same kind, which gradually died away.

But, behold! Richard Brothers arose! The Millennium was at hand! The Jews were to be gathered together, and were to re-occupy Jerusalem; and Sharp and Brothers were to march thither with their squadrons! Due preparations were accordingly made, and boundless expectations were raised by the distinguished artist. Upon a friend remonstrating that none of their preparations appeared to be of a marine nature, and inquiring how the chosen colony were to cross the seas, Sharp answered, "Oh, you'll see; there'll be an earthquake, and a miraculous transportation will take place." Nor can Sharp's faith or sincerity on this point be in the least distrusted; for he actually engraved two plates of the prophet Brothers, having calculated that one would not print the great number of impressions that would be wanted when the important event should arrive; and he added to each the following inscription: "Fully believing this to be the man appointed by God, I engrave his likeness: W. Sharp." The writing engraver, Smith, put the comma after the word "appointed," and omitted it in the subsequent part of the sentence. The mistake was not discovered until several were worked off; the unrectified impressions are in great request. Whether this be true, or only a hoax by Smith to put collectors on a false scent, has not been ascertained; there is no such impression in the British Museum. If the reader paused in the place where Sharp intended, the sentence expressed, " Fully believing this to be the man appointed by God,"—to do what? to head the Jews in their predestined march to recover Jerusalem? or to die in a mad-house? one being expressed as much as the other.

Brothers, however, in his prophecy, had mentioned *dates*, which were stubborn things. Yet the failure of the accomplishment of this prophecy may have helped to recommend "the Woman clothed with the Sun!" who now arose, as might be thought somewhat *mal à propos*, in the West. Such was Joanna Southcote. The Scriptures had said: "The sceptre shall not depart' from Israel, nor a lawgiver from between his feet, until Shiloh come; and to him *shall the gathering of my people be.*" When Brothers was incarcerated in a madhouse in Clerkenwell, Joanna, then living in service at Exeter, persuaded herself that she held converse with the devil, and communion with the Holy Ghost, by whom she pretended to be inspired. When the day of dread that was to leave London in ruins, while it ushered forth Brothers and Sharp on their holy errand, passed calmly over, the seers of coming events began to look out for new ground, and to prevaricate most unblushingly. The *days* of prophecy, said Sharp, were sometimes weeks or months; nay, according to one text, a thousand years were but as a single day, and one day was but as a thousand years. But he finally clung to the deathbed prediction of Jacob, supported as it was by the ocular demonstration of the coming Shiloh. In vain Sir William Drummond explained that Shiloh was in reality the ancient Asiatic name of a star in Scorpio; or that Joanna herself sold for a trifle, or gave away in her loving-kindness, the impression of a trumpery seal, which at the Great Day was to constitute the discriminating mark between the righteous and the ungodly. We shall hear more of Sharp in association with Joanna Southcote, presently.

Sharp died poor: he earned much money, but his egregious credulity accounts for its dispersion. He was an epicure in his living, he grew corpulent, and had gout; he died of dropsy, at Chiswick, July 25th, 1824, and was interred in the churchyard of that hamlet, near De Loutherbourg, for whom, at one period, he entertained much mystic reverence.

This great engraver, this William Sharp, was an enthusiast for human freedom. He engraved, from a liking for the man, Northcote's portrait of Sir Francis Burdett; and bestowed unusual care on an engraving after Stothard's beautiful bistre-drawing of "Boadicea animating the Britons." For many years preceding his death he was a wholesale believer in Joanna Southcote; as we have already seen—and he had implicit faith in mystical doctrines; of his portrait of Brothers, Horne Tooke well observed, that, coupled with its extraordinary inscription, it "exhibited one of the most eminent proofs of human genius and human weakness ever contained on the same piece of paper."

Burnet, the engraver, used to relate that Sharp had an ingenious way of carrying a proof print to a purchaser, in an umbrella contrived to serve two additional duties,—a print-case and a walking-stick.

When John Martin exhibited his picture of Belshazzar's Feast, Sharp called upon him at his house, introduced himself, praised his picture, and asked permission to engrave it. "That I was flattered by a request of the kind from so great an artist," says Martin, "you will readily imagine; and I so expressed myself." Sharp felt pleased. "My belief," said Sharp, "is, that yours is a divine work—an emanation immediately from the Almighty; and my belief further is, that while I am engaged on so divine a work, I shall never die." When Martin told this story, he added, with a smile, his eyes twinkling with mischief, "Poor Sharp! a wild enthusiast, but—a masterly engraver."[*]

Richard Brothers was born at Placentia, in Newfoundland, and had served in the navy, but resigned his commission, because, to use his own words, he "conceived the military life to be totally repugnant to the duties of Christianity, and he could not conscientiously receive the wages of plunder, bloodshed, and murder." This step reduced him to great poverty, and he appears to have suffered much in consequence. His mind was already shaken, and his privations and solitary reflections seem at length to have entirely overthrown it. The first instance of his madness appears to have been his belief that he could restore sight to the blind. He next began to see visions and to prophesy, and soon became persuaded that he was commissioned by Heaven to lead back the Jews to Palestine. It was in the latter part of 1794 that he announced, through the medium of the press, his high destiny. His rhapsody bore the title of "A revealed Knowledge of the Prophecies and Times,

[*] "New Materials for Lives of English Engravers," by Peter Cunningham. *Builder*, 1863.

Book the First. Wrote under the direction of the Lord God, and published by his sacred command; it being the first sign of warning for the benefit of all nations. Containing, with other great and remarkable things, not revealed to any other person on earth, the restoration of the Hebrews to Jerusalem, by the year 1798: under their revealed prince and prophet." A second part speedily followed, which purported to relate " particularly to the present time, the present war, and the prophecy now fulfilling : containing, with other great and remarkable things, not revealed to any other person on earth, the sudden and perpetual fall of the Turkish, German, and Russian Empires." Among many similar flights in this second part, was one which described visions revealing to him the intended destruction of London, and claimed for the prophet the merit of having saved the city by his intercession with the Deity.*

Brothers gained a great number of partisans, not only among uneducated persons, but among men of talent. We have seen Sharp, the engraver, as his devoted disciple. Among these followers was Mr. Halhed, who had been a schoolfellow of Sheridan at Harrow; they also had a sort of literary partnership, and they fell passionately in love with the same woman, Miss Linley. Halhed was a profound scholar, a man of wit, and a member of the House of Commons; he published pamphlets in advocacy of the prophetic mission of Brothers, and even made a motion in the House in favour of the prince of the Jews, as Brothers delegated himself.

Brothers took more of a political turn than his com-

---

* Sketches of Imposture, Deception, and Credulity. Second Edition. 1840.

panions. He had been a lieutenant in the navy, and during the years 1792–3–4, greatly disturbed the minds of the credulous with his *prophecies.* We have said that he styled himself the "Nephew of God," and predicted the destruction of all sovereigns; he also foretold the downfall of the naval power of Great Britain.

His writings, founded on erroneous explanations of the Scriptures, at length made so much noise, that Government found it expedient to interfere, and on the 14th of March, 1795, he was apprehended at his lodgings, No. 58, in Paddington Street, under a warrant from the Secretary of State. After a long examination before the Privy Council, in which Brothers persisted in the divinity of his legation, he was committed to the custody of a State messenger. On the 27th he was declared a lunatic, by a jury appointed under a commission of lunacy, assembled at the King's Arms, in Palace Yard, and was subsequently removed to a private madhouse at Islington. While here, he continued to see visions and to pour forth his rhapsodies in print. One of these productions was a letter of two hundred pages, to "Miss Cott, the recorded daughter of King David, and future Queen of the Hebrews, with an Address to the Members of His Britannic Majesty's Council." The lady to whom this letter was addressed had become an inmate of the same asylum with Brothers, and he became so enamoured of her, that he discovered her to be "the recorded daughter of both David and Solomon," and his spouse "by divine ordinance." Brothers was subsequently removed to Bedlam; but in the year 1806 was discharged by the authority of Lord Chancellor Erskine. He died in Upper Baker Street, on the 25th of January, 1824. He was seen in the street a few days before his death, walking with great difficulty, and apparently in the last stage of consumption. It is recorded that the minister who attended Brothers in his last moments died of a broken heart; and the medical man under whose care he had been confined, committed suicide.

Brothers appears to have unwittingly suggested to Coleridge and Southey the clever poem of the *Devil's Walk*, by the mad prophet asserting that he had seen the devil walk leisurely into London one day!

THE SPENCEANS.

Early in the present century there arose in the metropolis a religio-political sect, which took its name from an itinerant bookseller, named T. Spence, who formed a sort of Constitution on the principle that "all human beings are equal by nature and before the law, and have a continual and *inalienable property* in the earth and in its natural productions;" and consequently that "*every man, woman, and child,* whether born in wedlock or not (for Nature and Justice know nothing of illegitimacy), is entitled quarterly to an equal share of the rents of the parish where they have settled." This he called "the Constitution of *Spensonia;*" and the Abstract from which we have quoted he called "A Receipt to make a *Millennium,* or Happy World." By this reference and by some allusions to the Jewish economy, he also gave his system a slight connection with religion— but it was very slight; for he neither regarded the precepts of the moral law, nor the doctrines of the Gospel. He admitted, however, of a Sabbath every fifth day; but only as a day of rest and amusement—not for any purposes of devotion. A scheme somewhat similar to the above was formed in the time of the English Commonwealth, and it is probable Spence may have borrowed his system partly from that source.

Spence was punished for his vagaries; for, in 1801, he was sentenced to pay a fine 50*l.* and to suffer twelve months' imprisonment for publishing *Spence's Restorer of Society,* which was deemed a seditious libel. Spence died in October, 1814.

JOANNA SOUTHCOTE, AND THE COMING OF SHILOH.

This "dropsical old woman," Joanna Southcote, was a native of Exeter, and was born in April, 1750. She was employed chiefly in that city as a domestic servant, and up to the age of forty or thereabout, she seems to have aspired to no higher occupation. But having joined the Methodists, and become acquainted with one Saunderson, who laid claim to the spirit of prophecy, the notion of a like pretension was gradually communicated to Joanna. She wrote prophecies, and she dictated prophecies, sometimes in prose and sometimes in rhymed doggerel; her influence extended, and the number of her followers increased; she announced herself as the woman spoken of in the 12th chapter of Revelation, and obtained considerable sums by the sale of *seals*, which were to secure the salvation of those who purchased them. Her confidence increased with her reputation, and she challenged the bishop and clergy of Exeter to a public investigation of her miraculous powers, but they treated her challenge with contemptuous neglect, which she and her converts imputed to fear.

By degrees, Exeter became too narrow a stage for her performances, and she came to London on the invitation and at the expense of Sharp, the eminent engraver. She was very illiterate, but wrote numerous letters and pamphlets, and her prophecies, nearly unintelligible as they were, had a large sale. In the course of her Mission, as she called it, promising a speedy approach of the Millennium, she employed a boy, who pretended to see visions, and attempted, instead of writing, to adjust them on the walls of her chapel, "the House of God," a large building which adjoined the Elephant and Castle Inn, at Newington Butts. A schism took place among her followers, one of whom, named Carpenter, took possession of the place, and wrote against her; not denying her Mission, but asserting that she had exceeded it.

It may, however, be interesting here to describe what may be termed the *modus operandi* of the delusion. Great pains were now taken to ascertain the truth of her commission. "From the end of 1792," says Mr. Sharp, who, we have already seen, was the most devout of her believers, "to the end of 1794, her writings were sealed up with great caution, and remained secure till they were conveyed by me to High House, Paddington; and the box which contained them was opened in the beginning of January, 1803. Her writings were examined during seven days, and the result of this long scrutiny was the unanimous decision of twenty-three persons *appointed by divine command*, as well as of thirty-five others that were present, *that her calling was of God.*" They came to this conclusion from the fulfilment of the prophecies contained in these writings, and to which she appealed with confidence and triumph. It was a curious circumstance, however, that her handwriting was illegible. Her remark on this occasion was, " This must be, to fulfil the Bible. Every vision that John saw in heaven must take place on earth; and here is the sealed book, that no one can read! "

A protection was provided for all those who subscribed their names as volunteers, for the destruction of Satan's kingdom. To every subscriber a folded paper was delivered, endorsed with his name, and secured with the impression of Joanna's seal in red wax: this powerful talisman consisted of a circle enclosing the two letters J. C., with a star above and below, and the following words, "The sealed of the Lord, the Elect, Precious, Man's Redemption, to inherit the tree of life, to be made heirs of God and joint-heirs of Jesus Christ." The whole was authenticated by the signature of the prophetess in her illegible characters, and the person thus provided was said to be *sealed*. Conformably, however, to the 7th chapter of the Revelation, the number of those highly protected persons was not to exceed 144,000.*

Early in her last year, she secluded herself from male society, and fancied that she was with child—by the Holy Spirit!—that she was to bring forth the

* *Sketches of Imposture, Deception, and Credulity.* Second Edition. 1840.

Shiloh promised by Jacob Bryan, and which she pretended was to be the second appearance of the Messiah! This child was to be born before the end of harvest, on the 19th of October, 1814, at midnight, as she was certain it was impossible for her to survive undelivered till Christmas. The harvest, however, was ended, and Christmas came, without the fulfilment of her predictions. Some months previously, Joanna had declared her pretended situation, and invited the opinion of the faculty. Several medical men admitted her pregnancy, others doubted; and some, among whom was Dr. Sims, denied it. There was, indeed, the external appearance of pregnancy; and, in consequence, the enthusiasm of her followers, who are said to have amounted at that time to no fewer than one hundred thousand, was greatly excited. An expensive cradle was made, and considerable sums were contributed, in order to have other things prepared in a style worthy of the expected Shiloh. Among the costly presents made to her was a Bible which cost 40*l.*, and the superb cot or cradle 200*l.*, besides a richly-embroidered coverlid, &c.

It was now deemed necessary, to satisfy certain worldly doubts, that medical men should be called in to give a professional opinion as to the fact, from a consideration of all the symptoms, and without reference to miraculous agency. One of these gentlemen, Mr. Mathias, appearing incredulous of Joanna's pregnancy, was asked "if he would believe when he saw the infant at the breast?" He protested against a question so blasphemous; but his further attendance was dispensed with, as she had been answered, "that he had drawn a wrong judgment of her disorder." Mr.

Mathias, too, let out some strange information, showing that Joanna passed much of her time in bed, ate much and often, and prayed never; but to keep up the delusion that she was with child, she, like other ladies in that situation, had longings. On one occasion she longed for asparagus, and ate one hundred and sixty heads, at no small cost, before she allayed her liking.

Dr. Richard Reece* was now consulted by Joanna as to her pregnancy. He was not a proselyte to her religious views, but is thought to have been deceived by her symptoms, and declared to a deputation of her followers his belief of her being pregnant by some means or other. As her supposed time of deliverance approached, Joanna fell ill, and began to doubt her inspiration, most probably by her fears awakening her conscience; and as Dr. Reece continued in attendance, he witnessed the following scene:—"Five or six of her friends, who were waiting in an adjoining room, being admitted into her bed-chamber, she desired them," says Dr. Reece, "to be seated round her bed; when, spending a few minutes in adjusting the bed-clothes with

* Dr. Richard Reece was the son of a clergyman, and was articled to a country surgeon. In 1800 he settled in practice in Henrietta Street, Covent Garden, and published *The Medical and Chirurgical Pharmacopœia*; and having received a degree of M.D. from a Scotch university, he exercised the three professions of physician, apothecary, and chemist. He likewise published several volumes upon various medical subjects; and established himself in the western wing of the Egyptian Hall, Piccadilly. He assailed quackery with much boldness; hence his mistake as to Joanna Southcote was made the most of. He had also considerable practice, by which he gained money. He published *A Plain Narrative of the Circumstances attending the last Illness and Death of Joanna Southcote.*

seeming attention, and placing before her a white handkerchief, she addressed them in the following words: 'My friends, some of you have known me nearly twenty-five years, and all of you not less than twenty; when you have heard me speak of my prophecies, you have sometimes heard me say that I doubted my inspiration; but, at the same time, you would never let me despair. When I have been alone, it has often appeared delusion; but when the communication was made to me, I did not in the least doubt. Feeling, as I now do feel, that my dissolution is drawing near, and that a day or two may terminate my life, it all appears delusion.' She was by this exertion quite exhausted, and wept bitterly.

On reviving in a little time, she observed that it was very extraordinary, that, after spending all her life in investigating the Bible, it should please the Lord to inflict that heavy burden on her. She concluded this discourse by requesting that everything on this occasion might be conducted with decency. She then wept; and all her followers present seemed deeply affected, and some of them shed tears. 'Mother,' said one (it is believed Mr. Howe), 'we will commit your instructions to paper, and rest assured they shall be conscientiously followed.' They were accordingly written down with much solemnity, and signed by herself, with her hand placed on the Bible in the bed. This being finished, Mr. Howe again observed to her, 'Mother, your feelings are *human*; we know that you are a favourite woman of God, and that you will produce the promised child; and whatever you may say to the contrary will not diminish our faith.' This assurance revived her, and the scene of crying was changed with her to laughter."

Mr. Howe was not the only one of her disciples whose sturdy belief was not to be shaken by the most discouraging symptoms. Colonel Harwood, a zealous believer, entreated Dr. Reece not to retract his opinion as to her pregnancy, though the latter now saw the folly and absurdity of it; and when the Colonel approached the bed on which Joanna was about to expire, and she said to him, " What does the Lord mean by this ? I am certainly dying;" he replied, smiling, " No, no, you will not die; or if you should, you will return again."

About ten weeks before Christmas she was confined to her bed, and took very little sustenance, until pain and sickness greatly reduced her. On the night of the 19th of October, a very large number of persons assembled in the street where she lived—Manchester Street, Manchester Square *—to hear the announcement of the looked-for advent; but the hour of midnight passed over, and the crowd were only induced to disperse by being informed that Joanna had fallen into a trance.

Mr. Want, a surgeon, had warned her of her approaching end; but she insisted that all her sufferings were only preparatory to the birth of the Shiloh. At last she admitted the possibility of a temporary dissolution, and expressly ordered that means should be taken to preserve warmth in her for four days, after which she was to revive and be delivered. On December 27th, 1814, she actually died, in her sixty-fifth year, she

* One of Joanna's London residences was at No. 17, Weston Place, opposite the Small Pox Hospital.

having previously declared that if she was deceived, she was, at all events, misled by some spirit, either good or evil. In four days after, she was opened in the presence of fifteen medical men, when it was demonstrated that she was not pregnant, and that her complaint arose from bile and flatulency, from indulgence and want of exercise. In her last hour she was attended by Ann Underwood, her secretary; Mr. Tozer, who was called her high priest; Colonel Harwood, and some other persons of property; and so determined were her followers to be deceived, that neither death nor dissection could convince them of their error. The silencing of her preacher, Tozer, and shutting up of the chapel which he had opened, had by no means diminished the number of her believers.

While the surgeons were investigating the causes of her death, and the mob were gathering without-doors, in anticipation of a riot or a miracle, Sharp, the engraver, continued to maintain that she was not dead, but entranced. And, at a subsequent period, when he was sitting to Mr. Haydon for his portrait, he predicted to the painter, that Joanna would reappear in the month of July, 1822. "But suppose she should not?" said Haydon. "I tell you she will," retorted Sharp; "but if she would not, nothing should shake my faith in her Divine Mission." And those who were near Sharp's person during his last illness, state that in this belief he died. Even when she was really dead, the same blind confidence remained. Mrs. Townley, with whom she had lived, said cheerfully, "she would return to life, for it had been foretold twenty years before."

Mr. Sharp also asserted that the soul of Joanna

would return, it having gone to heaven to legitimate the child which would be born. Though symptoms of decomposition arose, Mr. Sharp still persisted in keeping the body hot, according to the directions which she had given on her death-bed, in the hope of a revival. Dr. Reece having remarked that if the ceremony of her marriage continued two days longer, the tenement would not be habitable on her return, "The greater will be the miracle," said Mr. Sharp. Consent at last was given to inspect the body, and all the disciples stood round, smoking tobacco. Their disappointment was excessive at finding nothing to warrant the long-cherished opinion, but their faith remained immovable.

Her corpse was removed on the 31st of December to an undertaker's in Oxford Street, where it remained till the interment. On the 2nd of January, 1815, it was carried in a hearse, so remarkably plain, as to have the appearance of one returning from rather than proceeding to church; it was accompanied by one coach, equally plain, in which were three mourners. In this manner they proceeded to the new cemetery adjoining St. John's Wood Chapel, with such secrecy, that there was scarcely a person in the ground unconnected with it. A fourth person arrived as the body was being borne to the grave; this was supposed to be Tozer. The grave was taken, and notice given of the funeral, under the name of Goddard. Neither the minister of St. John's, who read the service, nor any of the subordinate persons belonging to the chapel, were apprised of the real name about to be buried, till the funeral reached the ground. The grave is on the west side, opposite No. 44 on the wall, and twenty-six feet from it, where is a flat stone with this inscription :—

"In Memory of
Joanna Southcote,
Who departed this life Dec. 27, 1814, aged 65 years.

> While through all thy wondrous days,
> Heaven and earth enraptur'd gazed,
> While vain Sages think they know
> Secrets Thou Alone canst show ;
> Time alone will tell what hour
> Thou'lt appear to ' Greater ' Power.
>
> *Sabineus.*"

On a black marble tablet, let into the wall opposite to the above spot, is the following inscription, in gilt letters :—

"Behold the time shall come, that these Tokens which I have told Thee, shall come to pass, and the Bride shall Appear, and She coming forth, shall be seen, that now is withdrawn from the Earth."
2nd of Esdras, chap. 7, verse 26.

"For the Vision is yet for an appointed time, but at the end it shall speak, and Not Lie, though it tarry, Wait for it ; Because it will surely come, it will not tarry."
Habakkuk, chap. ii. ver. 3d.

"And whosoever is delivered from the Foresaid evils, shall see My Wonders."   2nd of Esdras, chap. 7th, ver. 27th.

(See her writings.)

This Tablet was Erected,
By the sincere Friends of the above,
Anno Domini, 1828.

The number of Joanna's followers continued to be very great for many years after her death : they believed that there would be a resurrection of her body, and that she was still to be the mother of the promised Shiloh.

The Southcotonians also still met and committed various extravagancies. In 1817 a party of the disciples, conceiving themselves directed by God to proclaim the coming of the Shiloh on earth, for this purpose marched in procession through Temple Bar, when the leader sounded a brazen trumpet, and declared the coming of Shiloh, the Prince of Peace; while his wife shouted, "Wo! wo! to the inhabitants of the earth, because of the coming of Shiloh!" The crowd pelted the fanatics with mud, some disturbance ensued, and some of the disciples were taken into custody, and had to answer for their conduct before a magistrate. A considerable number of the sect appear to have remained in Devonshire, Joanna's native county.

The whole affair was one of the most monstrous delusions of our time. "It is not long since," says Sir Benjamin Brodie, in his *Psychological Inquiries,* 3rd edition, "no small number of persons, and not merely those belonging to the uneducated classes, were led to believe that a dropsical old woman was about to be the mother of the real Shiloh." The writer, however, adds that Joanna was "not altogether an impostor, but in part the victim of her own imagination."

A small square volume of Southcotonian hymns was published, entitled, "Hymns or Spiritual Songs," composed from the prophetical writings of Joanna Southcote, by P. Pullen, and published by her order. "And I saw an angel," &c.—Rev. xx. 1, 2. The "Little Flock" are thus addressed by their "Poet Laureat:"—"By permission of our 'spiritual mother, Johanna Southcote,' I have composed the following hymns from her prophetic writings; and should you feel that pleasure in singing them to the honour and glory of God, for the establishment of *her blessed kingdom*, and the destruction of Satan's power, as I have felt in the perusal of her writings, I am fully persuaded that they will ultimately tend to your ever-lasting happiness, and I hope and trust to the speedy completion of what we ardently long and daily pray for, namely, 'HIS KINGDOM *to come, that* HIS *will may be done on earth as it is in heaven, and that we may be delivered from evil;*' that that blessed prayer may be soon, very soon fulfilled, is the earnest desire of your fellow-labourer, Phillip Pullen. London, 16th September, 1807."

"The reader of these Hymns," says a Correspondent of *Notes and Queries*, "will not feel the spiritual elevation spoken of by Mr. Pullen, unless, perhaps, he has, like him, drunk at that fountain-head, *i.e.* studied the 'prophetic writings:' the songs for the now 'scattered sheep' being rhapsodical to a degree, and intelligible only to such an audience as that some of your sexa-genarian readers may have found assembled under the roof of the 'House of God.' The leading titles to these Hymns are, 'True Explanations of the Bible,' 'Strange Effects of Faith,' 'Words in Season,' 'Communications and Visions,' not published, 'Cautions to the Sealed,' 'Answers to the Books of Garrett and Brothers,' 'Rival Enthusiasts,' and such like. Pullen, their poet, was formerly a schoolmaster, and afterwards an accountant in London, and is called by Upcott, in his *Dictionary of Living Authors*, 1816, an empiric.

"A couplet in the first hymn bears an asterisk, intimating that it is published at the particular re-quest of Johanna Southcote; it is short, and will afford at once a specimen of the poetical *calibre* of the volume, and the pith of the 'Spiritual Mother's' views :—

> " ' To FATHER, SON, *and* HOLY GHOST,
> *One* GOD *in power* THREE,
> *Bring back the ancient world that's lost*
> *To all mankind—and me.'* "

Joanna Southcote published many pamphlets, and one of her disciples, Elias Carpenter, issued several curious and mystical tracts. The lists of these publications are too long to be quoted here. Probably the most complete collection preserved of the extraordinary productions by and relating to this wonderful imposture, was that made by Sir Francis Freeling, together with cuttings from all the newspapers, and bound in 7 vols. 8vo, 1803 to 1815. The titles of the principal tracts fill a page of Thorpe's Catalogue, Part III., 1850. For another very rare collection, in 6 vols., 8vo, see J. C. Hotten's Catalogue for October, 1858. Perhaps the most tangible explanation attempted of Joanna Southcote's mission is that by Carpenter, in the *Missionary Magazine*, 1814. To Carpenter is attributed the following anonymous work, "The Extraordinary Cure of a Piccadilly Patient, or Dr. Reece physicked by Six Female Physicians, 1815."

THE FOUNDER OF MORMONISM.

Joseph Smith, "the Prophet," has left to the world a short sketch of himself and his system of Mormonism, which is one of the most remarkable movements of modern times. He was born in the State of Vermont, in 1805, and was brought up to husbandry. When about fourteen years old, he began to reflect upon the importance of being prepared for a future state, and inquiring into the plan of salvation. He tells us:—"I retired to a secret place in a grove, and began to call upon the Lord. While fervently engaged in supplication, my mind was taken away from the objects with which I was surrounded, and I was enwrapt in a heavenly vision, and saw two glorious personages, who exactly resembled each other in feature and likeness, surrounded with a brilliant light which eclipsed the sun at noonday. They told me that all the religious sects were believing in incorrect doctrines, and that none of them was acknowledged of God as his Church and Kingdom. And I was expressly commanded to *go not after them*, at the same time receiving a promise that the fullness of the Gospel should at some future time be made known to me."

This "fullness of the Gospel" was that revealed in the *Book of Mormon*, of the discovery of which and its contents he says:—"On the evening of the 21st of September, A.D. 1823, while I was praying unto God and endeavouring to exercise faith in the precious promises of Scripture, on a sudden a light like that of day, only of a far purer and more glorious appearance and brightness, burst into the room; indeed, the first sight was as though the house was filled with consuming fire. The appearance produced a shock that affected the whole body. In a moment a personage stood before me surrounded with a glory yet greater than that with which I was already surrounded. The messenger proclaimed himself to be an angel of God, sent to bring the joyful tidings, that the covenant which God made with ancient Israel was at hand to be fulfilled; that the preparatory work for the second coming of the Messiah was speedily to commence; that the time was at hand for the Gospel in all its fullness to be preached in power unto all nations, that a people might be prepared for the Millenial reign.

" I was informed also concerning the aboriginal inhabitants of this country (America), and shown who they were and from whence they came; a brief sketch of their origin, progress, civilization, laws, governments, of their righteousness and iniquity, and the blessings of God being finally withdrawn from them as a people, was made known unto me. I was also told where there were deposited some plates, on which was engraven an abridgment of the records of the ancient prophets that had existed on this continent. The angel appeared to me three times the same night, and unfolded the same things. After having received many visits from the angels of God, unfolding the majesty and glory of the events that should transpire in the last days, on the morning of the 22nd of September, 1827, the angel of the Lord delivered the records into my hands.

" These records were engraven on plates which had the appearance of gold; each plate was six inches wide and eight inches long, and not quite so thick as common tin. They were filled with engravings in Egyptian characters, and bound together in a volume, as the leaves of a book, with three rings running throughout the whole: it was partly sealed. With the records was found a curious instrument, which the ancients called *Urim and Thummim*, which consisted of two transparent stones set in the rim on a bow fastened to a breastplate. Through the medium of the *Urim and Thummim* I translated the record by the gift and power of God.

" In this important and interesting book, the history of ancient America is unfolded from its first settlement by a colony that came from the Tower of Babel, at the confusion of languages, to the beginning of the fifth century of the Christian era."

It should here be noticed that the Prophet's account of his early life, before the appearance of the angel and the discovery of the plates, is remarkably vague. He had been very rudely educated, and for some time got a living by trying for mineral veins by a divining rod; and some affirm that, like Sidrophel, he used " the devil's looking-glass—a stone," and was consulted as to the discovery of hidden treasures, whence he had come to be commonly known as the " money-digger ; " and on one occasion he had been, at the instigation of a disappointed client, imprisoned as a vagabond. He is also stated to have carried off and married a Miss Hales, during the interval between the first angelic visitation and the discovery of the plates of Nephi.

As to the *Book of Mormon* itself, the authorship has been claimed for one Solomon Spalding, a Presbyterian preacher, who, having fallen into poverty, composed a religious romance, entitled *The Manuscript Found*, which professed to be a narrative of the migration of the Lost Tribes of Israel from Jerusalem to America, and their subsequent adventures on the continent. The work was written, but Spalding could not find anyone who would print it, and ten years after his death, the manuscript was carried by his widow to New York, and was stolen by, or somehow got into the hands of, Smith, or his early associate, Rigdon. There is nothing in the book to contradict the supposition that it is the work of Smith himself—for as to its being a divine revelation, the most cursory examination of the book will convince an educated man of the utter improbability of that, if its possibility were otherwise conceivable. Be the author who he may, Smith having obtained the book—whether from Solomon Spalding's travelling-chest, his own brain, or the stone-box which the angel discovered to him—thought it behoved him to make his treasure known. At first he told the members of his own and his father's household, and they believed the truth of his mission and the reality of the gift. But, he says: "As soon as the news of this discovery was made known, false reports, misrepresentations, and slander flew, as on the wings of the wind, in every direction. My house was frequently beset by mobs and evil-designing persons: several times I was shot at, and very narrowly escaped; and every device was made to get the plates away from me, but the power and blessing of God attended me, and several began to believe my testimony."

Among these was a farmer, Martin Harris, whom Smith persuaded to conver this stock into money in order to assist in printing the book. But Harris wished first to consult some scholar, and Smith entrusted him with a copy of a portion of one of the golden plates to carry to New York. Harris took the copy to Dr. Anthon, who was unable to make out the characters, which he described to be "reformed Egyptian"—and this is one of the proofs "cited by Mormonite teachers of the authenticity of the book." But Dr. Anthon's account is very different: he tells us that from the first he considered the work an imposture, and his account of it is the only description which has been published, and is as follows: —"The paper was a singular scrawl. It consisted of all kinds of crooked characters disposed in columns, and had evidently been prepared by some person who had before him at the time a book containing various alphabets. Greek and Hebrew letters, crosses and flourishes, Roman letters inverted or placed sidewise, were arranged in perpendicular columns, and the whole ended in a rude delineation of a circle divided into various compartments, decked with various strange marks, and evidently copied after the Mexican calendar, given by Humboldt, but copied in such a way as not to betray the source whence it was derived."

No sooner was the discovery published than the faithful as well as unbelievers flocked to obtain a sight of the marvellous plates, and the prophet and his mother were driven to great shifts to conceal them. At length it was revealed to Smith that the desired sight should be vouchsafed to three witnesses, whose " testimony" is prefixed to every printed copy of the *Book of Mormon*. These witnesses aver, in their strange language, "that an angel of God came down from heaven, and he brought and lay before our eyes, that we beheld and saw the plates, and the engravings thereon." But a. more specific testimony was given by eight other witnesses, to whom Smith was permitted to show the plates. Mrs. Smith says that these eight men went with Joseph into a secret place, " where the family were in the habit of offering up their secret devotions. They went to this place because it had been revealed to Joseph that the plates would be carried by one of the ancient Nephites. Here it was that these eight witnesses, whose names are recorded in the *Book of Mormon*, looked upon and handled them." The witnesses themselves say :—" We have seen and hefted, and know of a surety that the said Smith has got the plates of which we have spoken." Of these eight witnesses, three were members of Smith's own family. After these witnesses had seen the plates, Mrs. Smith tells us, "the angel again made his appearance to Joseph, at which time Joseph delivered up the plates into the angel's hands;" and Joseph himself says:—"He (the angel) has them in charge to this day;" thus disposing of any demand to see the original plates. Smith carried on the process of *translating the plates* by retiring behind a screen, where he read the plates through the "curious instrument called the Urim and Thummim," while a scribe outside the screen wrote as he dictated.

The *Book of Mormon* was published in 1830. In the previous year Smith and his scribe had been baptized by an angel, and power given them to baptize others.

Smith may now carry on the narrative. On April 6, 1830, "The Church of Jesus Christ of Latter Day Saints" was first organized in Manchester, Ontario county, State of New York. Some few were called and ordained by the spirit of revelation and prophecy, and began to preach as the Spirit gave them utterance, and though weak, yet they were strengthened by the power of God; and many were brought to repentance, were immersed in the water, and were filled with the Holy Ghost by the laying on of hands. They saw visions and prophesied, devils were cast out, and the sick healed by the laying-on of hands. From that time the work rolled forth with astonishing rapidity, and churches were formed in the States of New York, Pennsylvania, Ohio, Indiana, Illinois, and Missouri. In the last-named State, a considerable settlement was formed in Jackson county. Great numbers joined the Church; "we made large purchases of land, our farms teemed

with plenty, and peace and happiness were enjoyed in
our domestic circle and throughout our neighbourhood;
but, as we could not associate with our neighbours—
who were many of them of the basest of men, and had
fled from the face of civilized society to the frontier
country to escape the hands of justice—in their midnight
revels, their Sabbath-breaking, horse-racing, they commenced at first to ridicule, then to persecute, and
finally an organized mob assembled and burnt our
houses, tarred and feathered, and whipped many of our
brethren [Smith himself was tarred and feathered], and
finally drove them from their habitations; these, house-
less and homeless, contrary to law, justice, and humanity, had to wander on the bleak prairies till the
children left their blood on the prairie. This took
place in November, 1833." The Government, he
says, "winked at these proceedings, and the result was
that a great many of them died; many children were
left orphans; wives, widows; and husbands, widowers.
Our farms were taken possession of by the mob, many
thousands of cattle, sheep, horses, and hogs were taken,
and our household goods, store goods, and printing-
presses were broken, taken, or otherwise destroyed."

Driven from Jackson, the Mormonites settled in Clay
county, and being threatened with violence, removed to
Caldwell and Davies counties. Here their numbers
rapidly increased: but troubles again came upon them;
their bank failed, and Smith was obliged to conceal
himself; and finally, by an "extraordinary order" of
the Governor of Missouri, in 1838, they were violently ejected from their homes, plundered of their
goods, and subjected, the women especially, to the most
frightful atrocities.

Being thus expelled from Missouri, they settled in Illinois, and in 1839, on the Mississippi, laid the foundation of their famous city, Nauvoo, or *the Beautiful*, which was incorporated in 1840. Smith dwells with great delight on this city, which he had seen rise up under his presidency from a wild tract to be a place of "1,500 well-built houses, and more than 15,000 inhabitants, all looking to him for temporal as well as spiritual guidance." He describes as provided for,—"the University of Nauvoo, where all the arts and sciences will grow with the growth and strengthen with the strength of this beloved city of the Saints of the Last Days." But the grand feature of the city was the Great Temple, which Smith thus sketches: "The Temple of God, now in the course of erection, being already raised one story, and which is 120 feet by 80 feet, of stone with polished pilasters, of an entire new order of architecture, will be a splendid house for the worship of God, as well as an unique wonder of the world, it being built by the direct revelation of Jesus Christ for the salvation of the living and the dead."

The progress of Nauvoo was even more rapid than that of any of the preceding places. Dangers of various kinds beset Smith, but he escaped from them all; and by a provision in the city charter, formed an independent civic militia, of which he was lieutenant-general: and he consolidated his spiritual government, and made careful provision for an ample succession of hardy as well as zealous missionaries. But Smith becoming embroiled with the civil authority of the State, got up a sort of social scheme of his own, and was actually in 1844 nominated for President. The storm now gathered around him; the "gentile" inhabitants of Nauvoo, who

had always been most troublesome, supported by some
of the dissatisfied among the saints, established an
opposition newspaper, which denounced the morals of
the Prophet, as well as his system of government ; the
city council condemned the newspaper to silence ; and
a mob broke into the office and destroyed the presses.
The proprietors charged some of the Mormon leaders
with inciting the mob to this act, and they were arrested,
but set at liberty. The injured parties now carried
their complaint to the Governor of Illinois, who had
long been waiting for a legal opportunity to crush the
power of Smith ; he was arrested on a charge of treason
and sedition, June 24th, 1844. He put Nauvoo into
a state of defence, and his militia was drawn out ; but
to avoid bloodshed, on the approach of the State troops
Smith surrendered, on a promise of safety till his legal
trial ; and he, with others, was committed to Carthage
jail. A guard, small in number, and purposely chosen
from among Smith's declared enemies, was set over
them ; but on the 27th of June, a mob of about two
hundred armed ruffians broke into the jail, and firing
at the door of the room, shot Smith's brother Hyram
dead at once. Joseph Smith attempted to escape by
the window, but was knocked down, carried out, and
shot. His dying exclamation is said to have been,
"O Lord my God." His body was given up to his
friends, and buried with great solemnity.

Smith had estimated his followers at 150,000, from
among almost every civilized people on the face of the
earth. He had become intoxicated with power and
prosperity, and was lustful and intemperate. In the
Mormon creed, polygamy is not referred to ; though
there is no doubt that in the last year of Smith's life

this was one of the charges brought against the Mormonites. Still, the doctrine of a *plurality of wives* was never openly taught until after Smith's death, and if he proclaimed it at all, he confined the revelation to the initiated. He is said, however, to have sealed to himself "*plural wives*," as the Mormons express it, about two years before his death; and the privilege may have been accorded to some of the chief of his followers.

He was still regarded as the glorified prophet and martyr. In Nauvoo the popular cry was for revenge, but this was changed to forbearance. Brigham Young was elected as Smith's successor; and he removed his people beyond the farthest settlements of his countrymen, convinced that only in a country far distant from societies living under the established forms, could the vision of the Prophet stand a chance of realization. They were allowed by their enemies to finish their beautiful temple ; and this being accomplished in September, 1846, the last band of the brethren departed from the land of their hopes to seek a new land of promise.

They chose the site of their new city beyond the Great Salt Lake, in the territory of Utah, to be their appointed Zion, principally governed by the maxims of the Mormon leaders, and Brigham Young, the Mormon prophet. We may here state briefly that the Mormons· profess to be a separate people, living under a patriarchal dispensation, with prophets, elders, and apostles, who have the rule in temporal as well as religious matters, their doctrines being embodied in the *Book of Mormon;* that they look for a literal gathering of Israel in this western land; and that here

Christ will reign personally for a millennium, when the earth will be restored to its paradisaical glory.

Nauvoo, after the departure of the Mormons, became the seat of a colony of French communists, or Icarians, under the direction of M. Cabet, who were, however, far from successful. The population has much dwindled. The great Mormon temple of Nauvoo was, in October, 1848, set on fire by an incendiary and destroyed.

HUNTINGTON, THE PREACHER.

William Huntington, who, by virtue of his preaching, came to ride in his coach, and marry the titled widow of a Lord Mayor, was no ordinary man. He was born in the year 1774, in the Weald of Kent, between Goudhurst and Cranbrook, where his father was a day-labourer. The boy worked in various ways, and having "a call," he became an Arminian preacher, at the same time that at Thames Ditton he carried coals on the river, at 10*s.* a-week: hence he was generally known as the *Coalheaver.* He preached inordinately long sermons, sometimes of two hours' duration; his prayers were mostly made up of Scriptural phrases.

It suited the purpose of Huntington to represent himself as living *under* the special favour of Providence, because he intended to live by it: that is, upon the credulity of those whom he could persuade to believe him: and the history of his success, which he published under the title of *God the Guardian of the Poor, and the Bank of Faith; or, a Display of the Providences of*

God, which have, at sundry times, attended the Author, is
a production equally singular and curious.

One reason which he gives for writing this marvellous
treatise is, that we are often tempted to believe that
God takes no notice of our temporal concerns.   " I
found God's promises," he says, " to be the Christian's
bank-note ; and a living faith will always draw on the
divine banker, yea, and the spirit of prayer, and a deep
sense of want, will give an heir of promise a filial
boldness at the inexhaustible bank of heaven." Accordingly, for great things and for little he drew boldly upon
the bank.   Thus, he was provided with game and fish.
One day, when he had nothing but bread in the house,
he was moved by the Spirit to take a by-path, where
he had never gone before ; but the reason was, that a
stoat was to kill a fine large rabbit, just in time for him
to secure the prey.   When his wife was lying-in, and
there was no tea in the house, and they had neither
money nor credit, his wife bade the nurse set the kettle
on in faith, and before it boiled, a stranger brought a
present of tea to the door.   At another time, a friend,
without solicitation, gives him half-a-guinea when he
was penniless ; and lest he should have any difficulty in
obtaining change for it, when he crossed Kingston
bridge, he casts his eyes on the ground, and finds a
penny to pay the toll.   He borrows a guinea, which he
is unable to pay at the time appointed, so he prays that
God would send him one from some quarter or another,
and forthwith the lender calls and desires him to consider it a free gift.   He wants a new parsonic livery :
" wherefore," says he, " in humble prayer I told my
most blessed Lord and Master that my year was out,
and my apparel bad ; that I had nowhere to go for

these things but to him; and as he had promised to give his servants food and raiment, I hoped he would fulfil his promise to me, though one of the worst of them." So, having settled it in his own mind that a certain person in London would act as the intermediate agent in this providential transaction, he called upon him, and, as he expected, the raggedness of his apparel led to a conversation which ended in the offer of a new suit, and of a greatcoat to boot.

He lived in this manner seven or eight years, not, indeed, taking no thought for the morrow, but making no other provision for it than by letting the specific object of his prayers and their general tendency always be understood, where a word to the unwise was sufficient. Being now in much request, and "having many doors open to him for preaching the Gospel very wide apart," he began to want a horse, then to wish, and lastly to pray, for one. "I used my prayers," he says, "as gunners use their swivels, turning them every day, as various cases required;" before the day was over he was presented with a horse, which had been purchased for him by subscription. The horse was to be maintained by his own means, but what of that? "I told God," says he, "that I had more work for my faith now than heretofore; for the horse would cost half as much to keep as my whole family. In answer to which this Scripture came to my mind with power and comfort, 'Dwell in the land, and do good, and verily thou shalt be fed.' This was a bank-note put into the hand of my faith, which, when I got poor, I pleaded before God, and he answered it; so that I lived and cleared my way just as well when I had my horse to keep as I did before."

Huntington was no ordinary man. The remarkable circumstance which occurred concerning a certain part of his dress has been told in various books. The old song says—

> "A light heart and a thin pair of breeches
> Go through the world, my brave boys;

but the latter qualification is better for going through the world on foot than on horseback; so Uncle Toby found it, so did Huntington, who, in this part of his history, must be his own historian: no language but his own can do justice to such a story.

"Having now," says Huntington, "had my horse for some time, and riding a great deal every week, I soon wore my breeches out, as they were not fit to ride in. I hope the reader will excuse my mentioning the word breeches, which I should have avoided, had not this passage of Scripture obtruded into my mind, just as I had revolved in my own thoughts not to mention this kind providence of God. 'And thou shalt make them linen breeches to cover their nakedness; from the loins even unto the thighs shall they reach. And they shall be upon Aaron and upon his sons when they come into the tabernacle of the congregation, or when they come near unto the altar to minister in the holy place; that they bear not iniquity and die. It shall be a statute for ever unto him and his seed after him.' Exod. xxviii. 42, 43. By which, and three others, namely, Ezek. xliv. 18; Lev. vi. 10; and Lev. xiv. 4, I saw that it was no crime to mention the word breeches, nor the way in which God sent them to me; Aaron and his sons being clothed entirely by Providence; and as God himself condescended to give orders what they should be made of, and how they should be cut. And I believe the same God ordered mine, as I trust will appear in the following history.

"The Scripture tells us to call no man master; for one is our master, even Christ. I therefore told my most bountiful and ever-adored Master what I wanted; and he, who stripped Adam and Eve of their fig-leaved aprons, and made coats of skin, and clothed them; and who clothes the grass of the field, which to-day is and to-morrow is cast into the oven, must clothe us, or we shall go naked; and so Israel found it, when God took away his wool and his flax, which he gave to cover their nakedness, and which they prepared for Baal: for which iniquity was their skirts discovered, and their heels made bare. Jer. xiii. 22.

"I often made very free in my prayers with my invaluable Master for this favour; but he still kept me so amazingly poor that I could not get them at any rate. At last I determined to go to a friend of mine at Kingston, who is of that branch of business, to bespeak a pair; and to get him to trust me until my Master sent me the money to pay him. I was that day going to London, fully determined to bespeak them as I rode through the town. However, when I passed the shop, I forgot it; but when I came to London, I called on Mr. Croucher, a shoemaker in Shepherd's Market, who told me a parcel was left there for me, but what it was he knew not. I opened it, 'and behold there was a pair of leather breeches, with a note in them! the substance of which was, to the best of my remembrance, as follows:—

"'Sir,—I have sent you a pair of breeches, and hope they will fit. I beg your acceptance of them; and if they want any alteration, leave in a note what the alteration is, and I will call in a few days and alter them.   I. S.'

"I tried them on, and they fitted as well as if I had been measured for them; at which I was amazed, having never been measured by any leather breeches maker in London. I wrote an answer to the note to this effect :—

" 'Sir,—I received your present, and thank you for it. I was going to order a pair of leather breeches to be made, because I did not know till now that my Master had bespoke them of you. They fit very well, which fully convinces me that the same God who moved thy heart to give, guided thy hand to cut : because He perfectly knows my size, having clothed me in a miraculous manner for near five years. When you are in trouble, Sir, I hope you will tell my Master of this, and what you have done for me, and He will repay you with honour.'

"This is as near as I am able to relate it, and I added :—

" 'I cannot make out I. S. unless I put *I* for Israelite indeed, and *S* for sincerity; because you did not sound a trumpet before you, as the hypocrites do.' "

The plan of purveying for himself by prayer, with the help of hints in proper place and season, answered so well, that Huntington soon obtained, by the same means, a new bed, a rug, a pair of new blankets, doe-skin gloves, and a horseman's coat; and as often as he wanted new clothes, some chosen almoner of the Bank of Faith was found to supply him. His wife was instructed to provide for her own wants by the same easy and approved means. Gowns came as they were wanted, hampers of bacon and cheese, now and then a large ham, and now and then a guinea, all which things Huntington called precious answers to prayer.

Some awkward disclosures were now made, and he became weary of Thames Ditton, and having a well-timed vision, he secretly wished that God would remove him from that place; and as London was the place where he might reasonably expect to work less and feed better, it was " suddenly impressed on his mind to leave Thames Ditton, and take a house in the great metropolis, where hearers were more numerous, and that this was the meaning of the words spoken to him in the vision." It was likewise suggested to his mind that the people had been permitted of late to persecute him more than usual, that they might drive him to this removal. "And I much question," says Huntington, "if ever God sends his word there again, for I think they are left almost as inexcusable as Chorazin and Capernaum!" The impression which he had now received was acknowledged as a plain and evident *call* by the good friends who negotiated his bills upon the Bank of Faith, and accordingly to London he and his family went.

His next draft upon the Bank was to a larger amount. During three years he had secretly wished for a chapel of his own, because, as he says, he was sick of the errors that were perpetually broached by some or other in Margaret Street Chapel, where he then preached with Lady Huntingdon's people. Much, however, as he desired this, he protests that he could not ask God for such a favour, thinking it was not to be brought about by one so very mean, low, and poor as himself. But fortune favours the bold. One of his friends looked at a suitable piece of ground, by particular impulse of Providence; and he took Huntington to look at it also. Another friend, under a similar impulse, planned a chapel one day while he was hearing Huntington preach a sermon; and he offered to undertake the management of the building without fee or reward. Thus encouraged, he took the ground and began to build Providence Chapel, when he was 20*l.* in debt, and had no other funds than the freewill offerings of his hearers, and the money which they were willing to lend him upon his credit with the Bank of Faith. The first offering amounted to no more than 11*l.*, which were soon expended on the foundations. He bespoke a load of timber, and going to the right person for it, it was sent him with a bill and receipt in full, as a contribution towards the chapel. Another "good man" came with tears in his eyes to bless Mr. Huntington for the good which he had received under his sermons, and to request that he might paint the pulpit, desk, &c., as a grateful acknowledgment. A bed-room was very handsomely furnished for him that he might not be under the necessity of walking home in the cold winter-nights. A looking-glass for his chapel study was presented by one person, a book-case by another, chairs for the vestry, a pulpit cushion, a splendid Bible, a set of china, and a well-stored tea-chest, were supplied in like manner: money was liberally lent as well as given; the chapel "sprang up like a mushroom;" and when it was finished, he says, "I was in arrears for 1,000*l.*, so that I had plenty of work for faith, if I could get plenty of faith to work; and while some deny a Providence, Providence was the only supply I had."

His never-failing friends settled him in a country-house, stocked his garden and his farm for him; and that he might travel conveniently to and from his chapel, they presented him with a coach and pair of horses, and subscribed to pay the taxes for both. To crown all, having buried his wife, the gleaner, he preached himself into the good graces of Lady Saunderson, the widow of the Lord Mayor, and married her.

His uniform prosperity received but one shock. The chapel in Titchfield Street, which he had raised from the ground and carried up into the air, when ground-room was wanting, was burnt down. This was thought by some of Huntington's followers to be a judgment upon him for having inclosed the free seats, and "laid out the whole chapel in boxes like an opera-house." But Huntington looked at this misfortune otherwise. Writing to one of his friends, he says: "Such a stroke as this twenty-seven years ago would have caused our hope to give up the ghost; but being a little stronger in the Lord, faith has heavier burdens laid on. The temple built by Solomon, and that built by Cyrus, were both burnt. It will cause a little rejoicing among the Philistines, as has been the case often: they once triumphed gloriously, when the ark of God was taken, supposing that Dagon had overcome the God of Israel; but their joy was short. This I know, that it shall work for our good, but how I know not; if I did, I must walk by sight, and not by faith." He then held out a sort of threat of removing into the country; but his London followers were presently in motion, "some looking out for a spot of ground, some bringing their offerings, others wishing the glory of the latter house may exceed that of the former." "But," says he, "it is to bear the same name: this I gave them to understand from the pulpit, and assigned the following reasons for it:—that unless God provided men to work, and money to pay them, and materials to work with, no chapel could be erected; and, if he provided all these, Providence must be its name." The chapel, accordingly, was built in Gray's Inn Lane, and upon a larger scale than the last: taught by his former experience, Huntington took care not to make himself responsible for any of the expenses, and when it was finished, managed matters so well with his obedient flock, that the chapel was made over to him as his own, for he is said to have refused to preach in it on any other conditions.*

The preacher had innumerable applicants for spiritual advice. To one person who consults him, he says:— "You need not have made any apology, as the troubled minds of sensible sinners are my peculiar province. I am authorized and commissioned by the God of heaven to transact business and negotiate affairs between the King of kings and self-condemned rebels." One madman assures him that he was actually electrified in body and soul by one of his books. This man saw a brilliant star over the head of Huntington while he was preaching, and Huntington publishes the letter and assures him that dreams (of which he has communicated a curious story) are from the Spirit of God. Sometimes he found that correspondents were troublesome, newborn babes being never satisfied when they desire the sincere milk of the word. A certain Mrs. Bull writes to him rather more frequently than is agreeable. Huntington lets Mrs. Bull know that he does not like her head-dress; he finds fault with her preposterous

* Selected and abridged from an excellent paper on Huntington's Works and Life, attributed to Southey; *Quarterly Review*, No. 48.

streamers, and her first, second, and third tier of curls; but tells her that a little more furnace-work will teach her to pull down those useless topsails. This prediction was verified rather more literally than it was meant, for the said Mrs. B., thinking it was not his business to interfere with her head-dress, was about to resent it in a sharp letter; "but," says she, "happening to fall asleep by the fire, as I was reading the Bible, the candle caught the lappet of my cap, and a good deal of my hair, and I own it a great mercy that I was not consumed myself, and you may be assured that you will see neither streamers, curls, nor topsails again."

Mr. Bramah, the celebrated engineer, appears among Huntington's controversial correspondents; and he tells him that he makes a good patent lock, but cuts a poor figure with the keys of the Kingdom of heaven.

Mr. Bensley, the printer, was one of his believers, which explains the handsome appearance of Huntington's collected works, in twenty volumes, octavo; his spiritual employer calls him dear brother in the Lord, and dear Tom in the flesh. Trader in faith as he was, there were some social qualities about him, which won and secured the attachment of his friends, even of those upon whom he drew most largely. He mentions particularly Mr. and Mrs. Baker, of Oxford Street, who, having no children of their own, kept caring and travailing many years for him; and though "sorely tried by various losses in business, bankruptcies, and bad debts, supplied him with money whenever he required it." "While the chapel was building," he says, "when money was continually demanded, if there was one shilling in the house, I was sure to have it. This couple and another, with whom he was on terms of equal intimacy, agreed, as they were bound together with their chosen pastor for life and for eternity, not to be divided in death; and accordingly they jointly purchased a piece of ground near Petersham, and erected a substantial tomb there, wherein they might rest together in the dust.

Huntington died in 1813, at Tunbridge Wells; he was buried at Lewes, in a piece of ground adjoining the chapel of one of his associates: it was his desire that there should be no funeral sermon preached on the occasion, and that nothing should be said over his grave. He indited his own epitaph in these words :—

> " Here lies the Coalheaver,
> Beloved of his God, but abhorred of men.
> The Omniscient Judge
> At the Grand Assize shall rectify and
> Confirm this to the
> Confusion of many thousands;
> For England and its Metropolis shall know,
> That there hath been a prophet
> Among them."

The sale of his effects by public auction took place soon after his death, at his elegantly-furnished villa, Hermes Hill,* Pentonville, and lasted four days. His friends and admirers, anxious to secure some memorial

---

* Huntington resided in the house built by the Swiss doctor De Valangin, who had been a pupil of Boerhaave, and practised in Soho Square. He removed thence to Cripplegate, and about 1772 he purchased ground at Pentonville, and there built himself a villa, which he named, from the discoverer of chemistry, Hermes Hill, then almost the only house on or near the spot, except White Conduit House. One of his medicines, *The Balsam of Life*, he presented to the Apothecaries' Company. He had, by his first wife, a daughter, who, dying at nine years of age, was buried in the garden at Hermes Hill, in a very costly tomb.

of Huntington, paid most fabulous sums of money for articles of no intrinsic value in the excess of their veneration. A mahogany easy-chair, with hair seat and back cushion in canvas, on brass-wheel castors, with two sets of flowered calico cases, sold for 63*l.*; an ordinary pair of spectacles sold for seven guineas; a common silver snuff-box, five guineas; every article of plate at from 23*s.* to 26*s.* per ounce; his library sold for 252*l.* 19*s.*; a handsome modern town coach for 49*l.* 7*s.* The aggregate of the four days' sale was 1,800*l.* 11*s.* 2½*d.* In a newspaper, October, 1813, we read:—"At the sale of the effects of the Rev. Mr. Huntington, at Pentonville, an old arm-chair, intrinsically worth fifty shillings, actually sold for sixty guineas; and many other articles fetched equally high prices, so anxious were his besotted admirers to obtain some precious memorial of that artful fanatic." One of his steady followers purchased a barrel of ale, which had been brewed for Christmas, "because he would have something to remember him by."

Huntington is described as having been, towards the close of his career, a fat, burly man, with a red face, which rose just above the pulpit cushion; and a thick, guttural, and rather indistinct voice. A contemporary says:—"His pulpit prayers are remarkable for omitting all for the King and his country. He excels in extempore eloquence. Having formally announced his text, he lays his Bible at once aside, and never refers to it again. He has every possible text and quotation at his fingers' end. He proceeds directly to his object, and except such incidental digressions as 'Take care of your pockets! Wake that snoring sinner! Silence that noisy numskull! Turn out that drunken dog!' he never deviates from his course. Nothing can exceed his dictatorial dogmatism. Believe him, none but him—that's enough. When he wishes to bind the faith of his congregation, he will say, over and over, 'As sure as I am born, 'tis so;' or, 'I believe the plain English of it to be this.' And then he will add, by way of clenching his point, 'Now you can't help it,' or, 'It must be so, in spite of you.' He does this with a most significant shake of the head, and with a sort of Bedlam hauteur, with all the dignity of defiance. He will then sometimes observe, softening his deportment, 'I don't know whether I make you understand these things, but I understand them well.' He rambles sadly and strays so completely from his text, that you often lose sight of it. The divisions of his sermons are so numerous that one of his discourses might be divided into three. Preaching is with him talking; his discourses, story-telling. Action he has none, except that of shifting his handkerchief from hand to hand and hugging his cushion. Nature has bestowed on him a vigorous, original mind, and he employs it in everything. Survey him when you will, he seems to have rubbed off none of his native rudeness or blackness. All his notions are his own, as well as his mode of imparting them. Religion has not been discovered by him through the telescopes of commentators."

Huntington's portrait is in the National Portrait Gallery, in Great George Street, Westminster. He " might pass, as far as appearances go, for a convict, but he looks too conceited. The vitality and strength of his constitution are fearful to behold, and it is certain that he looks better fitted for coal-heaving than for religious oratory."—*History of Clerkenwell*, 1865, pp. 529–531.

AMEN.

A Correspondent of the *Athenæum*, 1865, writes:—
" While some philosophers seek information in the Far
West, and others in the not-much-nearer East—one,
perchance, reducing eccentric arrow-heads to a civilized
alphabet; another metamorphosing emblematic pitch-
forks, tom-cats, &c., of 2,000 A.M. into sensation novels
of the period; a third studying the customs and annals
of pre-historic America by the aid of Aztec pots and
pipkins—it has been the happy lot of the undersigned,
with no greater effort than a short railway journey and
a pleasant walk, to light upon a treasure of antiquity,
which may not be without interest to some of your
readers. The internal evidence of the following lines is
sufficient to show what they purport to be—*viz*. the
epitaph of an accomplished parish officer at Crayford,
in Kent. They run as follows:—

" Here lieth the body of
Peter Isnell.
(30 years Clerk of this Parish.)

" He lived respected as a pious and mirthful man, and died on his
way to church to assist at a wedding on the 31st day of March,
1811; aged seventy years.
"The inhabitants of Crayford have raised this stone to his cheerful
memory and as a tribute to his long and faithful services.

" The Life of this *Clerk* was just threescore and ten,
Nearly half of which time he had sung out *Amen*;
In his Youth he was married, like other young men,
But his wife died one day, so he chanted *Amen*.

A second he took, she departed, what then ?
He married and buried a third with *Amen.*
Thus his joys and his sorrows were *Trebled,* but then
His voice was deep *Bass* as he sung out *Amen.*
On the *horn* he could blow as well as most men,
So his *horn* was exalted in blowing *Amen ;*
But he lost all his *Wind* after threescore and ten,
And here with three Wives he waits till again
The trumpet shall rouse him to sing out *Amen.*"

STRANGELY ECCENTRIC, YET SANE.

The study of psychology proves that hallucinations,
or illusions, may exist in man without the intellect
being disordered. In some instances, they can be produced by effort of the will. Dr. Wigan, in his able
work, *Duality of the Mind,* relates :—"A painter who
succeeded to a large portion of the practice, and (as he
thought) to more than all the talent of Sir Joshua
Reynolds, was so extensively employed, that he im-
formed me he had once painted (large and small) three
hundred portraits in one year. This would seem physically impossible, but the secret of his rapidity and of
his astonishing success was this : He required but one
sitting, and painted with miraculous facility. I myself
saw him execute a Kit-Kat portrait of a gentleman well
known to me in little more than eight hours; it was
minutely finished, and a most striking likeness. On
asking him to explain it, he said, ' When a sitter came,
I looked at him attentively for half-an-hour, sketching
from time to time on the canvas. I wanted no more—

I put away my canvas, and took another sitter. When I wished to resume my first portrait, *I took the man and sat him in the chair, where I saw him as distinctly as if he had been before me in his own proper person*—I may almost say more vividly. I looked from time to time at the imaginary figure, then worked with my pencil, then referred to the countenance, and so on, just as I should have done had the sitter been there. *When I looked at the chair, I saw the man!* This made me very popular; and, as I always succeeded in the likeness, people were very glad to be spared the tedious sittings of other painters. I gained a great deal of money, and was very careful of it. Well for me and my children that it was so. Gradually I began to lose the distinction between the imaginary figure and the real person, and sometimes disputed with sitters that they had been with me the day before. At last I was sure of it, and then —and then—all is confusion. I suppose they took the alarm. I recollect nothing more—I lost my senses— was thirty years in an asylum. The whole period, except the last six months of my confinement, is a dead blank in my memory, though sometimes, when people describe their visits, I have a sort of imperfect remembrance of them; but I must not dwell on these subjects.'"

It is an extraordinary fact that, when this gentleman resumed his pencil, after a lapse of thirty years, he painted nearly as well as when insanity compelled him to discontinue it. His imagination was still exceedingly vivid, as was proved by a portrait, for he had only two sittings of half-an-hour each; the latter solely for the dress and for the *eyebrows*, which he could not fix in his memory.

It was found that the excitement threatened danger, and he was persuaded to discontinue the exercise of his art. He lived but a short time afterwards.

A hallucination, although recognized and appreciated as such by the person who is the subject of it, may, by its vividness and long continuance, produce so depressing an influence on the mind as to be the cause of suicide. "I know," says Wigan, "a very intelligent and amiable man, who had the power of thus placing before his own eyes *himself*, and often laughed heartily at *his doubls*, who always seemed to laugh in turn. This was long a subject of amusement and joke; but the ultimate result was lamentable. He became gradually convinced that he was haunted by himself, or (to violate grammar for the sake of clearly expressing his idea) by his *self*. This other self would argue with him pertinaciously, and, to his great mortification, sometimes refute him, which, as he was very proud of his logical powers, humiliated him exceedingly. He was eccentric, but was never placed in confinement or subjected to the slightest restraint. At length, worn out by the annoyance, he deliberately resolved not to enter on another year of existence—paid all his debts—wrapped up in separate papers the amount of the weekly demands—waited, pistol in hand, the night of the 31st of December, and as the clock struck twelve, fired it into his mouth."

We read in Dr. de Boismont's very able treatise on Hallucinations (translated by Hulme):—"All mental labour, by over-exciting the brain, is liable to give rise to hallucinations. We have known many persons, and amongst others a medical man, who, when it was night, distinctly heard voices calling to them; some would stop to reply, or would go to the door, believing they heard the bell ring. This disposition seems to us not uncommon in persons who are in the habit of talking aloud to themselves.

We find in Abercrombie's work the case of a gentleman "who has been all his life affected by the appearance of spectral figures. To such an extent does this peculiarity exist, that, if he meets a friend in the street, he cannot at first satisfy himself whether he really sees the individual or a spectral figure. By close attention he can remark a difference between them, in the outline of the real figure being more distinctly defined than that of the spectral; but in general he takes means for correcting his visual impression by touching the figure, or by listening to the sound of his footsteps. He has also the power of calling up spectral figures at his will, by directing his attention steadily to the conception of his own mind; and this may consist either of a figure or a scene which he has seen, or it may be a composition created by his imagination. But, though he has the faculty of producing the illusion, he has no power of vanishing it; and, when he has called up any particular spectral figure or scene, he never can say how long it may continue to haunt him. The gentleman is in the prime of life, of sound mind, in good health, and engaged in business. Another of his family has been affected in the same manner, though in a slight degree.

It would be easy to mention many examples of illustrious men who have been subject to hallucinations, without their having in any way influenced their conduct.

Thus, Malebranche declared he heard the voice of God distinctly within him. Descartes, after long confinement, was followed by an invisible person, calling upon him to pursue the search of truth.

Byron occasionally fancied he was visited by a spectre, which he confesses was but the effect of an over-stimulated brain.

Dr. Johnson said that he distinctly heard his mother's voice call "Samuel." This was at a time when she was residing a long way off.

Pope, who suffered much from intestinal disease, one day asked his medical man what the arm was which seemed to come out of the wall.

Goethe positively asserts that he one day saw the exact counterpart of himself coming towards him. The German psychologists give the name of *Deuteroscopia* to this species of illusion.

STRANGE HALLUCINATION.

On the 25th of November, 1840, Mr. Pearce, the author of several medical works, was tried at the Central Criminal Court for shooting at his wife with intent to murder, and acquitted on the ground of insanity. He entertained the peculiar notion that his wife wished to destroy him, and that she had bribed persons to effect his death in various ways, the principal of which was that his bed was constantly damped or wetted. This idea seems to have haunted him continually. He was shortly after his acquittal taken to Bethlem Hospital. For some time he refused to leave the gallery in which his cell was situated, and go into the airing-ground; in order, as it appeared, that he might watch his cell door to prevent anything "villanous" being done.

In a letter addressed to the Governors of the Hospital, Pearce argued the point in a very serious and connected manner. "If," said he, in allusion to some of the witnesses, who at various times had stated they felt his bedding and found it dry, "the simple act of placing one's hand upon a damp bed, or even the immediate impression on a man's body when he gets into it, was infallible, how could it occur so frequently that travellers at times are crippled with rheumatism, or lose their lives by remaining all night in damp bedding? If the thing was so easily discoverable, no man of common understanding could be injured by such a proceeding or accident at inns.

"Technically speaking, the matter of which I complain is not a delusion; it is an allegation—a positive charge, susceptible of proof, if proper evidence could be brought to bear upon the fact, not warped or suborned by the man or men in whose power I hourly am. It would be a sad delusion for me to declare my bed was composed of straw instead of flocks, or that I was a prophet, or the Pope, or Sir Astley Cooper. I grant I have no such crotchets. My mind is perfectly sound, calm, and reflective; and I implore you to consider well the distinction between the things which cannot in nature physically be and the things which can physically be. It is a vital one in my sad case.

"It may be told you I have charged persons elsewhere with this atrocity of damping my bed. I have done so. At the private madhouse, near Uxbridge, whence I was brought here, my bed was kept almost wet for three months, and I only saved my life by sleeping on a large trunk, with my daily articles of dress to cover me. Some portion of this time, the cold was eight and ten degrees below freezing-point."

He then solicited that a lock might be put upon his cell-door to protect him from this annoyance; and concluded his letter with this appeal: "I beseech you to commiserate my hard lot. I have some little claim to the title of a gentleman, and have been estimated by persons of some consideration in society; I am now, by a wretched chain of circumstances, in a great prison hospital, dragged from my children and my home, and the comforts of social life, and doomed to herd with desperadoes against the State, the destitute, and the mad."

Mr. Pearce was afterwards introduced, and answered the questions put to him in a very collected manner. He then stated that since his marriage-trip to Boulogne, he had been subjected to the greatest abuse from his present wife, and on one occasion, had been struck by her, and insulted by the vilest epithets. He complained that when first brought to Bethlem Hospital, he had been "chummed" with Oxford, and objected, but had been compelled to associate with that ruffian. He had taught Oxford the French language, and tried to improve his mind. Oxford had conveyed to him matter of importance relative to the great crime of which he had been guilty, and which he (Mr. Pearce) thought of sufficient importance to be communicated to the Secretary of State, and had accordingly written a letter in Latin, detailing the several circumstances. It had, however, been taken from him, and he did not know whether it had ever been sent to Downing Street. He wished to show how Oxford boasted of having cajoled Sir A. Morrison and Dr. Monro into a belief that he was insane, and how he sent for such books as *Jack the Giant-Killer* in order to make the jury let him off on the ground of insanity. This was what he (Mr. Pearce) wished to tell the Secretary of State, and now the letter was used against him.

After some further remarks, Mr. Pearce was questioned by the jury, and persisted in the statement that his bed was damped, that deleterious drugs were applied to his clothes, and that a conspiracy existed against him. He produced from under his clothes a small packet, which he said contained portions of the shirt of which mention had been made, and a snuff-box, in which he stated he had kept parts of the shirt, and which he " demanded " to have submitted to the test of Professor Faraday or some other eminent chemist. He announced himself to be grand-nephew of Zachariah Pearce, Bishop of Rochester, and translator of Longinus, and prayed, in conclusion, the jury to relieve him from the situation in which he was placed.

The jury returned a verdict to the effect "that Mr. Pearce was of unsound mind, and that he had been so from the 16th of October, 1840."

"CORNER MEMORY THOMPSON."

In February, 1843, there died, at the age of 86, this remarkable person, whose eccentric success had become matter of public interest. John Thompson was a native of St. Giles's, where his father was a greengrocer ; the boy on carrying a salad to the house of an undertaker in the neighbourhood attracted attention by his ready and active manner, and the undertaker took him as errand-boy; then he became assistant, and next married his master's daughter, and thus obtained property. This was his *start* in life, and enabled him to commence business as an auctioneer and brewer's valuer, by which he amassed considerable wealth. As he advanced in life, he sought retirement, and on a spot just below Hampstead Church, built for himself, without plan or order, "Frognal Priory," an assemblage of grotesque structures, but without any right of road to it, which he had to purchase at a great price. Thence, Thompson often went to town in his chariot, to collect curiosities for his house; and he might be seen pottering about among the curiosity-shops: an Horace Walpole cheapened Dicky Bateman's chairs at half-a-crown a-piece for Strawberry Hill, so John Thompson collected his "items of taste and *vertu*" for Frognal Priory, and these, for a time, he would show to any person who rang at his gate. He was designated "Corner Memory," for his having, for a bet, drawn a plan of St. Giles's parish from memory, at three sittings, specifying every coach-turning, stable-yard, and public pump, and likewise the *corner shop* of every street. He possessed a most mechanical memory; for he would, by reading a newspaper over-night, repeat the whole of it next morning. He gained some notoriety by presenting to the Queen a carved bedstead, reputed once to have belonged to Cardinal Wolsey; with this he sent some other old furniture to Windsor Castle.

MUMMY OF A MANCHESTER LADY.

About the middle of the last century there died near Manchester a maiden lady, a Miss Bexwick or Beswick, who had a great horror of being *buried alive*. To avoid this, she devised an estate to her medical adviser, the late Mr. Charles White and his two children, *viz.* Miss Rosa White and her sister, and his nephew, Captain White, *on condition that the doctor paid her a morning visit for twelve months after her decease*. In order to do this, it was requisite to embalm her, which he did; she was then placed in the attic of the old mansion in which she died, and in which the doctor took up his residence. Upon his leaving it, she was removed to the house erected by him in King Street, Manchester, and which stood on the ground now occupied by the Town Hall. At the death of Mr. White, the doctor, she was sent to the Lying-in Hospital, where she remained until she was removed to her present resting-place, the Manchester Museum of Natural History, where the mummy is suspended in a case with a glass-door.

Mr. de Quincey, when a boy at Manchester School, at the beginning of the century, became acquainted with the mummy, and in one of his works mentions it being taken from the case, and the body of a notorious highwayman being substituted; but this is an embellishment or exaggeration of the already extraordinary story.

HYPOCHONDRIASIS.

In the year 1827 there was living at Taunton a person who had often kept at home for several weeks under the idea of danger in going abroad. Sometimes he imagined that he was a cat, and seated himself on his hind-quarters; at other times he would fancy himself a teapot, and stand with one arm a-kimbo like the handle, and the other stretched out like the spout. At last he conceived himself to have died, and would not move or be moved till the coffin came. His wife, in serious alarm, sent for a surgeon, who addressed him with the usual salutation, "How do you do this morning?" "Do!" replied he in a low voice, "a pretty question to a dead man!" "Dead, sir; what do you mean?" "Yes; I died last Wednesday; the coffin will be here presently, and I shall be buried to-morrow." The surgeon, a man of sense and skill, immediately felt the patient's pulse, and shaking his head, said, "I find it is indeed too true; you are certainly defunct; the blood is in a state of stagnation, putrefaction is about to take place, and the sooner you are buried the better." The coffin arrived, he was carefully placed in it, and carried towards the church. The surgeon had previously given instructions to several neighbours how to proceed. The procession had scarcely moved a dozen yards, when a person stopped to inquire who they were carrying to the grave: "Mr. ——, our late worthy overseer." "What! is the old rogue gone at last? a good release, for a greater villain never lived." The imaginary deceased no sooner heard this attack on his character, than he jumped up, and in a threatening posture said, "You lying scoundrel, if I were not dead I'd make you suffer for what you say; but as it is, I am forced to submit." He then quietly laid down again; but ere they had proceeded half-way to church, another party stopped the procession with the same inquiry, and added invective and abuse. This was more than the supposed corpse could bear; and jumping from the coffin, was in the act of following his defamers, when the whole party burst into an immoderate fit of laughter. The public exposure awakened him to a sense of his folly; he fought against the weakness, and in the end conquered it.

Here is an instance of a cure for hypochondriasis in Switzerland:—A wealthy and hypochondriacal farmer, who believed himself to be possessed by seven devils, applied to the Swiss doctor, Michael Schuppach, to rout the demoniac occupants of his distressed mind. "Friend," said Schuppach gravely, "you believe there are but seven devils in you; in reality there are eight, and the eighth is the captain of the band." To expel the eight unclean spirits the physician had recourse to an electrical apparatus, with which contrivance the farmer was of course utterly ignorant. For eight successive days the patient visited the doctor and underwent an electrical shock. At each of the first seven shocks the operator said, "There goes one of your devils." On the eighth day Schuppach said, "Now, we must relieve you of the chief of the evil spirits—it'll be a tough job!" As these words were uttered, a violent shock sent the patient fairly to the floor. "And now," cried the benevolent impostor, "you are free of your devils,—that last stroke was a settler!" The cure was complete.

Strange Sights and Sporting Scenes.

"THE WONDER OF ALL THE WONDERS THAT THE WORLD EVER WONDERED AT."

UNDER the title of "*Horæ Subsecivæ*," in the *Dublin University Review*, in 1833, vol. i., p. 482, by the late Dr. West, of Dublin, appeared the following amusing trifle :—

"Among Swift's works, we find a *jeu d'esprit*, entitled 'The Wonder of all the Wonders that the World ever Wondered at,' and purporting to be an advertisement of a conjurer. There is an amusing one of the same kind by a very humorous German writer, George Christopher Lichtenberg, which, as his works are not much known here, is perhaps worth translating. The occasion on which it was written was the following. In the year 1777, a celebrated conjurer of those days arrived at Göttingen. Lichtenberg, for some reason or other, did not wish him to exhibit there; and, accordingly, before the other had time even to announce his arrival, he wrote this advertisement, in his name, and had it printed and posted over the town. The whole was the work of one night. The result was, that the real Simon Pure decamped next morning without beat of drum, and never appeared in Göttingen again.

Lichtenberg had spent some time in England, and understood the language perfectly, so that he may have seen Swift's paper. Still, even granting that he took the hint from him, it must be allowed he has improved on it not a little, and displayed not only more delicacy, which, indeed, was easy enough, but more wit also.

"'Notice.

"'The admirers of supernatural Physics are hereby informed that the far-famed magician, Philadelphus Philadelphia (the same that is mentioned by Cardanus, in his book *De Naturâ Supernaturali*, where he is styled "The envied of Heaven and Hell"), arrived here a few days ago by the mail, although it would have been just as easy for him to come through the air, seeing that he is the person who, in the year 1482, in the public market at Venice, threw a ball of cord into the clouds, and climbed upon it into the air till he got out of sight. On the 9th of January, of the present year, he will commence at the Merchants' Hall, publico-privately, to exhibit his one-dollar tricks, and continue weekly to improve them, till he comes to his five-hundred-guinea tricks; amongst which last are some which, without boasting, excel the wonderful itself, nay are, as one may say, absolutely impossible.

"'He has had the honour of performing with the greatest possible approbation before all the potentates, high and low, of the four quarters of the world; and even in the fifth, a few weeks ago, before her Majesty Queen Oberea, at Otaheite.

"'He is to be seen every day, except on Mondays and Thursdays, when he is employed in clearing the heads of the honourable members of the Congress of his countrymen at Philadelphia; and at all hours, except from eleven to twelve in the forenoon, when he is engaged at Constantinople; and from twelve to one, when he is at his dinner.

"'The following are some of his common one-dollar tricks; and they are selected, not as being the best of them, but as they can be described in the fewest words:—

"'1. Without leaving the room, he takes the weather-cock off St. James's Church, and sets it on St. John's, and *vice versâ*. After a few minutes he puts them back again in their proper places. N.B. All this without a magnet, by mere sleight of hand.

"'2. He takes two ladies, and sets them on their heads on a table, with their legs up; he then gives them a blow, and they immediately begin to spin like tops with incredible velocity, without breach either of their head-dress by the pressure, or of decorum by the falling of their petticoats, to the very great satisfaction of all present.

"'3. He takes three ounces of the best arsenic, boils it in a gallon of milk, and gives it to the ladies to drink. As soon as they begin to get sick, he gives them two or three spoonfuls of melted lead, and they go away in high spirits.

"'4. He takes a hatchet, and knocks a gentleman on the head with it, so that he falls dead on the floor. When there, he gives a second blow, whereupon the gentleman immediately gets up as well as ever, and generally asks what music that was.

"'5. He draws three or four ladies' teeth, makes the company shake them well together in a bag, and then puts them into a little cannon, which he fires at the aforesaid ladies' heads, and they find their teeth white and sound in their places again.

"'6. A metaphysical trick, otherwise commonly called πᾶν, *metaphysica*, whereby he shows that a thing can actually be and not be at the same time. It requires great preparation and cost, and is shown so low as a dollar, solely in honour of the University.

"'7. He takes all the watches, rings, and other ornaments of the company, and even money if they wish, and gives every one a receipt for his property. He then puts them all in a trunk, and brings them off to Cassel. In a week after, each person tears his receipt, and that moment finds whatever he gave in his hands again. He has made a great deal of money by this trick.

"'N.B. During this week, he performs in the top room at the Merchants' Hall; but after that, up in the air over the pump in the market-place; for whoever does not pay, will not see.'" •

"THE PRINCESS CARABOO."

Early in the year 1865 there died at Bristol a female of considerable personal attractions, whose early history was amusing enough, yet took a strong hold upon credulous persons half-a-century since. She pretended to be a native of Javasu, in the Indian Ocean, and to have been carried off by pirates, by whom she had been sold to the captain of a brig. Her first appearance was in the spring of 1817, at Almondsbury, in

Gloucestershire. Having been ill-used when on board the ship, she had jumped overboard, she said, swam on shore, and wandered about six weeks before she came to Almondsbury. She appears next to have found her way to Bath, and there to have created a sensation in the literary and fashionable circles of Bath and other places, which lasted till it was discovered that the whole affair was a romance, cleverly sustained and acted out by a young and prepossessing girl, who sought to maintain the imposition by the invention of hieroglyphics and characters to represent her native language.

In 1817, there was published at Bristol a narrative of this singular imposition, "practised upon the benevolence of a lady residing in the vicinity of Bristol by a young woman of the name of Mary Willcocks, *alias* Baker, *alias* Bakerstendht, *alias* Caraboo, Princess of Javasu;" for which work Bird, the Royal Academician, drew two portraits.

It was ascertained that she was a native of Witheridge, in Devonshire, where her father was a cobbler. She appears to have taken flight to America, and in 1824 she returned to England, and hired apartments in New Bond Street, where she exhibited herself to the public at the charge of one shilling; but she did not attract any great attention.

On being deposed from the honours which had been awarded to her, "the Princess" retired into comparatively humble life, and married. There was a kind of grim humour in the occupation which she subsequently followed, that of an importer of leeches; but she conducted her operations with much judgment and ability, and carried on her trade with credit to herself and

satisfaction to her customers. The quondam " Princess"
died, leaving a daughter, who, like her mother, is
described as very beautiful.

There is, it should be added, a very strange story of
the Princess having got an introduction to Napoleon
Bonaparte at St. Helena, of which affair the following
account appeared in *Felix Farley's Bristol Journal*,
September 13th, 1817 :—

"A letter from Sir Hudson Lowe, lately received
from St. Helena, forms at present the leading topic of
conversation in the higher circles. It states that on the
day preceding the date of the last dispatches, a large
ship was discovered in the offing. The wind was strong
from the S.S.E. After several hours' tacking, with
apparent intention to reach the island, the vessel was
observed to bear away for the N.W., and in the course
of an hour the boat was seen entering the harbour. It
was rowed by a single person. Sir Hudson went alone
to the beach, and to his astonishment saw a female of
interesting appearance drop the oars and spring to land.
She stated that she had sailed from Bristol, under the
care of some missionary ladies, in a vessel called the
Robert and Anne, Captain Robinson, destined for
Philadelphia; that the vessel being driven out of its
course by a tempest, which continued for several successive days, the crew at length perceived land, which
the captain recognized to be St. Helena; that she immediately conceived an ardent desire of seeing the man
with whose future fortunes she was persuaded her own
were mysteriously connected; and her breast swelled
with the prospect of contemplating face to face an
impostor not equalled on earth since the days of Mohammed; but a change of wind to the S.S.E. nearly

overset her hopes. Finding the captain resolved to proceed according to his original destination, she watched her opportunity, and springing with a large clasp-knife into a small boat which was slung at the stern, she cut the ropes, dropt safely into the ocean, and rowed away. The wind was too strong from the land to allow of the vessel being brought about to thwart her object. Sir Hudson introduced her to Bonaparte under the name of Caraboo! She described herself as Princess of Javasu, and related a tale of extraordinary interest, which seemed in a high degree to delight the captive chief. He embraced her with every demonstration of enthusiastic rapture, and besought Sir Hudson that she might be allowed an apartment in his house, declaring that she alone was an adequate solace in his captivity.

" Sir Hudson subjoins : ' The familiar acquaintance with the Malay tongue possessed by this most extraordinary personage (and there are many on the island who understand that language), together with the knowledge she displays of the Indian and Chinese politics, and the eagerness with which she speaks of these subjects, appear to convince every one that she is no impostor. Her manner is noble and fascinating in a wonderful degree.'

" A private letter adds the following testimony to the above statement: ' Since the arrival of this lady, her manners, and I may say the countenance and figure of Bonaparte, appear to be wholly altered. From being reserved and dejected, he has become gay and communicative. No more complaints are heard about inconveniences at Longwood. He has intimated to Sir Hudson his determination to apply to the Pope for a dispensation to dissolve his marriage with Maria Louisa, and to sanction his indissoluble union with the enchanting Caraboo.' "

However, corroboration of this strange story is wanting.

FAT FOLKS.—LAMBERT AND BRIGHT.

About the centre of the new burial-ground of St. Martin's, Stamford Baron, is a black slate inscribed with gilt letters to the memory of that immense mass of mortality, Daniel Lambert, the most popularly known of " Fat Folks."

> " Altus in animo, in Corpore Maximus.
> In remembrance of that prodigy in nature,
> Daniel Lambert, a native of Leicester,
> Who was possessed of an exalted and convivial mind ;
> and, in personal greatness, had no competitor.
> He measured 3 ft. 1 in. round the leg ;
> and weighed 52 st. 11 lbs. !
> He departed this life on the 21st June, 1809,
> aged 39 years.
> As a testimony of respect, this
> Stone is erected by his friends in Leicester."

Daniel Lambert was born on the 13th of March, 1770, at Leicester. His parents were not persons of remarkable dimensions ; but he had an uncle and aunt on the father's side who were both very heavy.

At the age of 19, young Lambert began to imagine that he should be a heavy man. He possessed extraordinary muscular power, and at the above age could lift great weights, and carry five hundred-weight with ease. He succeeded his father in the office of keeper of the prison at Leicester, within a year after which his bulk began rapidly to increase, owing to his confinement and sedentary life. Though he never possessed any extraordinary agility, he was able to kick to the height of seven feet, standing on one leg.

About the year 1793, when Lambert weighed 32 stone, he walked from Woolwich to London, with much less apparent fatigue than several middle-sized men who were his companions. Upon this Mr. Wadd remarks: "It is clear, therefore, that he was a strong, active man, and continued so after the disease had made great progress; and I think it may fairly be inferred that he would not have fallen a sacrifice so early in life, if he had possessed fortitude enough to meet the evil, and to have opposed it with determined perseverance."

Lambert was very expert in swimming, and taught hundreds of the young people of Leicester. His power of floating, owing to his uncommon bulk, was so great that he could swim with two men of ordinary size upon his back. He proved a humane keeper of the prison, and upon his retirement from the office, the magistrates settled upon him an annuity of 50l. for life, without any solicitation.

He now lived a leisure life at Leicester, but his uncommon corpulence brought him many visitors; and he at length found that he must either submit to be a close prisoner in his own house, or endure the inconveniences without receiving any of the profits of an exhibition. He then determined to visit London; and as it was impossible to procure a carriage large enough to admit him, he had a vehicle built to convey him to the metropolis, where he arrived in the spring of 1806, and fixed his abode in Piccadilly. Here he was visited by much company. Among them was the celebrated Polish dwarf, Count Boruwlaski, who had before seen Lambert at Birmingham; the little man exclaimed that he had seen the face twenty years ago, but it was not surely the same body. In the course of conversation, Lambert asked what quantity of cloth the Count required for a coat, and how many he thought his would make him. "Not many," answered Boruwlaski; "I take good large piece of cloth myself—almost tree-quarters of a yard." At this rate, one of Lambert's sleeves would have abundantly sufficed for the purpose. The Count felt one of Mr. Lambert's legs, "Ah, mine Got!" he exclaimed, "pure flesh and blood; I feel de warm. No deception. I am pleased, for I did hear it was deception." Mr. Lambert asked if the Count's lady was alive; to which he replied, "No, she is dead, and I am not very sorry, for when I affront her, she put me on the mantel-shelf for punishment."

In September, 1806, Lambert returned to Leicester, but repeated his visit in the following year, and fixed his abode in Leicester Square. Here, for the first time, he felt inconvenienced by the atmosphere of the metropolis; accordingly, by the advice of Dr. Heaviside, his physician, Lambert returned to his native place. He then made a tour through the principal cities and towns of England, and proved as attractive in the provinces as he had formerly been in the metropolis. He now enjoyed excellent health, and felt perfectly at ease, either while sitting up or lying in bed. His diet was plain, and the quantity moderate. For many years he never drank anything stronger than water. He slept well, but scarcely so much as other persons, and his respiration was as free as any moderately-sized individual. His countenance was manly and intelligent; he possessed great information, much ready politeness, and conversed with ease and facility. He had a powerful and melodious tenor voice, and his articulation was perfectly clear and unembarrassed.

Lambert had, however, for some time shown dropsical symptoms. In June, 1809, he was weighed at Huntingdon, and by the Caledonian balance was found to be 52 stone 11 lb. (14 lb. to the stone), 10st. 4lb. heavier than Bright, the miller of Malden. His measure round the body was three yards four inches, and one yard one inch round the leg.

A few days after this measurement, on June 20th, he arrived from Huntingdon, at the Wagon and Horses Inn, St. Martin's, Stamford, where preparations were made to receive company the next day, and during Stamford races. He was announced for exhibition; he gave his orders cheerfully, without any presentiment that they were to be his last: he was then in bed, only fatigued from his journey, but anxious to be able to see company early in the morning. Before nine o'clock, however, the day following, he was a corpse! He died in his apartment on the ground-floor of the inn, for he had long been incapable of walking up-stairs.

His interment was an arduous labour. His coffin measured six feet four inches long, four feet four inches wide, and two feet four inches deep, and contained one hundred and twelve superficial feet of elm. It was built upon two axletrees and four wheels; the room-door and wall of the room in which he lay were taken down to allow of his exit, and thus his remains were drawn to the place of interment at St. Martin's, Stamford. His grave was dug with a gradual slope for several yards; and upwards of twenty men were employed for nearly half-an-hour in getting the massive corpse into its resting-place: the immense substance of the legs made the coffin, of necessity, at most a square case. The funeral was attended by thousands of persons from Stamford and the country many miles round.

At the Wagon and Horses inn were preserved two suits of Lambert's clothes: seven ordinarily-sized men were repeatedly enclosed within his waistcoat, without breaking a stitch or straining a button; each suit of clothes cost 20*l.* His name was remembered for a time as a tavern sign: one on the north side of Ludgate Street remained till within a few years.

The great weight of Edward Bright, the miller of Malden, has been incidentally mentioned. He died on November 10th, 1750, at the age of 30. He was an active man till within a year or two of his death; when his corpulency so overpowered his strength, that his life was a burthen to him; yet, as we have seen, he was ten stone four pounds lighter than Lambert. Mr. Wadd says it is supposed that Bright's weight at his death was forty-four stone, or 616 pounds.

Horace Walpole relates the following story of Bright's weight backed against that of the Duke of Cumberland: —"There has been a droll cause in Westminster Hall: a man laid another a wager that he produced a person who should weigh as much again as the Duke. When they had betted, they recollected not knowing how to desire the Duke to step into the scale. They agreed to establish his weight at twenty stone, which, however, is supposed to be two more than he weighs. One Bright was then produced, who is since dead, and who actually weighed forty-two stone and a half. As soon as he was dead, the person who had lost objected that he had been weighed in his clothes, and though it was impossible to suppose that his clothes could weigh above two stone, they went to law. There were the Duke's twenty stone bawled over a thousand times,—but the righteous law decided against the man who had won!"

Bright, when twelve years old, weighed one hundred and forty-four pounds; and there was another boy in Malden at the same time, fourteen years of age, who weighed as much.

There was, however, an Essex man, who not only attained a great weight, but lived to a great age, which is remarkable among persons of this class. This was James Mansfield, a butcher, who died at the village of Debden, on November 9th, 1862, in his 82nd year. Though not above the ordinary height, he measured nine feet round and weighed thirty-three stone. When sitting in his chair, made specially for his use, his abdomen covered his knees and hung down almost to the ground. When he lay down, it was necessary to pack his head to prevent suffocation : he could only lie upon one side. He was exhibited, in 1851, in Leicester Square, as " the greatest man in the world." In a suit of his clothes four ordinarily-sized men might be comfortably buttoned up. Mansfield, just before his death, was a hale old man, of good constitution, and a sanguine and happy temperament.

Corpulency naturally subjects its bearers to some of

" The thousand natural shocks .
That flesh is heir to."

Among these inconveniences is the absolute prohibition from horsemanship, and the difficulty of transportation from place to place, which may be illustrated by the following anecdotes, related by Mr. Wadd, in *Brande's Journal*, 1828 :—

Mr. B.——, of Bath, a remarkably large, corpulent, and powerful man, wanting to go by the mail, tried for a place a short time before it started. Being told it was full, he still determined to get admission, and opening the door, which no one near him ventured to oppose, he got in. When the other passengers came, the ostler reported that there was a gentleman in the coach; he was requested to come out, but having drawn up the blind, he remained quiet. Hearing, however, a consultation on the means of making him alight, and a proposal to " pull him out," he let down the blind, and laying his enormous hand on the edge of the door, he asked, who would dare to pull him out, drew up the blind again, and waiting some time, fell asleep. About one in the morning he awoke, and calling out to know whereabout he was on the journey, he perceived, what was the fact, that to end the altercation with him, the horses had been put to another coach, and that he had spent the night at the inn-door at Bath, where he had taken possession of the carriage.

A similar occurrence took place at Huddersfield. A gentleman went to a proprietor of one of the coaches to take a place for Manchester, but owing to the enormous size of his person he was refused, unless he would consent to be taken as lumber, at 9*d*. per stone, hinting at the same time the advantage of being split in two. The gentleman was not to be disheartened by this disappointment, but adopted the plan of sending the ostler of one of the

inns to take a place for him, which he did, and in the
morning wisely took the precaution of fixing himself in
the coach, with the assistance of the bystanders, from
whence he was not to be removed easily. There placed,
he was taken to his destination. The consequence was,
on his return he was necessitated to adopt a similar process, to the no small disappointment of the proprietors,
who were compelled to convey three gentlemen who
had previously taken their places in a chaise, as there
was no room beside this importunate passenger, who
weighed about thirty-six stone.

A CURE FOR CORPULENCE.

In 1863, a philanthropist laid before the public the
narrative of a man who was tremendously fat, who tried
hard for years to thin himself, and who at last succeeded. Mr. Banting, the gentleman who had the
courage and good feeling to write and publish this
narrative, not long before measured 5ft. 5in., and
weighed about 14½ stone. He owns that he had a great
deal to bear from his unfortunate make. In the first
place, the little boys in the streets laughed at him; in
the next place, he could not tie his own shoes; and,
lastly, he had, it appears, to come down-stairs back-
wards. But he was a man who struggled gallantly, and
whatever he was recommended to do, he honestly tried
to carry out. He drank mineral waters, and consulted
physicians, and took sweet counsel with innumerable
friends, but all was in vain. He lived upon sixpence

a-day, and earned it, so that the favourite recipe of Abernethy failed in his case. He went into all sorts of vapour baths and shampooing baths. He took no less than ninety Turkish baths, but nothing did him any good; he was still as fat as ever. A kind friend recommended increased bodily exertion every morning, and nothing seemed more likely to be effectual than rowing. So this stout warrior with fat got daily into a good, safe, heavy boat, and rowed a couple of hours. But he was only pouring water into the bucket of the Danaides. What he gained in one way he lost in another. His muscular vigour increased; but then, with this there came a prodigious appetite which he felt compelled to indulge, and consequently he got fatter than he had been. At last he hit upon the right adviser, who told him what to do, and whose advice was so successful that Mr. Banting could soon walk down-stairs forwards, put his old clothes quite over the suit that now fitted him, and, far from being made the victim of unkind or ill-judged chaff, was universally congratulated on his pleasant and becoming appearance. The machinery by which this change was effected was of a very simple kind. He was told to leave off eating anything but meat. It appears that none of his numerous friendly advisers, and none of the physicians he consulted, penetrated so far into the secresy of his domestic habits as to have discovered that twice a day he used formerly to indulge in bowls of bread and milk. The Solomon who saved him cut off this great feeder of fat, and since then Mr. Banting has been a thinner and a happier man.—*Abridged from the Saturday Review.*

EPITAPHS ON FAT FOLKS.

In the year 1755, died the great tallow-chandler whose life and death are thus laconically recorded on his tombstone :—

> " Here lies in earth an honest fellow,
> Who died by fat, and lived by tallow."

Another corpulent person is thus lamented :—

> " Here lies the body of Thomas Dollman,
> A vastly *fat*, though not a very tall man ;
> Full twenty stone he weighed, yet I am told,
> His captain thought him worth his weight in gold :
> Grim Death, who ne'er to nobody shows favour,
> Hurried him off for all his good behaviour ;
> Regardless of his weight, he bundled him away,
> 'Fore any one ' Jack Robinson ' could say."

A moral lesson is given in the following :—

> " But why he grew so fat i' th' waist,
>   Now mark ye the true reason,
> When other people used to fast,
>   He feasted in that season.
> So now, alas ! hath cruel Death
> Laid him in his sepulchre.
>   .   .   .   .
> Therefore, good people, here 'tis seen,
>   You plainly may see here,
> That fat men sooner die than lean,
>   Witness fat Johnny Holder."

The son of a Dean, a man of very spare habit, expressing to the son of a Bishop his astonishment at the great difference of the size of their fathers, the Bishop being very fat, he explained the reason in the following extempore parody of the old song :—

> " There's a difference between
> A Bishop and a Dean,
> And I'll tell you the reason why :
> A Dean cannot dish up
> A dinner like a Bishop,
> To feed such a fat son as I."

COUNT BORUWLASKI, THE POLISH DWARF.

One of the best attested cases of dwarfish existence on record is that of Joseph Boruwlaski, the Polish dwarf, who was the delight of our grandfathers, and who, after the age of *seventy*, suddenly found himself able with his hand to raise the latch of a door which up to that period he had always raised with a stick. How many inches he grew is not recorded, but the fact of his growth is sufficiently astonishing, and is only paradoxical so long as we continue to hold the general opinion that "men do not grow after reaching maturity," whereas, in strict language, we must admit that they *grow* as long as they live, but do not normally surpass the standard of maturity ; growth continues, but only to supply the waste, not enough, as in childhood, to supply the waste and furnish *surplus* for the increase.

Count Joseph Boruwlaski is, in many respects, the most interesting dwarf of whom we have accurate records, and he has written his own memoir to complete

our interest. He has given us his height at various
epochs as follows :—

						Ft.	In.
At one year old he measured			.	.	.	0	11
At three	„	„	.	.	.	1	2
At six	„	„	.	.	.	1	5
At ten	„	„	.	.	.	1	9
At fifteen	„	„	.	.	.	2	1
At twenty	„	„	.	.	.	2	4
At twenty-five	„	„	.	.	.	2	11
At thirty	„	„	.	.	.	3	3

Here he stopped until he was seventy. He was born
at Chaliez, in Russian Poland, November, 1739, of
noble parents, who were richer in pedigree than in
land or money. They were both well formed, healthy,
and of the ordinary size; yet of their six children, three
were dwarfs; and, to add to the singularity, the
dwarfs *alternated* with well-formed children. Joseph was
eight inches in length when born, yet perfectly well
formed, and he sucked with infantine success, walking
and talking at about the usual age.

On reaching his ninth year, he lost his father, who left
a widow and six children very ill-provided for. Luckily,
a friend of the widow, a Madame de Caorliz, adopted
Joseph, and with her the boy spent four happy years.
His benefactress then married, and this event produced a
change in his fortunes. A dwarf so remarkable was
naturally enough an envied possession; and the Countess
Humieska, a very great person indeed, felt the desire
natural in so great a person, to have this among her
curiosities. Domiciled with the great Countess, Joseph
began to taste the splendours and luxuries of courts.
They travelled through Poland, Germany, and France,
and everywhere he was the lion of the hour. At Vienna

he was presented to Maria Theresa, who, pleased with his courtly compliments, kissed him, and complimented the Countess on her travelling companion. On another occasion, Joseph, in the lap of the Empress, who had sixteen children of her own, and doted on them, was looking at the hand in which his own was clasped, and which flashed light from a ring bearing her cipher in brilliants. She asked him if he was pleased with the ring; he told her it was the *hand* he looked at, and at the same time raised it to his lips. The flattered Empress insisted on giving him the ring; but alas! it was too large, whereupon she called to a young lady of about six years old, and taking from her a fine diamond ring, placed it on Joseph's finger: this young lady was Marie Antoinette.

From Vienna the travellers proceeded to Munich, and thence, after countless fêtes, they went to Luneville, the court of Stanislas Leckzinski, titular King of Poland. Here Joseph met the dwarf Bébé, of whom Boruwlaski gives this account:—" With this prince (Stanislas) lived the famous Bébé, till then considered the most extraordinary dwarf that was ever seen; and who was, indeed, perfectly well proportioned, and with a pleasant physiognomy, but who (I am sorry to say it, for the honour of us dwarfs) had all the defects in his mind and way of thinking which are commonly attributed to us. He was at that time about thirty,* and his height two feet eight inches; and when measured, it appeared that I was much shorter, being no more than two feet four inches. At our first interview he showed

---

* Joseph is in error here; Bébé was two years his junior, but precocity of development made him appear to be thirty, though really only about seventeen.

much fondness for me; but, on perceiving that I preferred the company and conversation of sensible people,
and above all, when he perceived that the King took
pleasure in my society, he conceived the most violent
jealously and hatred of me; so that I escaped his fury only
by a miracle. One day, we were both in the apartment
of his Majesty, who caressed me, and asked me several
questions, testifying his pleasure and approbation of my
replies in the most affectionate manner. Then addressing Bébé, he said: 'You see, Bébé, what a difference
there is between him and you. He is amiable, cheerful,
entertaining, and instructed, whereas you are but a
little machine.' At these words I saw fury sparkle in
his eyes; he answered nothing, but his countenance and
blush proved how violently he was agitated. A moment
after, the King having gone into his cabinet, Bébé
availed himself of the opportunity to execute his re-
vengeful projects; and slyly approaching, seized me by
the waist, and endeavoured to push me on to the fire.
Luckily, I laid hold with both hands of the iron prop
which sustained the tongs and poker, and thus prevented
his wicked intentions. The noise I made in defending
myself brought back the King to my assistance. He
afterwards called the servants, and ordered Bébé corporal
punishment. In vain did I intercede."

On quitting the court of Stanislas, Boruwlaski visited
that of Versailles, where the Queen, the Duke of
Orleans, and other distinguished personages, made as
much of him as vanity could desire. The Count Orginski,
finding he had a taste for music, provided him a master
for the guitar. At the table of this nobleman, he one day
allowed himself to be concealed in a large vase, which
was placed amid the dishes, and to which the attention

of the guests was directed, till their curiosity was fairly
roused, expecting some rarity surpassing all the delicacies of the already sumptuous banquet; and then Joseph
suddenly stood up, amid shouts of laughter.

From Paris he went to Holland, and thence back to
Poland. His reception in Warsaw was enthusiastic;
and as travel and reading had given polish to his
manners and culture to his intellect, his society became
sought after for something more than mere curiosity.
He now attended the theatre, and became fascinated
with the actresses. His first love was a French actress,
who, amused and flattered, pretended to return his
passion, and for a time he was in a delirium of happiness;
but an unlucky discovery of her having talked about
his passion with mockery, cruelly dispelled his brief
dream. To be in love with an actress, and to find that
she has been laughing at the passion she has inspired,
and only feigning to return it for some object of her own,
is what many young men have had to experience; but
perhaps in none could the mortification of self-love have
been so cruel as in the little dwarf, who knew the ridicule which must necessarily attend his presumption in
claiming the privilege of a man. But the heart having
once known the bitter-sweet of love, will not long be
kept from it; and Joseph soon fixed his affections on
Isolina, a *protégée* of the Countess Humieska, who,
living under the same roof with him, was much astonished
to observe that he allowed every *other* lady to take him
on her lap and caress him; she accused him of not
liking her, because to her only he was reserved and shy.
Now, he had not forgotten the ridicule of the French
actress: for a whole twelvemonth he continued loving
in silence, in doubt, and in trouble. His health suffered;

at last, passion triumphed over his fears; he declared his love, which the lady treated as the love of a child. "Really," said she, "you are a child, and I cannot help laughing at your extravagance." He tried to convince her that he was no child, and would not be loved like a child; when she burst out laughing, told him he knew not what he said, and left the room.

This was a ludicrous situation, but with a tragic aspect; a young and lively woman receiving a passionate declaration from a being not taller than a child three or four years old, may be excused if her sense of the ludicrous prevented her understanding the seriousness of the passion she inspired. Joseph was hurt, but not altogether dissatisfied. The secret no longer pressed its uneasy burden on his mind. She know of his love; she could now interpret his reserve—his melancholy—his silent adoration. In time she might be touched. For the first few days, indeed, there seemed little hope of such an issue. She bantered him incessantly, and the more he tried to speak to her as a man, the more she persisted in treating him like a child. The effect of this was a serious illness; for two months he was in danger. He recovered, and she, from that time, gave up the dangerous game; and they were eventually married.

We must now accompany Boruwlaski to England, where he was received by the Duke and Duchess of Devonshire, and was presented to the King and Queen, and patronized by the Prince of Wales and the nobility.

Among the remarkable persons whom the Count met was O'Brien, the Irish giant. "Our surprise," says Boruwlaski, "was mutual—the giant remained a moment speechless with astonishment, and then stooping halfway, he presented his hand, which could easily have contained a dozen of mine, and made me a very pretty compliment." When they stood beside each other, the giant's knee was nearly on a level with the dwarf's head. They both resided together some time at an inn at Epping, where they often walked out together, greatly to the amusement of the townsfolk.

Mathews, the comedian, was a friend and admirer of Boruwlaski, and contrived to get an interview arranged with George IV. for the presentation of a copy of the Count's *Memoirs*, published in 1788. Mathews and his little charge were ushered into the presence of the sovereign: the King rose and met Boruwlaski, raised him up in his arms, in a kind embrace, saying, " My dear old friend, how delighted I am to see you !" and then placed the little man upon a sofa. But the Count's loyalty not being so satisfied, he descended with the agility of a schoolboy, and threw himself at his master's feet, who, however, would not suffer him to remain in that position for a minute, but raised him again upon the sofa. In the course of the conversation, the Count, addressing the King in French, was told that his English was so good it was quite unnecessary to speak in any other language ; for his Majesty, with his usual tact, easily discerned that he should be a loser in resigning the Count's prettily-broken English, which (as he always thought in his native language, and literally translated its idioms) was the most amusing imaginable, and totally distinct from the imperfect English of other foreigners. . . . The King, in the course of conversation, said, " But, Count, you were married when I first knew you : I hope madame is still alive, and as well as yourself." " Ah, no ! Majesty ; Isolina die thirty year ! *Fine* woman ! *sweet, beauty* body ! You have no *idea*, Majesty." " I am sorry to hear of her death; such a charming person must have been a great loss to you, Count." "Dat is very true, Majesty; *indid, indid,* it was great sorrow for me!" His Majesty then inquired how old the Count was, and on being told, with a start of surprise, observed, "Count, you are the finest man of your age I ever saw. I wish you could return the compliment." To which Boruwlaski, not to be outdone in courtesy, ludicrously replied, "Oh! Majesty, *fine* body! *indid, indid; beauty* body!"

The King, on accepting the book which the Count wished to present, turned to the Marchioness of Conyngham, and took from her a little case containing a beautiful miniature watch and seals, attached to a superb chain, the watch exquisitely ornamented with jewels. This the King begged the Count to accept, saying, as he held the *Memoirs* in the other hand, "My dear friend, I shall read and preserve this as long as I live, for your sake; and in return I request you will wear this for mine." His Majesty said to Mathews, in the absence of the Count, "If I had a dozen sons, I could not point out to them a more perfect model of good breeding and elegance than the Count; he is really a most accomplished and charming person."

It appears that, by the kindness of friends, Boruwlaski had purchased an annuity, which secured him independence for the remainder of his life. Out of this transaction arose a laughable incident. One day he called at the insurance office with Mr. Mathews, and on being asked how he was, he replied, with the vivacity of eighteen, "Oh, *never* better! *quite* vel!" and he ran out of the office from the gaze of the aged insurer, scarcely able to restrain his merriment till he got out of hearing.

He then told Mr. Mathews, during his convulsions of laughter, that the person they had just seen was the granter of his annuity. "Ha! ha! ha! O Mattew, I cannot help! Oh *poor devil*, poor *hold* body! It *maks me laffing*, poor *hold hanimal!* Oh he say prayer for me die, often when he *slip!* Oh you may *d*epend—ha! ha! ha! but Boruwlaski *never* die! He *calcoolated dat* dwarf not live it long, *et* I live it forty year to *plag* him. Oh he is in a *hobbel debblishly!* I *tellee dat!* He fifty year *yonger den* Boruwlaski; *mintime* he dead as soon as me. Oh yes, you may be sure *dat—dat* is my *oppinnon*. Boruwlaski never die," playfully nodding his little head, "you may *d*epend." Mr. Mathews asked him if the old man had any family (feeling some compassion for his hard case), to which the Count cried out, "Oh he have it *shildren* twenty, like a pig, poor *devel! mintime* he *riche* body! Oh he have it *goold et wast* many bank *nott*. *Bote* he have it *greet prepencity* to keep him fast hold, poor idi*ot!* It *macks me laffing!* "—(See the *Memoirs of Charles Mathews*, by Mrs. Mathews.)

To these characteristics we are enabled to add that of an English letter, written by the Count in his *eighty-ninth* year, the handwriting of which is singularly firm and steady, resembling that of a schoolboy of about fourteen. We shall copy it *literatim* from the autograph letter in the possession of Lord Houghton. It is addressed to Miss Emma George, at Miss Bird's, Pitt Street, Edinburgh, and runs thus:—

"Dear Emma.—I am a fraid you will think me negligent in not answering your kind Letter which I received both. which made me delay write soonere I was en a visite at Newcastle, and I remain rathere to lon. and with the acceident happing when I burn your Lette in

which been your derection, when I do so after reading,
for alwais afraid of aney mischiefe at homes, what you
know my situation, in which I remain to this day. and
increas dayli more and more unhappy. I have maney
things to tell you and you wish to know about me, but
I cannot trust to a Lettere to disclos, and gave you
picture of my precise state of my of my Life with extended Field, to make description of my trouble but
only I may say truly. That I find myselfe without
friend in a Stranger Country. Yet from the aspect of
flattering appearance. I thought aftere a very fatiging
journey in the begonning of my Life, that no kind of
vexation would distourb my present State of happiness
at Durham. Upon which my mind being grounded, in
expectation of all feliesity. But here what to say of my
sorrow with astonishment, when I found overeeting,
when I behod now nothing but betterness of heart, and
so heavy a Cloud over my existance in misery. So I
have not on friend, but I have wakeful body who watch
all my motion. So I have my share to be partner with
you and support on othere, when we are left to our-
self in a Pilgrimage in which we are engaged so severely.
To be sure I feel the disappointments of my situation.
Yet I have experience that I cannot help thinking that
it was well that Providence had blessed me, to alowd
me kindly as litll as it is; Yet to accommodated Dear
Emma according to fortune which God gave me, which
Dear Emma will receive next month your 5l. I beg
Dear Emma make your selfe happy and not uneasy if
some time I delay in answering your Lettere. Notwith-
standing you most know me now to trust me and have
Confidence in me that I ame not Changable nature, but

U 2

remain, and believe me, your sincer affectiont, Joseph Boruwlaski.

"*Durham* 17 *March* 1828."

This singular being lived to the extraordinary age of ninety-eight; a great age for an ordinary man, and quite without example in the history of dwarfs. He died at Bank's Cottage, near Durham, on the 5th of September, 1837, and his remains were placed near those of Stephen Kemble, in the Nine Altars of Durham Cathedral. It is stated in the *Gentleman's Magazine* (Oct., 1837), that the cottage was the gift of some of the prebendaries of Durham, who also allowed him a handsome income. They may have given him the cottage, but the income came, as Boruwlaski himself informs us, from the Misses Metcalfe. In the parish church of St. Mary-the-Less is a mural tablet of white stone, with an inscription, erected in memory of the Count, who long resided in the city, and has, indeed, given his name to a bend in the river, known as "Count's Corner."—(Walker's *Brief Sketch of Durham*, 4th edition, 1865.) If the reader attentively considers the story we have narrated, he will perceive that the Count, although an anomaly in respect of size, was in all other respects a perfectly formed man, and is distinguished from most other dwarfs by longevity, paternity, and intelligence. The anomaly, therefore, could not have been deeply seated. He was a perfect copy of nature's finest work in duodecimo. A full-length portrait of him may be seen in the Hunterian Museum, life-size, leaning against a chair.

It may be interesting to narrate a few more examples of dwarf life, from accredited sources.

M. St. Hilaire relates from the *Philosophical Trans-*

actions, 1751–2, the case of a dwarf named Hopkins, who, at fifteen years of age, stood only 2 ft. 7 in., and weighed between 12 and 13 lbs. He had all the signs of old age. He was bent, deformed, and troubled with a dry cough. His hearing and sight were bad; his teeth almost all decayed. He was very thin, and so weak as scarcely to be able to stand. Till the age of seven he had been gay, healthy, and active; nor at that age did he show any indications of stopped growth. He was well formed, and weighed nineteen pounds, *i.e.* six pounds more than he weighed at fifteen. From that period his health declined, and his body wasted. He came from healthy parents of ordinary stature, and was the second of six children, another of whom also was a dwarf.

Dantlow, the Russian dwarf, was only thirty inches high; he was without arms, and had only four toes on each foot. With his feet he made pen-and-ink sketches rivalling etchings; and knitted stockings with needles made of wood. He fed himself with his left foot; learned with great facility, and was eager to learn.

M. Virey describes a German girl, exhibited in Paris in 1816. She was of parents above the average height, who had previously produced a male dwarf. At eight years old she weighed no more than an ordinary infant; her height was eighteen inches. In temper she was gay, restless, and excitable. Her pulse normally was at ninety-four.

M. Virey also relates the following example:—Thérèse Souvray, was destined to become the bride of Bébé, to whom she was solemnly affianced in the year 1761; but death snatched the bridegroom from her, and as the *fiancée* of this celebrated man, she was exhibited in Paris during the year 1821. She was then seventy-three years of age; gay, healthy, lively, and danced with her sister, two years her senior, and measuring only three feet and a half, French measure.

In 1865, there died in Paris the dwarf Richebourg, who was an historical personage. Richebourg, who was only 60 centimètres high, was in his sixteenth year placed in the household of the Duchess of Orleans (the mother of King Louis-Philippe). He was often made useful for the transmission of despatches. He was dressed up as a baby, and important State papers placed in his clothes, and thus he was able to effect a communication between Paris and the *émigrés*, which could hardly have taken place by any other means. The most suspicious of *sans culottes* never took it into his head to stop a nurse with a baby in her arms. For the last thirty years he lived in Paris in one of the houses in the remotest part of the Faubourg St. Germain. He had a morbid dread of appearing in public, and it is recorded that during this long period he never put his foot outside the house. He received from the Orleans family a pension of 3,000 francs per annum. He had attained the ripe age of ninety-two.

A writer in *Fraser's Magazine*, August, 1856, from the above and other examples of dwarfs quoted by him, sets down these few general conclusions upon the question of their organization:—"In doing so," he remarks, "it will be well to bear in mind that the very fact of dwarfs being *anomalies*, renders any generalization respecting them subject to many qualifications in each particular instance. Thus, although it is true, as a general fact, that they are short-lived and unintelligent, we see examples of more than ordinary intelligence in

Boruwlaski and his brother, and Jeffrey Hudson, and of longevity in them. One may assert, indeed, that longevity and intelligence are intimately allied in the dwarf organization ; for, whenever the anomaly of growth is not profound enough to affect the health, it is presumably too superficial to affect the intelligence ; and, *vice versa*, when we see a being passing rapidly from childhood to old age, we may be certain that the organization is too aberrant from the normal type to permit the free development of intelligence. Another general fact about dwarfs, and one to which we know of no exception, is, that they are very excitable, and consequently, irascible ; when in good health, lively, restless, and turbulent. This, indeed, is a characteristic of men and animals of the small type."

THE IRISH GIANT.

This extraordinary person, whose height was eight feet seven-and-a-half inches, was born at Kinsale, in Ireland. His real name was Patrick Cotter. He was of obscure parentage, and originally laboured as a bricklayer. His uncommon size rendered him a mark for the cunning of a showman, who, for the payment of 50*l.* per annum, had the privilege of exhibiting Cotter for three years in England. Not contented with his bargain, the huckster underlet to another speculator the liberty of showing him ; and poor Cotter, through resisting this nefarious transaction, was saddled with a fictitious debt, and thrown into a spunging-house in Bristol. In this situation he was visited by a gentleman of the city, who, compassionating his distress, and having reason to think that he was injustly detained, generously became his bail, and investigated the affair, and not only obtained Cotter his liberty, but freed him from all kind of obligation to serve his taskmaster any longer. He was then but eighteen years old. He retained, to his last breath, a due sense of the good offices of the Bristol stranger, conferred upon him when he was sorely in need; and the giant did not forget his benefactor in his will.

It happened to be September when Cotter was liberated; and by the further assistance of his benefactor, he was enabled to exhibit himself in the St. James's fair at Bristol; and in three days he found himself possessed of thirty pounds English money. He now commenced a regular exhibition of his person, which he continued until within two years of his death, when having realized sufficient money to enable him to keep a carriage, and live in good style, he declined to exhibit any more, which was always irksome to his feelings. He was unoffending and amiable in his manners; was possessed of good sense, and his mind was not uncultivated; he long kept a journal of his life, which a whim of the moment induced him to commit to the flames. He died in his forty-sixth year, September 8th, 1806, at the Hotwells, Bristol. He was buried in the Roman Catholic chapel, Trenchard Street, at six o'clock in the morning, this early hour being fixed on to prevent as much as possible the assemblage of a crowd; but it is stated that at least 2,000 persons were present. The coffin, of lead, measured nine feet two inches in the clear, and the wooden case four inches more; it was three feet across the shoulders. No hearse could be procured long enough to contain the coffin, the projecting end of which was draped with black cloth. Fourteen men bore it from the hearse to the grave, into which it was let down with pulleys. To prevent any attempt to disturb his remains, of which Cotter had, when living, the greatest horror, the grave was made twelve feet deep, in a solid rock. A plaster cast of his right hand may be seen at the College of Surgeons, Lincoln's Inn Fields.

BIRTH EXTRAORDINARY.

On Sunday, the 23rd of October, 1836, occurred an event interesting to physiologists. The wife of a dwarf, Don Santiago de los Santos (herself a dwarf), was delivered of a well-formed male infant, at their residence, No. 167, High Holborn, near Museum Street. The accoucheurs were Mr. Bowden, of Sloane Street, Chelsea, who had before attended Donna Santiago on a similar occasion; and Dr. Davis, of Savile Row. Both gentleman had for some time been very assiduous in their attentions to the little lady; but the infant, though it came into the world alive, did not survive above half-an-hour. Its length was thirteen and a half inches; its weight one pound four ounces and a half (avoirdupois); it was in every respect well formed; and the likeness of the face to that of its father was very striking. It was carried in a coffin to St. George's Church, Bloomsbury; but being there refused sepulture, it was taken home, preserved in spirits, and subsequently exhibited. Dr. Davis was anxious to have it submitted to dissection, and to lecture upon it in the theatre of University College; this, however, was objected to by the Lilliputian parents, who appeared poignantly to feel the proposition.

Don Santiago, who was only twenty-five inches high, was at this time in his fiftieth year. He was a native of the Spanish settlement of Manilla; in one of the forests of which he was exposed and deserted, on account of his diminutive size. He was, however, miraculously saved by the Viceroy, who was hunting in that quarter, and humanely ordered him to be taken care of, and nursed with the same tenderness as his own children, with whom the little creature was brought up and educated, until he had attained the age of *manhood*. His birth dated from the period of his exposure, which was in 1786. His parents, it was ascertained, were farmers; and were, with their other children (sons daughters), of robust frame, and rather above the usual height.

When the Don was twenty years of age, his humane protector died; and attachment to the place of his birth prevented his accompanying his foster brother and sisters to Old Spain. This wilfulness cost him dearly; neglected by his parents and family, he suffered hardships and privations of the most afflicting nature. At length, he found his way to Madras, and was, in the year 1830, brought to England by the captain of a trading vessel. During the voyage he was washed overboard by a heavy sea; but hencoops and spars being thrown out, and other assistance afforded, his life was saved.

On his arrival in northern latitudes, he suffered severely from cold, and even when accustomed to the climate, he could not swallow cold water. Still, he

never went near a fire, although he felt sensibly if his
room was not kept warm. He was stoutly built, and
generally in cheerful spirits and good health. His
complexion was of a slight copper colour, and the expression of his countenance was pleasing and intelligent.
His habits were temperate, and he seldom drank anything but warm water; but on birth days and other
anniversaries, he indulged in a few glasses of wine. He
was fond of music and dancing, and gallant to the ladies;
but his ruling passion appeared to be a fondness for
jewellery and silver plate, to which ornaments he had
been accustomed in the house and at the table of the
Viceroy of Manilla. His mind appeared to be deeply
impressed with the tenets of the Roman Catholic
church, in which his foster-father took care to have him
instructed. He read his prayer-book and psalter morning and evening, very devoutly crossing himself, and
performing his genuflexions and the other ceremonies
inculcated by the teachers of that faith. Once or twice
a month, he went to the Spanish Ambassador's chapel,
where, secluded from observation, he worshipped with
the sincerity and devotion of a good Catholic. Besides
his native tongue, he spoke an Indian *patois*, conversed
freely in Portuguese, and in English indifferently well.

He became acquainted with his little wife in Birmingham, of which town she was a native. Her name
was Ann Hopkins; her height was thirty-eight inches,
or thirteen inches taller than her dwarf spouse. She
was thirty-one years of age, and was a pretty little
creature, possessing much symmetry and grace. Her
father stood six feet one inch and a half out of his
shoes; her mother was of middle size, and her
brothers and sisters, nine in number, were all tall
and robust. The little Don and Donna lived to-

gether very affectionately, their attachment having been mutual and at first sight; their only difference of opinion being, that she being of the Protestant faith, they did not worship together. They were married on the 6th of July, 1834, in the Roman Catholic chapel at Birmingham; and two days after, at St. Martin's church, in the same town, by the Rev. Mr. Foy; the high bailiff giving away the bride. The crowd of spectators was so great that the assistance of the police was necessary to secure the ingress and egress of the little couple into and out of the church. Much uneasiness was caused to the bridegroom by the refusal of one clergyman to ratify his marriage in the Protestant Church, on the supposition that it was contrary to the canon law; but this difficulty was ultimately arranged.—*Abridged from the Morning Advertiser.*

WILLIAM HUTTON'S "STRONG WOMAN."

William Hutton, the Birmingham manufacturer, was accustomed to take a month's tour every summer, and to note down his observations on places and people. Some of the results appeared in distinct books, some in his autobiography, and some in the *Gentleman's Magazine*, towards the close of the last century and the beginning of the present. One year he would be accompanied by his father, a tough old man, who was not frightened at a twenty-mile walk; another year he would go alone; while on one occasion his daughter went with him, she riding on horseback, and he trudging on foot by her side. Various parts of England and Wales were thus visited, at a time when tourists' facilities were slender indeed. It appears from his lists of distances that he could "do" fifteen or twenty miles a day for weeks together; although his mode of examining places led to a much slower rate of progress.

One of the odd characters which Hutton met with at Matlock, in Derbyshire, in July, 1801, is worth describing in his own words. After noticing the rocks and caves at that town, he said, "The greatest wonder I saw was Miss Phœbe Bown, in person five feet six, about thirty, well-proportioned, round-faced and ruddy; a dark penetrating eye, which, the moment it fixes upon your face, stamps your character, and that with precision. Her step (pardon the Irishism) is more manly than a man's, and can easily cover forty miles a day. Her common dress is a man's hat, coat, with a spencer about it, and men's shoes; I believe she is a stranger to breeches. She can lift one hundred-weight with each hand, and carry fourteen score. Can sew, knit, cook, and spin, but hates them all, and every accompaniment to the female character, except that of modesty. A gentleman at the New Bath recently treated her so rudely, that "she had a good mind to have knocked him down." She positively assured me she did not know what fear is. She never gives an affront, but will offer to fight any one who gives her one. If she has not fought, perhaps it is owing to the insulter being a coward, for none. else would *give* an affront [to a woman]. She has strong sense, an excellent judgment, says smart things, and supports an easy freedom in all companies. Her voice is more than masculine, it is deep toned; the wind in her face, she can send it a mile; has no beard; accepts any kind of manual labour, as holding the plough, driving the team, thatching the ricks, &c. But her chief avocation is breaking-in horses, at a guinea a week; always rides without a saddle; and is supposed the best judge of a horse, cow, &c., in the country; and is frequently requested to purchase for others at the neighbouring fairs. She is fond of Milton, Pope, Shakspeare, also of music; is self-taught; performs on several instruments, as the flute, violin, harpsichord, and supports the bass-viol in Matlock church. She is an excellent markswoman, and, like her brother-sportsmen, carries her gun upon her shoulder. She eats no beef or pork, and but little mutton; her chief food is milk, and also her drink—discarding wine, ale, and spirits."—*From the Book of Days.*

WILDMAN AND HIS BEES.

In Winchester Place, now Pentonville Road, near to the south-east corner of Penton Street, stood "Prospect House," so called from the fine view which it commanded over London and the circumjacent country. In the British Museum is a fine pen-and-ink drawing of a view of London from Pentonville, by Antonio Canaletti; and we find "Prospect House" in the rate-books in 1669; there were bowling-greens attached to it for "gentlemen bowlers." Subsequently the house was named from its proprietor, and became popularly known as Dobney's, or D'Aubigny's. Mrs. Dobney, who kept the house for many years, died in 1760, at the age of eighty-six. It then passed to a new proprietor, a Mr. Johnson, who built on the bowling-green, which was near the corner of Penton Street, an amphitheatre for equestrian performances, *al fresco,* and engaged one

Price, who had been starring at the Three Hats, a rival house close by, to exhibit his original feats of horsemanship. In 1769, the house was the scene of Philip Jonas's exhibition of "dexterity of hands;" and about this time was shown here the skeleton of a whale sixty feet long. In 1770, the house was taken for a boarding school, but was soon closed. It was then re-opened as the Jubilee Tea Gardens (from the Jubilee got up at Stratford-upon-Avon, by Garrick, in honour of Shakspeare); the interiors of the boxes were painted with scenes from some of his plays.

In 1772, the celebrated Daniel Wildman exhibited here his bees every evening (wet evenings excepted). He made several new and amazing experiments; he rode standing upright, one foot on the saddle, and the other on the horse's neck, with a curious *mask of bees* on his head and face. He also rode standing upright on the saddle with the bridle in his mouth, and by firing a pistol, made one part of the bees march over a table, and the other part swarm in the air and return to their proper hive again. Wildman's performances of the "Bees on Horseback" were also thus described:—

> " He with uncommon art and matchless skill
> Commands those insects, who obey his will ;
> With bees others cruel means employ,
> They take their honey and the bees destroy ;
> Wildman humanely, with ingenious ease,
> He takes the honey, but preserves the bees."

Wildman also sold bees from one stock in "the common or newly-invented hives." He published a "Guide for Bee Management" at his Bee and Honey Warehouse, No. 326, Holborn. In 1774, the gardens were much neglected, the walks not being kept in order, nor the hedges properly cut; but there were several good apartments in the house, besides handsome tea-rooms; but the ground was cleared about 1790, and the present handsome dwelling-houses in Winchester Place were built upon part of the site. The gardens, though much shorn of their beauty and attractiveness, continued in existence until the year 1810, when they disappeared; and the only memorial that remains on the site of this once famed place of amusement, is a mean court in Penton Street, known as Dobney's Court. Mr. Upcott, of the London Institution, had in his collection a drawing of Prospect House, taken about 1780.—*Pinks's History of Clerkenwell.*

LORD STOWELL'S LOVE OF SIGHT-SEEING.

Lord Stowell loved manly sports, and was not above being pleased with the most rude and simple diversions. He gloried in Punch and Judy—their fun stirred his mirth without, as in Goldsmith's case, provoking spleen. He made a boast on one occasion that there was not a puppet-show in London he had not visited, and when turned fourscore, was caught watching one at a distance with children of less growth in high glee. He has been known to make a party with Windham to visit Cribb's, and to have attended the Fives Court as a favourite resort. "There were curious characters," he observed, "to be seen at these places." He was the most indefatigable sight-seer in London. Whatever show could be visited for a shilling, or less, was visited by Lord Stowell. In the western end of London there was a room generally let for exhibitions. At the entrance, as it is said, Lord Stowell presented himself, eager to see "the green monster serpent," which had lately issued cards of invitation to the public. As he was pulling out his purse to pay for his admission, a sharp but honest north-country lad, whose business it was to take the money, recognised him as an old customer, and knowing his name, thus addressed him: "We can't take your shilling, my lord; 'tis the old serpent which you have seen twice before in other colours; but ye shall go in and see her." He entered, saved his money, and enjoyed his third visit to the painted beauty. This love of seeing sights was, on another occasion, productive of the following whimsical incident. Some thirty years ago, an animal, called a "Bonassus," was exhibited in the Strand. On Lord Stowell's paying it a second visit, the keeper very courteously told his lordship that he was welcome to come, gratuitously, as often as he pleased. Within a day or two after this, however, there appeared, under the bills of the exhibition, in conspicuous characters, "Under the patronage of the Right Hon. Lord Stowell;" an announcement of which the noble and learned lord's friends availed themselves, by passing many a joke upon him; all of which he took with the greatest good humour.

Lord Stowell was a great eater, and, says Mr. Surtees, "the feats which he performed with the knife and fork were eclipsed by those which he would afterwards display with the bottle." His habits were slovenly and unclean. "The hand that could pen the neatest of periods was itself often dirty and unwashed; and the mouth which could utter eloquence so graceful, or such playful wit, fed voraciously, and selected the most greasy food." Then, again, he was an unquestionable miser. He kept a very mean establishment. Fond as he was of his wine, he would drink less at his own than at other tables. "He could drink any *given* quantity," as was wittily observed by his brother, Lord Eldon, but was abstemious where he had to pay. The most painful fact that remains to be recorded respecting him is, that when his only son William had formed an attachment that was unexceptionable, he, though it may be said he rolled in riches, would not make him a sufficient allowance to enable him to marry. It has been stated that this son died from the effects of intemperate habits; and it must be added, that but for this disappointment the young man might have lived. In despair he plunged into excesses. His father just survived him, and his great wealth was gathered up by collaterals. Perhaps his fondness of poking about London visiting cheap shows was connected more with his avarice than with his curiosity. After his elevation to the peerage, he was actually seen coming out of a penny show in London—cheap excitement! Like Lord Eldon, though a great friend of the church, he never attended public worship. What had been said of his brother might have been said of him, that he was more properly a buttress of the church than a pillar, for he was never seen inside it. At the same time there is no reason to doubt that he was a good Christian; probably, like many other University men, he had a surfeit of chapels when at college, and shuddered at the thought of again entering one. With all his failings, and notwithstanding his avarice, which increased with his years, Lord Stowell must be regarded as having been, after a peculiar sort, a kindly, amiable man.

JOHN DAY AND FAIRLOP FAIR.

In the Forest of Hainault, in Essex, about a mile from Barking side, stood the famous Fairlop Oak, which the tradition of the country traces half-way up the Christian era. This forest possesses more beautiful scenery than, perhaps, any other forest in England. Fifty years since the oak was still a noble tree. About a yard from the ground, where its bole was thirty-six feet in circumference, it spread into eleven vast arms, yet not in the manner of an oak, but rather in that of a beech, its shade overspreading an area of 300 feet in circuit. Around this fine old tree, eighty years since, archery meetings were held by the gentry of the district, with pic-nics in tents, bands of music, &c.; and then to protect the old oak it was enclosed with a spiked paling, inscribed as follows: "All good foresters are requested not to hurt this old tree, as a plaister has been put to its wounds." The extremities of its branches had been sawn off, and Forsyth's composition applied to them, to preserve them from decay.

But the tree has a more popular history. Upon a small estate, near the oak, in the last century, there dwelt one John Day, a well-to-do block and pump maker, of Wapping, who used to repair annually, on the first Friday in July, to the forest, and there meet a party of his neighbours, and dine under the shade of the famous oak, on *beans and bacon*. In the course of a few years, Day's rural feast induced other parties to follow his homely example, and suttling booths were erected for their accommodation. In addition to the entertainment given to his friends, Mr. Day never failed, on the day of the feast, to provide several sacks of beans, with a proportionate quantity of bacon, which he distributed from the trunk of the tree to the persons there assembled. About the year 1723, the scene on the first Friday in July exhibited the appearance of a *regular fair*, such as John Gay, in one of his *Pastorals*, almost contemporaneously describes in these lines :—

> "Pedlers' stalls with glitt'ring toys are laid,
> The various fairings of the country maid :
> Long silken laces hang upon the twine,
> And rows of pins and amber bracelets shine.
> Here the tight lass knives, combs, and scissors spies,
> And looks on thimbles with desiring eyes.
> The mountebank now treads the stage, and sells
> His pills, his balsams, and his ague spells.
> Now o'er and o'er the nimble tumbler springs,
> And on the rope the vent'rous maiden swings ;
> Jack-pudding, in his parti-coloured jacket,
> Tosses the glove and jokes at every packet ;
> Here raree-shows are seen, and Punch's feats,
> And pockets picked in crowds, and various cheats."

For several years before the death of the generous founder of this fair and public bean-feast, the pump and block makers of Wapping went annually to the fair in the forest, seated in a boat of one entire piece of fir, covered with an awning, mounted on a coach-carriage, and drawn by six horses; attended with flags and streamers, a band of music, and a great number of persons on foot and horseback. The number of carriages was then increased to three, two of them being rigged as ships. At six o'clock precisely they all paraded round the oak, singing a glee composed for the occasion; after which the holiday-keepers returned to town.

A few years before Mr. Day's death, the Fairlop Oak lost a large limb, out of which he had a coffin made for his own interment. He died on the 19th of October, 1767, at the age of eighty-four. His remains, pursuant to his own request, were conveyed to Barking by water, attended by six journeymen pump and block makers, to each of whom he bequeathed a new leather apron and a guinea. There is a memorial of him in Barking church-yard.

The fair long survived the patriarchal pump-maker, good John Day, as did also the oak. It was enclosed, as we have stated, at the commencement of the present century. But, notwithstanding the appeal to the " good foresters," and the respect due to the veteran of the forest, the rabble broke down the palings and lit their fires within the trunk in the cavities formed by the roots, and several of the limbs were broken off. The space within the trunk may be estimated by the evidence of a resident in the neighbourhood. " When a boy," he writes, " I have driven in a hot day from out of the hollow three or four horses, and sometimes four or five cows." But the tree received the greatest injury on the 25th of June, 1805, when a party of sixty persons, who came from London to play at cricket, &c., kindled a fire, which, after they had left, spread very considerably, and caught the tree. It was not discovered for two hours, and though a number of persons brought water to extinguish it, yet the main branch on the south side and part of the trunk were consumed. Fifteen years later, the high winds of February, 1820, brought the massive trunk and limbs to the turf which the tree had for so many ages overshadowed with its verdant foliage. Its wood was very much prized : a pulpit was made of it for Wanstead Church ; the rest of the timber of the Fairlop Oak was purchased by Mr. Seabrook, the builder, who formed with it the very handsome pulpit and reading-desk for the church of St. Pancras, in the New Road, then in course of erection.

The fair was still continued, though the loss of the oak, and the assemblage of booths and shows, and theatrical exhibitions, which bordered the area in the forest, destroyed the simplicity that was originally intended to be preserved by the founder. As the fair was held on Friday, it became a great point to extend it to Sunday, when shoals of visitors came ; and, though the shows were interdicted, the refreshment resorts grew to such licence as it became necessary to curb. Of the fair of 1843, we have a special remembrance. The block-makers, sail-makers, and mast-makers, as usual, came to "gay Fairlop," in their amphibious frigates, gaily decorated and mounted on carriages, each drawn by six horses ; and the wives of the men in their holiday gear followed in open landaus. But the Essex magistrates had now by notice restricted the fair to *one day*. The booths and shows were less numerous than on former occasions, but the gipsies were in great numbers; the knights of the pea and thimble were vigilantly routed by the police. The Lea Bridge and Ilford roads were crowded with horses and vehicles ; and many persons went by railway to Ilford, and thence to the forest. But there came a heavy July rain to spoil the sport, and the fair grew flat. The booths and shows could not be removed till Monday, but nothing was allowed to be sold after Friday, and the exhibitions were closed. Nevertheless, the Sunday visitors came in thousands.

By these curtailments, Fairlop Fair was gradually brought to an end, though not until it had existed for a century and a quarter.

A PRINCELY HOAX.

In the autumn of 1785, when the Prince of Wales was at Brighton, he was much in the company of Mr. and Mrs. Lawrell; of whom and the Prince, Lady Llanover, in her *Memoirs of Mrs. Delany*, relates the following piquant story, which she received from a gentleman, as well as from Miss Burney, who had it from Lady Rothes, Sir Lucas Pepys' wife.* It happened one afternoon that Mrs. Lawrell alone was of a party with the Prince of Wales, Lady Beauchamp, and some other fine people. Mrs. Lawrell, like a good wife, about nine o'clock, said she must go home to her husband. The Prince said he and the party would come and sup with them; the lady received the gracious intimation with all the respect that became her, and hastened home to acquaint her husband and make preparation. Whether Mr. Lawrell was more or less sensible of the honour that was designed him than his wife I don't know, but he said he should not come if he could help it, and if he did come, he should have nothing to eat. It was in vain Mrs. Lawrell remonstrated; he continued inflexible, and she had nothing for it but to put him to bed, and wrote a note to Lady

---

* Sir Lucas Pepys was physician in ordinary to the King, and seven years President of the College of Physicians. He had a seat at Mickleham, in Surrey. One day, at Dorking, he inquired at a druggist's what all his varieties of drugs were for. To prepare prescriptions, was the reply. "Why," said Sir Lucas, "I never used but three or four articles in all my practice."

Beauchamp, informing her Mr. Lawrell was taken suddenly ill, and begging she would entertain the Prince in her stead. Between one and two o'clock in the morning, when the company were pretty merry, the Prince, whether he guessed at the reason or was concerned for the indisposition of his friend, said it was a pity poor Lawrell should die for want of help, and they immediately set about writing notes to all the physicians, surgeons, and apothecaries they could think of in the place, informing them as from Mr. L. that he was taken suddenly ill, and begged their immediate assistance; these notes very soon set the medical body in motion towards Mr. L.'s doors; a few of the *most alert apothecaries* came first, but they were got rid of by the servants, who assured them it was a mistake, that their master and mistress were well and asleep, and that they did not care to wake them. Soon after came Sir Lucas Pepys, who declaring that "*nobody would presume to impose upon a person of his character,*" insisted on seeing Mr. L., and was pressing by the maid towards his bedchamber; she was then forced to waken her mistress, and Mr. L. being very drowsy and disinclined to rise, his lady was obliged to appear in great deshabille, and with the *utmost difficulty* persuaded Sir Lucas he *was* imposed upon, and prevailed with him to retire. During their dispute the staircase *was filled* with the rest of the faculty arriving in shoals!

INDEX

TO THE FIRST VOLUME.

———◦◦◦———

END OF VOL I.

London: Printed by W. CLOWES & SONS, Stamford Street and Charing Cross.

POPULAR WORKS
BY THE AUTHOR OF MODERN ECCENTRICS.

A CENTURY OF ANECDOTE from 1750. By
JOHN TIMBS, F.S.A. 2 vols. Five Portraits. 21s.

"The best collection of anecdotes which modern times have produced."—*Athenæum.*
"As good and full a miscellany of curious, amusing, modern anecdote as anywhere to be found."—*Examiner.*
"An admirable collection of the best modern anecdotes, under the heads of court and fashionable life, political life, men of letters, clerical life, law and lawyers, eccentric persons, and players and painters."—*Reader.*
"The work contains a world of entertainment, wit, and pleasantry. We turn from page to page half dazzled and bewildered by the richness.—*Daily News.*"

CLUB LIFE of LONDON. With Anecdotes of
the Clubs, Coffee-houses, and Taverns during the Seventeenth, Eighteenth, and Nineteenth Centuries. By JOHN TIMBS, F.S.A. 2 vols. crown 8vo. 21s.

"The book is one of anecdotes, redolent of the social wit and manners of the clubs during past and present times. To the club *habitué* of to-day, and the general reader, the book is entertaining and interesting."—*Globe.*

BY THE SAME AUTHOR.
ROMANCE of LONDON: Strange Stories, Scenes,
and Remarkable Persons of the Great Town. In 3 vols., post 8vo. 31s. 6d.

"Most entertaining volumes. This work is a creditable monument of Mr. Timbs's perseverance and taste."—*Reader.*
"Mr. Timbs has an amount of industry and a knowledge of his subject which few men possess. He has put together anecdotes and short histories of London, which, to all the interest of romance, add the information of history."—*Star.*
"These volumes are most fascinating. Once opened, the reader finds it very difficult to close them. He is drawn on from one strange narrative to another, until he is forced to the conclusion that this painstaking writer has furnished a very powerful rival, in the way of absorbing interest, to the latest fictions of Mr. Wilkie Collins and Miss Braddon."—*London Review.*

ANECDOTE LIVES of PAINTERS. With Portraits.
Post 8vo. 6s.
*** Used in the Art Department of the South Kensington Museum.

ANECDOTE LIVES of the DISTINGUISHED
STATESMEN, LORD CHATHAM and EDMUND BURKE. With Portraits. Post 8vo. 6s.

"This volume presents an agreeable variety of style, from the light, caustic gossip of Walpole, to the deep, sonorous periods of Macaulay and Brougham."—*Post.*

ANECDOTE LIVES of WITS and HUMORISTS.
2 vols., post 8vo. With Portraits. 12s.

"The cream of a dozen interesting biographies."—*Saturday Review.*
"Executed in Mr. Timbs's best manner."—*Daily News.*

RICHARD BENTLEY, NEW BURLINGTON STREET,
Publisher in Ordinary to Her Majesty.

www.ingramcontent.com/pod-product-compliance
Lightning Source LLC
Chambersburg PA
CBHW021258050726
47498CB00003BB/899